Next to Forever

SHATTERED INNOCENCE TRILOGY

Book Three

A. L. LONG

wordclay

Next to Forever

Wordclay books may be ordered through booksellers or by contacting:

Wordclay
1663 Liberty Drive
Bloomington, IN 47403
USA
www.wordclay.com
877-886-7051

Because of the dynamic nature of the Internet, any web addresses or links contained in this book may have changed since publication and may no longer be valid. The views expressed in this work are solely those of the author and do not necessarily reflect the views of the publisher, and the publisher hereby disclaims any responsibility for them.

Any people depicted in stock imagery provided by Thinkstock are models, and such images are being used for illustrative purposes only. Certain stock imagery © Thinkstock.

ISBN: 978-1-5079-0039-0 (sc)
ISBN: 978-1-5079-0040-6 (e)

Print information available on the last page.

Wordclay rev. date: 12/30/2015

Table of Contents

Prologue

"How could she do this? After everything we had together." He contemplated his next move as he paced back and forth in the small hotel room that he had no choice but to check into. He wanted to give her so much. He knew he shouldn't have stayed away so long. Now he couldn't stay away. Not anymore. How could she find someone so soon? And for it to be the one man who had everything to offer. He couldn't let this continue. Rade will not have her. She belonged to him. He will get her back if it's the last thing he does. He just needed a plan. A way to get her alone. He had to make her understand that everything he did was for her, so they would never have to worry about anything ever again.

First, he needed to find a way to get rid of Rade Matheson. If he was ever to have another chance with her, Matheson had to go away. He couldn't wait to have her again. This time he wouldn't wait. It would be different. Every inch of her would be his. The only sound that would come from her mouth would be his name as she screamed in pleasure. He couldn't wait to be deep inside her. She would desire and want him just as much as he wanted her. She would beg him for more. Her need for him would be like a drug she'd never be able to live without. He would control her. There would be nothing that she wouldn't do for him. He would finally have her beneath him like it should have always been. She will forget about Rade Matheson, because once he took her, he would be the only person she thought about. The only person she would desire. The last person who would take her. Rade Matheson might have power and money, but soon she would forget. None of that would matter once she was his. He could give her all those things and more. She would want for nothing. They would have kids together and live in a big house with a big dog. Maybe out in the country where no one could bother them. He would demand she home school their children so she would always be near him. He would never let her go. He had been so gentle with her before. No more. It was time she experienced everything he was going to do to her. He wished she was with him right now. How good it would feel to have her lips wrapped around his cock, licking and sucking him until his seed slide down her perfect throat.

He only saw her before him. Picturing her kneeling before him, he imagined her mouth taking every inch of him. There was no mercy, the intense pleasure took over his body. He only wished it was Dylan pleasuring him. He would take her every day, at least once maybe more.

Chloe would soon have Rade and he would soon have Dylan. Soon Dylan would be his.

Chapter One

It's strange how one life could change with a blink of an eye. Everything she knew about this man was gone. The man she loved, the man she could see herself spending the rest of her life with, gone. *How many more secrets were there? How could they ever be together now?* Dylan promised that she would never leave Rade, but when she heard the news that he and Chloe were going to have a child together, all bets were off.

It didn't take her long to pack once she pulled herself together. She must have cried for what seemed like hours before she had shed her last tear. Rade was frantically knocking at the door the whole time. She couldn't face him, so she ignored his pounding fists against the door. When the door to the bedroom opened, everything in her body told her to run.

Rade saw the hurt and confusion as he looked at Dylan. The last thing he wanted was to cause her so much pain. Pain that he knew he would never be able to take back. He knew he should have told Dylan everything. Now his chance was gone. The last thing he expected was for Chloe to show up on his doorstep. She had taken everything from him. Everything that mattered to him. Rade couldn't let Dylan leave. She needed to hear what he had to say. It was his last chance.

"Dylan," Rade said softly as he approached her.

"Rade, I need to go. I can't be near you right now," Dylan muttered.

"Before you go, would you please let me explain," Rade pleaded taking her by the hand. If he could let her know what happened, maybe she would understand how this could have happened and how he would never be with that woman by choice.

Dylan didn't resist Rade as he walked her over to the bed. Pulling her to his side, he sat down on the bed. Dylan looked beyond hurt. She looked as though the news she heard was the end of the world for her. Rade wasn't about to let that happen. There was more to this whole thing then he even knew. It just didn't make sense.

"When I was taken, Alex was the one who kept me drugged. I don't ever remember seeing Chloe at the house. It's starting to make sense Dylan. She must have been there," Rade declared, rubbing Dylan's hands as he held on to her. "I would never willingly be with her. She knew that I wouldn't resist her in a drugged state. That must have been when she seduced me."

The more Rade explained his theory, the more it sounded farfetched. But he knew Chloe and how she liked playing games.

"Rade, do you know how crazy that sounds?" Dylan argued. "Why would she do that? When they rescued you, there was no sign that she was even there."

"I know how it sounds Dylan, but I'm telling you, I would never sleep with that woman. She was there. I'd bet my life on it. I'm going to prove to you that she was," Rade confirmed. "When I found out she was pregnant, she told my father that I had raped her. She said that she had pictures to prove it. Dylan you know me. I would never do that to any woman. I'm going to find out the truth and what her game is."

"I want to believe you Rade. I need time to think. This is too much," Dylan replied. Standing to her feet, she started walking to the bedroom door, leaving Rade sitting on the bed.

Before she left the room, Rade murmured softly, "You can stay at the penthouse. I'll stay here. Take the Audi." Removing the keys from his pocket, Rade walked to where Dylan was standing. Placing the keys in her small hand, he leaned over. "I will give you all the time you need Dylan, but please let me show you that I'm telling you the truth. Have faith in me. Have faith in us." Rade cupped Dylan's face in his hands wanting her to know the pain he was feeling. She was his life and no one, not even Chloe was going to take her away from him.

Dylan left Rade's home feeling numb. Her thoughts were all over the place. She no longer knew what was real and what wasn't. She wanted to believe Rade. She knew how evil Chloe was. Maybe she was there at the house with Rade. Dylan remembered the doctor in Bethel saying that the drug given to Rade had Rohypnol and something else mixed with it that they were unable to identify. All she knew was she needed time to sort through everything.

It was late by the time Dylan pulled into the parking garage at Rade's penthouse. She was completely exhausted from everything that was going through her mind. Grabbing her small bag from the trunk, she headed to the elevator. Just as she was getting ready to step on, Richard was coming off. Richard was the last person she wanted to see. With everything going on, she wondered how much he knew about Rade and Chloe. Taking a chance, she decided to find out.

"Hey Richard," Dylan said softly.

Richard knew the minute he looked at her, something was wrong. "Ms. Adams. I thought you and Mr. Matheson were at his home in Hampton Bay."

"Yeah, well, Chloe showed up. Did you know about them? I mean the baby," Dylan asked.

"Mr. Matheson informed me earlier today," Richard began. "Dylan, I've known Mr. Matheson since he was a child. Whatever Chloe says, I'm pretty sure Mr. Matheson had no part in. At least not willingly. You need to trust him. He will find out the truth."

"How can you be so sure Richard?" Dylan replied unconvinced.

"Because, he loves you. Before you, the only person he ever loved was his brother Isaac. You are the only person that showed him to love again. Don't give up on him Dylan," Richard pleaded.

When Dylan entered the penthouse, she felt an emptiness consume her. Her heart hurt. She no longer had any more tears to shed. Her life was beginning to crumble. Piece by piece, her heart was falling apart. She no longer had the strength to keep doing this. She felt broken and all the kings' men would never be able to put her back together again. With everything going on, she remembered that she no longer had a place to stay even though Rade insisted she stay at the penthouse. When she agreed to move in with Rade, she ended her lease on her small apartment. Rade paid for the early termination fee to get her out of her lease. Even though she argued, he kept pointing out that she didn't need her place, and since he requested she move in with him right away, he should be the one to cover the fee. Dylan wished she wouldn't have given in. She couldn't even stay with Lilly. Lilly already had someone renting her apartment while she was away in Paris. This is when it finally hit her. Her best friend was gone and she had no one that she could talk to. Sure, she could call her dad, but how would she explain what happened without him wanting her to come home. Besides she couldn't do that to her dad. Not while he was still recovering from his near fatal accident.

Tomorrow, she would put her life back in order. She needed to get in touch with Keeve and Mason and see if she could get her job back. She knew they hadn't hired anyone yet to fill her position, so it was a matter of letting them know that her plans had changed. Then there was the issue about staying with Rade. She wasn't sure what was going to happen now that a new life was coming into the picture. She wasn't even sure what Rade's plans were with the baby, Chloe, or them.

Thinking there were no more tears to shed, Dylan's tears came down once again. It only took one thought of Rade to bring on the waterworks. When Rade confessed to her that he loved her, she dreamt so many things for them. A house that they would share together. Sharing the birth of their first child. Only that wasn't going to happen, at least the part where she would be carrying his child. It would be Chloe. His first child would be from a woman that had no right to be a mother. Chloe even took that away from her. How would she even feel knowing that the child belonged to the one woman she hated more than anyone, and was also a part of the man she truly loved? *Would she even be able to look at the child knowing that it was Chloe's? Could she love the child even though it was still a part of Rade?*

Dylan's thoughts tormented her well into the morning. Somehow she needed to get past this. She knew how she felt about Rade. She knew she still loved him and that she would never be able to stop loving him. She just wasn't sure if she could be with him.

Taking everything she had, Dylan pushed from her bed and headed to the bathroom. As much as she wanted to wallow in her pity, she knew she couldn't. She had to do something to get her mind off of everything. She thought that if she could focus on getting back into a routine, she would be able to take her mind off of Rade and the baby. Taking a long hot shower, Dylan tried to clear her mind of all the pain and misery her body absorbed in the last twelve hours.

Dressed and looking halfway presentable, Dylan left the penthouse with a purpose. She needed to see two men about getting her job back. She knew at the very least, Mason would be at the office.

Getting to the BlackStone office in record time, Dylan parked the Audi in her designated parking spot. She was glad to see that they hadn't yet removed her name signage from the plate attached to the concrete wall. Grabbing her purse and locking the car, she headed to the elevator. Dylan could feel the vibration of her phone inside her purse as the elevator doors shut. When she pulled it out, she could see that Rade was calling her. She wasn't ready to talk to him. She didn't even know what she would say to him. She was still hurt by the news. She was even more hurt that he kept it from her. Declining the call, she tossed her phone back inside her purse.

The office reception area was quiet. Dylan didn't see Jessica or Lucy behind the reception desk. The more she looked around, the office seemed empty, a least until Mason rounded the corner. He was so preoccupied with a document that he didn't notice Dylan standing only a few feet away from him.

Clearing her throat, Mason looked up. "Dylan, I wasn't expecting to see you here."

"Yeah, I wasn't expecting to be here either," Dylan confessed. "Do you have a minute to talk?" Dylan was nervous about asking Mason for her job back. She knew they wouldn't hesitate to take her back. She just wasn't ready for the explanation she had to give him.

"Sure, let me make a copy of this and I'll meet you in my office," Mason replied.

Dylan waited in Mason's office for what seemed like forever. When he finally appeared, she could feel her palms getting sweaty and her chest tighten.

"So, tell me what this is about?" Mason asked as he took a seat behind his desk.

Dylan didn't know where to begin. She didn't want to explain the sordid details of her love life, so she just explained what she was only willing to share. "I wanted to see if you would consider taking me back. I might have been a little hasty in giving you my two weeks' notice."

"Well this is unexpected. May I ask what changed your mind?" Mason asked.

"I would rather not go into it, but let's just say my plans didn't turn out the way I wanted them to," Dylan admitted. At least, she was telling him the short version of her situation.

"We would love to have you back. Technically you are still an employee here. Your things are still in your old office. I will let HR know that you won't be leaving after all." Mason wished that he knew why the change in circumstance. He suspected that it had to do with Rade Matheson. He hoped to get to know Dylan better and he didn't mean the employee to boss relationship. He really liked Dylan and he wanted to share so much more with her.

Dylan felt an enormous amount pressure being lifted from her shoulders. At least she knew she had her job back. With that problem out of the way, she would be able to focus on what she was going to do about her situation with Rade. She wished she had a crystal ball so she could predict what was going to happen between them. Mostly she just wanted to know how things would end. *Were they going to be okay? Was this whole thing just a bad dream and soon she would wake up?*

One thing she knew for sure was she would never let Chloe be the person that tore them apart. Dylan could never give her the satisfaction knowing that she finally got to her.

Dylan decided to spend the rest of her day doing what she loved. As soon as she was back at the penthouse, Dylan changed her clothes, putting on a pair of shorts and a tank-top, and headed out to Central Park. It was still early enough in the morning that the temperature was still fairly cool. One thing she loved about Rade's place in the city was that it was only a few blocks from the park. Finding her favorite running mix on her iPod, she headed out on her venture.

Dylan was halfway around Central Park when she was stopped dead in her tracks. *"Chloe, that bitch."* Dylan was about to turn around in the other direction when she saw an older woman walk up to her. Dylan wished she was a fly, so she could hear what the two were discussing. Taking her place behind a large tree, Dylan looked over to the two women. Chloe pulled something out of her purse. It looked to be a manila envelope. What surprised Dylan the most was what was inside. Money and a lot of it. It looked to be at least twenty grand. Chloe and the woman shared a few words and then parted ways with the woman heading straight for Dylan. Dylan rounded the tree as the woman came closer. Dylan didn't know why she was hiding since the woman walking towards her didn't know her, nor did Dylan know the woman. Dylan decided to follow her and see if she could find out where she was going. If she was in any way associated with the likes of Chloe Dupree, Dylan knew it couldn't be good.

Dylan followed her until she walked up to silver BMW that was parked in the parking area of the park. As soon as the woman got into the car and backed up, Dylan took a glance at the license plate. She didn't have anything to write the plate number on, but it wasn't that difficult to remember considering they were personalized with *"#1-DOC"* spelled across the plate. Something was definitely going on.

Dylan ran back to the penthouse where she left her phone. She knew there was one person that could help her find out who this woman was and why Chloe was paying her. By the time she opened the door, she was out of breath. Once she was able to catch her breath, she went in search for her phone. Finding it in the bathroom, she dialed Richard.

"Ms. Adams, this is a surprise. Is everything okay?" Richard asked concerned.

"Yes...yes. I need to see if you could do something for me. I ran into Chloe at the park. She was talking to a woman." Dylan started. "I wouldn't have thought anything of it, except she handed her an envelope that was filled with a lot of money."

"Did you get a good look at the woman?" Richard asked.

"I did. She was tall with blond hair. She couldn't be more than forty. That's not all Richard, I got her plate number. I thought maybe Peter or someone you know could find out who the woman is," Dylan suggested knowing that Richard had connections to people that would be able to find out information.

After Dylan gave Richard the information, she settled on the couch. Maybe what Rade had been telling her was the truth. It was beginning to make sense. Her only hope was that Richard would be able find out something with the information she gave him. Lost in her thought, Dylan's cell started ringing. Still in her hand, she looked down at the screen to see the caller. Debating on whether to let it go to voicemail or answer it, she stared at the picture of Rade.

"Hello," Dylan said hesitantly.

"Dylan, Richard told me what happened today in the park. Based on your description of the woman you saw in the park, it had to be the OB/GYN at the clinic where I gave my blood sample. We'll know for sure once the plates are ran. I'm glad you got in touch with Richard, you didn't have to do that," Rade said with compassion.

"I didn't do it for you Rade. I needed to know the truth. I needed to know what really happened to you in that house. I thought that finding out who that woman was would give me that," Dylan choked. "I have to go."

"Dylan, wait..." Before Rade could finish, the line went dead. He tried calling her back, but it went to voicemail. "Dammit."

Rade's thoughts were on Dylan and what she must be going through. He never wanted to hurt her and now the threat of losing her was becoming more realistic. He couldn't sit and wait until he lost the one thing that meant everything to him. Grabbing his leather jacket, he walked to the garage and hopped on his Ducati. It was time he took back control of his future. The first thing he needed to do was find out about the doctor. Pulling out of the iron gates, he headed back to the city.

Rade knew Dylan would refuse to see him. As much as it pained him, he needed to give her time. He decided to go to his office and put his life back together, but before he did anything, he contacted Peter to meet him there.

Peter was already waiting in the parking garage at RIM Global when Rade pulled up on his bike. Removing his helmet and placing it on his seat, he looked over to Peter leaning against his Camero as he walked over to him.

"Thanks for meeting me here," Rade said shaking his hand.

"It sounded important," Peter commented.

"It is. Let's go to my office and I'll fill you in," Rade suggested, pushing the button for the elevator.

The office was quiet. No one usually worked on Saturdays. No one except Rade. Taking a seat behind his desk, Rade looked over at Peter, seated in one of the chairs across from him.

"So tell me, what I can do for you?" Peter asked.

"I need you to look into Chloe Dupree's past. I think you will come up with some very interesting information. I also need you to look into a certain OB/GYN. Her name is Cali O'Brien. I don't trust her. I think she has a few skeletons in her closet as well," Rade said.

"Shouldn't be too difficult to find out what you need. How long do I have?" Peter asked.

"Yesterday," Rade said sarcastically unwilling to wait any longer than he had to. As Peter started to leave Rade added, "Oh, and Peter, see what medical records you can find on Chloe Dupree. I want to know everything about her down to the medication she's taking."

"You got it," Peter acknowledged.

If there was anything to dig up on these two women, Peter would find it. Just then, Rade remembered he needed to get in touch with Chris, but he would need to wait until Monday since it was the weekend. He needed a hacker and Chris was the best. He could get into anything.

By the time Rade left his office, he was pretty confident that he had all his bases covered. Peter was looking into Chloe and Dr. O'Brien. Richard was instructed to stick by Dylan, not only to protect her, but also to keep track of her movements. The last thing Rade needed was for Dylan to get hurt by satisfying her curiosity. He knew Dylan all too well. She would never think of her safety first if it meant she could find the answers she needed.

There was one last thing Rade needed to do before he went home, he needed to see his father. As much as it pained him to do so, he needed to see the pictures that Chloe had of him. If he could get his hands on them, maybe he could figure out if they were photo-chopped. He had no doubt they were. Chloe was full of surprises. Rade had a pretty good idea what he was dealing with. He wished he'd never set eyes on her.

Chapter Two

Rade pulled up to the Four Seasons hotel shortly after hanging up with his father. His father didn't seem to be surprised that Rade needed to talk to him given the circumstance for the visit. When Rade asked where Chloe was, Garrett informed Rade that Chloe was away taking care of matters and that she wouldn't be returning to the hotel until later that evening. When Rade asked about the photos, Garrett assured him that they were safely locked away in the hotel room safe.

Stepping off the elevator, Rade walked up to his father's suite. Knocking, he waited for him to open the door. It took everything Rade had not to lay into him when the door finally opened. As much as Rade hated this man, he hated Chloe more. Looking at his father, Rade could see that something was up with him. Wanting to get this over with as soon as possible, Rade walked past him and snickered, "I just need to see the pictures then I'll be out of here."

Garrett looked at his son with remorse. Not only because of their past history, but also because of the guilt weighing on him. "Son, I might have jumped to conclusions. I took another look at those pictures Chloe showed me. I think it's someone else in them." Garrett walked over to the small desk and picked up the folder holding the pictures. Holding them out to Rade he continued, "Take a look for yourself."

Rade went to where his father was standing and took the folder. Taking a seat on the sofa, he examined the photos. Rade knew something was wrong from the very beginning. Something just wasn't right and the photos just confirmed it. He saw right away that it wasn't him towering over Chloe's body while her hands were bound to the headboard. The man before him did have the same build and hair color, but had something that Rade didn't. A faint line of a tattoo was evident on the man's left shoulder. Rade could barely make it out since it was concealed with some sort of make-up, but the closer Rade looked, it appeared the tattoo was some sort of dragon. Looking through all the photos, he could clearly see it wasn't him. The scenes in the photos looked like they were staged. Even though Chloe's face looked to be badly bruised with blood running down her lip, it could have been made up. Rade also saw that her tied wrists had red marks circling them which could have been self inflicted. Her naked form looked to be aroused at what the man was doing. His body was hard and displayed over hers. Rade could see that he was fucking her. Chloe's legs were bent and being held in place by her accomplice. Every picture looked like it was faked. There was nothing real about them.

Before his dad could say a word, Rade looked over to him. "I'm guessing you saw the same thing I did."

"I'm sorry for not trusting you Rade. I should have never doubted you." Garrett took a seat across from Rade pulling his hands through his already mused hair. "When she came to me looking as she did, I thought for sure she was raped. Then when she produced the pictures, you supposedly took, they looked like you son."

"This is so fucked up. How could I have taken them, when the person pretending to be me was in clear view?" Rade cursed.

"I asked the same thing. She told me that you used a tripod and put the timer on so it would take the pictures while you were fucking her," Garrett explained.

"Oh my God! Are you serious? Do you know how stupid that sounds? I don't believe this. Alex had control of my phone the whole time." Rade was becoming infuriated with this bullshit.

Gathering the pictures and placing them back inside the folder, Rade left his father's suite no happier than when he got there. One thing was for sure, Chloe was done playing games with him. He needed to find out who the guy was in the photos and he needed to find out who took those photos. As he entered the elevator, he pulled his phone from his pocket. He was glad that he was able to retrieve the SD card from his phone he threw against the wall. Looking through his saved data, he could see there were no photo's saved or even taken with his phone. It wasn't to say they weren't deleted. He would need to ask Chris if there was a way he could get into the deleted memory and find out if there were any photos taken to begin with.

Just as Rade was about to close out his gallery app, a picture of Dylan filled the screen. He remembered taking this picture at the penthouse when she was staring out the window in only his shirt. God, she was so beautiful. Even though it had only been 24 hours since she'd left his house in Hampton Bay, it seemed like an eternity. He missed her so much. He knew he needed to do everything he could to get her back. This was going to be the last time that Chloe would be come between them. This time he was going to make sure she would be out of their lives for good.

* * * * *

It was Monday morning and Rade woke with a new purpose. No longer was he going to let people dictate how his life was going to be lived. The only person he cared about was Dylan. He wasn't about to wait until she decided she had enough time only to inform him that they were done. He wasn't about to let that happen. Slipping on his charcoal suit jacket, Rade left his Hampton home to get back what was his. No sooner he stepped out the door, Richard was there to greet him.

"What are you doing here Richard? I thought I made it clear that you were to stay near Dylan," Rade said confirming his disapproval.

"Ms. Adams is in good hands. Josh is watching her," Richard confirmed. "I thought you might want to know that we were able to trace the plate we got from Ms. Adams. The car belongs to Cali O'Brien. But I'm sure you already knew that."

"I knew. I just needed to be sure," Rade admitted. "Do you have anything else for me?"

"Peter is still looking into the doctor and Ms. Dupree. Should hear something back from him later today," Richard said knowing how much Rade wanted the information he requested.

"Good. I've got to get going. I have a meeting with Chris this morning to discuss some computer work I needed to have done. In the mean time, I need you to get back to Dylan." Even though Rade knew that Josh was more than capable of watching over Dylan, he preferred Richard to cover her.

As soon as Rade entered the office, not only was he greeted by Gwen's bright smile, Chris was also waiting for him. Looking over to Gwen, Rade instructed her to hold his calls. He didn't want to be disturbed.

Rade and Chris headed to Rade's office. Once inside, Rade quickly shut the door to make sure they wouldn't be interrupted. The first thing he needed Chris to do was look at his phone to see if there was any information that may have been deleted. Handing him his phone, Chris took the phone and plugged it into the equipment needed to retrieve deleted files. Rade was pretty sure he knew what he would find. Absolutely nothing. Chris confirmed Rade's suspicion. There were no recent photos taken, nor were there any photos deleted from his phone. Chris went one step further to see if there was any software downloaded on Rade's phone which could access his personal information. Once again, he came up empty. Rade's phone was clean of any unwanted apps or tracking software.

"Your phone is clean Mr. Matheson. I'm going to install a tracking device on your phone. It will alert you if anyone tries to access your phone remotely. I have set it up to alert you on your phone as well as on your computer," Chris informed Rade.

"Good. I have one more thing I need you to do for me. I need you to hack into Chloe Dupree's personal computer," Rade asked.

"You know I could get into trouble if I get caught," Chris confirmed looking at Rade with concern.

"I know the risks Chris, but I wouldn't ask if it wasn't important," Rade admitted. "What do you need to get this done?"

"I would need to find out what her IP address is. If I could get that, then it would be a piece of cake," Chris confirmed.

"Well, that my friend is a little harder to do, if not impossible." The only way to get the information Chris needed would be to get close enough to Chloe to get it. Rade knew that wasn't going to happen. His only other option was to ask his father to get it for him. "Is there any other way you can get into her computer?" Rade asked.

"There is, but it could take awhile and there is an even higher chance of getting caught," Chris added.

The last thing Rade wanted was to put Chris in a situation where he could get caught. The last thing Chris needed was to get into trouble again. Rade had been kind enough to bail Chris out when he was a minor. He did it as a favor to an old friend. He might not be so lucky this time and didn't want to risk it.

Rade knew what he had to do. He contacted his father. To his surprise, his father agreed to get him the information he needed. His father told him that he no longer trusted Chloe and wasn't willing to play her games either. There was no way he would be taken by a woman. Rade thought it was funny coming from his father, especially since he was taken by Evan's mother and ended up with a son he didn't even know he had until recently.

It was getting close to five o'clock when Rade decided to check in with Richard. Even though Dylan refused to see him, at least he could make sure she was being protected. It killed him not being able to see her. To hold her. To take in her scent. Ever since the day at the mansion, Rade tried to hold back his urge to knock down her door and take her into his arms. Without being able to see her, the last forty-eight hours were filled with only thoughts of her. Every nerve in his being craved her. He would do anything to get back what they had. He needed to have her in his bed again. He needed to have her beneath him. Pleasuring her. Satisfying her every need.

Rade couldn't stand being so far away from Dylan. It seemed like they were worlds apart. Since he couldn't stay at the penthouse, his only other option was to get a suite at The Ritz. Rade got in touch with Gwen to make arrangements which would allow him to be closer to Dylan.

Entering his suite, Rade tossed his keys on the coffee table and poured himself a scotch. Even though it wasn't his preferred brand, it did the job. Before Rade knew it, he had consumed half the bottle. The amber liquid masked the helplessness he felt, leaving him numb in its place. He could only hope that soon he would have the answers he needed. Soon he and Dylan would be together again.

Taking his cell from his pocket, he entered his code and went to his favorite contacts to bring up her name. Looking at her picture, he contemplated giving her a call. He needed to make sure she was okay. More than that, he just needed to hear her voice. Hitting the call icon, he waited for her to answer.

"Hello," Dylan spoke softly.

"Hey Sweetness. I know you needed time, but I just needed to hear your voice," Rade confessed, unsure if he would be talking to dead air or her soft voice. "I miss you. I miss having you near me."

"I miss you too Rade. I just don't know how to deal with this anymore. Every time I think about it, I start to breakdown. You're going to be a father Rade. I thought it would be you...." Dylan broke off. She couldn't think about the one thing she would never have with this man. "I can't talk about this Rade. Not now."

Dylan hung up on Rade to soon. His heart ached knowing this thing with Chloe was causing her so much pain. He didn't know how to fix it. All he knew was he needed her. The erection he was possessing was proof. His only reprieve was to ease some of the pain. Walking to the bathroom, he turned on the water to the shower. He undressed while the water began to heat. Stepping inside the confines of the small space, he let the water stream down his tense body. Grabbing hold of his hard shaft, he stroked the tight skin. Increasing his movements, he closed his eyes as thoughts of Dylan filled his mind. It was only her he saw as her luscious lips wrapped around his engorged cock. He imagined that it was her mouth sliding up and down is length coating the taut flesh. He could feel her tiny hand cup his sac as she gently caressed the stretched skin. Unable to hold back his desire for her, he increased his movements feeing her mouth wrap around him. His legs started to buckle underneath him when he gave into his release. The minute he gained control, images of her were gone and reality settled in. It had been a long time since Rade had to take care of his own relief. He felt like a horny teenager again.

It was still early enough in the evening so Rade decided to check in with Peter. He was pretty certain that Peter wouldn't have any new information for him since he talked to him less than twelve hours ago. He needed to do something and drinking was no longer an option for him. Just when he was about to dial Peter, his phone began ringing. Rade didn't recognize the number.

"Matheson," Rade answered hesitantly.

"Rade, its Evan. I just had the strangest visit by a Chloe Dupree," Evan said not sure how Rade was going to take what he was about to share with him. "She seemed to be pretty interested in my relationship with Dylan. Do you know why she would be asking me?"

"Evan. I know we have only recently found out about our family ties, but I need to warn you, that woman is pure evil. I would suggest you stay far away from her." Rade only knew one thing. Evan's recent visit with Chloe was nothing but trouble. Rade didn't know what her agenda was with Evan, but whatever it was, he knew it wouldn't be good.

"Yeah well, I got that impression the minute she mentioned Dylan's name. She also mentioned that you two were going to have a child together. I didn't know whether to believe her or not," Evan claimed.

"I'm not sure how accurate that actually is. Everything is pointing towards me being the father of the child she's carrying, but I'm not one-hundred percent convinced that I am. I'm working on getting additional information." Rade continued to explain Chloe's underhandedness to Evan. He only hoped that after his explanation, Evan would agree with him. The more people he had in his corner the better.

"If you need me to do anything. Let me know," Evan declared. Even though they got off to a bad start, Rade was still his brother. With no other family, he knew he needed to put his feeling for Dylan aside and build a relationship with Rade. After all you can't help whom you fall in love with.

"I will Evan," Rade asserted. "Thanks for the offer."

"Before I forget, I wanted to let you know that I'm having a grand opening at *Riley's* on Saturday. I'd like you to come," Evan asked.

"I'll be there bro."

No sooner did Rade hung up with Evan, a knock came at his door. When he opened the door, his heart was filled with hopefulness as he looked down on her. All he could see was sorrow reflected in her eyes. Without a second thought, he pulled Dylan to him and held her body close to his. He could feel the tremble of her body as her emotions took hold. Nothing could have prepared him for how he felt at that very moment. Dylan's head gently pressed into his chest as each moan of sadness escaped. The only thing he could do was to sooth her pain by holding her close to him. When her trembling finally stopped, he understood the love she had for him. Lifting her chin, he was met by her beautiful, but grief stricken eyes. He lowered his lips to hers and consumed her pain. His only hope was that he could absorb the torment that they held. If he could he would have taken it all.

Dylan's arms embraced him as their kiss deepened. Every part of her soul was taken by him. No words could explain how she felt at that very moment. Fully consumed by her, Rade gently lifted her into his arms and carrying her to his room. He needed to have more of her. He needed to feel every inch of her perfection.

Unable to speak, Dylan tucked her head in Rade's neck. This was where she needed to be. With everything that had happened in the last forty-eight hours, this was home for her. As Rade lowered her body to the bed, Dylan was unwilling to let him go. She was afraid that if they parted for just one second, she would be unable to find this place again.

"Sweetness, you need to let me go. Just for a second," Rade whispered tenderly.

"I can't Rade. I'm afraid if I let go, what we have will be gone forever," Dylan cried.

"You will never lose me Sweetness," Rade confirmed knowing that he would be only hers.

Even though he needed to be buried inside of her, he was content just holding her. If this was what she needed, he couldn't deny her. As much as his heart ached. As much as he needed to take her, this was about what she needed. Slowly he lifted his body from hers and pulled her gently to his side as he engulfed her being.

No matter how close they were, Dylan still felt her world was coming down. She wished everything that happened a few days ago was just a bad dream and soon she would wake up and find just the two of them. Just as they were right now. Dylan knew the love she had for him was stronger than anything she ever felt before. But was her love for him strong enough to get them through this. The more she thought about it, the more she knew what she needed to do. As much as it pained her, she knew she could never give herself completely to him. Because for her to do that, she would need to accept him completely and that meant his relationship with Chloe and their child.

Chapter Three

It was morning and Dylan woke still embraced by Rade's arms wrapped around her. Lifting her head, she took in his features as she watched him sleep. God, he was beautiful. Just as she was ready to push her body from his, she felt him stir. His arms wrapped tighter around her as though he couldn't let her go. Dylan didn't protest. No matter how she felt last night, she needed him to hold her tight and never let her go. Rade slowly rolled over and placed her body beneath his. They had fallen asleep in their clothing and all Rade wanted was to feel her skin next to his. He wanted so badly to take what was his last night, but he knew Dylan only needed the contact of his body next to hers. But now it was his turn. He needed to feel her. Rade lowered his body closer to hers and placed his head against hers thanking God that she was back. Kissing her forehead, he whispered, "I thought I lost you." Dylan ran her hand along his cheek reassuring him that she was here and that was all that mattered. Her soft touch spoke louder than words. Rade knew she was his.

Pulling her closer, he rolled over lifting her small frame to his lap as he gently pulled her t-shirt over her head. There was a soft moan as Rade sucked and kissed the area between her neck and her ear. He could feel her heart beating as he lowered his mouth to her chest. With his hand, he gently lowered the cup of her bra and began tenderly consuming her breast. He would never get tired of the softness of her skin he caressed in his hand. Placing his other hand to her back, he quickly unhooked her bra and lowered the straps down her soft shoulders. Her beautiful breasts instantly popped free. Rade knew then that she wanted him. Dylan's back arched giving him free access. He lowered his lips to her pert nipple and gently kissed and sucked until it hardened into a taut peak. Caressing the other breast, he laid her back carefully onto the bed and worked to unzip her jeans. Her moans filled the air as he tweaked her nipple between his fingers. Raising her butt from the bed, he pulled down her jeans along with her lacy panties baring her sweet thighs. His hands moved away from Dylan, no longer than necessary until he could shed his own clothing. In a matter of seconds he was over her once again kissing and licking every inch of her soft body. Raising her above him, he spread her legs wider and positioned his body between them. Once again her body straddling his lap. Her red hair flowed down her naked back as her head fell back.

Rade took hold of her hair and pulled her closer to him. His lips trailed down her neck kissing and sucking her, consuming her sweet scent. He could feel every inch of her body tremble with every touch his lips had laid on her sensitized skin. Nothing and no one would ever take this woman away from him. He was never going to let her go. He was mesmerized by her beauty. Every curve and line of her body was pure perfection. Unable to withstand the separation, Rade gently lifted Dylan hips from his body and carefully lowered her onto his hard shaft. This was what he had been waiting for. All he wanted to do was feel her. He didn't want to feel the pain anymore. He didn't want to deal with the shit that was knocking him down at every turn. Right now, this moment was all he wanted. Dylan in his arms. Him inside her. Feeling only her.

Dylan's soft moans sounded as her tight walls took every inch that Rade had given her. He could feel her body let go. Her arms wrapped around his neck and he felt the pull she had on him. He continued thrusting inside her. Wanting only to take her deeper, faster, Rade pulled from her, flipping her over so he was now positioned behind her. "On your knees Sweetness," he demanded pushing lightly on her back. Dylan obeyed by lowering her head to the pillow while tucking her arms underneath her. With a quick thrust, Rade was inside her once again where he belonged. She was so wet with arousal that his big cock slipped right back into place. Grasping her hips with both hands, Rade tightened his grip and pulled her against him as he drove forward. He was so deep inside her, that he was certain he was going to explode. Moving his hand up her spine, he locked onto her red hair and pulled her head back. He could hear her whimper as he continued to glide inside her.

There was nothing that Dylan wouldn't give him. She knew he had her heart. Broken or not, she could only be with him. Dylan was about to explode with her release, when Rade pulled from her body. Frustration filled her mind at the loss of contact. It was only until she was up in the air and flipped over once again that she knew she would be given what she craved. Leaning over her, he took her arms and raised them above her head. With one strong hand he held them tightly as he once again entered her. Drawing a breath, he moaned, "God, you're so tight." Dylan was so close, but deprived of what she needed. Rade slowed his assault on her knowing that she was about to unleash. He wanted this to last. He needed to show her that he controlled her orgasms.

Dylan's hips started to move harder against Rade's slow pace. She needed more friction. She needed more of him. Trying to fight for what she needed, but unable to get there, she pleaded with him. "Rade, please."

"Please, what Sweetness?" Rade asked.

"Harder, I need more," Dylan cried.

"Tell me what you need more of. I want you to say it." Rade knew all too well what she wanted. But in order to give it to her, she had to earn it. And in order for her to earn it, she needed to tell him exactly what she needed.

"I needed you to fuck me harder." Dylan all but spelled it out for him.

Rade drove his cock faster and deeper inside her. As much as he wanted to savor this moment, he needed to take what was his. Dylan's body shattered with her release. Rade got what he desired. It was only her pleasure that he needed. So when his own pleasure took hold, it was only icing on the cake.

Taking in her form, Rade slowly released Dylan's wrists and pulled her body close to his. "I will never let you go Dylan Adams." Those words were all he needed to say. For she was his and nothing could ever break them.

* * * * *

It was late afternoon by the time Dylan had enough nerve to talk to Rade about their situation and how they were going to deal with it. Rade had been in the living area of his suite all morning working while Dylan spent most of her morning in the bedroom reading, claiming that she didn't what to distract him. But the truth was, she needed to give herself time to figure out how she was going to approach Rade with how she truly felt. She had horrible thoughts about the baby and what it would do to their relationship. How she felt about the child being Chloe's and how she was afraid she would never be able to accept the child even if it was a part of him. Dylan hoped that he would understand, especially knowing that she wanted his first child to come from her and not Chloe.

Closing her book, Dylan decided she couldn't put off what she had to say any longer. It only made her angrier the more she thought about it. This was something she needed to confront him with if they were ever going to be able to be together. Rade was deep in thought when Dylan walked into the room. She knew he didn't hear her, because his head was still buried in whatever he was looking at. Nervous, Dylan began walking towards him.

Standing in front of him, she lost all courage to tell him what she so desperately needed to say. Rade still hadn't looked up at her. This was her only escape, so she quickly turned and headed back to the bedroom. Startled by his voice, Dylan stopped just shy of the door. "Did you need something Sweetness?" Rade asked amused by her sudden jolt.

Dylan turned back to face Rade. He was still looking at the document in front of him. "I needed to talk to you." Dylan explained as she walked back to where Rade sat.

"I'm listening," Rade answered not looking up at her.

"Rade, I needed to have your attention. If you need to finish whatever you're working on, I'll come back later," Dylan offered. She needed to have his undivided attention for what she was about to tell him. She wasn't sure she could repeat it again if he wasn't fully listening to her.

Placing his pen on the coffee table, Rade stood from his chair and walked over to where Dylan was standing. He could tell by the look in her eyes that whatever was on her mind was making her uncomfortable. Taking her by the hand, he pulled her over to the leather couch. Once she was settled, he took her other hand and pulled her onto his lap. If what she was about to tell him was as important as she claimed, he wanted to make sure she was as comfortable as possible.

"Now tell me what's on your mind," Rade asked.

"I need you to really listen to what I have to say. This is really hard for me and I don't think I can say it more than once," Dylan began as she waited for Rade's response.

"You have my undivided attention Sweetness," Rade declared pulling her in closer.

"I want to take about this thing with you and Chloe," Dylan confessed.

28

"Sweetness you don't need to worry about me and Chloe. We are never going to have a thing," Rade confirmed.

"That's just it Rade. You two will be sharing a child together in seven months. You will always have a connection to her. Even if you don't want to admit it. She will always be a part of your life." Dylan tried saying what she needed to say without falling apart. It wasn't helping that Rade was holding her in his arms. If she was to finish what she needed to say, she needed to pull away from him, otherwise she would end up crying and that would be the end.

Pushing from his lap, Dylan stood and walked to the other side of the room where Rade could still see her. Standing, Rade walked over to where she was. This was not how Dylan wanted this conversation to go. "Stop Rade. I need to get this out and I can't do that when you're so close to me," Dylan demanded.

Rade stopped a few feet from where Dylan stood. He was trying to understand what this was about. "Talk Sweetness," he said softly.

Dylan looked up at him knowing he was hurt that she didn't want him near her. "I love you Rade with my whole being." Dylan wasn't sure how she would tell him what she was about to say. She decided to just come out with it. "I don't know if I can love a child that you are going to share with a woman I hate more than anything." There, she said it. It didn't come out the way she wanted it to, but now he knew.

Rade was speechless. This was something he would have never expected to come from a woman with a heart of gold. So when those words erupted from her lips, it was all he could do not to leave the room. If he could have changed the circumstances between Chloe and himself, he would have, but he couldn't, at least not yet. He was trying really hard to understand how Dylan felt. He wished he wouldn't be having a child with any woman let alone Chloe. He didn't want children at all. He would never be able to bear the pain after he lost his brother so young, Moving in on Dylan, he didn't stop until he was standing inches from her, face to face. He wasn't sure what he was going to say, but he knew for a fact that he loved her more than anything. Cupping her face with his hand, he lowered his lips to hers. She was his life. He didn't want to lose her. This child would be a part of him no matter how she felt. The part of him he knew Dylan would eventually accept. He hated Chloe just as much as she did, if not more. Even though he would be a father, he didn't want that to come between them.

"Dylan, I can't change what happened. I understand you not wanting to share anything that is a part of Chloe. This child, no matter what, is my responsibility. I can't ask you to accept that, but I pray that you would. Don't let an unborn child come between us." Rade said softly as he waited for Dylan's response.

Dylan's eyes filled with tears. How could she have been so selfish knowing that this was just as hard on Rade as it was on her? How could she ask him to give up his responsibility to this child for her? If they had any chance at all, she needed to stand beside him and put her feeling aside. Maybe it would be different once the child was born. Nodding her head, Dylan placed her hand over his. She knew how this was tearing Rade apart. Rade lowered his mouth to hers and kissed Dylan passionately. Not only to show the love he had for her, but also to show her the understanding he had knowing she was giving herself to him unconditionally.

* * * * *

Dylan left later that night for the penthouse. With everything going on with them, she needed time to think. She knew Rade was right about the child being his responsibility. The child was going to be a part of his life. The part of him that she wasn't sure she could love.

Rade insisted on staying with her at the penthouse and Dylan didn't have the heart to tell him no. Soon he would be home thinking that their life would begin where it left off a few days ago. The only problem with that was, Dylan had reservations. It was like Rade was telling her how she should feel. As much as she wanted to give him what he wanted, she didn't know if she could. She had six months to figure it out.

Dylan was getting a glass of wine when she heard the door to the penthouse open. Even though she left Rade not more than an hour earlier, he looked like he had the weight of the world on his shoulders. His hair was messy and his otherwise perfect appearance was just as messy with his tie hanging low and his jacket slung over his shoulder. Something must have happened after she left him.

Walking up to him, Dylan grabbed his jacket and placed it on the bar stool. Taking a good look at him, his forehead was crinkled with worry. She hated seeing him like this. Taking his hand, she led him to the living area and willed him to take a seat on the couch. Rade watched her as she poured him a tumbler of his favorite fifty year scotch. Holding the crystal glass out, Rade reached for it as Dylan settled down beside him.

Before Dylan could ask him what was going on, Rade blurted out, "Chloe called me after you left. She wants to name the child Isaac if it's a boy and Liza if it's a girl. She also wants me to go to London with her to meet her parents. I didn't even know they were still alive."

Dylan could tell Rade was angry. Why would Chloe even think that Rade would be okay with her naming their child after the two people he lost only to be reminded of them? He would never let their child bear the name of either of them. Those names were special to only him. He would never share that part of him with Chloe. There was no love in conceiving the child, only hate.

Dylan tried to comfort Rade, but he was filled with so much rage and hurt that the only sound she heard was the breaking of glass as Rade threw his drink against the wall.

"Rade, you don't have to agree to what she wants," Dylan said softly.

"You don't understand Dylan. She has the power to do whatever she wants. She doesn't care one way or another about the people she hurts along the way," Rade cursed. "That bitch will do whatever it takes to have me."

"What is that suppose to mean?" Dylan asked.

"It means... she knows exactly what she's doing. There are things she can use against me to get what she wants," Rade muttered pulling his hand through his thick hair.

"Like what things Rade? What does she have that makes her think she has you?" Dylan looked at Rade confused. *What could Chloe possibly have over Rade? She's the one who is evil.* Dylan knew everything that happened to Rade was somehow her doing.

Rade walked from the living area to where he placed his briefcase in the entryway. Dylan was confused by his sudden retreat. She was ready to question him, when she saw him walking back holding a manila folder in his hand. She wasn't sure what he was about to show her, but knew more than likely had to do with Chloe. Rade held out the folder waiting for Dylan to take it from him. Dylan looked at the folder and then to Rade.

"Take it Dylan. It will explain everything," Rade admitted.

With shaky hands, Dylan took the folder from Rade. Flipping open the folder, Dylan could see picture after picture of Chloe bound to a bed with Rade on top of her. Her face was bruised and bloodied. It looked as though she was being raped. Dylan's hands shook as the folder and its contents fell to the floor. She could only stand there, unable to move, unable to breathe. Rade bend down and picked up the photos. He knew then that Dylan thought it was him in the pictures. The one person he expected, more than anyone, to see right away that it wasn't him, was crumbling before him.

"Dylan, are you okay?" Rade asked looking down on her. Taking her by the hand, he gently pulled her to his body. She wouldn't move. He had no other choice but to lift her from where she stood and place her on the couch. He cupped his hand on her cheek willing her to look at him. "Dylan, you need to look at me. You need to listen to what I'm about to say."

Dylan did everything she could not to break down. She couldn't believe what she saw. There had to be a mistake. It couldn't be Rade in all those pictures. She knew in her heart, he couldn't have done those things to Chloe. Lifting her head so that her eyes met his, she looked deeply trying to find the man she loved with all her heart. The minute she saw him, she knew. "It can't be you in those pictures. I know you would never do anything like this."

"It's not me Sweetness. But if you could be fooled, then imagine what would happen if they got into the wrong hands," Rade confessed.

"Who is it? In the photos," Dylan whispered.

"I don't know. But I'm working on finding out," Rade said with confidence. The man in the pictures was the key to everything. "All I know is, he has a tattoo on his shoulder of a dragon. It's hard to see, but it's there."

Dylan took the photos from Rade and looked more closely at the man hovering over Chloe. She didn't know how she could have missed it the first time, but there it was, the outline of a dragon on the left shoulder. She knew Rade could never do anything so vicious. Chloe was setting him up. After looking at the photos, it was clear that Chloe was after Rade. *Was she so obsessed with him that she would do anything to have him?* Dylan didn't have a vindictive bone in her body. She assumed that everyone was good and if they weren't, they should at least be given a second chance. But with Chloe, she didn't deserve a second chance. She didn't even deserve to breathe the same air as them.

Dylan placed her hand on Rade's cheek. She knew with all her heart the man she fell in love with would never do such awful things to a woman. Giving Rade the reassurance he needed, Dylan shifted her body so that she was straddling his lap. With a gentle touch she placed her lips on his and kissed him. Rade felt the love she had for him. He cupped her face and pressed his lips harder against hers. He was consumed by her. Every inch of her succulent mouth made him wither. Slipping his tongue between her soft lips, he explored the warmth within. Licking and sucking her bottom lip, he deepened their kiss. He needed her now more than ever. Even though it had only been an hour, every minute he spent without her seemed like an eternity.

Rade gently lifted Dylan with ease while still holding on to her. Nothing could separate them as he walked carefully to the bedroom. Placing Dylan on her feet, he tugged her t-shirt over her head exposing her lacy bra. He took in her curves as he grazed soft kisses down her shoulder, to her neck where his lips rested just above her right breast. Taking care, he unclasped her bra and lowered the thin straps down her silky arms. His gaze fell upon her breasts as he met her beautiful pink buds. If he was an artist, she would be the most magnificent subject he could have ever captured on canvas. Every line, every curve of her body was flawless. God couldn't have created a more perfect being than what was in front of him. Lowering his mouth, he took her taut nipple between his teeth and tugged lightly on the pink flesh. Dylan moaned with pleasure as her need for him started to intensify. Rade could feel the small tremble of her body as he continued to assault the other nipple, making sure to give it the same, if not more, attention.

Dylan's need for him grew with every moment. Unable to hold back her own desire for him, she reached between them and began frantically undoing his belt and lowering the zipper on his slacks. In one swift movement, she pulled down on his silk boxers and his pants, freeing his impressive hard-on from the confines of the material. Dylan wrapped her hand around his engorged shaft while placing soft butterfly kisses along his chest. Tightening her grip, she stroked his cock the best she could with her small hand. She loved the way his length felt in her hand. So soft and velvety. Like silk running against her palm.

Rade couldn't take it anymore. If he let Dylan continue, he would let loose in her hand and he didn't want that. He wanted to be deep inside her when he came. He wanted the feel of her tight walls around him when he pumped in and out of her wet channel. Gliding his hands down her back, Rade gently grabbed her ass and raised her body from the floor. Dylan's legs automatically wrapped around Rade's waist as he deposited her onto the bed. No words were said as their eyes met. They knew the feeling between them was more than words could ever describe. Rade tried desperately to remove Dylan's jeans, but when he lost hope of a quick removal, he gripped the two sides of the thick material and with one forceful pull, the fabric tore in two giving him immediate access to her sex. He didn't give Dylan time to protest about the damage done to her hundred dollar jeans, nor did he care about the damage he was going to inflict on her lacy underwear. One tug of the delicate material and she was completely bare. He had to be inside her. His animal hunger took over all his senses. Positioning himself above her, he took hold of his hard shaft and plunged it inside her wet folds. There was nothing that could describe the feeling of his cock entering her silky channel. It was euphoria. It was unlike anything he had ever felt before.

Dylan was already lost in her own pleasure that she didn't care that Rade's animalistic tendency took not only her jeans but her underwear in its wake. All she cared about was this moment and how good he felt inside her. Wrapping her legs around his waist she locked her ankles tightly together needing to get him deeper inside her. All it took was one more hard thrust and she exploded with such force, swearing that her heart stopped beating. This wasn't enough for Rade. He wanted more. There was no way she was going to get away with only one orgasm. Slowing his assault on her, he gently took hold of her clamped legs and put them over his wide shoulders. With his hands under her ass, he began once again pumping inside her. Driving his hard shaft deeper and deeper within her tight channel. He loved her in this position. He could get deeper inside, feel every curve of her pretty cunt. He was so close to his own release, but he only wanted to feel her explode once again. Removing one hand from her ass, he snaked his hand down her stomach placing his finger on her swollen clit. Rolling his finger in small circular motions, her moans grew louder. "Yes, Oh God yes." Her back began to arch at the same time he felt her walls clinch tighter around his hard cock. It took everything he had not to lose it. Unable to hold out any longer, Rade pulled free from inside her and quickly flipped Dylan's body over. He needed to take control of her body. "Place your hands behind you back Sweetness." When her hands came back, Rade clinched them with one hand while holding onto her hip with the other. Pulling her back, he pushed inside her soaked channel. Once again he could feel the tight grip of her muscles consuming him with each drive inside her. Before he gave her permission to come, she exploded with yet another orgasm, this one more intense than the last. Rade held back as long as he could, until he also violently exploded spilling his seed inside her.

Chapter Four

Rade prepared breakfast the next morning while Dylan got in the shower. Last night was the beginning of their life together. He would have Dylan in his bed for good. With breakfast ready, Rade turned on the television as he waited for Dylan to finish her shower. He regretted turning it on, because what he was hearing made him lose his appetite.

"Officials have located Chloe Dupree. Ms. Dupree went missing over a week ago. When asked where she was, Ms. Dupree verified that she was staying with Garrett Matheson, father of Rade Matheson. It seems there was a misunderstanding according to Ms. Dupree. Rade Matheson and Ms. Dupree are having their first child together. Ms. Dupree went on to say that they were very much in love and would be making wedding arrangements in the near future. She also stated that they would be making a trip to London to visit her parents and possibly hold the wedding there. Ms. Dupree elected not to talk about the events leading to Rade Matheson's kidnapping. Her only comment was that she didn't know Alex Moreno as well as she thought and she was glad that the ordeal was over so she and Rade could begin their new life together."

Rade was beyond furious. Without even thinking he threw the remote at the flat screen which only tipped it before it settled back on its stand. When Rade turned around, Dylan stood in the hallway, her body slumped to the floor, helplessness raining in her eyes. The last thing Rade wanted was for Dylan to hear the lies being told about his relationship with Chloe.

Taking the few steps towards her, Rade pulled her into him and wrapped his arms around her limp body. As he held her, her tears fell, soaking his thin t-shirt. Holding her at arm's length, he lifted her chin so she could see the truth he was about to confess.

"Sweetness, no matter what you hear on the news or in the papers, please know that I will only love you. Chloe means nothing to me. She will never have my heart or my soul they way you do." Rade brushed his hand along her cheek as he wiped away a stray tear from her eye.

"I want to believe you Rade. I just don't know how to do that anymore with everything that has happened between us," Dylan muttered softly.

"You need to trust me. Trust us. I will never allow that woman to take what we have together," Rade admitted.

Pulling her body closer, Rade placed his mouth over hers in what began as a soft tender kiss. Then the kiss deepened as if to say that nothing would separate them. Not even Chloe would be able to break them.

Placing his palm on her cheek, he helped her to her feet hoping that she would trust what he said. Rade turned to shut of the TV while Dylan went back into the bedroom to finish getting dressed.

They ate their breakfast in silence. Nothing they could have said would make this day any better. Dylan only knew that she was confused by everything that was happening. She knew she loved Rade deeply. She just didn't know if it was going to be enough to keep them together. Everything they had together needed to be placed on trust and a little faith. One thing she did know was that Chloe was going to be a problem for them. She wasn't going to make this easy on either of them.

Rade and Dylan left the penthouse together needing a reprieve. The best way for Dylan to get her mind off things was to think about something else. That's when Rade decided a day of sightseeing was in order. Just as Rade helped Dylan into the passenger side of the Audi, his cell rang. Looking down at the screen, it was Peter. He had Peter checking on things for him regarding Chloe. He hoped that he would have some good news for him.

"Hewitt, I hope you have some news for me," Rade asked sternly.

"I do sir. I found out some very interesting things about Ms. Dupree. It seems Ms. Dupree was pregnant once before, but lost the child. She got pregnant during her sophomore year in college. She was dating a senior at the time. The medical records showed that she had some sort of genetic abnormality in her DNA. I'm trying to find more information on this," Peter confirmed. "There's something else you might find interesting, Ms. Dupree spent time at the Hawthorne Institution for Women shortly after she miscarried. I'm working on getting those records as well."

"At least that's something. Let me know what else you find out," Rade knew Chloe's life wasn't squeaky clean. "What about the doctor? Were you able to find anything on her?"

"Nothing yet, sir. I'll let you know what I find out as soon as something comes up," Peter said regretfully, wishing he had more answers for Rade.

Rade felt better after talking with Peter. He knew Chloe and how deceitful she was. He hoped that Peter would be able to come up with something on the doctor. This whole thing with Chloe and the baby just didn't sit right with him. He wanted to make sure every avenue was covered before he committed fully to this unborn child.

Dylan sat in the seat beside Rade wondering what Peter had found out about Chloe and the gynecologist taking care of her prenatal care. Ten minutes passed when Dylan couldn't stand it anymore. She thought for sure Rade would have said something to her.

"Are you going to tell me what Peter found out about Chloe and the doctor or are you going to keep that from me as well?" Dylan didn't mean for her words to come out so crass, but she was tired of being the last one to know anything.

Rade looked over at her shocked by her sass. He knew he kept things from her, but only because the right time never presented itself to come clean. He still didn't even know how he was going to explain Michael to her. He knew it would only be a matter of time before Michael showed his face again. It would be a matter of time before the truth came out. Finding out he was going to have a child with Chloe tore Dylan apart, but this would certainly end their relationship forever.

Placing his hand over hers, he gently took it and pulled it to his lips gently kissing the back. Reverting his gaze back to the road, he started explaining his conversation with Peter. "Peter was able to find some information about Chloe. Seems she was pregnant once before when she was in college. Needless to say, she lost the baby. She had some sort of genetic abnormality. Peter is going to try and get more information on this."

Dylan looked toward Rade as he explained. Even though he kept his eyes on the road, Dylan knew something else was on his mind. Before she could ask he continued. "Chloe was admitted to the Hawthorne Institution for Women shortly after she lost the baby. Hopefully Peter can come up with something. It would certainly explain her psychotic behavior."

Dylan's jaw fell open. It was then that she realized why Chloe was such a nut case. She was institutionalized. It explained everything. She was obsessed with Rade. Everything she did proved it. The incident at *The Castle*, the staged photos, the baby. Everything was clear as day. Even though it still had to be proven, it made Dylan more convinced that she played a big part in Rade's kidnapping. It all made sense. She had to have been the one who ordered Alex to drug Rade. She could stay in the background while Alex did everything for her. *No wonder Rade couldn't remember ever seeing her at the house.* Then when he was good and drugged, she went in for the kill. Just thinking about how she took advantage of him made Dylan's stomach turn. She could no longer hold it down.

"Rade pull over," Dylan cried.

When Rade looked over at her, she looked sick. Her face turned pale and her forehead began to bead with sweat. Rade pulled the car into the nearest alley. Before he had the car fully stop, Dylan had her seatbelt off and her hand on the door handle. With all the strength she had, she pushed open the door and quickly got out of the car. Stumbling her way to the front bumper, she placed one hand on the hood to support herself as heaved the full contents of her breakfast on the dirty asphalt. Just when she thought she couldn't spill any more, another burst of nausea seeped up her throat. Rade immediately took her in his arms knowing that something he said must have triggered her attack. Dylan pushed Rade away from her as she once again began spilling her guts. Rade was right beside her holding her hair from her face. He had never seen her like this.

When she was finally finished and only dry heaves remained, Rade lifted her from the pavement and carried her back to the front seat of the car. Being careful, he lowered her exhausted body onto the seat. He took the silk pocket square from the breast pocket of his suit jacket and gently wiped it across Dylan lips and then her forehead. As soon as he was sure that she was okay, he rounded the front of the Audi and got behind the wheel.

* * * * *

By the time they arrived back at the parking garage at the penthouse, Dylan was totally drained. Her emotional attack took over causing her body to submit to total exhaustion. Rade put the Audi into park careful not to wake her. Exiting the car as quietly as possible, he opened her door and gently lifted her from her seat.

Nothing could have satisfied him more than to feel her body so close to his, but to have her in this state was torture. That was until her arms wrapped around his shoulders and her head nestled in the crook of his neck. Rade tenderly kissed the top of her head as he patiently waited for the elevator to open.

Moments later, Dylan was sleeping comfortably in their bed wearing only her bra and panties. It took Rade little effort to strip away her clothing once he had her on the bed. She was dead to the world. Covering her, he leaned down and kissed her forehead whispering softly, "I love you Sweetness."

Rade headed out of the room taking one last look at Dylan as she laid peacefully on the bed. As much as he hated leaving her alone, he knew he needed to make some calls. With everything going on over the past few days, his mind wasn't on work. His thoughts were only on Dylan and how he would be able to fix things between them. When Dylan showed up at his hotel room, he knew she still loved him and their love for each other was all they needed.

He only hoped that it wasn't too much for Dylan. Everything that had happened to her over the past months was more than anyone should have to endure. But he knew his Sweetness, she was strong and unwilling to give up. She was also stubborn, which drove him crazy at times. They would get through this together.

No sooner Rade got to his study, he cell began to ring. He didn't recognize the number, but thought it best to answer the call.

"Matheson, can I help you," Rade greeted the caller.

"That's something you need to be asking yourself," the caller snickered.

"Who is this?" Rade demanded.

"Let's just say, someone you needed to be very careful of. You will never have her Matheson. All of your efforts will be for nothing," the caller advised sarcastically.

"Tell me who the fuck this is?" Rade had enough of these games. Whoever was calling, sound like he was threatening him and he didn't take kindly to threats.

"All in good time. All in good time." The caller hung up before Rade had a chance to tell him to "fuck off."

There was something about the caller that made Rade very suspicious. He was pretty certain he knew exactly who the caller was. Pulling up his contacts, he dialed Richard. Once Richard answered, he demanded that he find out who the number belonged to. Rade rattled off the number to Richard, knowing that the caller probably used a disposable phone. He still had to try even though he had better odds betting on a cock fight than finding the caller.

Rade finished his calls and got his schedule set up for the week. He had been so focused on Dylan the past week that he was neglecting his work. Gwen set yet another appointment with Mr. Henderson which cost Rade a two-hundred dollar bouquet of flowers which Gwen justly deserved. He also touched base with a few companies requesting to meet with him for a potential investment. Some looked to be very promising, while others were just fighting a losing battle. Even with that, he was still willing to meet with them to see what they had to offer. He also got in touch with Keeve Black and Mason Stone to see how things were moving along with the Spectrum transition. They seemed to be very pleased with the progress aside from the expansion of a new facility in New York. Rade assured them, he had a location picked out and that he would get with them by the end of the week to show them the new location. He wanted to make sure Dylan was on board with his plans before he rushed into anything. After all it was her hard work that brought them all together.

There was a light knock on the door just as Rade shut down his laptop. When he looked up, Dylan was standing in the doorway wearing one of Rade's button-down shirts. If ever there was a more beautiful sight, he hadn't experienced it. It would never compare to the beauty standing before him. The shirt she wore hung just above her knees with only the middle three buttons done. When she walked toward him, he could see a hint of her lacy panties as she stepped forward. Her nipples were taut against the thin lace of her bra and the starched fabric of the shirt causing them to become more prominent the more she tugged on the bottom hem. Her hair was a mess and piled high on top of her gorgeous head. She had that sleepy look that showcased her hooded lids as she rubbed them delicately with her finger trying to wake up fully. Just the sight of her made him hard.

Slowly, Rade rounded his desk and approached Dylan. She was the most beautiful thing he had ever seen. Closing the distance, he stepped in front of her and began undoing the three buttons on her crisp white shirt. He took hold of the opened ends and pushed the shirt down Dylan's shoulders. Her perky nipples rose to attention even with her bra on. That soon came off as well. He wondered if she was as excited as he was. There was one way to find out. Cupping her sex, he found his answer. Even in her tired state, the heat radiated from the minuscule material of her panties. Slipping his hands inside the waistband, he lowered her underwear until they fell to the floor. Without hesitation, Dylan lifted her feet one at a time and kicked them out of the way.

Rade pulled one of her legs to his waist slipping one and then another finger inside her moisten channel. He loved how she was always ready for him. Pushing his fingers deeper inside her, he could hear her soft moans. Rade lowered his head sucking and biting her earlobe. "Are you ready to play Sweetness?" There were no words from her. Only the sweet sounds of pleasure filled the space between them. Dylan's body was on fire with need. She wanted Rade more than ever. She was so overcome with desire that she exploded with a violent orgasm from the assault of his fingers. Although Rade smiled at her lack of self-control, for this she would be punished. "My little minx needs to show a little more control," Rade whispered as he removed his fingers from her vagina. Dylan moaned with frustration. She needed more from him. Her orgasm came to quickly leaving her wanting more.

A feeling of emptiness hit her as she watched Rade leave the study. She was ready to go after him when she heard his voice coming from just outside the door. "Don't move Sweetness. If you want more, you'll do as I say."

Dylan's frustration turned into anger. He was playing with her. It was a test. Her only choice was to do as he commanded. Dylan remembered how she felt the first time he used his dominance on her. Her body heated like a roman candle. She also remembered the pleasure he gave her when she gave herself completely to him. In all her nakedness, she stood where she was and didn't move. Her body began to chill as the cool air hit her naked body, but still burned knowing what would be waiting for her. Twenty minutes passed, then thirty, thirty-five. Dylan watched as the clock slowly moved. Dylan could feel the tightness in her chest as her anger began to boil. Forty-five minutes had past when Dylan was ready to give Rade a piece of her mind. Just as she was ready to leave the study, she felt the warmth of his hand on her shoulder. She was ready to turn around to face him, when he placed a black scarf over her eyes. "You will do exactly as I say Sweetness or your pleasure will be denied. Do you understand?"

Dylan nodded her head, but Rade demanded an answer. "You need to tell me that you understand Sweetness."

"I understand," Dylan answered.

"Good girl," Rade said smiling as he stood behind her.

Taking Dylan by the hand, he led her to his desk. The front of Dylan's legs bumped the edge causing her to stop her movements. It was then that Rade's strong hand pushed down on her lower back willing her to lower her chest down on the cold surface. Gliding his hand up and down her spine, he leaned over her back and said softly, "Put your hands behind you back Sweetness and spread those sexy legs for me."

Dylan did as she was told. She knew it would be a matter of time before Rade would be controlling her body. There was a quick tug on her wrists letting her know that he was binding them together. It wasn't tight, but she knew she wouldn't be unable to free herself from the restraints. Surprised and startled, a quick slap landed on her ass taking her breath away. Slap, slap, slap, this time on the other cheek. The slaps weren't painful. Just a small sting filtered through her skin. With each swat to her ass, the burning of her skin intensified leaving her wanting more. The wetness that pooled between her spread legs only confirmed her desire. If her hands were free, she would have pleasured herself. She was so close to the edge, she could feel the tingle from head to toe. Rade's warm breath soothed her ass taking the sting away, like a child being comforted with a scrapped knee. "Your ass is nice and pink for me Sweetness. Do you know why I have punished you?"

Dylan's mind was elsewhere. It took her a moment to think. "Because I came before you gave me permission."

"Good girl," Rade smiled. "Remember Sweetness, your pleasure is mine and only I can give you permission to come."

Dylan missed the way Rade took control. She loved the dominant side of him. With everything that happened over the past month, she didn't realize how much she actually missed having her body controlled by him. Relishing the thought, Dylan let out a small moan as Rade slip his finger between her slick folds. Gathering her juices, he moved his finger to her perineum, circling the outer pucker with the tip of his middle finger. With his other hand he reached around her waist until he found her clit. Pinching and rubbing the sensitized nub, he stared down at her body as her back began to arch. This is how he wanted her. She was his to command. Carefully, Rade added a little more force to his middle finger and slowly pushed the tip further inside the tight pucker. He could feel Dylan's body tense at the invasion. "Relax Sweetness," he whispered lowering his mouth to her shoulder while gently biting the skin just at the juncture of her neck. Dylan took a deep breath and tried to relax.

Rade continued his assault on her tight passage making sure his finger was well lubricated with her juices to allow him easier access. Adding more pressure, he pushed his finger inside up to the first digit. There was a slight resistance, but then her muscles relax letting him in further. As his finger penetrated her, his other hand glided between her folds soaking up the wetness of her sweet honey. Rade gently slipped his finger inside her wet channel and hooked it upward in order to find her special spot. He knew he had found gold when her walls began to tighten.

There were no words to describe the pleasure mixed with pain that Dylan was feeling. She felt full from the invasion at both ends, yet totally taken. She needed to hold back her release. It was getting harder and harder with every push and pull of Rade's fingers. She couldn't hold on much longer. The thought of Rade buried deep inside her only heightened her need. Just when she was about to explode, Rade quickly pulled away leaving her unfulfilled. Her body ached for release. Tears began forming in her eyes from the torment of being denied the pleasure when she was so close to ecstasy. She could have screamed at him for not giving her what she needed. "No, no, please. I need to come," Dylan cried. No sooner she spoke, Rade was deep inside her, filling her tight channel with his thick hard cock. Desperation filled her, but she knew only he could let her come. Her only salvation was to beg for it. "Please Rade, let me come."

Rade stood behind Dylan smiling, knowing that he indeed had control over her. She had learned well that only he controlled her body. Leaning over, he whispered softly, "Come."

Chapter Five

Keeve and Mason were waiting in the conference room for their weekly meeting. Dylan was surprised to see them both seated already. Normally she would have been the first one to the meeting, but today she was a little late getting to work, no thanks to Mr. Wonderful.

Normally, the weekly meetings included some of the other co-workers, so Dylan was confused when she didn't see anyone else seated.

"Where is everyone? Did the meeting get switched to another day?" Dylan asked confused.

"No, the meeting is still on for today," Keeve explained. "We just felt this meeting didn't pertain to the other associates."

Dylan took her seat and opened her leather note jogger for the meeting. There was a moment of silence before the phone in the conference room started to ring.

"Right on time," Mason said as he put the call on speaker. "Mr. Matheson, we are all here. Are you ready for your presentation?"

Dylan was once again confused. She had no idea why Rade would be included in today's meeting. The Spectrum transition was almost finished. The only thing left to do was to find a new location for the facility in New York. Maybe this was the topic of the meeting.

"Thank you gentlemen, Ms. Adams," he began. "I'll try not to take too much of your time."

When Dylan heard the voice coming over the speaker, she knew right away that it wasn't Rade. The only other man she knew that went by Mr. Matheson was Rade's father, Garrett. What she couldn't understand was why he would be calling during their meeting?

"I know that you're all curious as to why I've asked for this meeting." Garrett knew what he was about to say was going to shock the socks off them. "It has come to my attention that my son may have been a little hasty in his decision to split the shares of Spectrum between you three. Unfortunately, there is a small problem with his generosity. As you know, I am a secret partner in BlackStone Industries which would give me the option, if I so desire, to partake in the distribution of those shares. Since I own fifty-one percent of BlackStone Industries, I see it only fitting that the majority of those shares should go to me."

"What are you trying to say Mr. Matheson?" Keeve asked.

"What I'm saying is that unless you have the capitol to buy out my shares of BlackStone Industries, I believe that twenty-six percent of the Spectrum shares should go to me. The remaining shares would be twenty-five to my son and twenty-four and a half to each of you. Now if you three decide to give Dylan the ten percent that was agreed upon, that's on you. Either way you look at it, I would have controlling interest in Spectrum giving me control over any and all decisions."

"Why are you doing this Garrett?" Dylan asked irritated by his arrogance. "Why would you do this to your own son?"

"It's business Ms. Adams. My son, more than anyone, will understand that. Anyway, I will have my attorney draw up a new contract. I'll let you know when it's ready." Garrett knew he had them by the silence on their end of the phone. "Good day gentlemen, Ms. Adams." With that Garrett ended the call.

Dylan was in shock. She couldn't believe what just happened. She really thought that Rade's father was a changed man. She trusted him when he said he would do anything in order to get back his relationship with Rade. Rade was right about him. Garrett Matheson only did things for his own personal gain. She needed to let Rade know. When she got back to her office, she looked at her phone and thought for a moment before she dialed Rade's number. If she knew Rade, he would have already been informed of the low blow by his father.

* * * * *

"Son of a bitch! That low life motherfucker," Rade yelled as his temperature began to boil. He knew that everyone in his office could hear him cursing. *How could he have been so stupid to believe that his father was making an effort to get back in his good graces?* He should have went with his first instinct and never let his guard down.

As Rade was trying hard to tame is anger with a shot of scotch, there was a soft knock on the door. Rade was still pissed by the audacity of his father. "Come in," he spat, not caring about the tone of his voice.

Gwen hesitantly opened the door and poked her head inside. She was afraid to enter his office completely. She knew something had set off his anger and she didn't want to make it any worse than it already was. In a soft voice she murmured, "Mr. Henderson is here to see you sir."

Rade looked up at Gwen with apologetic eyes. He knew she was only doing her job and that he needed to stop taking his frustrations out on her. "Give me a moment before you send him back," Rade said with a softer tone then a few minutes ago.

When Gwen closed the door, Rade pushed from his chair and went to his liquor cabinet to pour another drink. Before he could down the contents, a knock came at his door. Mr. Henderson no doubt.

With everything that had taken place in the last hour, Rade was surprised to find his meeting with Dwight Henderson went seemingly well. He managed to tone down his temper enough to get through the meeting. The last thing he wanted was to lose a potential relationship with someone he might be willing to invest in. Mr. Henderson was the owner of a freight company that mostly did business off shore. Of the many companies Rade had invested in, this was one company that he needed to learn more about. He wasn't in the habit of investing in off shore freight liners, but there could be a possibility to expand some of that business closer to home. Even though the meeting was a good distraction, he needed to focus on his father's announcement. He set his mind on doing just that.

"Gwen, I'm leaving for the day. I can be reached on my cell if you need me," Rade said.

"Very well Sir," Gwen replied keeping her eyes on her computer.

Richard pulled up to the BlackStone office building shortly before five o'clock. Rade insisted on allowing Richard to drive them to work when they left this morning. He wanted to spend as much time with Dylan as possible. He missed not being able to sit next to her during the short drive.

When they arrived at BlackStone, Rade suggested that Richard wait in the Bentley while he went up and got Dylan. There were some things he needed to talk to Keeve and Mason about regarding his father and his secret partnership with their company. He wanted to know why this was never brought to his attention when the contract was negotiated on the Spectrum deal. Rade needed to know what, if any, what his father's actual rights were. He needed to see a copy of the contract that spelled out the agreement with his father. Rade was hoping that his attorney would be able to find some sort of loophole that may have been overlooked.

Stepping off the elevator, Rade was greeted only by Jessica. He wasn't sure where her shadow was, nor did he care. His only concern was getting to Dylan and talking with Black and Stone. Entering her office, he found she wasn't there. He waited for a while for her to came back. Fifteen minutes passed, but she still hadn't returned. It was then that Rade decide to look for her. To his surprise she was sitting alone in the conference room. Rade tapped lightly on the door, careful not to startle her. When she looked up at him, he saw a sadness to her eyes.

Leaning down he gave her a soft kiss on the lips. "Dylan, you look like you lost your best friend," Rade said concerned.

"I'm guessing you've heard. I should have never trusted your father Rade. How could he do this to you?" Dylan replied.

"Because he is a selfish bastard," Rade admitted. "Everything he does, is for his own personal gain. Nothing more. It doesn't matter to him how many people it affects."

"What are you going to do?" Dylan asked.

"I need to talk to Keeve and Mason. Hopefully there is a clause in the agreement outlining what he can and can't do as a secret partner." This was Rade's only hope other than buying out his father's shares.

Rade spent a few minutes with Keeve and Mason going over how they came to meet Garrett Matheson and how he was able to become a secret partner. Come to find out, his father had been in some pretty shady deals with other investors which he claimed he never knew about until he was already neck deep. By the time he realized it, it was too late to bail, especially with the amount of money he had tied up. His bad investment decisions caused his reputation to be tarnished. So when he entered into an agreement with BlackStone Industries, he didn't want their business affected by his stupid mistakes, hence the secret partnership. BlackStone needed the funds and Garrett Matheson needed a legitimate company to invest in. It was a win, win situation for everyone. Keeve produced a copy of the partnership agreement and gave it to Rade. Rade informed them that he wanted his attorney to look it over. Hopefully he would be able to find something that his friends had missed.

Rade sat silent going over the partner agreement while Richard drove him and Dylan back to the penthouse. He wanted to take a look at the document so that when he called his attorney, he would have some knowledge of what to expect. When he got to the bottom of the agreement, he noticed an additional provision. As he read through it, he knew he may have found the kink he was looking for. The provision stated that in order for the contract to be valid, the secret partner had to attend quarterly board meetings, re-invest five percent of the annual gross profits back into the company, and attend any and all acquisition meetings either in person or by phone.

Rade was pretty confident that his father did none of those things and it wouldn't be too hard to prove. Certainly there were board minutes taken during the meetings and financial statements to show whether or not his father made any additional contributions back into the company. Attending acquisitions wasn't a problem to prove since Rade knew for a fact his father was not present during any of the meetings with Spectrum in person or by phone. To be sure, Rade still wanted his attorney to confirm his discovery.

Dylan scooted closer to Rade trying to get a closer look at the agreement. Rade had gone through each page so quickly; she thought for sure he was some sort of speed reader. It was only after he stopped on the last page that she was able to read its contents. As she read the provisions, a smile came over her.

"Rade, if this agreement has any weight on the partnership, then your dad doesn't have any say or right to anything," Dylan said excited knowing there was a chance she was right.

"I hope your right Sweetness. I want my attorney to look at it though, just to be sure," Rade declared.

It had been a long day for Rade and Dylan. All Dylan wanted to do was soak in a bubble induced bath for at least an hour. She still couldn't believe that Garrett Matheson would do something so underhanded. He seemed so sincere when she first met with him. Just the thought of him playing on her sympathy made her angry.

While Dylan was soaking mindlessly in her bath, Rade was on his cell with his attorney. Miles Carter had been a friend of Rade's since his college days at Stanford, where Rade had studied business and Miles studied law. It was Miles that Rade turned to when he first started RIM Global. Rade trusted him more than anyone. Miles requested that Rade scan the documents over to him, so he could take a look at them. Once he confirmed that he received the document, Rade headed to the bedroom to check in on Dylan. He had his own idea on how to decompress.

The bedroom door was closed, so Rade lightly tapped on it. When there was no answer, he turned the knob and opened the door. Dylan wasn't inside the bedroom, but he knew she wouldn't be far. When he opened the door to the bathroom, he knew he had died and gone to heaven. If heaven was like this, then he would die a million times over. Dylan was lying in the tub with the bubbles only covering half her body, exposing her soft creamy breasts. She was beyond beautiful. Everything about her was perfect. Rade was surprised to see that she had dosed off. The last time that happened, she almost ended up drowning herself. Quietly, Rade walked over to the giant tub and gently rubbed her cheek with his thumb. Her eyes fluttered open as she hummed.

"Hey," she said softly.

"Can I join you?" Rade asked, already removing his clothing before she could refuse him.

Without saying a word, Dylan moved forward so that Rade could slide in behind her. Rade stripped off the last of his clothing and carefully slipped in. This had to be his most favorite time with her. He pulled her close to him, both of them relaxing, think of nothing but how good it felt to be together. Dylan turned her body so that they were facing each other. Dylan looked up at Rade with softness in her eyes. She wondered if it would always be like this with him or would his time with her be taken away by his unborn child. She didn't know if she would ever be ready for the what the future would bring for them. The only thing she did know was that she wanted to spend it with him. Rade knew the minute she looked at him that she loved him as much as he loved her. Lowering his head, he gently kissed her soft lips. When their lips met, heat surged between them. Nothing would ever tear them apart. Rade slowly lifted Dylan so that she was straddling him.

He loved the way she smelled, the way her body felt on his. How they fit so perfectly together. They were virtually inseparable. There was something different though. The way Dylan clung to him was pulling him under. He could feel the desperation radiating from her body. Regretfully, Rade pulled from her. When their eyes met, he could see the moisture building in them. He wasn't sure what caused her uneasiness. Brushing his thumb against her cheek he said, "What is it Sweetness?"

Dylan tried turning her head so she wasn't looking at him. She could bear for him to see her so tormented. That worked for only a moment before Rade placed his hand on her cheek forcing her to look at him. "Everything is so messed up Rade. It seems every time things are going good, something bad happens," Dylan choked trying to keep her tears hidden.

"Everything will work out Sweetness. I promise." Rade wasn't sure how convincing he sounded, but he knew he hated seeing Dylan this way.

The water was getting cold and Rade was ready to take her to his bed. Getting out first, Rade wrapped a towel around his waist while grabbing another for Dylan. Dylan stood in the tub knee deep loving the way Rade wrapped the warm towel around her chilled body. Before she could protest, Rade tucked his arm under her knees and lifted her from the cool water. Dylan's only response was to tuck her head under his chin. Even though her arms were nestled within the confines of the soft towel, she loved how he held her in his arms. She not only felt loved, but she felt protected.

Exiting the bathroom, Rade laid Dylan gently on the bed. Her towel came open, giving him a perfect view of her glorious body. Dylan was no longer the shy woman he met months ago. He knew every curve and line of her body down to the small scar on her right knee. He wanted her so badly that the blood in his cock began to surge. He wasn't ready to take her just yet. He had something else in mind for her. He wanted to pleasure her like she had never been pleasured before. Going to his walk-in closet, he grabbed a few things and went back to the bed. Dylan knew he was up to something. It didn't matter what it was, she would always trust him.

Holding a black scarf in front of her, he softly asked. "Do you trust me Sweetness?"

He needed to hear the words from her, so when she nodded he asked again. "Sweetness, I need to hear you say that you trust me."

"I trust you Rade." Her eyes showing him, she trusted him completely.

Sitting beside her on the bed, he placed the black scarf over her eyes and secured it behind her head. "How does that feel? Is it too tight?" Rade asked.

"No, it's fine," Dylan confirmed.

"Good. I need you to lie down on your back, hands in front of you," Rade demanded.

She did as he ordered. Scooting her body back farther onto the bed, Dylan felt for the pillows knowing this would be the head of the bed. Once she was comfortable with her body stretched out and her head on the pillow, she held her hands in front of her.

"God, you're beautiful," Rade confessed as he took in the sight of her submission to him.

Rade reached behind him and took a long silk red rope in his hand. He had learned the technique of *"Kinbaku"* when he was younger. If done correctly, it could heighten a woman's arousal. Taking the soft piece of rope, Rade began intricately weaving the rope between Dylan's hands. When he was finished with her hands, he began wrapping the rope around Dylan's upper body. Lifting her this way and that, he made sure the rope was placed where it needed to be in order to put a hint of pressure on her breasts. Knotting and tying the rope, he tugged slightly to make sure he had the right amount of tension. He needed to make sure her binds weren't too tight. If they were too tight, it would defeat the purpose of intricate binding. When he was finished with her breasts, he moved on to her legs. Once again he masterfully tied the rope making sure to set the knots in just the right areas. Looping the rope just above her pubic area, he took the end and brought it between her legs making sure he placed a knot over her clit. With just enough pull, she would feel the firmness of the knot as it rubbed against her swollen nub. Finishing, he spiraled the last length of rope around each thigh taking the ends around her ankles and securing them to the hooks he had built into the frame at the foot end of the bed. Rade never used this technique on Dylan, but knew she would enjoy the pleasure he was about to give her. Staring down at her body, she was beautiful with the rope wrapped around her body. The red of the rope contrasting to the creamy color of her body was breathtaking.

Rade leaned over her and whispered as he took hold of her earlobe between his teeth. "I am going to pleasure you until you scream my name Sweetness."

Those words alone made Dylan's body quiver. The placement of the rope on her breast and on her clit had her so aroused that the tiniest movement would set her off.

Rade took his time with her. He wanted to take her in. He had to admit his handiwork was magnificent. The way her breasts were on display for him, made him hard at just the sight. Her nipples were so red from the constriction of the rope, he knew one flick of his tongue across the sensitive peak would send her spinning. The knot he placed on her clit was saturated with her sweet juices that it had him wanting to taste her. As much as she was aroused, his arousal was doubled. The pressure building in his cock was to the point of ripping him wide open. He wasn't sure how much longer he could wait. This was about pleasuring her first.

Adjusting his form, he positioned his body between her legs. Beginning at the top of her head, he softly and slowly placed wet kisses on her, breathing in her essence along the way. When he got to her neck, he could feel her push into him as her back arched. Her breasts were pushed so far upward that he could feel her taut peaks rub against his chest. Taking her hands, he loosened the slip knot he had done and pulled her arms above her head, putting more tension on the knot at her clit. He liked that he had the option of placing her hands where he wanted them to be.

With her back still arched, Rade placed a kiss on her sensitive nipple gently sucking and licking the taut bud. When he had given it enough attention, he moved to her other one. Dylan was so aroused that all she wanted to do was come. The knot over her clit, stimulated her just enough to drive her crazy. What she really wanted was to have Rade deep inside her.

"Rade, please, I need you," Dylan breathed.

"Tell me what you need Sweetness," Rade said softly continuing his assault on her over-sensitive nipple.

"I need to have you inside me," Dylan panted.

At that moment, Rade bit her nipple lightly sending a surge of pleasure to her core causing her to explode. He wasn't ready to quit. He needed more from her. With a feverish desire, Rade captured Dylan's lips in a heated kiss. Her body began to buckle underneath him as another wave of pleasure hit her. He would never get over how sensitive her body was to his touch. Nipping at her bottom lip, Rade continued to kiss her softly, colliding his tongue with hers, until he could feel her body relax. While her body calmed, Rade continued his exploration of her luscious mouth. Swiping his tongue with hers, he wanted to preserve this moment. Her soft moans excited him in such a way, he knew she was his. Needing to taste more of her, he broke their kiss and slowly moved down her body. The ropes were taut against her skin and he could see the indentations beginning to form. Reaching her mound, he gently moved the rope that was snug between her legs to the side and began devouring her sweet nectar. Her clit was swollen beyond belief. He had never seen anything more beautiful. He didn't want her to come again so soon, so he only gave her clit a quick lap of his tongue before moving to her slick folds. His tongue plunged inside her tight channel as he continued to suck and lick her. One hand fell to her ass while the other explored her wet folds. Following the movement of his tongue, he glided his middle finger inside her slick channel while his thumb slowly circled her anus. He knew she would soon be delivering another orgasm when her hips began moving frantically. Before Dylan knew it, Rade had her ankles untied from the foot of the bed and her body turned so that she was now lying on her stomach. Rade lifted her hips causing the rope between Dylan's legs to tighten. The knot was pressed firmly against her clit causing a sensation she had never felt before.

Before she could respond to the stimulation, Rade had two fingers inside her tight channel. Curling them upward, he found her special spot. Dylan began rocking her hips back and forth needed more of him. Rade was pleasuring every sensitized area of her body. The only place left was her tight passage which he wanted to penetrate with his hard cock. It had been a while since he had taken her there. Taking hold of his cock, he moved his fingers from her channel and slowly dipped his shaft inside her, just enough to arouse her, but not enough to make her come. With her juices now coating his engorged cock, he slipped from her and rubbed his cock against her tight opening. There was a slight movement of Dylan's hips before she settled. "Relax Sweetness. I need to go slow so I don't hurt you."

Dylan took in a deep breath and tried to relax her muscles. Her body was so overwhelmed with pleasure, she wasn't sure how much more she could take. Rade had given her so much; her body was on blissful overload. More than anything she wanted to give him a piece of the pleasure he had given her. Rade slowly inched his way inside her tight passage pulling out each time only a fraction. She was so tight for him that he had to bite his lip in order not to come. Dylan started to push back against him. The feeling of fullness increasing the more of him she took. With his free hand, Rade slipped his finger inside her wet heat moving it in and out mimicking the motion of his cock as he pulled and pushed further inside her anus. Rade lost control when Dylan exploded once again screaming his name. He continued to move slowly, deeper inside her tight passage not wanting to hurt her. Her scream of satisfaction filled the room again as she was once again consumed by her desire. Rade watched as his balls hit her sweet cunt, sending him closer and closer to the edge. It only took a few more thrusts before he too exploded with violent fury.

With their bodies fully spent, Rade gently flipped Dylan's body over and began untying the ropes expertly wound around her body. As he removed the rope, he was greeted with the indentation that the bindings left. It was breathtaking. Dylan was only the second person he used this technique of bondage on. His first was Chloe, but he would never let Dylan know that. He didn't want her to know that Chloe had this part of him first even though it meant nothing to him. Nothing could compared to how he felt when tying Dylan and the mark it left on her body was nothing but electrifying. His mark. The more Rade undid the ropes, the more of her beauty was on display. She laid before him in silence as he looked upon her. It was only after he removed the rope from her nipples did Dylan whimper. He knew the lack of blood flow to her taut buds was beginning to rush back. Bending over, he gently placed a kiss on each nipple hoping to relieve some of the pressure that built inside them. His tender touch caused another shudder as Dylan's body was once again consumed with utter pleasure.

Rade smiled knowing he could cause her so much pleasure. He knew this wouldn't be the last time he would be tying her up this way.

Chapter Six

Rade was staring at the ceiling when his phone began to vibrate. Slipping on his pants, he grabbed his phone and quietly left the bedroom leaving Dylan to sleep. It was early morning and he gritted his teeth at the early intrusion. When Peter's number appeared, his body relaxed knowing he informed Peter to call anytime, day or night if he had any new information.

Rade swiped the screen and greeted Peter. "I hope you have some information for me Peter."

"I do sir. We found out information on Dr. O'Brien. Seems she has a business on the side. She runs an adaption service. She also specializes in infertility and artificial insemination," Peter explained.

"What about her credentials?" Rade questioned.

"She's highly sought after. She holds several honors in the medical field and also in embryonic stem cell research," Peter paused. "There's something else sir. There were several malpractice suits filed against Dr. O'Brien, but they were never brought to trial. I'm not sure what the reasons were behind the suits, but I'm hoping to have that information soon."

"Let me know what you find out," Rade said, ending his call with Peter.

With the information he just received, his head began to spin with all kinds of what ifs. *What if Chloe wasn't really pregnant?*

What if a sample of his sperm was taken while he was drugged and implanted inside her? What if she had plans to adapt a child pretending it was theirs when it came time for her to deliver?

He was thinking erratically. All he knew, he needed to find answers. Something about this whole ordeal just didn't sit right with him, especially knowing that Chloe was pregnant once before and lost the child. Nothing made sense to him. *How would he be able to prove she wasn't carrying his child when he couldn't even prove she was at the house with him? There had to be a way.* The more he thought about it, he only had one option. Make a trade. Before he made any abrupt decisions, he needed to run it by Dylan.

The best way to get Dylan to agree with his plan was to fix her a phenomenal breakfast. He was hoping that the saying, *"the best way to a man's heart is through his stomach"* also held true for women. At least one woman in particular. If he was going to make an amazing breakfast she wouldn't forget, he had better get started before she woke up. Another way to a woman's heart was having breakfast served in bed, at least by his standards.

By the time Rade finished cooking breakfast, he had fresh raspberry crêpes with a sweet cream sauce, crisp bacon, oven brown seasoned potatoes, and fresh squeezed orange juice, waiting to be served. He went an extra step, and fired up his espresso machine, making Dylan a very special vanilla latte with chocolate shavings on top. Placing everything on the breakfast tray, he looked at his masterpiece with a smile and headed back to their bedroom. *God, how he loved the sound of that. Their bedroom.* Dylan was still asleep as he entered the room. He knew he had worn her out last night. Her body was pushed beyond the limit. He might have felt a little selfish, if it wasn't for the multiple orgasms he gave her.

Placing the tray on the night stand, Rade crawled into the bed beside her. She was so warm, wrapped up in the sheet and comforter. Snaking his hand under the covers, he searched for her breasts. When she rolled over, he knew he had been caught trying to cop a feel. He didn't care because as soon as her eyes opened, he saw the most magnificent shade of green. He could have sworn that Dylan's eyes were greener and clearer than he had seen them for a long time.

"Good morning Sweetness," Rade said softly as he pulled her closer to his body.

"Mmmm, I like this. You next to me when I wake up," Dylan said snuggling closer to him.

"I brought you breakfast. Are you hungry?" Rade asked.

"Starving," Dylan replied.

Rade slid from under the covers while Dylan position herself in a sitting position. When Rade placed the tray on her lap, Dylan couldn't believe the display of food before her. Rade must have slaved all morning to make her such a wonderful breakfast.

"Rade, how long have you been up? This looks amazing." Dylan licked her lips as her eyes feasted on the food in front of her.

"It's just something I whipped up," Rade replied taking the napkin from the tray and placing it across Dylan's chest.

Dylan didn't believe him. No one could just whip up a breakfast like this. She knew firsthand what goes into making crêpes alone. Taking her first bite, her taste buds were doing a happy dance as the sweet cream and fruit hit her tongue. "Oh my God, Rade. This tastes incredible."

"I'm glad you like it Sweetness." Rade smiled, watching Dylan devour her breakfast. Her moans and groans of delight almost set him off as he watched her lips wrap around the fork.

* * * * *

It was Saturday and the grand opening of Evan's newly remodeled pub. Dylan almost forgot about it when his name came up on her phone. Dylan hadn't told Rade about the opening. Not because she was hiding it from him, but because with everything that had been going on, it simply slipped her mind. She wasn't sure if she really wanted to go. The look on Evan's face was more than enough for her to know he was not happy seeing her with Rade when he came to the penthouse for his blood test.

Dylan thought it would be better to talk to Rade about the event first before she talked to Evan. So instead of answering his call, she swiped the decline and let the call go to voice mail. Rade was in the kitchen cleaning up the mess from his awesome breakfast. Dylan offered to help him, but he refused to let her, instead she took a much needed shower. After their night of blissful, beyond paradise, love making, she needed to rid herself of the remnants. Rade was already finished cleaning the kitchen and had settled down on the couch by the floor-to-ceiling windows when she entered the living area. Dylan walked over to where Rade was sitting. His thoughts were on something else because he didn't notice that she had walked up to him. Touching his arm to get his attention, Rade's eyes slowly drifted to hers.

"You look like you have the weight of the world on your shoulders Rade," Dylan said.

"I've been thinking about what to do about Chloe. I want to get another blood test done, but in order for her to agree to it, I think I might have to bribe her in a trade-off," Rade confessed.

"What kind of trade-off.?" Dylan asked concerned. She wasn't sure if she was ready to hear what he had to say.

Taking Dylan by the hand, he swung her around and pulled her close before pulling her down onto his lap. He knew it would be better if she was sitting. Taking in a deep breath, he laid out his plan to her. "I think I should agree to go to London with her to meet her parents, but only if she agrees to have another blood test done," Rade hinted. "If she refuses, than it will only make her look like she's hiding the real truth about being pregnant. It would be something I could use against her."

"So what you're saying is that you will agree to go to London with her if she agrees to another blood test?" Dylan wasn't sure how she felt about his plan. She didn't want Rade anywhere near that bitch, let alone flying off to London with her.

"Yes, but there's a catch. She would have to submit to the blood test first. That way when it came time to go to London, you would be going with me. She wouldn't need to know," Rade began. "What I really want, is for the blood test to come back negative and prove that I'm not the father or better yet that she wasn't pregnant after all."

"Do you think it will work? What if she finds out what you're up to?" Dylan was concerned that Rade's plan would fall apart.

"It doesn't matter, either way we win. If she refuses, it only makes her look like a liar and if she agrees, she will learn she can't have me and you're the only person I love."

"What if she is really pregnant and she finds out I'm going to London with you. She could keep you from ever seeing your child," Dylan argued.

"Not that it matters to me one way or the other, but it will never happen Sweetness. With the information we have regarding her past, we can use that against her," Rade assured her.

* * * * *

Dylan sat beside Rade as he talked to Chloe. Rade contemplated on meeting her in person, but he didn't want to deal with the drama, nor did he want to be near her. It took some convincing, but Chloe finally agreed to have another blood test taken. Instead of having Julia Foster administer the test, they decided to use a doctor they could both agree on. Someone who had good credentials and neither one of them knew. They decided it was best for their attorney's to handle the details. The appointment would be scheduled for early next week and the truth would finally come out. Good or bad, Rade was ready.

Rade and Dylan were surprised when Chloe agreed to another blood test. Even though it would have been better if she refused, showing she was a liar, Rade would soon find out the truth.

As they sat on the couch, Dylan thought it was a good time as any to tell Rade about the grand opening at *Riley's*.

"Rade, with everything that's been happening over the last week, I forgot to tell you that Evan is having a grand opening at *Riley's* tonight. I was hoping that you would go with me. Lilly was supposed to go, but since she's currently in Paris, that's impossible," Dylan asked looking at Rade.

"It completely slipped my mind. Evan called me a couple of days ago and told me about it. I already told him that I would be there," Rade replied.

"Good. I'm glad that you two are trying to build a relationship together despite your father's transgressions," Dylan admitted.

Rade agreed with Dylan. Evan and he were just innocent bystanders. It shouldn't matter that they shared the same father, no matter how much Rade hated him. Rade was actually looking forward to seeing Evan. Rade had been to *Riley's* several times and noticed the changes Evan made to the place. He was impressed by his younger brother's accomplishments. At least hard work and perseverance were traits they had in common.

Rade pulled Dylan close to him needing to tame down his erection which was now occupying the constricting area of his jeans. It didn't matter if he was sitting next to her or just thinking about her, she managed to get to him. Needing some relief, he lifted Dylan onto his lap, positioning her right above his throbbing cock. There was too much clothing between them. Taking hold of the zipper to Dylan's frilly skirt, he pushed it down until he was able to lift the fabric up over her head. Dylan's knit top went with the skirt leaving her in her dainty lacy panties and bra. It didn't take long for Rade to rip the delicate material of her panties from her bottom. *Yep, he definitely needed to replenish her supply of panties.* It was a small price to pay not to lose the contact his heavy shaft had against her soft cunt. Cupping his hands over her firm breast, Dylan moaned feeling the pressure he was applying. Dylan's head fell back the moment his mouth took hold of her nipple through the thin lace of her bra. Rade slid the lacy cups down off her breast exposing the creamy mounds. Dylan's breasts were the perfect size. His strong hands fit around them perfectly. Mouth to pert breast, Rade began seducing her nipple until it rose to a perfect peak. Dylan's moans of pleasure filled the room as Rade continued his assault on one, then the other taut bud.

Dylan's body was feeling the wrath of Rade's touch all the way to the tip of her pretty pink toes. She needed for him to be inside her. Shifting her body, she gently took hold of his hard length, and positioned it between her slick folds. Ecstasy was the only word to describe how her body felt with him planted inside her. Dylan began slowly moving her body up and down, relishing every movement of his cock sliding in and out of her. She wanted to be filled by him, so the more he gave, the more she took. The warmth between them grew into a heated rush as the friction of his shaft pumping in and out of her increased.

Dylan was close to her release, but wanted to hang on to it. It was Rade who told her, the longer she could hold out, the sweeter the benefits would be. Concentrating on only him, Dylan delighted him by covering his body with tender wet kisses, from the base of his neck to the hard bud of his nipple. This was where she rested her eager mouth, making sure to satisfy the need she had for him as well. Before Dylan could move to the other side, Rade lifted his body from the couch, taking hers with him. It was unexpected, but Rade walked over to the floor-to-ceiling windows pressing Dylan's body against the hard surface as he continued pumping inside her. Dylan's hands went to Rade's shoulders as she tried to balance herself to meet his thrusts with her own. He wanted nothing more than for the world to see that she belonged to him, even though it would be impossible through the tinted glass.

Their need for each other grew the harder they hammered together. Dylan's body pressed firmly against the cool glass as Rade's pressed against the soft curves of her body. Rade knew he hit the right spot when Dylan's release took over and her body trembled with fury. This is what Rade loved more than anything. To have the woman he loved, come undone in his arms. Knowing that he gave that to her. Knowing that no one else would ever have her. The sound of satisfaction spreading, drenching her with pure ecstasy.

After showering for an hour, Rade and Dylan finally retreated from the shower. They were like two teenagers unable to keep their hands off each other. It would've been easier for them to dress themselves, but being unable to separate, Dylan managed to dress Rade in a pair of black jeans, a grey t-shirt and a dark jacket. It was more difficult for Rade considering he couldn't take his hands off Dylan's body long enough to get past her lacy underwear and bra.

It was almost nine o'clock by the time they left the penthouse. Rade thought it best for Richard to drive them to the opening. Arriving thirty minutes later, Dylan's face lit up at the line of people waiting to get inside the pub. This was going to be a successful opening for Evan. Dylan was happy so many people had shown up for the opening. Even though she wasn't looking forward to standing in line to get in, she wouldn't have missed this for the world. It wasn't until Rade took Dylan by the hand and led her to the alleyway that she realized his plan. When he knocked on the back door and Evan appeared, she knew they must have made arrangements beforehand so they wouldn't be waiting to get in.

Rade and Evan did a quick hand shake before Evan moved to the side to let them enter. Dylan felt uncomfortable that Evan didn't make eye contact with her. She was pretty sure it wasn't her imagination, but when the air got very cold in a matter of minutes, she knew he still had ill feelings towards her.

The music was blasting to the sound of retro music as Evan led them inside the small pub. Evan took them to a small table with a reserved seating sign sitting on top. Within minutes a waitress came by with a glass of red wine and a small glass containing a double shot of scotch. Dylan was disappointed when Evan excused himself from their table. She wanted them to be on better terms, but she had a funny feeling that his abrupt departure had to do with the animosity he still had towards her. More than anything Dylan was hoping she would be able to talk to him and sort things out. The last thing she wanted was for Evan to be mad at her.

The pub was jammed packed. Rade and Dylan could hardly hear themselves talk above the loud music. Rade moved his chair closer to Dylan so they wouldn't be yelling at each other across the table. Dylan was amazed at the number of people that showed for the opening. Granted the place wasn't small, but every inch of the bar was covered with bodies making it feel claustrophobic inside. If Dylan had to guess, there were at least a hundred to a hundred-fifty people inside, mingling and enjoying themselves.

Dylan took a sip of her wine when the waitress brought them each another drink. If the drinks kept coming at the rate they were, Dylan knew she would be two sheets to the wind before the night even began. Scanning the area, Dylan sought out any familiar faces she might have recognized. There were so many people; surely she would have spotted someone she knew.

Everyone was getting into the beat of the music. Some of the woman made themselves known by climbing up onto the bar and dancing on the slick top. That was until a hefty bouncer escorted them off. The last thing Evan needed was for things to get out of hand. With all the drinking taking place, it wouldn't be good publicity for him if the police were called in to hall off drunken bodies.

The music switched to a more subtle song allowing the men patrons to pull their dates or significant others closer. Dylan watched the dancers sway and rock to the music. It was at that moment that Rade grabbed Dylan's hand and led her to the area being used as a dance floor. There was barely any room to dance, but Rade managed to find a spot and pulled Dylan close to his body. Dylan could have stayed this way all night. She loved the way Rade held her so close. Dylan closed her eyes as she took in the words to the song. It was one of her favorites, *"I don't want to miss a thing,"* by Aerosmith.

When the song ended, Rade led Dylan back to their table. Sitting down, Dylan suddenly got a chill up her spine. She felt like someone was watching them. Looking around, Dylan only saw people either dancing or conversing with others. Turning her head, she scanned the other side of the room. Still everyone seemed to be enjoying themselves. No one stood out. Reaching for her drink, she noticed the napkin under her drink had been written on. Pulling it from underneath her wine glass she began to read the message.

You belong only to me.

Soon the time will come when we will be together again.

Us together, inseparable.

Rade must have read Dylan's expression because no sooner she read the note, he took it from her hand. As Rade read the words, he knew it could be only one person who could have left it for Dylan to find. Rade folded the napkin and slipped it into his pocket. Dylan watched confused by the little message.

"Rade, what does it mean?" Dylan asked.

Holding back his anger, Rade replied, "I don't know, but I'm going to find out."

CHAPTER SIX

Rade's ability to control his anger was becoming harder with each passing minute. Someone was able to get near Dylan without Rade noticing. This was unacceptable. Rade knew exactly who that someone was, but more importantly, Peter and his men were not doing their job. This was going to be the last time that Michael Stewart was going to come near Dylan.

Chapter Seven

Rade instructed Richard to take Dylan home while he stayed behind to look at the security footage from *Riley's*. Rade and Evan went through the footage several times to see if they could see anyone coming near their table. Rade knew exactly what he was looking for. He requested Evan to stop the recording several times thinking he may have seen something, only to come up short. Even though the pictures were clear, there was no way of telling if Michael was there. The bar was dark and the angle of the cameras didn't show the table they were seated at. It was when they looked through the footage of the entrance that Rade was able to see Michael enter *Riley's*. He could have ripped the computer monitor from Evan's desk. As much as it angered him, Rade couldn't reveal that he got his answer.

He knew then that someone needed an ass chewing. Rade walked from Evan's office down the hallway with his cell in his hand. The grip he had on his phone was so tight, revealing the anger he carried. Barely able to see straight, Rade finally brought up Peter's contact and waited as the phone rang.

Peter answered, "Hewitt." He would have been better off letting it go to voicemail than take what Rade was about to lay on him.

"Are your men just fucking irresponsible or are you that ignorant to hire total fuck-ups?" Rade shouted.

"Do you want to tell me what this is about?" Peter snapped.

"Are you fucking kidding me," Rade started. "Maybe you should ask the man you had assigned to Dylan, because I'm pretty sure he wasn't where he was supposed to be."

"I thought you were with Dylan sir?" Peter said in a cocky voice.

"Don't push me Hewitt. I specifically requested Dylan be watched 24/7. What part of that request didn't you understand," Rade blurted. "I don't care if she's with me or the US Marine Corp, you will stay close to her."

By the time Rade hung up with Peter, he could feel his chest tighten and his blood rushing. He needed to cool off before he went home. The last thing he needed was for Dylan to see him this out of control. Walking down the sidewalk, Rade slipped into a bar three blocks up the street and ordered a double scotch, neat. One drink led to another, and another, before Rade finally calmed down enough to call Richard to pick him up.

It was two in the morning by the time Rade stumbled back to the penthouse. He not only felt like shit from the cheap scotch he drank, but also smelt like it. Taking a chance not to wake Dylan, Rade quietly went to the bathroom to take a much needed shower. As the water pounded on his tense body, he could only think about what could have happened if Dylan would have gone to *Riley's* alone. He couldn't imagine how badly it could have turned out.

Rade wasn't sure how long he was lost in his thoughts, but it must have been long enough because the water had turned cold. Grabbing the towel he placed on the hook next to the shower, Rade quickly dried his body then wrapped the damp towel around his waist. When Rade looked in the mirror, he could see a different man in front of him. The tension was evident by the creases on his forehead and the tightness at the base of his neck. Rade took his toothbrush from its base and added a dab of toothpaste. One thing that did make him smile was seeing Dylan's pink toothbrush next to his. It was amazing to him how much product a woman had to have to make themselves look gorgeous. Not that Dylan needed any of it. It also comforted him, knowing that she was here living with him. She was here to share everything with him. If only he could share his secrets.

After spending more than enough time in the bathroom, Rade turned off the bathroom light and slipped into bed next to the warmth he longed for. Spooning her body to his, Rade lightly kissed Dylan's temple and held her close.

With the amount of liquor Rade consumed, he thought for sure he would fall asleep in a matter of minutes. Unfortunately for him, he was still awake when the sun peeked through the blinds. Staring at the ceiling, Rade's thoughts went back to last night at *Riley's*. He blamed Peter for not keeping a closer eye on Dylan, but mostly he wondered how Michael Stewart knew they would be there. The only reasoning he had, was that Michael must have been following Dylan. This led to another concern. *What if Michael had been following Dylan all this time?* It would mean that he knew Dylan's habits. It would mean Michael knew where she would be and when. Even Rade knew Dylan's daily routine. It wouldn't be that hard to find her. She was a creature of habit. She never took a different route to work or frequent a different coffee shop for lunch. She wouldn't even think about arriving at work later or leaving earlier just to change things up.

Rade pushed from the bed regretting having to leave the warmth of Dylan's soft body. Careful not to wake Dylan, Rade opted to make a few calls before she woke up. After taking another quick shower, Rade headed to his study. His first call was going to be to Chris, his IT guy. He needed to check the status of hacking into Chloe's personal computer. Rade was able to get her IP address from his father before the thing with Spectrum came up, which was another thing he needed to handle.

"Chris, its Rade. Sorry to bother you so early and on a Sunday, but I need to know your progress with Ms. Dupree's computer," Rade admitted.

"I haven't been able to access it yet. It's going to take some time. Her computer isn't on all the time, so it's close to impossible to get her information. Once I'm in though, I can change her security settings to gain access," Chris explained.

"Well let me know the minute you find anything." Rade was hoping Chris would have something for him. His patience was starting to run thin. Not having any information was driving him insane.

His next call was to his attorney. He knew Miles wouldn't be in his office today, but he had his cell on speed dial.

"Rade. I was hoping you would call. You were right about the BlackStone partnership. Your father doesn't have a leg to stand on. He has already breached his right to make any decision concerning BlackStone," Miles advised.

"Well at least that's something. I'll let Keeve and Mason know. My father would be stupid to fight it," Rade interjected. "How about the appointment for the blood test? Has that been worked out?"

"Yes. Looks like Wednesday is the big day. I'll email you the time and place. The doctor we agreed on has been checked out. Dr. Kincaid is clean and very reputable," Miles affirmed.

"Good. Let me know the details once you have them."

Rade hung up the phone knowing that soon he would have the truth regarding Chloe's pregnancy. If he was in fact the father, then he was ready to take full responsibility for it. But if she had been lying the whole time, then the wrath of Matheson would be coming down on her.

Just as Rade was ready to contact Peter, He heard a soft knock on the door. He knew it could only be one person. Rising to his feet he walked over to the door to open it. Seeing Evan instead of Dylan surprised the hell out of him. "Evan, I wasn't expecting to see you here."

"I hope this isn't a bad time?" Evan asked.

"No, not at all," Rade assured him, still wondering what he was doing there and how he got in. "Please have a seat."

"This won't take long. I know we haven't been on the best of terms, but after last night, I was hoping I could change that by offering you my help. Dylan seemed pretty upset about the message she was left. I just wanted to let you know I'm here if you need anything," Evan said sincerely.

Rade wasn't ready to let Evan in on everything that was going on, even though it seemed Evan was being sincere about helping him out. He just didn't know why. It could have been because Evan didn't have any one else in his life. With his mother gone and no other siblings, his only other family was Garrett. That was even a stretch considering he didn't know what type of relationship Evan and their father had.

Trying to make an effort, Rade invited Evan to stay for breakfast. It was still early and Dylan had yet to wake-up. The two of them headed down to the kitchen where Rade prepared coffee. Evan took a seat at the breakfast bar and waited while the coffee began brewing. While Evan sat, Rade grabbed some items from the fridge and began chopping and slicing onions, peppers, ham, mushrooms and tomatoes. Evan watched as Rade displayed his culinary skills.

"You know, if you ever get tired of running a multi-billion dollar empire, I could always use a good chef," Evan said teasingly.

"I keep that in mind bro," Rade replied smiling.

It felt good spending time with Evan. The only other male in Rade's life was Richard. Richard was a good man, but he could be as headstrong as Rade. If it wasn't for Richard though, Rade probably wouldn't have got his shit together and probably would have end up on the streets. He was more of a father to Rade then Garrett Matheson had ever been.

Rade and Evan were chatting about their childhoods when Dylan appeared. Evan's back was towards her, so he didn't immediately see her, but when Rade greeted her, He knew right then she was there.

"Hey Sweetness, I hope we didn't wake you," Rade said.

"Not at all. Why didn't you wake me? I didn't know Evan was coming over," Dylan said.

"I wanted to let you rest. After last night, I thought you needed it," Rade answered.

Dylan nodded her head as she rounded the counter to get herself a cup of coffee. She didn't realize how inappropriately she was dressed until she saw both men looking at her like they were ready to pounce on her. Taking her coffee cup, she headed back to the bedroom to take a shower as well as hide the blush of embarrassment she suddenly wore.

Rade and Evan just smiled as she left. They both knew how beautiful she was and how it showcased her innocence. Rade knew Evan still felt something deeper for Dylan than just friendship. He could tell by the way he looked at her when he saw her. Rade saw it, because it was the exact same look he had when he first laid eyes on her. To this day, Rade still didn't know how things changed between them in such a short time. He was thankful everyday that she came into his life and he didn't follow through with his initial plan. The more he thought about it, the more he realized he was more like his father then he cared to admit. Rade's intension was solely to get what he wanted from Dylan, and then leave her. He was glad that changed. She had changed him. He wasn't that person, at least not when it came to Dylan. He had to thank Michael in a fucked up way, because if it weren't for him, he would have never met Dylan. A chance meeting of sorts.

Breakfast went by in a blur. Rade wasn't sure what the conversation between them had even been about. He only heard bits and pieces thinking only about Dylan and his brother's reaction to her. He knew by the way Dylan was looking at Evan; she didn't share the same feeling. Sure she listened intently to what he was saying, but her look was more interest than desire.

Evan left a short time after breakfast. In a way Rade was glad. He wanted to spend the rest of the day alone with Dylan. So when he gathered her up in his arms, it was no surprise to her what he wanted. Dylan of course didn't protest. It took everything she had not to jump his bones at breakfast, especially when his warm hands landed on her thigh and somehow slipped under her skirt. The heat radiated from between her legs. She was surprised she didn't spontaneously combust.

Ending up back in bed, Rade quickly peeled Dylan's clothing off layer by layer. It was only after she was completely naked that he began ripping off his own clothing. He was more than ready to take her. When he felt her thigh during breakfast and then the moisture between her legs, it took everything he had not to swoop her up and take her to their room. Now that he had her, he wasn't going to waste one more minute. Spreading her legs so that she was open for him, Rade glided his hands up her silky thighs just to the apex of her sexy cunt. Grabbing her hip with one hand and sliding two fingers inside her with the other, he knew she was ready for him. His shaft was raging by the sheen of wetness coating his fingers. Working his fingers deeper inside her, he lifted her leg over his shoulder splaying his hard body over her, being careful not to crush her. "God, I love the way you feel beneath me." Her back arched reeling in the pleasure he was giving her. Moving his hand up her body, he took hold of her pink bud caressing it firmly, not hard, between his fingers. Rolling it into a taut peak, he lowered his head and lapped his tongue around the hard bud before planting his mouth on her breast surrounding her areola while he continued to kiss and suck her firm nipple.

Dylan's body slowly began to melt as Rade continued his magic on her breast. Her eyes closed taking in each movement of his fingers inside her. She was in heaven. The pleasure he was giving her was like the warmth of a tropical island. Paradise. Dylan's hands tightened around Rade's wide biceps as the movement of his fingers increased. Angling his middle finger just right, he found the spot that would drive her over the edge. The scream of his name from her lips signaled she was close to letting go. Pulling his hand from her wet channel, she let out a moan of frustration. Dylan should have known he would end his assault on her as quickly as he began. This was his new trademark, leaving her wanting more.

Rade had other plans, he had her bottom side-up before she could protest his abandonment. Easing inside her, his cock filled her and the feeling of fulfillment was back. Dylan moaned with pleasure, taking in each surge of Rade's cock in her tight channel. Adjusting her hips, Dylan could feel the hardness of his cock as it rubbed against her g-spot. She was floating with need. Every region of her body was on fire with desire for this man. One more thrust was all it took before Dylan reached her summit. She was flying high with so much pleasure, she wasn't sure if she was ever going to be able to land.

Hitting her peak, Rade could feel the pulsating of her walls as they tightened around his thick shaft. He never felt anything like it. It was like having Dylan for the first time. Every taste of her body was better than the last. Every orgasm, more intense than the one before. Every kiss. Every touch. Every moment. Better beyond words. Indescribable.

* * * * *

Dylan and Rade laid around most of the day. After the mind blowing sex, what else was there to do. Dylan loved days like this. Nothing but each other to focus on. When they weren't in bed making love, they were in his study, christening his desk or his couch. They did managed to work out in the gym. Only no equipment was used other than the exercise bands which Rade used to tie Dylan up with.

A sudden knock on the door brought them to reality, making them realize they were both naked standing in the kitchen eating from a container of Dylan's favorite flavor of *Ben and Jerry's* ice cream. Rade looked at Dylan laughing watching as she panicked to get to the bedroom to put some clothes on.

The person at the door was still knocking. The knocking was getting louder by the minute exhibiting the visitor's irritation that no one had answered the door yet. Rade tried pulling his jeans on while frantically hurrying to the door. If he would have known it was his father on the other side, he would have never opened the door. He should have known better then to open it without looking at the monitor in the kitchen.

Garrett pushed inside the door, before Rade could stop him. "What the hell do you want?" Rade asked infuriated by his father's presence.

"Do you hate me that much that you would interfere with my partnership with BlackStone Industries?" Garrett hissed.

"Your partnership with them is nothing but a joke," Rade laughed. "If you were so concerned about your precious partnership, maybe you should have read the additional provisions to your agreement." Rade was furious with his father's assumptions, no matter how true they were.

"That's where you're wrong son. Maybe you should ask Keeve and Mason to give you the rest of the agreement, because the one I have makes that little provision you're referring to null and void," Garrett snickered. "Before I leave, a word of advice. You may want to do a little digging into Keeve Black and Mason Stone. I'm sure what you find will be very interesting."

Dylan was standing in the hallway getting wind of the full conversation between Rade and Garrett. When Garrett left, she walked to the entry area where Rade still stood. "Rade," Dylan said walking up to him. "What do you think he meant by that?"

"I'm not sure. Knowing my father, he's after something. He wants me to question my decision to partner with BlackStone on the Spectrum deal," Rade replied.

"Maybe you should have someone look into it. I don't think they will find anything, but it wouldn't hurt." Dylan couldn't believe Keeve and Mason would do anything underhanded when it came to their company. Even though she only worked for them for a short time, there was no way they were dishonest.

Dylan wasn't sure where the day went, but night time was already upon them. After Garrett left, Rade prepared a hardy dinner which they devoured. Dylan cleaned the dinner dishes while Rade put the leftovers in containers and placed them in the fridge. With everything cleaned and put away they settled on the couch to watch a movie. Only they weren't really watching anything except each other. The only thing Dylan remembered about the movie was an empire being destroyed by robots and that was before Rade slipped his hand under the shirt she was wearing. It was pretty easy access for him considering it was his shirt she was wearing and nothing else.

When his hand eased up her shirt latching on to her breast, it sent a tingle all the way to the top of her head down and back down to her toes. She didn't know what it was about his touch, but she was fully his. Dylan opened wider for him, giving Rade what he needed. When he slipped a finger inside her wet channel, she knew she would be fully drenched in a matter of seconds. Rade began kissing and nibbling on her earlobe while his finger worked back and forth inside her. Rade added another finger sending her on the way to pure ecstasy. Within minutes Rade had removed his own clothing and hoisted her body over his allowing him to enter her. The hold of her wet channel was so tight, he could have come at that very moment. Holding onto every inch of control he had, he moved one hand from her hip and began kneading her plump breasts. Dylan's head fell back, feeling every movement as Rade push deeper and deeper inside her.

Soft moans escaped her lips with every thrust of his thick shaft. Dylan was about to unleash when Rade lifted her from his cock and gently placed her on the soft cushions. With Dylan on her back, he lifted her legs over his shoulders and resumed his assault on her sweet cunt. Her juices coated his hard cock, warming him, as he pumped deeper and deeper inside her. Leaning over her perfect body, he brought his lips to hers and kissed her like there was no tomorrow. Like it was the last kiss he would ever get. A feverish rush consumed him the minute her tongue laced with his. There was such hunger between them that all Rade wanted was more. Even if his whole body took her over, it would never be enough for him. He was never so addicted to one person as he was to Dylan. She was the beating of his heart. Every breath he took, was hers. Only she could keep him alive. Only she would have his heart. His body. His soul. He was hers and she was his. Nothing and no one would ever take that from him.

Chapter Eight

Dylan wasn't sure what the day would bring. Rade had set up an early meeting with Keeve and Mason to find out exactly what was going on with the contract they had with his father. When they pulled up to the BlackStone building, something wasn't right. There were police cars everywhere. Even a SWAT team had been dispatched. Rade tried contacting Keeve by cell, but it went straight to voice mail. He tried the same with Mason, but no luck there either.

The front of the building was blocked off with barricades and yellow crime scene tape. There was no way Richard was going to get close enough to the building to let Dylan and Rade off. Rade wasn't even sure they could get inside. With the amount of commotion going on outside and the crowd of people gathered in the street, Rade knew their chance of getting inside the building was better from the parking garage. He just needed to find a way in.

"There has to be another way inside?" Rade contemplated. "Sweetness, is there another way inside the parking garage without driving in?"

Dylan had to think for a moment. She knew there was an exit door from the building to the garage, but couldn't remember ever seeing an exit door that led outside. That's when she remembered the set of steps by the security entrance. She never knew where they led, but it had to lead somewhere.

"I don't know if this helps, but I remember there being a set of stairs going down by the security entrance. Sometimes I would see people coming up the steps. I guess I really never paid that much attention to where they were coming from," Dylan confessed.

Rade advised Richard to turn left at the next block. If his suspicions were right, he was pretty sure that there was a walkway under the street which allowed pedestrians to walk to the other side of the street or in this case from parking garage to parking garage. When Richard rounded the corner to the next street, they spotted a parking garage. It looked to be unguarded by an attendant. There was still a gate arm, but it could be accessed by pulling a parking ticket from a small box.

Richard quickly pushed the green button on the small box which instantly spit out a parking ticket. Driving past the gate, Rade spotted a set of steps leading down a few feet from the attendant booth. Richard quickly pulled the Bentley in the first available spot. Before they could all exit the car, Rade turned to Dylan, "You need to stay in the car."

Dylan was not going to remain in the car only to be left wondering what was going on inside the BlackStone Building. Looking at Rade displeased by his command, she said, "No way. I'm not staying here wondering what is going on."

"Sweetness, the last thing I want is for something to happen to you. You're safer if you stay inside the car. Don't push me on this," Rade demanded.

Richard looked back and forth between Dylan and Rade as they argued. "You two need to decide if Dylan is staying or going."

"I'm going," Dylan asserted.

Rade took one look at Dylan. He knew this was a no win for him. He knew Dylan wasn't about to stay in the vehicle no matter what he said. " One condition, you stay near us. Do you understand?"

Dylan nodded her head as Rade took her by the hand and helped her out of the Bentley. Richard pushed the lock on the key fob and adjusted his coat. Dylan could see that Richard was carrying a gun. As soon as he stood, she saw the bulge on his left side. Rade knew right away she had seen Richard's gun. "It's just a precaution Dylan. Nothing more," Rade assured her.

As they approached the steps, Rade was thankful that the police didn't have the entrance to the tunnel leading across the street blocked off. This was a good sign that they would be able to make to the other side without being stopped. Once they reached the BlackStone parking garage, Richard scanned the area to make sure there were no cops patrolling the area. Richard could see a couple of officers with their backs to them standing in front of the garage entrance. Evidently, they were more concerned about people getting in than the people already inside.

Richard signaled to Rade and Dylan by putting his index finger to his lips and then pointing the same finger towards the two officers. Dylan had worn her Louboutins and decided it would be better to remove them so she wouldn't be heard. The last thing she wanted was to be heard walking across the cement parking floor or fall on her derrière.

Rade was pretty sure the lobby area would be swarming with cops. Instead of drawing attention, he motioned for Richard and Dylan to follow him to the stairwell. It would be their only chance to get to the fifteenth floor undetected. Rade opened the door leading to the lobby from the stairwell before they made their decent up the fifteen floors. He was hoping he could at least hear what was going on.

There was a group of detectives talking. They weren't close enough to hear everything. He could only hear bits and pieces, but from what he could hear, someone had reported shots being fired in the BlackStone office. There was one casualty and several people hurt. While Rade was still listening to the conversation, Jessica and Lucy appeared, getting off the elevator with a policewoman.

He knew whatever took place on the fifteenth floor must have been pretty bad. Jessica and Lucy were both covered in blood. Being that they weren't handcuffed, Rade knew the two girls must have been innocent bystanders. Now more than ever, he needed to get to the BlackStone office. As soon as he rose to his feet, he took one last look through the stairwell window only to see that the paramedics were now in the lobby. There were three of them and they were each pushing a stretcher. This told him at least three people were injured.

It was at that point, Rade urged, "Let's go."

"What's going on Rade?" Dylan whispered trying to keep her voice low so she couldn't be heard by anyone but Rade and Richard.

"I don't know, but I guessing two people got hurt and one killed. We need to find out who," Rade confessed.

By the time they got to the fifteenth floor, Dylan's feet were throbbing. Half way there, she had to remove her shoes once again. Four inch heels and stairs didn't mix. Taking a seat on the fifteenth floor landing, Dylan began rubbing her aching feet. Rade and Richard were already at the stairwell door. Richard looked through the rectangular window to see if he could see anybody. There were numerous suited men and uniformed police officers coming in and out of the office. Richard ducked from the window, just as a man in a suit was heading their way. Pushing Rade back to his side, he once again held his finger to his lips signaling them to be quiet.

That was too close for comfort for Richard. When he could see that the coast was clear, Richard opened the door. There had to be a way to get closer to what was going on in the office. Another man in a suit walked by the exit door, Richard had to take his chance. Opening the door, he pulled the guy into the stairwell and applied pressure to his neck. Within seconds he was out. Richard searched his body and found his badge. Placing it in full view on his waistband, he exited the stairwell and headed to the BlackStone office.

Dylan and Rade waited patiently while Richard went to investigate. Dylan was nervous just thinking about what could have happened. She wasn't normally a nail biter, but given the circumstances, it was the only thing she could do to remain calm. That was until Rade pulled her hand to his lips and kissed her. Time stood still as they waited for Richard to come back. Dylan looked down at the man, wondering if Richard would get back before the guy woke up.

Richard had been gone for about thirty minutes when the guy on the floor started to stir. Rade had no other choice but to place a sleeper hold on him. When the guy went unconscious again, Rade carefully placed his head back down on the hard concrete. Looking at Rade, Dylan couldn't believe that Rade would know how to do what he just did. Just like that the guy was out.

Trying to make light of the situation, Rade looked over to Dylan staring at him. "He is going to have on hell of a headache when he wakes up."

"That's not funny Rade," Dylan said, crossing her arms over her chest.

Forty-five minutes later, Richard finally came through the stairwell door. Not wasting any time, Richard started down the steps. He wasn't ready to explain to Rade what he had found. He wanted to make sure Rade was sitting before he let him know. Rade helped Dylan to her feet, following close behind Richard. Rade wasn't sure what was going on with Richard, but he knew it was bad by the way he moved down the stairs.

They got back to the Bentley safely unnoticed. Once inside, Rade was ready to come unglued. Richard didn't say one word about what happened. Rade needed answers and he wasn't going to wait another second.

"What the hell happened? You better start talking," Rade demanded.

"Sorry sir, I needed to wait until we got back to the car to tell you. Mason Stone was shot during some sort of altercation. Keeve Black was also shot. They've both been taken to Mount Sinai. They were shot pretty bad," Richard confirmed.

What about the other person?" The detectives said there was one casualty. Who was the other guy Richard?" Rade urged.

Richard lowered his eyes unable to look at Rade. "It was you father, Rade. Whoever killed him, shot him in the face. His face was unrecognizable. They were only able to identify him by the ID in his wallet. I'm sorry Rade," Richard said placing his hand on Rade's shoulder.

Dylan's mouth gaped open. She couldn't believe what she was hearing. Tears began pooling in her eyes knowing Rade's father was dead. Her heart broke for him. Dylan placed her hand on Rade's face. Even with everything going on between Rade and his father, Dylan knew this was the last thing Rade expected. Looking in his eyes, she could see pain plaguing them. She knew he was hurting no matter how hard he tried to cover his feelings. "Rade, I'm so sorry."

Rade looked at Dylan, " Where are they taking his body?" Rade was addressing Richard while still looking at Dylan. He couldn't fathom that the man with his face shot off was his father until he saw him for himself. He knew his father well. There was only one way to tell if it truly was his father heading to the hospital morgue.

"Mount Sinai," Richard replied.

* * * * *

On the way to the hospital, Richard began explaining what he heard along with information he found out himself. "An unknown man entered the BlackStone office while Jessica and Lucy were in the back office making copies that Keeve requested for an upcoming meeting. When they heard shots, they hid in the copy room, praying they wouldn't be found. As soon as the coast was clear, they went to check out the office. It was then they found Keeve and Mason. Both shot. Jessica was helping Keeve, while Lucy helped Mason. There was so much blood. Jessica was the one who called 911. Shortly after, the police arrived and then the paramedics. Neither one of them saw the shooter. They didn't realize that Garrett Matheson had been the dead body until an officer pointed it out to them."

When Richard finished telling Rade what happened, Rade knew then his father could have been the one killed. As much as he hated his father, this was the last thing he would have wished on him.

Rade was looking out the window trying to hold back his feelings. When Richard pulled up to the hospital, Rade couldn't move. He didn't know if he was ready to face what was waiting for him. Dylan gently took him by the hand. Richard exited the Bentley first. Rounding the hood, he opened the back passenger door and assisted Dylan out. She still had a hold of Rade's hand as she stepped out.

Dylan could feel the anxiety in Rade's touch as she continued to hold tightly to his hand. Entering the hospital, they went to reception, where they were directed to the hospital morgue. There were a couple of officers standing outside the ME's examining room. Since Rade couldn't speak, Richard did the talking.

"This is Rade Matheson, I believe Garrett Matheson was brought in. His son would like to confirm that it's his father lying on the table," Richard stated.

The officers stepped aside so Rade, Dylan and Richard could enter the room. Rade's chest began to tighten. When the ME removed the white sheet from the lifeless body, Dylan's face turned pale. Her stomach began to heave. Turning her body from the killer's brutality, she searched for something she could spew in. Dylan spotted a small trash can in the corner and spilled her guts. Rade was standing right beside her, holding her hair back from her face as she expelled the contents from her stomach. He knew it was a bad idea letting Dylan come into this room with him. When Dylan was done heaving, Richard led her out of the room so she could get some fresh air

Rade was still in the examining room. He about lost it himself when he saw the condition of the man's face. It looked like it had gone through a shredder instead of taking a bullet. There wasn't a piece of flesh that hadn't been affected. Rade lowered the sheet down the man's body searching for the one thing that would tell him if this was his father or someone else. It was a tattoo his father had inked on his chest right below his heart. It read *"Forgiveness."* When Rade saw the tattoo, his emotions took over. Deep down he never really stopped loving his father. Rade fell to his knees and the ME was right there to assist him in a chair.

"Sir, are you all right?" the medical examiner asked.

"Yeah," Rade said softly.

The ME headed back to the table. It was pretty evident what the cause of death was, so the examiner didn't feel the need to continue his examination. The bullet fragments had already been removed so it was a matter of identifying the weapon used and who the gun was registered to. The examiner proceeded to clean the mess in front of him. Taking the sprayer, he began rinsing the blood from the body. Rade couldn't move. All he could do was watch as the water spilled over his father's body. Rade watched as the red water ran down the side of his father's mutilated face. He watched as the examiner wiped down his body. Rade was in a daze still not accepting that his father was dead. He also felt the guilt inch inside him for not making amends with him.

Standing, Rade walked over to his father's body to tell him one last goodbye. It was only then that he saw the faded tattoo. Rade looked over to the ME and back down to his father's chest. "What the hell? This isn't my father."

"It seems the tattoo wasn't permanent," the ME said as he continued to rub the area. "This changes everything. I need to do a thorough examination of this body. He's no longer Garrett Matheson but a John Doe until we can identify him."

Rade couldn't be happier. Even though he felt bad for the man lying on the table, he was thankful that it wasn't his father. There had to be a reason for this cover-up. Why would someone want to make it look like this was Garrett Matheson? Rade needed to get out of there.

Heading back down the hall to the reception area, Rade found Richard and Dylan sitting next to the entrance door. Dylan still looked peaked from the sight of the man on the table. She also looked as though she had been crying, no doubt for him. He hated seeing her this way. He knew once he told her the news, it would make her feel better.

When Rade reached her, he took the seat beside her and pulled her into his body. "Are you all right Sweetness?"

"I've never seen anything like that before. I've never even seen a dead body before. I'm so sorry someone did this to your father Rade." Dylan said softly.

"I'm sorry you had to see that, but the man lying on the table isn't my father," Rade confirmed. "My father had a tattoo etched on his body after my mom and brother died. I will never forget it."

"So he didn't have the tattoo? The man in that room?" Dylan asked

"Oh he had it, only it wasn't real. Someone drew it on him to match the one my father had," Rade explained. "I just need to find out why."

* * * * *

One the way home, Rade thought about the guy lying on the table. His brain was going in circles trying to figure out what this whole thing meant. It also made him think that maybe, just maybe, his father had something to do with this. Keeve and Mason were still in ICU and in critical condition. Keeve had been shot twice. Once in the shoulder and again in the gut. They expected that he would make a full recovery since no vital organs were hit. Mason wasn't so lucky, he was shot in the chest. Even though he was alive, he may never truly recover. Rade wished he had his hand on the asshole who shot them. He would like to know what possessed him to go on a shooting rampage.

Dylan snuggled up to Rade while he was in deep thought. God, he was glad he had her. She made everything in his life so much better. Wrapping his arm around her shoulder, he pulled her in closer and kissed her gently on the head. He could feel her pull away from him only to see her tender eyes looking at him. Lifting her chin he lowered his head and placed his lips on hers. Dylan's lips were soft and still swollen from her emotional turmoil. Rade parted her lips with his tongue. Her warmth took him in, leaving him wanting more. Nudging her closer, Rade placed his hand along her neck, caressing the soft skin on her jaw. God, he loved this woman. He could feel the pressure building, as the mass of his cock started to rise. He needed to get Dylan home and fast.

"Step on it Richard," Rade ordered.

"Yes, Sir," Richard replied with a smirk.

Chapter Nine

Tomorrow would be the day that Rade went in to get his paternity test done. Dylan didn't know how she felt about it. As she stared out the window onto Central Park, there was one thing she did know, she was completely in love with Rade, so when he stepped behind her and asked her to strip and wait for him in the bedroom, she had no problem submitting to his command. This was something they both needed and desired. Removing her heels, Dylan bent over to pick them up giving Rade a view he couldn't resist. He could have taken her right then, but instead he moved to the liquor cabinet in the living area. Her little display was going to cost her a little alone time.

Knowing that Rade would be a while, Dylan decided to do a little preparation for what she knew would be a long night. Striping off her skirt, then her blouse, she went to the bathroom to freshen up. When she looked in the mirror, it was a wonder that Rade didn't run for the hills. She looked devilish. Like something out of a zombie movie. Washing her face as quickly as she could, she reapplied a little mascara and her favorite smoky eye shadow. With a little touch of lip gloss, her look was now that of a woman ready to be ravished. Checking her appearance once more before she left the bathroom, Dylan sprayed a small amount of perfume on her wrists and rubbed them together.

Surprised, Dylan sucked in a breath, seeing Rade's form in the doorway of the bedroom. Before she could move, he said sternly, "You were supposed to wait for me on the bed."

"I…needed to freshen-up first," Dylan explained.

Rade slowly walked to where Dylan was standing. *God, she was beautiful*, he thought to himself as he shortened the distance between them. Lifting her from the floor, he carefully set her down on the bed so that her body was sitting just on the edge near the foot of the bed. "Don't move," Rade ordered, loosening his tie and walking to the enormous closet.

Dylan wasn't sure what he was searching for, but when he finally appeared, he held a small box in his hands. Placing the box on the nightstand, Rade began to unbutton his shirt. Dylan's eyes drifted down his chest as he undid each button. Her fixation on his strong muscular body ended when she heard him speak. "Eyes on your lap Sweetness."

Dylan quickly turned her eyes from his body and moved them to her lap where her hands were neatly folded. She didn't know how she got to this point, but every nerve in her body tingled. The moisture pooling between her legs was surely beginning to drip from her inner thighs. Only Rade could make her this hot.

Without looking up, Dylan could feel Rade's presence before her. The scent of his masculinity filled the air. Before she could raise her head to look at his beautiful body, Rade had her on her feet, turned and facing the bed. His hands were on her, wrapped around her neck, slowly gliding down the plain of her back. Every nerve in her body was going crazy with desire. She tried focusing on the expensive painting above the headboard, but all she could think about was his touch and wanting more of him. No longer able to resist, she turned to face him and slowly fell to her knees. Placing her hands first on his muscular thighs to balance herself, she began unzipping his pants. Slowly removing them down his legs, she could only think of one thing. Kissing only the tip of his perfect cock, she playfully moved her tongue up and down his long shaft. When she heard him groan, she knew she had him. Moving her hands up his leg, feeling the taut flesh beneath them, there was no more waiting as she placed one hand on his tight ass while the other cupped his scrotum. She was the one in control of his desire. Lowering her head, she continued lapping her tongue up and down his shaft quenching her thirst with every inch of his perfection. While her hand kneaded the firm skin of his ass, the other caressed his sac. "Sweetness you need to stop, I don't think I can last much longer," Rade moaned in a throaty voice.

As much as she wanted to submit to Rade's request, she couldn't nor did she have the desire to. She needed this as much if not more than he did. Ignoring his request, she continued her assault on him. Taking him in her mouth, a drop of pre-cum fell upon her tongue, greeting her with a taste of what was awaiting her. Dylan only took enough of his cock in her mouth to tease him. She wanted to savor every inch of him. Flattening her tongue, she began going down on him. He was too big for her to take him fully, but she knew whatever she was doing was making him come undone. With her other hand still on his sac, Dylan tightened her grip while caressing his balls in her palm. Lilly had once told her that there was an area just below a man's sac that caused extreme pleasure. Pressing her middle finger and index finger just behind his sac, Dylan could feel Rade's movements increase. She knew he was getting close."Fuck, Sweetness. What are you doing to me?" Rade asked with a heated moan.

Before Dylan could finish the job, Rade had her up off the floor and on the bed with such force, she didn't realize until he was deep inside her what was happening. His animalistic instinct took over as he held her in place and fucked her from behind. Dylan could feel every muscle in his body as he continued to propel inside her. He was so deep, she thought for sure she was going to bust at the seams. The pleasure was beyond any pain her body was enduring. All she knew was that she needed more.

"Rade, please, harder," Dylan moaned.

"It's my turn Sweetness," Rade commanded.

"I need more Rade, please," Dylan begged.

"You are mine Sweetness. I want to hear you say it."

"I'm yours Rade, only yours," Dylan cried.

"Your body is mine to take Sweetness in any way that pleases me. Say it."

"My body is yours to take any way," Dylan said barely able to get the words out. Her body was on fire. All she wanted was release.

Just when she thought she would get what she needed, Rade pulled from her leaving her feeling empty. Dylan felt a shift in the mattress letting her know that Rade was leaving her unfulfilled. She didn't know what was happening. One minute he was ready to come unglued and in the next he was gone. It was dark in the room except the light coming from the walk-in closet. Dylan was just about to go after him when she saw him enter the room carrying a bowl. When he brought it to the nightstand, she could see that it was filled with ice. She didn't know what possessed him to bring ice, unless he was going to use it on her. It was at that point she knew, their play was only just beginning.

Rade sat next to Dylan on the bed with a hunger she'd never seen before. She knew she only belonged to him, but the look on his face showed much more than that. It was as if he was staking his claim on her. There was something different in the way he was looking at her. Concerned, Dylan placed her hand on his cheek. Brushing her thumb across the rough texture of his unshaven face, she asked, "Rade, what is it?"

At that moment it was over. The look on his face changed. With a tortured grin he said, "Hands above your head Sweetness."

Dylan knew she couldn't deny him. Rade opened the small box and pulled out two pieces of rope. He dangled them in front of her, he was telling her that he was in control now. Taking one piece of rope, he wrapped it snuggly around her right wrist. When the rope was secure, Rade pulled at Dylan's hips adjusting her position so that she was laying flat on the mattress. With the other rope he bound her left wrist and secured it to the headboard. There was nowhere for Dylan to go. She felt helpless yet excited for what was going to happen next. Her anticipation was evident by the moisture now gathering between her legs.

Rade turned his body so he could pull something else from the box. Dylan couldn't see what he had in his hand. All thoughts were lost when Rade's mouth clamped around her right nipple. The coldness shook her. Her body became electrified. She now knew the purpose of the ice. It was like nothing she ever felt before. The tip of his tongue circled her taut nipple. Every sensation was on overload. Rade pulled his cold mouth from her pert bud only to replace it with a nipple clamp. The sensation was overwhelming. Dylan had to take in a deep breath. Breathing slowly, Dylan's body finally adjusted to the added pressure.

Rade tenderly massaged the decorated breast, while giving attention to Dylan's bare one. Her nipple became taut within seconds, thanks to the ice cube Rade rubbed over her hard bud. Adding the second clamp, Dylan once again took in a deep breath before her body adjusted to the invasion. Rade lifted his head looking deep into Dylan's eyes. "Absolutely fucking beautiful," he said lowering his mouth to hers.

The kiss was intense, not only because of the clamps on Dylan's breast, but because the need for each other, was doubled with every breath they took. Rade pulled his mouth away and swiped back a strand of hair from her face. With added tenderness he whispered, "Good?" He meant it as a question so when Dylan didn't answer, he asked again, "Sweetness, are you good?"

"More than good," Dylan confirmed.

Her confirmation sent Rade back to tranquil bliss. With every kiss he placed on her body, a slight tremor followed. Her body was over-sensitized not only by the clamps on her breasts, but also from the tingling sensation she felt between her legs. She didn't know how much longer she would be able to hold on. Rade's mouth skimmed every inch of her body, leaving nothing but heated energy in its path. Dylan heard the clatter of the ice, letting her know more ice cubes were going to be used. Slowly and gently Rade kissed her freshly shaven mound, taking in her glorious scent while feeling her arousal penetrate his being. The sensation of the cold on Dylan's heated clit was almost too much for her. She could have exploded right then. Slipping his finger between her folds, her body began pushing against him with a dying need to be satisfied. He knew every touch he placed on her would bring her closer to the one place she needed to be. He wasn't ready to let her go. As much as he wanted to take her over the edge, he wanted to worship her more. Adding another finger to join the one between her slick folds, he entered her wet channel. Grabbing more ice, Rade began inserting one, two, three small cubes into her tight channel. Dylan could feel her orgasm ignite before he even entered her.

Dylan's back arched at the intrusion. It was too much for her. "Rade, I can't hold on any longer. I need you." Dylan's declaration rippled in a breathless plea.

"I got you baby. Let go." Rade's words were like Christmas and the Fourth of July all lumped together. Never had Dylan's body felt more buoyant then it did at that moment. It was like everything was washed away. There was no more turmoil, no more worry. It was just them.

Rade kissed Dylan tenderly on her inner thigh as he slowly pushed her knees to her chest. He could see the sheen of her wetness displayed in front of him. Lifting her hips to give him better access, he began to devour her sweetness. Dylan's back arched off the bed giving him even more of her sweet pussy. Diving in, Rade circled her clit in slow lapping movements with his tongue, making it impossible for her to move. Grabbing her hips, Rade held her tightly letting her know that he was in control of her next orgasm. He may have let her have the first one, but this one was on him. Dipping his tongue between her folds, only pure pleasure was waiting for her. There was nothing more beautiful then to see Dylan submit to him. He knew every detail of her body. He knew exactly where to touch her. Even her moans were carved in his mind. There was nothing about this woman he didn't know.

Releasing his grip on her hips, Rade leaned back on his heels so he could get a better view of Dylan's gorgeous body. "Do you know how beautiful you are?" Rade asked.

Dylan couldn't answer. All she wanted was to come. Her body was seething with arousal. She knew if she could just rub her legs together, she would be able to get the release she needed. Rade must have read her thoughts, because no sooner she craved it, he was over her. Placing his hands on either side of her small frame, Rade grabbed yet another cube and gently glided it into her tight channel. Her body trembled at the sudden coldness to her already sensitized cunt. Pushing his thick cock between her wet folds, he could feel her walls tighten with every push and pull of his cock. He could feel the ice melting as her body's heat thawed the tiny crystal. The feeling of his cock inside her cool channel was unmistakably the most remarkable sensation his dick had ever felt. Supporting his body with one hand, he took the other and held on to her ass, trying to get deeper inside her. It didn't matter how deep he went, he would never be able to get enough. In one swift move he had her face down on the bed and resumed his position behind her. He loved the shape of her ass. He loved the way it moved as he thrust deep inside her. Leaning over her body, Rade untied her and lifted her body onto his. Her back was to his front, but it didn't matter because he could feel all of her. Rade wrapped his arms around Dylan's waist and pulled her even closer to him. He drew his hand to her breast and removed first the right and then left nipple clamp. Dylan screamed his name with such force, that her tight pussy clamped down hard on him causing him to surrender to his own piece of heaven.

Rade gently lifted Dylan and placed her across his lap so she was now facing him. Her eyes were glazed over and Rade knew she was just as jaded as he was. Gently kissing her on the lips, Rade adjusted her body placing her on the bed. Looking down before leaving her, he inspected her body. He could see that her wrists were pink from the rope he used to bind her, which he expected from the way in which she moved. It was her nipples that caught his attention. They were a crimson color and more gorgeous than before, if that was possible. Unable to resist, he lowered his head and gently kissed the bright red peak. First the right and then the left. Dylan shook at the tenderness the clamps left behind, but welcomed Rade's touch.

Rade came back to the bed with a warm washcloth. He gently wiped her body clean of any remnants left of their uncontrollable passion. When he was satisfied she was clean, he stepped back into the bathroom to deposit the soiled cloth into the laundry hamper. Returning to the bed, Rade glanced over only to see that she was sound asleep. He knew he pushed her body to the limit. Sliding in beside her, Rade pulled her body close to his and wrapped his arms around her. Exhaustion took over and within minutes he was out.

* * * * *

Rade heard a pounding in his head. He thought it may have been from the drink he had earlier. Grabbing his cell, he looked at the time only to find that it was two in the morning. Fully awake, he realized that the pounding wasn't in his head, but coming from the front door. Pulling on a pair of pajama pants, he made his way to the annoying sound. When he looked at the camera, he could see the intruder was his father.

Rade opened the door. By the look of his father appearance, he hadn't showered for a couple of days. His suit was rumpled and his white dress shirt looked even worse. His shirt was buttoned wrong and blood stains covered the front.

"What the fuck happened to you and what the fuck happened at BlackStone?" Rade cursed.

"I'll explain everything, but first I need a drink," Garrett mumbled.

When Garret walked into the penthouse, Rade could tell that something wasn't right with his father. It was only after he collapsed on the hard marble floor that he knew he was right. Leaning over his father's body, Rade could see that the blood on his father's shirt was coming from him. Rade quickly unbuttoned his father's shirt and pulled it open. Garrett had a knife wound on his side, about four inches wide. Someone got him really good. Rade couldn't leave his father on the cold floor, so he carefully lifted his body over his shoulder and took him to the couch. Rade needed to think. His only choice was to call Richard.

"Richard, I need you to come to the penthouse. My father showed up. He's got a pretty good slice to his gut," Rade stated.

"On my way sir," Richard replied.

Richard arrived at the penthouse within minutes. It wasn't far for him to travel considering he lived one floor down from Rade. The door was still open to the penthouse, so Richard walked in without knocking. Richard saw Rade sitting on the coffee table trying to get the wound on Garrett's stomach to stop bleeding. Richard let Rade know he was there by gently placing his hand on Rade's shoulder. Rade looked up at him.

Richard patted Rade on the shoulder and said, "Stay here, I'll run and get more bandages."

Richard returned minutes later with a hand full of gauze and bandages. He also came back with what looked like antiseptic and a bottle of liquor. "We need to move him to the bedroom," Richard suggested.

"We can take him to guest room," Rade confirmed.

As they began to lift Garrett from the couch, Dylan appeared from the bedroom with only a sheet wrapped around her. Running her hand through her hair, she asked still half asleep, "What's all the noise about? Do you real….. Oh my God…. What happened Rade?" Dylan couldn't believe her eyes.

"I was just about to find out myself when he collapsed to the floor. He's been stabbed," Rade replied, still holding on to his father's limp body.

Dylan immediately moved out of the way so Rade and Richard could take him to the guest bedroom. When they were clear, Dylan followed behind them until they were in the bedroom. Rushing to the bed, Dylan pulled back the covers before they put Garrett on the bed. Richard worked to get Garrett's shirt off while Rade held on to his father's limp body. Once Garrett was settled, Richard went back to the living area to get the items that he brought.

Dylan had never seen so much blood. She was thankful that she didn't lose her lunch at the sight. Richard came back to the room carrying some bandages, antiseptic and a small bag that appeared to be full of medical tools. Pulling a chair beside the bed, Richard began working on Garrett, but before he did, he twisted the top of the whiskey bottle and took a large swig. He handed the bottle over to Rade, who also took a large drink. Whiskey wasn't his liquor of choice, but considering the circumstances, it didn't matter.

Richard did the best he could with what he had to patch up Garrett. He was thankful that his military training didn't escape him once he left the Seals. Even though it wasn't his best handiwork, at least he got the cut stitched and the bleeding to stop. Based on the amount of blood on Garrett's shirt, Richard knew he lost quite a bit. What Garrett needed now was rest. Richard would know more in the morning if what he did worked.

Dylan gathered all of the bloody items and took them to the kitchen where she dumped them into a garbage bag. The smell of the blood just about made her sick, but she struggled through it. She knew none of them would be going back to sleep, so she decided to make coffee. As she was filling the coffee maker with water, she kept wondering what could have happened to Rade's father. She was pretty certain it had something to do with the shooting at BlackStone Industries yesterday morning.

Rade and Richard were talking in the study when Dylan appeared with a tray holding three cups of coffee. Placing the tray down on the small table at the end of the couch, Dylan bent over and grabbed two of the cups handing one to Rade and the other to Richard. She wasn't sure what she missed, but she was done being left in the dark.

"So what do you think happened to him?" Dylan blurted out.

Rade looked over at Dylan unsure what she expected to hear. "We really don't know. We're trying to figure that out. We're pretty sure it has something to do with what happened at BlackStone."

"Do you have an idea who might have shot Keeve and Mason and why the shooter would have blown the face off of the other guy?" Dylan asked.

"Richard is going to see what he can find out. He has an old navy buddy that works for the NYPD. Maybe he'll be able to give us some answers. In the meantime, I need you to stay clear of this Dylan," Rade ordered. "The last thing I need is for something to happen to you."

Dylan stood from her seat rolling her eyes, "I'm going to check on Garrett." Just as she turned she heard Rade.

"This isn't a game Dylan. I need you to let us handle this," Rade demanded.

Rade hoped Dylan's stubbornness wasn't going to get the best of her. The only thing he could think about was keeping her safe. Just the thought of something happening to her made his heart ache. It could have been her that got shot. If they had arrived at the BlackStone building an hour earlier, who knows what the outcome would have been.

"Damn, that woman is going to get the best of me," Rade said between gritted teeth.

"I think we have bigger problems than Ms. Adams," Richard confessed handing Rade his cell.

Rade took Richard's cell from his hand and looked down at the screen. This was almost the breaking point for him. "Fuck," came from Rade's throat. Before he lifted his arm to throw Richard's cell across the room, Richard pulled back on his arm stopping him in time. The last thing Richard needed was to replace his phone.

"Sir, you need to calm down. We need to find out all the facts before we believe the press. I'll get in touch with my friend at the NYPD and find out what is really going on," Richard suggested. The last thing he wanted was for Rade to worry for no reason. Especially since he knew it wasn't his dad laying in the morgue. Maybe the cops were keeping it out of the press. Maybe they had an angle. Either way Richard's buddy would be able to shed some light on the matter. Rade needed to revert his focus on getting his father better so he could get some answers.

"Sir, can I suggest you check in on your father, while I make some calls. I'll let you know if I find out anything from my friend."

Rade took Richard's advice. His father was the only person who could answer his questions. He needed to make sure that he was well taken care of. As much as it pained him to see his father in such a helpless state, he still couldn't get past his feelings towards him. Rade wasn't sure if he would ever be able to let go of what his father had taken from him. Maybe his father had lived with the guilt long enough. It was evident that it stared at him every day by the tattoo he had branded on his chest. Maybe *forgiveness* was the key to his happiness.

Chapter Ten

It was a little past six in the morning, and Rade needed to get ready for his appointment with Dr. Kincaid. Rade checked in on his father. He seemed to be resting comfortably. Hopefully by the time he returned, Rade would be able to get the answers he needed from him.

It was a little after seven, and Rade needed to leave if he was going to make his eight o'clock appointment. Kissing Dylan on the lips, he gave her Dr. Foster's contact information in case his father's condition got worse. Dylan was reluctant to stay. She wanted to be with Rade when he took the paternity test. But she knew Rade needed her to stay with Garrett.

When Rade arrived at the clinic, Chloe was already there waiting. "Hello loverboy," she said with a smile.

"Let's just get this over with Chloe. No need for the pleasantries," Rade hissed.

"The only reason I'm here is because of you," Chloe asserted.

"Come on Chloe. You're only here because I agreed to meet your parents."

There was no love lost between the two of them, at least for Rade. He knew agreeing to go to London with her was the only way he would get her to agree to another test. Little did she know, Dylan would be part of his planned trip to London.

Pulling Rade from his thoughts, a young nurse appeared, breaking their tense conversation. If it had been a minute longer, Rade would have called the whole thing off.

"Ms. Dupree," the young nurse inquired.

Chloe stood from her seat. The dress she was wearing was just tight enough that Rade could see the small bump at her waistline affirming that it was going to be the longest nine months of his life.

Rade had been waiting in the waiting area for about an hour when the same nurse appeared. She called his name just as she had with Chloe. Rade rose to his feet and followed the young nurse through the door back to the examining area. All Rade knew was that he wanted to get this over with. His only hope was that this test would show that he wasn't the father of Chloe's child.

The young nurse escorted Rade to a small room with a chair, a computer and a counter displaying various vials. Rade was directed to take a seat while he waited for the phlebotomist to show. He couldn't believe that his life came to this. Lost in his thoughts, an older woman about fifty appeared. She seemed to be having a bad day.

"Mr. Matheson," she said sternly.

"Yes," Rade replied.

"Good, I need you to remove your jacket and roll up the sleeve of your left arm," She ordered.

Rade did what she said, and placed his suit jacket on the back of his chair. Removing his cufflink from his sleeve, he put it inside his shirt pocket and proceeded to neatly roll up his sleeve.

"Quickly Mr. Matheson. I don't have all day," she barked.

The way the phlebotomist was talking to him, Rade hope this wasn't going to be a sign as to how she was going to insert the needle into his arm.

The grouchy nurse placed a rubber tunicate around his upper arm and began thumping on his forearm. By no means was she gentle. When the desired vein appeared, Nurse Ratchet pushed the needle through the skin. Rade was surprised at how gently she eased the needle in. The only pressure he felt was a small prick. Rade watched as his blood filled the vial, When it was about half filled, the cranky phlebotomist released the tunicate. It was only when she was finished that she made eye contact with him. Rade could see something in them. She wasn't as shrewd as he thought. There was compassion behind them.

Rade left the clinic before Chloe, at least that's what he thought until he saw her approaching him. He tried to avoid her, but when he heard his name roll of her lips, he knew she spotted him. Turning his body, he waited for her.

When she was within talking distance, Rade cursed, "Whatever you have to say Chloe, save it."

"Do you hate me that much, because you certainly didn't when you fucked me?" Chloe hissed.

"I don't know what your game is Chloe, but you're going to end up losing," Rade snapped back.

"Is that what you think? That this is a game. We're going to have a child together for God's sake," Chloe cried.

"If I'm the father of the child you're carrying, I'll do my part to support he or she anyway I can. As for you, you will never have me."

"I still have the pictures," Chloe hissed.

"Don't threaten me Chloe. You and I both know those pictures were staged."

"Yeah, we'll see what happens when the authorities get a hold of them."

Rade took Chloe by the arm. He had enough of her threats. "Go ahead and show them, see what happens. My guess is that you'll be giving birth to that child in jail for falsifying evidence."

Chloe pulled her arm from Rade's grasp. The last thing she needed was to cause a scene with him. Although if she did, she might be able to get him to bend to her will. Unfortunately she had other plans for him. Turning around, Chloe headed down the sidewalk in the other direction. Rade watched as she slipped into a black sedan. The driver looked to be about Rade's age and build. It was then that he recognized him. As the driver got closer, Rade snapped a picture of the guy with his cell and sent the picture to Peter. Rade had a sneaky suspicion that the driver has something to do with the charade Chloe was playing.

It was late morning when Rade pulled up to Crystal Hill Tower. He had left Dylan with his father and his decision to do so was justified by the uncomfortable interaction he had with Chloe at the clinic. The last thing he needed was for Dylan to get upset.

Entering the penthouse, Rade could smell something wonderful in the air. As he rounded the corner, he saw his woman standing by the stove stirring the contents inside a big pot. Walking over to her, he wrapped his arms around her waist to see what she was up to.

"Mmmm, that smells heavenly," Rade whispered as he nibbled at her ear lobe.

"Mmmm, you feel heavenly. I missed you," Dylan replied. "I thought I would make something light for your dad when he woke up."

"Chicken noodle soup?" Rade questioned Dylan's remedy choice.

"Yeah. A good hot bowl of CNS cures all. Didn't your mother....." Dylan stopped mid-sentence realizing what she was about spill before it was too late. "I'm sorry... I didn't mean..."

Before Dylan could finish, Rade had her body turned to his and his lips on her gorgeous mouth. The stirring spoon fell to the floor with a loud clank as Dylan wrapped her arms around Rade's neck. Her hands automatically ran through his thick hair as their kiss became more than just a friendly peck. Moving Dylan away from the stove, Rade lifted her by her ass and carried her bear style to the adjacent counter where he set her down.

It didn't matter where they were, their bodies were like magnets. Rade lifted the thin t-shirt from her body. Cupping her breast, he could feel the tender peaks of her nipples already giving way to his touch. Pulling the cups of her bra down so they were resting under her breasts, Rade lowered his head attaching his mouth over her nipple. Just the scent of her, had him coming undone. It was hard for Dylan to focus on the pot of soup which was now boiling, just like the heat between her legs. The hot liquid was sizzling on the burner as it boiled over the top of the pot.

"Rade, I need to turn the temperature down," Dylan said breathing heavily.

"Just feel Dylan, Give yourself to me," Rade commanded.

"Rade the soup on the stove, its boiling over," Dylan advised.

With his free hand, Rade reached behind him and turned the knob on the burner without interrupting the enjoyment he was having consuming Dylan's breasts. Gathering her in his arms, he lifted her body from the granite counter top. With everything that was going on, only Dylan could make him forget about his problems. She was like the sunlight after the storm. Setting her down, Rade groaned with pleasure dipping his hand lower to her tight stomach and then to the zipper of her jeans. Dylan leaned back on the counter adjusting her body so that Rade could easily remove her jeans. As he pulled her jeans down, she watched him struggle to get her jeans off her body. With a frustrated look he whispered, "No more jeans. As a matter of fact no more clothing period while you're here with me."

Dylan had to giggle at his request. She knew he was being ridiculous thinking that she would walk around the penthouse naked all day to appease his sexual demands.

When Rade finally had her naked, aside from her bra which was still bunched under her beautiful breasts, he needed to free the heat bellowing beneath his pants. As he lowered his pants, it was visible that he wanted her as much as she wanted him . The hardening of his shaft was fully displayed at the waistband of his boxers. Dylan bit her bottom lip wanting nothing more than to take him inside her mouth. Her wish was soon granted when Rade lifted her onto the cold counter and sunk his finger inside her tight cunt causing her body to unravel with pure bliss.

Nothing could pull them apart. Knowing that Garrett Matheson was only a few feet away and could walk in on them at any moment didn't stop them. The only focus they had was on each other. Rade lifted Dylan by the ass feeling the coldness the counter had left on her cheeks. He knew the minute he plunged deep inside her, those cheeks would be warmed instantly. Bracing her body to his while using his other hand to guide his length inside her wet cunt, Rade felt Dylan submit to him, pulling her body even closer.

This was the perfect position for Rade. Even though she was so tight, she took every inch of him as he drove his cock deeper inside her. Her soft slick walls possessed him, harnessing his mass tighter and tighter with each push.

Positioning his hands on her back, Rade slowly leaned forward causing Dylan's back to hit the cold stone. Her back arched from the sharp temperature, but his assault on her cunt launched her body into a blaze, like a towering inferno. She could no longer hold back her desire as her body shuddered with her release. Even though she was spent, Rade didn't cease his assault on her body. His movements increased causing her yet another orgasm.

Rade was nowhere near done with her. Turning the kitchen faucet on, Rade grabbed the sprayer and lightly began spraying Dylan's sated body with the water. Rade watched as her body arched to connect with the warm water streaming down her chest to her stomach and them between her legs where their bodies were attached. This was like no other sensation she had ever felt. It was a mixture of hot and cold, pleasure and pain. Dylan wasn't sure how much more her body could take even though her mind was saying more. With the heat of the pussy wrapped around his cock, Rade could feel his own release take flight. Just a few more thrusts and he would be hers. Lowering his hand between their connected bodies, Rade pinched Dylan's clit as he continued driving inside her. Her body shook as Rade took another orgasm from her. His desire for release came as she too took another for herself.

By the time they finished their little interlude in the kitchen, Dylan had to reheat the soup on the stove. Leaving her side, Rade went to check on his father. When he got to his room, he could see that he was no longer in bed. Rade walked over to the bathroom and knocked on the door lightly. When there was no answer, Rade pushed the door open to find that Garrett was hunched over the sink. This should have concerned Rade, but the only thing it did was infuriate him. Not because his father was standing there, but because he needed his father to rest so he could find out what happened to him.

"What are you doing? You should have called someone to help you," Rade exploded with anger.

Garrett barely had enough strength to lift his head to address his son. "I don't want to be a burden to you. I know how much you love having me here," Garrett said sarcastically.

"The sooner you get back on your feet, the sooner you can leave," Rade advised. "You need to get back into bed. Dylan made you some soup. It will help you get your strength back."

Rade helped his father back to bed. Once he was settled, Rade could see blood had seeped through the bandage Richard had done for him. The movement to the bathroom must have irritated the wound causing it to bleed. Taking a closer look, Rade thought it best to re-dress his father's wound.

Dylan walked into the bedroom with a tray holding a bowl of her chicken noodle soup and crackers. Rade shifted his body so that Dylan could place the tray on the table next to the bed. Dylan could feel the tension in the room. Pulling up a chair, Dylan positioned herself so that she could better assist Garrett with his meal. Rade wasn't very happy that Dylan was giving so much attention to his father. If it would have been him, he would have left his father to fend for himself or starve.

Rade sat in the far corner of the room as he watched Dylan feed his father. He wasn't enjoying the sight, but he wanted to stick close by so that he could question his father once he was finished eating. Rade was ready to get to the bottom of what happened at the BlackStone building and what part his father played in it.

Dylan finished with taking care of Garrett's needs, taking the tray with the empty bowl with her as she left the room. This was a good time as any to began his interrogation on his father. Standing at the edge of the bed, Rade looked down at his father wanting more than anything to see him gone from his home.

"So, are you going to tell me what the fuck happened to you?" Rade barked.

"You don't waste any time," Garrett replied.

"I'm done playing your games. You're the one who came to me." Rade was losing his patience with his father.

"I'm not sure what I can tell you son that you don't already know."

"Well for starters, you can tell me who stabbed you and why you're identification was on another man's body."

Garrett rubbed his forehead as he began to explain. "A man walked into the BlackStone office. I was waiting in the conference room to have a meeting with Keeve and Mason about the terms of our partnership. Just as he was heading towards Keeve's office, another gentleman about my height and built got off the elevator. The other guy didn't have a chance. The gunman shot him in the face. That's when Keeve stepped out of his office to see what was going on. He should have stayed put. The guy shot Keeve twice. He kept asking Keeve if he knew me and where I was. I thought it best to say out of sight. I think he would have shot Keeve again, but Mason appeared. Mason must have seen what was going on, because he ran back to his office. The gunman saw Mason. It was too late. This was my chance. I took the dead guy's wallet and replace it with mine and quickly scribbled *"Forgiveness"* on his chest. Since the shooter didn't take the time to check his identity, I thought that if he saw my identification, he would have no reason to keep looking for me. I had to make everyone believe it was me lying on the floor. Just before I got to the stairwell, another shot was fired."

"This is all fucked up. Why would anybody be looking for you?" Rade asked.

"I don't know and I wasn't going to stick around and find out," Garrett confirmed.

"Did you get a good look at the shooter?"

"I couldn't see his face. He wore a ski mask, but he was short and heavy. The stupid fuck was dumb enough to wear glasses over his mask."

"How about the wallet from the dead guy? Do you still have it?" Rade asked hoping his father held on to it.

"I tossed it in a dumpster. His name was Paul New.., something or another, Newhouse. His name was Paul Newhouse. Did you know him?" Garrett asked.

"No," Rade spat, forking his hands through his hair. Turning towards his dad he asked, "It still doesn't explain how you got stabbed."

"A homeless person was digging through the dumpster when I opened the lid to throw the wallet inside. I must have scared him, because the next thing I knew, he stabbed me with a knife," Garrett confessed.

"Fucking hell are you kidding me? You got stabbed by a fucking homeless person," Rade laughed irately.

Chapter Eleven

The events from the last couple of days left Rade on edge. Not only because of what happened to his father, but also because the paternity results were in. The blood test came back positive confirming that Rade was the father of Chloe's child. He couldn't bring himself to share this information with Dylan. He didn't know how he was going to let her know. All he knew was that he needed to let her know gently. Maybe he would take her away for the weekend. Some place where they wouldn't be bothered. A place where there wouldn't be any way to get in touch with them. It was still warm enough so maybe he would charter a boat. A weekend out on the open sea would be perfect.

Making the final arrangements for his surprise getaway, Rade headed down the steps to where Dylan awaited him in the bedroom. He knew that she was exhausted with everything that happened at the BlackStone office. The investigation was still underway. Rade's father finally went to the police to let them know what he saw and to let them know the true identity of the man whose face was blown off. The police continued to mislead the press into thinking it was Garrett Matheson that was shot. Garrett was taken to a safehouse until the authorities could find out who the shooter was. Even the FBI were called since the man killed was a Federal employee, an IRS investigator.

Needless to say, Dylan's first day back to work was filled with questions relating to the incident. A new IRS investigator was assigned to finish the investigation into Keeve and Mason's financial records which also put added pressure on Dylan. Dylan provided what she could to the investigator, not really sure what he was looking for. She couldn't imagine any tax evasion taking place.

After dinner, Rade left Dylan soaking in the tub, hoping all the stress of the day would be washed away. He wanted to go to the BlackStone building with her to help deal with the shit left behind, but his focus needed to be on another issue before it got out of hand. Thankfully between Richard and Peter, Dylan was safe.

Opening the door to the bathroom, Rade walked in just as Dylan was getting out of the water. God, she looked beautiful. He wanted nothing more than to lean her body over the smooth surface of the counter and fuck her until she screamed his name. He could tell by her stance that she was still worried about the day and what it brought. Feeling her anxiety, Rade lifted her from the floor and took her to the bed. He was going to get her to relax, no matter what it took.

"What are you doing?" Dylan asked letting him continue his strides to the bedroom.

"I'm going to get you to relax Sweetness," Rade said with a grin.

When Dylan was settled on the bed, Rade went back to the bathroom to grab the lavender oil from the cabinet. Walking back to the room he commanded, "Rollover on your stomach Sweetness."

Without hesitation, Dylan turned over. She had a pretty good idea what he was going to do. Placing a generous dollop of the oil in his palm, he rubbed his hands together and began smoothing it over her soft skin. Rade loved the feel of Dylan's soft skin under his hands. This was the difference between her and him. Where he was hard, she was soft. Rade gently pressed his hands into her flesh causing her to moan with satisfaction.

"God, that feels so good," Dylan breathed with gratification.

"Not as good as it would feel with my body pressed against yours, rubbing every inch of you," Rade whispered as he continued to knead his hands gently into her soft skin.

The thought of covering her oiled body with his, sent an electric surge to the tip of his shaft. Rade could feel his excitement build the longer he caressed her body. This was suppose to help her relax, but instead it made him harder and harder for her. If he didn't stop he would soon have his cock deep inside her. Rolling her over onto her back, he couldn't deny himself any longer. He needed to take what was his. Lowering his body over hers, he placed his lips over hers and began devouring her sweetness. The heat between them ignited as Dylan took what he was offering. Slipping her tongue into his mouth, Dylan explored the confines of his warmth. He tasted of scotch and something sweet. Sucking and nibbling his bottom lip, she drew him in further. With a heated rush, Rade pulled his mouth from hers only to settle it on her right breast. This was where he found more of heaven. Her heaven. Lapping his tongue around her areola, Dylan's body began to respond to his assault. Her body arched as she gave more of herself to him. Gliding his hand down her firm stomach, he felt her body relax beneath him. "Maybe this, what we have now should have came first," Rade whispered hearing her quiet moan of pleasure.

Dylan didn't care what he did. As long as he didn't stop, she would be satisfied. Wrapping her legs around his waist, Dylan wanted, no needed to feel more of him. This, right now, was her tranquility and only Rade could give it to her. Thinking of nothing more than his touch, she felt Rade gently slip his middle finger inside her wet pussy. The fiction was all it took to free the stress within. Her body surrendered, letting the weight of the day stream from her body. Dylan screamed his name when another finger entered her soaked channel causing another blast of ecstasy to pour from her body.

With the weight of the world released from her body, Dylan had no problem falling asleep. Rade had left her fully satisfied and utterly exhausted. Rade laid with her until her eyes closed. He loved the feeling of her body pressed to his. As much as he hated to leave the comfort of her warmth, he needed to check the progress of Michael Stewart's whereabouts. Rade had spoken to Peter earlier that day, there was a hit on a credit card that he and Dylan once shared. Dylan probably didn't know it was still active since it was under his name. Since Michael's body hadn't officially been found and he hadn't been pronounced legally dead, all of his accounts were still active. This meant that the police also had access to track the use of any credit cards.

One thing that Rade couldn't understand was why Michael would be in Connecticut? He has no known ties to the state, let alone Waterbury. Peter assured him that he would be sending Josh that way to see what he could find. Rade knew that Michael was up to something. With the threats he received and the recent note to Dylan, he needed more than ever to keep her close. Nothing would please him more than to have all these loose ends tied up before the weekend. He knew that was only wishful thinking since the weekend was only three days away.

Rade poured a much needed scotch as he watched the sun set over the Manhattan skies. It was nights like these that made him appreciated how much he loved New York. Rade was about to pour another drink when his cell rang. Looking at the screen, Chris from IT appeared as the caller.

"Hey Chris," Rade answered

"Hey Rade," Chris greeted him on a first name bases. "Ms. Dupree finally logged into her computer and I was able to get some information for you. With her keystrokes, I was able to get the passwords to her bank accounts and credit card information. After logging into her account at World National Bank, I was able to get a copy of her most recent statement. There were some pretty hefty withdrawals. Five in all, in the amount of twenty thousand dollars each. She also has a pretty nice balance in her account, two-hundred thousand and change. Other than a safe deposit box, there are a couple of brokerage accounts and a savings account. I'm still working on her email account which should be pretty easy to get into. I thought I would give you an update before I did anything else."

"Good work Chris. When you access her email account, let me know right away if anything looks out of the ordinary especially if it has anything to do with Dr. O'Brian," Rade advised.

"Will do. Have a good evening," Chris said as he ended the call.

Rade knew something wasn't right with Chloe. Thinking about what Chris had found, he wondered where Chloe's sizable bank balance came from. He also wanted to get inside her safe deposit box. Maybe there would be something there that would give him the evidence he needed to prove she had a part in his kidnapping.

* * * * *

Rising out of bed the next morning, Dylan felt energized. She was ready to tackle whatever the day would bring. She knew there was still a lot to do with the financial situation. After her relaxing night, she had a better grasp on what needed to be done.

Rade wasn't next to her when she woke up, so she assumed he was already dressed and in his study or living area. Pushing herself from the bed, she decided to seek him out.

Stopping short of the kitchen, she laid her eyes on him as she stared at his perfect form reading what she assumed was the Wall Street Journal. She was in such a good mood that the mischievous side of her decided to sneak up on him. Tip-toeing to where he sat, Dylan was about to place her hands over his eyes when he turned around and said, "Boo!" Dylan was so surprised by his unexpected scare tactic that she stumbled backwards causing the chair, she was holding onto, to tip over, spilling the contents of her purse on the hard marble floor.

Rade reached out just in time to grab her by the waist before she also tumbled to the floor. He didn't realize that his playful behavior would cause her to jump.

"Oh God, Sweetness. I didn't mean to scare you," Rade said.

"I guess I shouldn't have snuck up on you like I did," Dylan replied.

Rade pulled Dylan in closer. Lowering his head, he gently kissed her on the lips taking in her scent. Biting her bottom lip, Rade felt her body melt into his letting him know he was forgiven for his naughtiness. Breaking their embrace. Dylan lowered her body so she could gather the contents that spilled from her purse. Rade stooped beside her helping her with her things. Grabbing a lone key, Rade looked at Dylan with a questionable look on his face. "Sweetness, I didn't know you had a deposit box."

"I totally forgot about that key. I found it in Alex's desk at BlackStone when you went missing," Dylan confirmed. "I was going to try and find where he had his accounts, but with everything going on, I completely forgot."

"Let me figure it out," Rade said kissing Dylan on the lips.

This was the kiss of all kisses that ended up returning much more. Rade's little gratitude cause Dylan to be an hour and a half late for work. When she did arrive, she was greeted by the irritated look of the IRS investigator. If he could have spit fire, it would have been directed at her.

"Mr. Metcalf, sorry to keep you waiting. An emergency came up," Dylan said knowing he could see right through her little lie.

"I hope you don't make a habit of being late. My time is very valuable Ms. Adams," he stated in a heavy tone.

Dylan walked back to her office to settle in while Mr. Metcalf walked to the conference room to continue with his review. Dylan joined him a few minutes later with an office box filled with financial documents. Even though the review was a tedious process, the investigator didn't come up with anything substantial. Nothing that rendered tax evasion. This was good news for Dylan because it meant that Keeve and Mason were on the up and up.

Breaking for lunch, Dylan asked that Richard take her to the hospital so that she could check in on Keeve and Mason. Keeve was moved to a regular room, while Mason remained in ICU. It would be sometime before Keeve would be able to return to work, but that didn't mean that Dylan couldn't communicate with him on everything taking place in the office including the IRS audit.

Richard pulled up to the front doors of Mount Sinai allowing Dylan to exit while he searched for a parking spot. When Dylan went through the automatic doors, she was surprised to see Rade standing in the waiting area.

"Rade, I wasn't expecting to see you here," Dylan said giving he a small kiss on the lips.

"Richard contacted me to let me know he was heading here. I hope you don't mind the company," Rade asked.

"Of course not," Dylan said reassuring Rade by taking hold of his hand.

Keeves new room was on the fifth floor, so when an available elevator opened, Rade and Dylan quickly stepped inside. Dylan could already feel the electricity radiating between them. Even though it had only been a couple of hours since they laid hands on each other, she could feel the warmth between her legs rising, filling her with desire for the man next to her. Rade must have felt the same way.

"If we weren't in a hospital elevator at the moment, I would have you pushed up against the wall thrusting my needy cock inside your sweet tight cunt," Rade confessed.

"Patience. Isn't that what you always say?" Dylan knowingly whispered taming down her own desire for him.

Before Rade could comment, the elevator dinged letting them know they had arrived on the fifth floor. Rade gently placed his hand on Dylan's lower back guiding her down the hallway to Keeve's room. Once they arrived, they took in the appearance of Keeve's body as his long frame extended the length of the hospital bed. His eyes were closed, which meant he was either sedated or resting. Keeve must have been resting, because as Dylan stepped closer to the bed, Keeve's eyes opened.

"Hey you. How are you feeling?" Dylan asked.

"Good, tired," Keeve said in a raspy tone.

Rade moved closer to the bed making sure that Keeve would be able to see him. "I know this is insensitive of me to ask, but I really need to know. Do you have any idea who the man was that shot you?" Rade said getting to the point.

"Rade," Dylan said looking over to Rade none too happy. "Can't he answer your questions when he gets stronger?"

"I'm sure Keeve wants to know as much as we do who shot him," Rade countered.

"It's Okay Dylan," Keeve began as he adjusted his body to a sitting position. "I wasn't able to see him with the ski mask he wore. But there was something about him. His voice, like I had met him before."

"Is there anything else you remembered about him?" Rade quizzed.

"Not really. Hopefully it will come to me once I remember that voice." Keeve paused. "Rade, he was looking for your father. I remember that Garrett was waiting for us in the conference room. I heard a shot before I blacked out. God, tell me he didn't get to him."

"My father is fine. The man who shot you, also shot Mason. That's the gun shot you heard . Mason is still in ICU." Rade wasn't sure how much Keeve knew or how much he was told. He did know that Keeve needed to know what happened to his partner.

"Bastard, If I ever get my hands on the son of a bitch, I'll make sure he doesn't see the light of day," Keeve hissed, the pain from his gun shots spreading like fire across his body.

"You need to calm down Keeve. We're doing everything we can to find the shooter. You need to focus on getting better," Rade advised.

Dylan sat back as Rade and Keeve argued about who was going to take out the gunman. It wasn't much of a match seeing as how Keeve could barely move. Dylan left the two men arguing to find out how Mason was doing. Even though he was still in ICU, his condition was improving. This was a good sign. They changed his status from critical to stable. Even though he still wasn't out of the woods, at least he was on his way to recovery.

Dylan got back to the office just in time to see the IRS investigator quizzing Jessica about some files he was holding in his hand. Dylan could see that Jessica was dumbfounded by what he was asking.

"I'll handle it from here Jessica," Dylan said looking straight at the investigator. "Mr. Metcalf, if you have any questions regarding your review, I would appreciate you directing them to me instead of asking our receptionist."

It wasn't long that Dylan had the investigator back in the conference room answering his questions. Some of them were so off the wall that Dylan had to laugh at the stupidity of them. It was only when he asked who the secret partner was, that Dylan quit laughing to herself. The investigator held up the partnership agreement which Dylan immediately recognized. Clearly he could see that Garrett Matheson was the secret partner. Dylan found it odd that the agreement would be among the financial statements when it should have been kept in a safe place.

"What does BlackStone having a secret partner agreement have anything to do with your investigation Mr. Metcalf?" Dylan questioned.

"It has everything to do with the investigation. It clearly states that in the event one of the partners, namely Keeve Black or Mason Stone, enters into any agreement without the other partners knowledge then any additional provisions on the initial contract will become null and void and the secret partner will retain fifty-one percent interest while any other partners would split the remaining forty-nine percent interest evenly," the investigator recited from the agreement.

"I can't believe that. Let me see the contract," Dylan claimed, grabbing the document from his hands. As she scanned the document, she could clearly see that the agreement in her hand was drawn up three months after the initial partnership was signed. This couldn't be happening. If what she read was true, then Garrett Matheson would be getting his piece of the pie. Her next question was, which one of the men had gone against the other and engaged into business without the others knowledge. This must have been what Garrett knew and kept from Rade.

Dylan headed back to her office to grab her things. "Where are you going Ms. Adams. We aren't finished here," the investigator barked.

"We'll have to commence again tomorrow. I need to take care of something," Dylan replied.

Dylan was out of the office and hailing a cab before the investigator knew what hit him. She needed to get to Rade and show him the revised contract that Keeve and Mason neglected to share with them. This would change everything pertaining to the Spectrum deal. It seemed the only thing that Rade could do was to back out of the deal he made with BlackStone. Dylan wouldn't blame him if he did since they weren't exactly forthcoming regarding the secret partnership and the deal that was made.

By the time Dylan reached Rade's office, her nerves were going a mile a minute. She couldn't believe that this information had been hidden from them and it took an IRS investigator to find it. She also wondered how much more information he was going to be digging up during his review.

Stepping out of the cab and onto the curb, a chill ran up Dylan's spine. It was the same feeling she got the night of the grand opening at *Riley's*. Looking around, she spotted what or more like who had her feeling uneasy. Standing across the street was a tall man, medium built looking right at her. She couldn't tell if she recognized him since he was wearing a hoodie and a pair of sun glasses. He was definitely trying to hide his identity. *Who wears a hoodie when it's nearly eighty degrees outside?* Dylan yelled at the guy as she began to approach him. Just as she crossed the street, he ducked into an alley where he disappeared out of sight. Dylan couldn't run after him even if she wanted to. Coming from work, she wasn't exactly dressed to chase down the guy.

Walking back across the street, Dylan was greeted by an agitated face. She knew all too well that look meant disapproval. Looking up at Rade, Dylan tried to explain, but was taken by the arm before she could.

"What the hell are you doing here Dylan? And why did I just see you climb out of a cab instead of waiting for Richard to bring you here?"

"I couldn't wait, I needed to talk to you right away," Dylan responded.

"Whatever it is, it doesn't justify your safety," Rade barked. "Who were you running after a moment ago?"

" I'm not sure. I got the same feeling I did at Evan's grand opening. I thought I….. I don't know what I thought. Just forget it," Dylan said, pulling her arm free from Rade's grasp.

The minute Dylan pulled from him, Rade had her pulled even tighter against his body. "Nothing is more important to me than your safety Dylan. Next time you are not to leave without Richard or myself. Clear." Rade stood silent as he waited for a response that never came. "Sweetness are we clear?"

"Yes," Dylan said hesitantly. She was tired of being a burden to Rade and especially Richard. She was sure he had more important things to do than to escort her everywhere she needed to go.

Richard must have pulled up with the Bentley while they were having their little dispute, because when Dylan pulled from Rade's embrace, he was already holding the back passenger door open for them. Rade took hold of her hand and led her to the passenger door of the SUV and assisted her inside.

On the way home Dylan wondered what would be waiting for her when they got there. She could tell by Rade's silence in the SUV that he was still angry with her for leaving work without letting Richard know. Just the thought of what her punishment would be made her body tingle with anticipation. A small smile appeared on her face at just the thought. Looking beside her at the man she loved, she was met with his dazzling smile. She knew he must have been thinking the same thing. Needless to say, she never got a chance to tell him about the purpose of her surprise visit to his office. Instead she decided to wait until she could find out all the facts.

Chapter Twelve

It was Friday and Rade couldn't be happier. He was finalizing his get-a-way plans with Dylan for the extended weekend. His only goal was to worship her every waking hour. By the time the extended weekend was over, she would be thoroughly fucked. Lost in his thoughts, a knock came at the door. Rade didn't have any appointments scheduled for the rest of the day and Gwen usually called when she needed him. Thinking nothing of it, Rade commanded, "Come in."

Look at the door, waiting for his visitor to appear, Rade's day just got shitty in a matter of seconds.

"Chloe, what the fuck do you want?" Rade hissed.

"Is that any way to talk to the mother of your child?" Chloe asked.

Chloe made herself comfortable by taking a seat in front of Rade's desk. She knew Rade was watching her every move, so she added a light swing to her step. Being pregnant had its perks. With the prenatal vitamins she was taking, everything about her glowed. Even though Rade hated to admit it, pregnancy did look good on her.

"Say what you came to say and then leave," Rade ordered, turning his attention back to his computer.

"Since I kept my end of the bargain and agreed to another blood test, I think it's only fair that we make plans for our visit to

London. I just dropped by to check your schedule," Chloe smiled knowing Rade would soon be hers.

"I'm perfectly aware of what I said Chloe. Let me know when you want to leave and I'll have Gwen make the arrangements," Rade replied with distaste.

"Very well. I can't wait till you meet my parents. They are going to love you," Chloe gloated as she rose from her seat.

Rade fisted his hands wanting to hit something. He didn't know what possessed him to agree to go to London with Chloe. His only absolution was that his days in London would be spent with Dylan by his side. Chloe was going to be in for a big surprise. He wanted to let her know that an additional guest would be accompanying him to visit her parents in London, but he couldn't spoil the surprise. Rade couldn't wait to see Chloe's face when Dylan arrived with him in London.

Rade needed to push his thoughts aside and concentrate on the trip he had planned with Dylan. A few more hours and they would be alone together on the blue water. A few more hours and she would be his for two glorious days. Not even Chloe could ruin what he had planned.

There was another knock on the door. *What did that bitch want now?.*

"I having nothing more to say to you Chloe," he said looking toward the closed door.

When the door opened he was surprised to see it wasn't Chloe standing before him. It was Richard and the look on his face was strained.

"Sorry to disturb you sir, but we have some information on Mr. Stewart's credit card. Turns out his credit card was stolen. His parents have been monitoring the charges and reported it stolen to the authorities. Sorry to say, we've come up empty," Richard said regretfully.

"I knew it was too good to be true. He would have been too stupid to use his card," Rade declared.

"We aren't giving up sir. Soon he will make a mistake and we will be right there when he does." It may have been wishful thinking on Richard's part, but Rade knew he needed to do whatever it took to have Michael Stewart in his control. It was then that he remembered the key that fell out of Dylan's purse. Pulling it from his pocket, he held it up as if it held all the answers he needed.

"Richard, I need you to find out where this key goes to. Dylan found it among Alex Moreno's things. I'm pretty certain it's a safe deposit key. You may want to check World National Bank," Rade suggested.

"Very well sir. I'll let you know what I find out," Richard assured him.

Rade was ready to head out. What started out being a good day turned into a day from hell. As bad as it was, Rade wasn't going to let it put a damper on his plans. He knew that Dylan would still be working and he wanted to make sure he was there to pick her up. She had no idea what he had planned for her, and he didn't want to waste anymore time then necessary to begin his little surprise.

All the arrangements were in place. Rade made sure Dylan didn't need to worry about anything, other than getting sunburn. Rade manage to locate a two hundred foot yacht he could charter. The owner and Captain of the boat was all too happy to accommodate Rade's request when he found out how much he would be getting paid for the short notice. It didn't take the Captain long to find a crew with enough experience to man the large vessel. All Rade had to do was sit back and enjoy. The

Captain assured Rade that the weather would be perfect for their little adventure. He also assured them that the staff would leave them to their privacy and they wouldn't notice them on board. If everything went well, Rade might even purchase the yacht and arrange for permanent employment for the Captain and the crew.

Pulling up to the BlackStone building, Rade drove to the parking garage and entered the lobby through the stairwell. Punching the button to the fifteen floor, he watched as the floors increased on the LED display on the elevator panel. Jessica and Lucy were sitting behind the reception desk like two bookends on a bookshelf. As soon as Rade entered the glass doors, their heads popped up and huge smiles swept across their faces.

"Good afternoon Mr. Matheson," they said in unison.

"Good afternoon ladies," Rade replied with a smile.

Walking down the hallway, Rade thought back to how lucky it was that Dylan wasn't around when the shooting took place. It was karma that she decided to go into work later that morning. It could have easily been her that got shot. Rade hoped that soon Richard and Peter would have some information for him as to who the man was that pulled a gun and let loose.

When Rade got to Dylan's office, he could see she was deep in thought. He knew that convincing her to give up her job and come to work for him would be out of the question. At least not until Keeve and Mason were back on their feet. He would love nothing more than to have access to her. He would make sure that her office was right next to his with an adjoining door. Nothing like a quickie in the middle of the afternoon.

Yanked from his thoughts, he was greeted with Dylan's beautiful smile. "Rade, what are you doing here?" Dylan asked surprised.

"I'm here to take you away. I have a surprise planned for us and I wanted to pick you up personally," Rade confessed.

"What kind of surprise?" Dylan asked, cocking her head to the side wondering what he was up to.

"If I told you, it wouldn't be a surprise Sweetness." Rade knew no matter how much Dylan begged to get the answer she needed, he wasn't willing to let her know.

Rounding her desk, he took her by the hand and led her out of her office. He was glad that she didn't protest. Once they got to his car, he pulled out a black scarf that he had tucked inside his suit pocket.

"Turn around Sweetness," he said with a smirk.

"What is this Rade?" Dylan asked confused.

"Part of your surprise," Rade replied.

With the scarf securely tied behind Dylan's head, Rade carefully lowered her into the car. Once she was settled, he reached across her body and buckled her in while taking advantage to gently brush her pert breasts. A smile appeared on Dylan's face acknowledging his playful deed. The touch alone set Dylan's body on fire. Unable to resist, Rade lowered his lips to hers and captured the kiss he was waiting all day for.

"This weekend is going to be just you and I. No phones, No work, and most of all no clothes," Rade whispered to her.

With a small giggle, Dylan was somehow able to capture his mouth with hers, pulling him in for another much needed kiss. Rade took advantage of her warmth and deepened their embrace. This is where he wanted to be, thinking of nothing but her. The problem was that he couldn't wait. Turning into a vacant alley, Rade gave into his desire. Dylan could feel his touch as he gently pulled her from her seat and positioned her over his lap. Finding the electric seat button, Rade pushed the button until his seat was fully extended allowing him full access to her body. With her on his lap, he eased his right hand between their bodies until he found her warm heat. With heated fervor, he slowly slipped his hand between her soft flesh, soaking in the wetness that was waiting for him. "What are you doing to me Sweetness? I will never get enough of you," Rade moaned unable to contain his own hunger. Lifting her body from his, he took hold of her hips and placed his hands under her skirt. Without warning, he took hold of her lacy panties and ripped them from her body. His uncontrollable need took over leaving her wanting him even more.

"Rade please take me. I'm yours," Dylan moan with a need she could no longer deny.

Soaring to unlimited heights, Rade adjusted his position, settling Dylan's warm cunt over his willing cock. He knew there was no other place he wanted to be. It didn't matter that he was in an unfamiliar place, he only knew he needed to satisfy his desire for this woman.

In tune with each other, Rade slipped his hardening length inside the burning tinder waiting for him. With precise thrusts, Rade slowly consumed the fire Dylan emanated as he accepted the hold she had on him.

Their bodies were as one as they embarked in the pleasure that overtook their senses. Dylan screamed his name, while Rade moaned his own release. He was certain that everyone could hear their ultimate release within a five mile radius. Holding her in his arms as they slowly came down from their explosive release, Rade said with complete bliss, "I will never love any other woman the way that I love you."

Rade regretfully pulled Dylan from his body and gently placed her in the passenger seat. He knew he had to break their little love session before he couldn't control himself.

Rade slowly removed the blindfold seeing the softness behind her eyes. Dylan looked over to him with adoration knowing she would never love a man more than she loved him.

* * * * *

When Rade drove to the pier, Dylan couldn't believe the massive yachts that were docked. She had no idea what Rade had in store for her, but she knew their weekend together would be one of total bliss. It wasn't until they walked up to one of the larger yachts that she gasped with excitement.

"Rade, is this boat yours?" Dylan asked in amazement. She had never seen anything so beautiful in her life.

"Unfortunately no, but that doesn't mean it couldn't be," Rade declared.

As they boarded the vessel, a stocky man with red hair and a scruffy beard greeted them. He couldn't have been more than forty. Dylan knew that he must have been the Captain by the white uniform he was wearing.

"Welcome aboard Mr. Matheson. I'm Captain Talbot, Ms. Adams. It's so nice to have you aboard. I'll have one of our crew members show you to your suite," the Captain offered.

Soon a young steward appeared leading them to where they would be spending most of their time. As they headed down the narrow hallway, a door was opened for them by the steward. Looking inside, the suite was more than Dylan dreamed. It hosted a king sized bed with a light blue duvet on top. The room was surrounded with deep wood trim and plush carpeting. Off to the left was a row of windows that extended the width of the room. There was a glass door which Dylan assumed led to the massive deck. Since Rade didn't give a hint as to where they were going, Dylan didn't have the opportunity to pack, but when she pulled open the door to the walk-in closet, she should have known it didn't matter. The only clothing inside were a few dress shirts and nightgowns.

Opening yet another door, Dylan was greeted with a jetted tub the size of a small Jacuzzi. The room was breathtaking with its shiny marble surfaces and mirrored ceiling. Dylan could see her and Rade spending a lot of time in it.

"This is amazing Rade. I could definitely get use to this," Dylan said.

"This little get-a-way is just what we needed," Rade replied.

Even though he still hadn't told Dylan about the results of his blood test, he hoped that this trip with her would soften the blow.

An announcement came over the speaker from the Captain letting them know that they would departing the port in fifteen minutes and that cocktails and hors d'oeuvres would be served on the main deck. Rade's mind was far from thinking about food. The only refreshment he was searching for, stood right in front of him ready to be devoured.

Stepping up to Dylan, he cupped her face and lowered his lips to hers. The softness hit him like cotton candy. Sweet and delicious. Feeling her submit to him, he deepened his assault taking in her warmth. Rade began nibbling on her bottom lip bringing her body even closer to his. Slipping his tongue between her parted lips, he explored every inch, lapping his tongue with hers.

Rade gently lifted Dylan from the floor and carried her over to the plush bed waiting for them. He gently set her upon it, taking in the sight of this beautiful woman. His only mission was to make sure she was beneath him for the next forty-eight hours. Grabbing her hands, he slowly lifted them above her head while nipping at the base of her soft neck. Dylan's body reacted with fervor as her back arched into his. Holding on to her wrists with one hand, Rade took each tiny pearl button of her blouse between his fingers and released them from the confines of the material. Once all the buttons were freed, he released his grip and pulled the soft material from her body leaving her ivory skin exposed for him. He slowly eased the soft material down her shoulders. While kissing her, he lowered the strap of her lacy demi bra and captured her nipple, sucking and licking until it peaked. Moving to the other side while caressing her now taut nipple, he began his decent on her soft bud.

Rade loved how responsive she was to his touch. Her body hummed with arousal as he kissed every inch of her. He needed her naked and beneath him. With untamed desire, he lowered his hand down her body freeing her of her skirt and panties in one swift movement. This is how he wanted her, naked and stretched out for the taking. Taking what was his, he consumed her. Lapping and sucking, kissing and nibbling. Worshipping her body like it was a sacred piece of work.

"This is how I want you. Naked and beneath me," Rade breathed.

"Take me Rade, I need you to take me," Dylan demanded.

Rade didn't know how much longer he could control his need to take her. He only knew, he wanted this to last. Lifting her body, Rade brought her closer to him guiding her body over his. Feeling her heat, he gently positioned his shaft between her slick folds. His control gave way, as he slowly lowered her body on to his throbbing length. It was heaven. Every slow movement of her hips took him deeper and deeper inside. Inch by inch, she blanketed him with her warmth, drawing him closer and closer to the edge. She knew exactly what she was doing to him. Reaching between her legs, Dylan could feel the moisture building. She needed more. Gliding her hand lower, she rested it on her swollen clit. With added pressure, Dylan moved her finger up and down her sensitized nub. "That's it Sweetness. I love watching you touch yourself," Rade groaned with his own pleasure. Dylan was so close to her release when Rade grabbed her hips and raised her from his cock. All he could hear was her scream of protest. He knew she was close. He wanted her first orgasm at sea to be memorable.

Dylan watched with dismay as Rade rose from the bed. She wasn't sure what his game was, but when he reached out to her, she knew it was only her he wanted. With little effort, Rade pulled Dylan's body to his. Placing his hands under her firm cheeks, he lifted her.

Walking to the glass doors, Rade held Dylan with one arm while opening the door with his free hand. The breeze coming off the water drew a sudden breath from Dylan sending an arctic rush through her body. Rade held her tightly as he placed her on the lounger waiting for them on the glistening deck. Shielding her from the crisp air of the ocean, he placed his lips to hers. Within minutes her body heated with an infinite flame that only Rade could deliver. Pulling her closer, Rade took what was his. His love for her unleashed, bringing him to a place he thought he would never leave again. Moving his hands down her body, Rade could feel her quiver beneath him with each kiss that touched her silky body. Adjusting his position, Rade spread her legs wider allowing him to nestle between them. Placing his hands on her ass, he lifted her hips slightly from the lounger, draping her legs over his shoulders. "This is a night to remember Sweetness. Nobody will ever give you what I can," Rade breathed as he tenderly kissed her lips. Dylan was so consumed by the desire she had for this man that the chill of the air no longer felt like ice against her skin. Instead she felt warmed. "I love you Rade," she confessed with parted lips as Rade slowly pushed inside her. Nothing mattered more to him then her. This moment with her was all he wanted.

Moving his hips, Rade slowly thrust his shaft inside Dylan's warm channel. He loved the way her tight walls surrounded him as he drove deeper inside. Rade knew she was close. Her body was his. Dylan lowered her legs from his shoulders and wrapped them tightly around Rade's waist. It was her means to bring him closer, but it was still not enough to satisfy her need. Pulling him closer yet, Dylan wrapped her arms around his shoulders taking everything he had to offer. They were as one as their bodies moved together. With pure immeasurable love, Dylan's body shattered, leaving her overpowered with a need her heart ached for.

Dylan turned her head to the side so Rade couldn't see the emotional torment she had for him. The love she had for him went beyond everything she knew. It was so deep that her very being hurt.

Pulling her from her thoughts, Rade lowered his lips to hers and kissed her. Wrapping her in his arms, he lifted her from the lounger. "We better get inside before you freeze to death."

Dylan was afraid to say anything. The last thing she wanted was for Rade to know that she just had an emotional breakdown. Instead, she tucked her head to his chest and took in his scent praying her tears wouldn't fall.

Chapter Thirteen

Dylan had slept better then she had in weeks. She wasn't sure if it was because of the fresh air or the rocking of the boat. Stretching her body, Dylan reached across the bed only to find that Rade wasn't next to her. Instead a single white rose rested upon his pillow. Taking it in her hand, Dylan brought it to her nose and took in the scent. With a smile, she pushed from the bed in search for something to cover herself with.

Opening every drawer in the built in dresser, Dylan found there were only bikinis and board shorts. Walking to the closet, Dylan remembered the only items inside were white dress shirts and a couple of nightgowns. Dylan giggled to herself, *"He really did mean no clothes."* With a limited selection to choose from, Dylan slipped on a barely there black bikini and a white dress shirt. Pulling her hair in a pony, she decided this was going to have to do.

Leaving the bedroom, Dylan went to find Rade. Even though the boat was huge, she didn't think it would be too difficult to locate him. Searching the large boat, she found that she was wrong. She had no idea where she was. She felt as though she had been going in circles. She also found it strange that she didn't run into any of the crew. Going back the same way she came, Dylan decided to make another round. It was at that moment she felt a warm hand wrap around her waist. Taking in his scent, she knew exactly who it was.

"I've been looking all over for you," Dylan said leaning into Rade's body.

"I know. I was watching you from the bridge. Didn't you realize you were walking in circles?" Rade smiled, turning Dylan to face him.

"I knew I wasn't going crazy," Dylan confessed.

"Breakfast is ready for us on the deck. You must be starving after all that walking," Rade smirked.

"Very funny," Dylan said pinching Rade on the stomach.

Turning in the other direction, Rade led Dylan to a set of stairs. "I'll take you on a tour of the boat when we finish breakfast."

Dylan was almost ready to comment, but the view in front of her took her breath away. Looking at Rade's backside would never get old. With each step he took, she could see the muscles in his legs and butt flex. It was pure heaven. Getting to the top of the steps, Rade veered to the right, where a table was set for two. Dylan was in awe at the setting before her. The table was covered with a while linen tablecloth and white china, trimmed in gold, sitting on top. In the middle of the table was a centerpiece with a beautiful arrangement of white roses and pink lilies. This made Dylan smile, wondering if her single rose was from this very arrangement.

As they sat taking in the warm sun, a young man dressed in black slacks, a white shirt and a black vest appeared. He was balancing a large tray on his shoulders. With a quick turn of the tray, he began placing the covered plates on the fine china. Dylan always wondered why that was done. It seemed like a waste of dishes when they weren't going to get dirtied. The waiter continued placing various items on the table which included a basket of toasted breads, some sweet rolls and an assortment of jams. When he lifted the domes from the plates, Dylan's eyes came to life. Sitting on her plate were two strawberry crêpes with a mound of cream on the top. There was also a small bowl filled with pineapple, cantaloupe and mango. Her eyes just feasted on the display of food she was about to consume.

After they finished their breakfast, Rade kept his word and took Dylan on a tour of the boat. She must have seen at least a dozen bedroom suites. All of them nicely decorated in light colors and dark wood. Rade showed Dylan where the kitchen was in case she felt the need for a late night snack. There was also a large dining room, theatre room, game room and even a small pool on the upper deck. No wonder she got lost when she went searching for Rade.

It was mid-afternoon and Dylan was enjoying herself on the upper deck. Her body was relaxed and warmed by the sun. This was the life she could get used to. Looking over, she watched Rade as he stood on the other side of the deck practicing his marksmanship. Every time Dylan heard him yell *"Pull,"* her body tensed knowing that there would soon be a shot fired. It was amazing how good Rade was at hitting the small clay disc flying through the air.

The sun was setting and Dylan was ready for a nice long bath. Rade had left the upper deck sometime ago. Dylan thought maybe he was going to get something to drink and join her afterwards, but he didn't. When Dylan got to the room, Rade wasn't there. She assumed he was probably lounging in the game room having a drink. Stepping out of her barely there bikini, Dylan felt a warm breath on her neck. "On the bed Sweetness. I've been waiting all day to devour you," Rade whispered softly.

Dylan walked over to the bed and waited for Rade to take her, only he wasn't behind her. The room was empty. Dylan had no idea where he could have gone. Feeling frustrated, she pushed from the bed. Just as she was ready to stand, Rade appeared from the closet. Looking down on her with a hint of displeasure, Dylan quickly moved back to the middle of the bed. Whatever Rade had planned, made Dylan's body quiver with anticipation.

Walking to the edge of the bed, Rade pulled his hands from behind his back and dropped what he was holding on to the comforter. Dylan's eyes lowered to scan the objects. There were three things splayed on the bed before her. She recognized the black scarf and the silky red rope, but the last object she had never seen before. It was long and shiny with a small curve on the end and marble like balls spaced about an inch apart down the shaft. Looking back at Rade, a grin from here to Texas appeared on his face. Dylan wasn't sure what he had planned, but she knew she trusted him completely.

"Turn around Sweetness, with your hands behind your back," Rade demanded.

Without hesitation, Dylan turned away from him so that she was facing the front of the bed. Dylan could feel Rade shuffling on the bed as his hands took hold of her wrist. She knew the silky rope would soon be binding her wrists together. Next came the black scarf which Rade placed over her eyes causing the room to go black. Dylan could feel Rade behind her, pushing his body close to hers. Even though he was still dressed, she could feel the hardness of his cock pressed against her butt. All she wanted was to feel him. "Rade," Dylan moaned, stricken with need.

"Tell me what you want Sweetness," Rade said softly, holding back his desire for her.

"You, only you," Dylan muttered feeling the heat building.

"You have all of me Sweetness." She did have him. His body, his heart, and his soul. Picking up the shiny new toy, Rade gently rubbed the object between her slick folds. Willing her to lower her body, he gently placed his hand on her back. Once she was in his desired position, he spread her legs wider so he could have better access to her pussy. With a gentle nudge, he slipped the toy inside her awaiting cunt. A moan of pleasure broke from her mouth at the new invasion, letting Rade know her new toy was a good choice.

Rade adjusted the wand so that the small curve hit her g-spot. Dylan began rocking her hips against the toy causing his already hard mass to throb more. Sliding it further inside her tight channel, Dylan was becoming unhinged. She didn't know how much longer she could hold back her release. With an ushered plea she panted, "Rade, please. I need to come."

"Not yet, Sweetness. Soon," Rade declared moving the objected further inside leaving only the ring on the end exposed.

As each round ball entered and rescinded, her body became more and more inflamed. She needed to let go. Rade could feel her desperation for release. He knew she was close. Just a few more thrusts in and out, and she would be his. Without warning, Rade quickly yanked the shiny toy from her cunt. With a searing explosion, Dylan's body gave way to an earth shattering orgasm igniting a flame inside her.

Rade was nowhere near done with her. He had kept his hands free from her all day knowing he would have her completely, and thoroughly fucked. Freeing his engorged cock from his shorts, Rade eased inside her wet heat. With each slow thrust, he could feel her body begin to come alive. Every push deeper inside her was met with the push of her hips against him. "God Sweetness, you feel so fucking good," Rade moaned in ecstasy.

Holding her by her bound wrists for support, Rade mercilessly thrusted harder and deeper inside her. Dylan pulled him deeper and deeper the harder he pushed. Close to his own release, Rade endured the grip her posse had on his shaft. Her hold on him was unyielding. He was a prisoner, yet unwilling to break free. The scream of his name from her lips filled the room as she propelled into a freefall. Unable to suppress his own rhapsody, Rade spilled his seed inside her warm channel.

* * * * *

After a glorious weekend of blissful sex, it was hard to believe that their time together alone was almost over. The beautiful yacht was headed back to Liberty Landing Marina. Dylan was sad to see their weekend rendezvous come to an end. There had been nothing but them. No worries, no interruptions, just complete focus on each other. Even the crew stayed out of sight. Dylan didn't even see most of the crew. It was only when they brought them their meals did she know they existed.

Pulling into port, Captain Talbot's voice came over the intercom. "The yacht should be docked and secured in fifteen minutes. The crew and I would like to thank you for sailing with us. We hope you have enjoyed your trip. We hope to have you back again."

Getting off the boat, Richard was already waiting for them on the pier. Rade assisted Dylan down the gang plank while Richard took what little luggage they had. Dylan was sad to say goodbye to the beautiful boat. Turning to Rade she asked, "Can we go again?"

"We can go whenever you want Sweetness," Rade confirmed kissing Dylan on the head as he pulled her closer.

The ride back to the penthouse was one sided. Dylan was doing all of the talking. She wasn't sure what was going on with Rade, but she could feel something different in his mood. He seemed to be miles away. Taking hold of his hand, Dylan said with concern, "Rade, you seem so far away. What's on your mind that has you so quiet?"

Rade's initial plan was to tell Dylan about the blood test, but she was having such a wonderful time, he couldn't bring himself to tell her. He couldn't remember the last time he saw her so relaxed. "The blood tests came back. I was going to share the results with you on our weekend outing, but I just couldn't ruin your weekend."

"What are you trying to say Rade," Dylan asked.

"The tests show that I'm the father of Chloe's child. I thought for sure she was playing a game. I never thought it would come back positive." Rade knew the moment he told Dylan, her spirit would be broken.

"So I guess this means you're going to be a daddy," Dylan said hopelessly. More than anything she wanted the test to show that Rade wasn't the father of Chloe's child.

"I've made arrangements with Chloe to go to London to meet her parents. I want you to go with me. We leave in two weeks," Rade confirmed.

Dylan didn't know what to say to Rade's admission. She only knew that she felt empty and hurt inside. Even though Rade assured her Chloe would never have his heart, Dylan felt like a third wheel in this relationship. Knowing that Rade loved her didn't make her feel any better. It didn't matter how much they loved each other, Chloe was always going to be a part of their life. This was something that Dylan couldn't accept, especially after everything that happened.

Getting closer to the penthouse, it was Dylan who remained quiet. Her heart ached. She knew weeks ago that there was a good chance that Rade would be a father, she just kept telling herself, that it wasn't true and it was only Chloe's attempt to get her claws into Rade.

Rade could feel Dylan's uneasiness as he tried to assist her from the Bentley. He knew her heart was hurting. He wished he could find a way to make it better. Maybe with time and his love, it would heal.

Entering the penthouse Dylan softly said, "I'm going to lay down for a bit. It's been a long day."

Pulling Dylan near him, Rade kissed her tenderly on the lips. There were no words from Dylan, only a soft whimper. "We will make this work Sweetness. Please don't give up on us," Rade vowed.

Consumed with emotion, Dylan pulled from Rade's embrace and headed down the hall to the bedroom. Stripping off her clothes, Dylan walked to the closet and pulled one of Rade's dress shirts from the hanger. Putting in on, she pulled the collar to her nose and breathed in his scent. Just the thought of not being with him made the tears fall. Once they began, Dylan couldn't control them. Slipping into bed, she grabbed Rade's pillow and pulled it to her chest. With one last tug of air, her eyes fell shut.

Rade was in his study trying to think of ways he could make this up to Dylan. He needed to let her know that no one mattered to him as much as she did. Taking a sip of his Glenfiddich, his cell began to ring.

"What is it Richard. I'm really not in the mood to talk," Rade admitted.

"Sorry sir, but I think you'll want to hear what I have to say," Richard paused. "Some new information surfaced while you were away with Ms. Adams. We got a tip on the guy who delivered the packages to Ms. Adams. He's the same guy in the photo's you showed to me of Ms. Dupree. He's also the same guy we spotted in front of Mr. Wu's place in Chinatown."

"How did you find out about him?" Rade questioned.

"It's the funniest thing. My navy buddy at the NYPD told me. He said his body washed up under the Brooklyn Bridge. Based on his body's decomposition, he's been dead for at least a week, tattoo and all," Richard explained. "I don't know about you, but with this information, it's looking like Ms. Dupree's skeletons are beginning to come to life."

"I knew it would only be a matter of time. If we could just tie her to my kidnapping," Rade cursed.

"There's more sir. You were right about the key. It does belong to a safe deposit box. We just need to figure out how to get inside the bank to retrieve its contents. We are certain that it is from World National Bank." Richard explained.

"Do whatever you need to do. Even if you need to open an account to gain access," Rade demanded.

It was getting late and Dylan was still asleep. Rade decided it was best to check up on her. When he got to the room, his heart tore in two. Dylan was laying curled up holding his pillow close to her. He knew the news of the paternity test had been a great blow to her. If he could take what happened back, he would. His only hope now was with the information that Richard shared with him, they would be able to nail Chloe for everything she did, not only to him but to Dylan. He no longer cared if she was pregnant.

Dylan must have heard Rade enter the room, because her eyes slowly opened. Walking up to her, Rade lowered his body next to hers on the bed. Pushing away a strand of hair from her face, Rade lowered his lips to hers. They were so warm, he couldn't help but take her in. Pulling her closer to deepen the kiss, he noticed that she had put on one of his white dress shirts. Unbuttoning it, Rade slipped it slowly off her, exposing her beautiful pink nipples. As much as he loved seeing her in his shirt, he loved seeing her naked more. Taking in her beauty, he pulled his mouth from hers and captured her pink nipple in his mouth. The warmth of her body sent a burning ache down his body. Rade felt her arms wrap tightly around him, cinching him closer to her body. When he felt her body tremble, Rade pulled away to find the torment in her eyes. "What is it Sweetness?" Rade asked with worry.

"I'm afraid that I'm going to lose you," Dylan cried.

"Oh Sweetness. You can never lose me. My heart will always be yours," Rade said as he kissed her swollen lips.

The passion between them ignited with such emotion that Rade finally understood what it really meant to love someone, heart, body and soul. He would die if he ever lost Dylan.

With vehement love, Rade took Dylan's sweet mouth to his and kissed her with intense passion, even the god's above couldn't separate them. Reluctant to release her, he quickly removed his clothing. His only desire was to be inside her. To feel every inch of her body next to his. Leaning over her body, he sweetly whispered in her ear, "You are my everything Sweetness. I will never stop showing you how much I love you." With those words, Rade lowered his lips to hers and once again kissed her with all the passion and love within him.

Aligning his body between her legs, Rade gently spread them wider so he could consume all of her. With a gentle thrust, he slid his shaft inside her wetness as he continued his assault on her mouth. Taking in her warmth, he slowly began moving his hips back and forth while his tongue played a rhapsody with hers. He would never get enough of her. Dylan whimpered softly as she began feeling the onset of her arousal. With added movement, she slowly rocked her hips to the beat of Rade's shaft as he continued his slow movements inside her.

This is where she wanted to be. Like this, with him. Forever. A breath escaped her, feeling the loss of Rade's body on hers. When she opened her eyes in search of him, she found him kneeling in front of her. His hand was on his cock, stroking it like a finely tuned instrument. Dylan watched with desire, needing to touch him. Rising to her knees, she moved closer to him. Placing her hands on top of his, Dylan too began stroking his length. She needed more. Lowering her head, she kissed the tip of his shaft while still continuing to stroke along with him. Tasting a drop of pre-cum, Dylan knew that he was close. Gently removing his hand from his beautiful manhood, she took him in her mouth. The velvety softness felt like heaven as her tongue began lapping up and down his length. Unable to take him fully, Dylan wrapped her small hand around the base of his shaft and began caressing him. Dylan could feel the pulsation of his cock, hearing his moans of pleasure. "God, I love your mouth Sweetness." With a few strokes of her tongue, his seed hit the back of her throat. When Rade was fully drained, he lifted her onto his lap and eased inside her, still needing more of her. With fervent desire, Rade took her with no mercy. Thrust after thrust, her tight walls milked him. It was only after she screamed his name, did Rade realize what their undying love met. His seed mixed with her sweet nectar. For a single moment, he wished it was Dylan having his child. Then the memory of loss crept in and he remembered how long it took him to get over it. All he needed was Dylan. Only her. The woman he loved more than life itself. His Sweetness. The one thing he vowed never to lose.

Chapter Fourteen

Dylan woke the next morning not feeling any better than she did the night before. She felt now more than ever, that Chloe was going to be the center of her life with Rade. She had yet to learn about the life style he was accustom to, at least the one he shared once with Chloe. Dylan needed to change this. She wanted to be everything that Rade desired.

Dylan knew that this new found ambition of hers needed to be carried out soon. With only two weeks till their trip to London, this didn't give her much time. It was then she decided to mention it again to Rade, only this time it wasn't going to be forgotten.

Slipping on her robe, Dylan made her way to the living area in search of Rade. With her head held high, she spotted him sitting at the breakfast bar reading the morning copy of the Wall Street Journal. Taking her place next to him, Dylan took a sip of coffee from his cup.

Rade could feel her presence as soon as she entered the room. He knew of it because his shaft came to life. It was like sonar the way it hardened when she was close.

"Good morning Sweetness. How did you sleep?" Rade asked still reading the stock report.

"Wonderful. Thanks for asking." Dylan replied. "Rade, can I ask you something?"

Rade wasn't sure where this was going, but he went along with it. "Sure Sweetness, you can ask me anything."

"When is your birthday?" Dylan inquired setting her plan in motion.

"January 24th. Why? When is yours?" Rade asked. He realized that all the time they had been together, he didn't know her birthday either.

"September 15th," Dylan answered in a mischievous voice.

"Dylan, that's only ten days away. Why didn't you say something sooner?" Rade said, perturbed that she hadn't told him.

"It's not a big deal," Dylan said unconvincingly.

"When it comes to you Sweetness, Everything is a big deal. I can't believe you didn't say anything," Rade blurted, standing from the barstool. "What do you want to do? You name it and we'll do it." This was the least Rade could do for her. Somewhere in the back of his mind, he remembered knowing her birthday. It was on the background check he had done on her when he first laid eyes on her. Of course, he could never let her know that.

"Really, anything!" Dylan said with surprise.

"Anything Sweetness," Rade confirmed.

"Then there is only one thing I want." Dylan wasn't sure how she was going to lay this on him, so like every other woman, she began seducing him. Placing her arms around him, she positioned herself between his legs and began kissing him on the neck.

"Whatever you want Sweetness," Rade moaned.

"*The Castle*. I want to go to *The Castle* for my birthday," Dylan confessed.

Rade took her arms from around his shoulders and held them to his lips. He wasn't expecting her to ask this of him. Even though he said he would give her anything, he had second thoughts about giving her this. "Dylan, I'm not sure that's such a good idea. Isn't there something else you want?"

"You said anything and that's what I want." Dylan said standing her ground.

"I know we've talked about this, but I'm beginning to think maybe we should wait. Just a little longer Sweetness." Rade wanted to put off their visit to *The Castle* as long as he could.

"I have waited. It's been five months since that night. I need to know I can go back there without any flashbacks," Dylan pleaded.

"Tell you what Sweetness, Let's get this trip with Chloe out of the way and then we can talk about going. Now, what else do you want?" Rade asked hoping she would agree to his proposal.

"Nothing," Dylan answered, pulling her body from Rade's embrace.

Dylan was hoping that Rade would agree to take her back to *The Castle*. Somehow she needed to get him to take her there before they left for London. She had less than two weeks to think of a way to change his mind.

* * * * *

Dylan was so happy to see Keeve back in his office when she got to work that she almost forgot about her disagreement with Rade yesterday morning. Dylan learned that the doctor released him while she was with Rade on their weekend getaway. Unfortunately, it would be awhile before Mason would be coming back to work. Even though he was no longer in ICU at Mount Sinai, he still had a long way to go. Keeve thought that he would be able to leave the hospital in a couple of weeks. The most important thing to Dylan was that he was alive. Nothing mattered more than life.

The IRS investigator was finishing up his review of the BlackStone's financial records. He only found a few discrepancies in the accounting, but nothing to warrant a full inquiry into the company. This was a relief to Keeve. The last thing he wanted was to have the IRS following their business transactions for the next five to ten years.

Dylan was working on a spreadsheet when Keeve entered her office. "Excuse me Dylan, but do you have a few minutes to talk," Keeve asked.

"Sure Keeve, have a seat," Dylan said, watching him as he took a seat in front of her desk.

"I know you have been working really hard while Mason and I have been out. I just wanted to thank you for everything that you've done for BlackStone Industries. I don't know what we would have done without your help," Keeve confessed.

"You know you don't have to thank me Keeve. I love working here. I care about this company," Dylan stated. "I do have one question though."

"What's that?" Keeve questioned.

"When the investigator was reviewing the financial records, he came across an amended partnership contract between BlackStone and Garrett Matheson. It stated that if any of the partners, namely you two, ever entered into a business agreement without the others knowledge, then the provisions to Garrett's contract would become void. So my question to you is, did you?" Dylan asked hesitantly.

Dylan knew there was something up by the way Keeve ran his hand through his hair.

"You have to understand. It was nothing against Mason. He is the best partner I've ever had. I just couldn't pass this opportunity up. I knew he wouldn't agree to it. He would have thought it was too risky, so I took a leap of faith without his knowledge. To this day he still doesn't know. You can't let him know Dylan. It would kill him," Keeve confessed.

"This changes everything Keeve. What you did, allows Garrett to take controlling interest in your company. I'm afraid of what will happen to Spectrum once Rade finds out. He has to be told. I can keep this information from Mason, but I can't keep it from Rade," Dylan admitted.

"I understand, but before you tell Rade, please let me tell Mason. I don't want it to be a surprise to him when Rade backs out of the Spectrum deal," Keeve insisted.

"Okay, but don't wait too long to tell him. I don't know how long I can keep this from Rade."

When Keeve left Dylan's office, she was torn between doing what she knew was right and protecting her boss. She wished Keeve had come clean in the beginning about his business transaction and the revised secret partnership contract with Rade's father. Everything could have been out in the open without having to keep secrets from one another.

Dylan hadn't heard from Rade all day. She started to think it may have been because of the way she left their conversation about *The Castle*. Even last night when she went to bed, Rade stayed up till who knows when. Dylan suspected that he didn't even make it to bed. She knew this only because his side of the bed looked to be untouched when she woke. Finding him gone only added to her regrets about their conversation.

When Dylan got to the penthouse, she was hit with silence. She called out for Rade, but knew he wasn't home. Calling him on his cell, her effort went straight to voicemail. Exhausted, Dylan decided to go to bed. It was after midnight and she was too tired to wait until Rade decided to come home.

* * * * *

Getting herself ready for work, she thought about not having Rade next to her. His touch on her as the water spilled on her body. Caressing her skin as the water streamed down their bodies. She knew she wouldn't have this because once again she woke alone.

Within minutes she was showered and ready to start her day. Even though she missed sharing her morning with Rade, she knew she needed to get to work and work on a game plan. She needed to work things out with Rade. His disappearing act was getting old. She also knew eventually she needed to confront Rade about what Keeve had told her about his business agreement.

When Dylan left the penthouse, she was greeted by Richard who was waiting for her in the parking garage. She wasn't sure how early Rade had left, but was determined to find out.

"Richard, did you take Rade to his office this morning," Dylan asked, not sure what answer she would receive.

"I'm sorry Ms. Adams, Mr. Matheson didn't request my service this morning. He only requested that I be available for your transportation," Richard confessed.

"I thought for sure you may have taken him to work. When I woke this morning, he was already gone." This was unlike Rade to leave the penthouse without letting her know. And for it to happen two mornings in a row was beginning to piss her off.

Pulling her cell from her purse, Dylan called Rade to find out what was going on. The call went right to voice mail. Dylan left a message letting Rade know that she wasn't happy that he left this morning without saying good bye.

Dylan arrived at work a little later than she had wanted. Jessica and Lucy must have been busy elsewhere because when Dylan stepped into the office, neither one was manning the front desk . Not thinking too much about it, Dylan headed back to her office. Settling in, Dylan booted her computer and began working.

Most of the morning went by without a hitch until Rade appeared at her door. When Dylan looked up and saw his appearance, she wondered if he had even gone to bed at all over the last couple of days. He looked exhausted.

"Rade, you look horrible. What's going on with you," Dylan asked with concern.

"I needed to clear my head," Rade said.

"For two days? I was worried about you," Dylan confessed.

"I didn't mean to worry you. I've done some thinking about your birthday request. I think it would be a much better idea if we stayed away from *The Castle* for awhile.

"How long are we talking about Rade?" Dylan asked.

"I don't know. All I know is, it might be better if we never go back," Rade said.

"Rade did something happen? You seem different. Distracted," Dylan asked.

"No," Rade blurted out.

Dylan wasn't sure what was going on with him, but there was no way she was going to let this go.

"I don't believe you. Something is going on with you. It's not like you to leave for two days with no word. I've never seen you like this before," Dylan said looking at Rade's tired eyes.

"It's nothing Dylan," Rade barked.

The last thing that Rade wanted was for Dylan to find out the real reason behind his mood change. When he left Dylan the morning of their argument, he received another threat. This one more threatening than the last. He knew it could only be Michael. The text message came in from an unknown caller. *Your days with Dylan are numbered. Soon she will be mine and you will never find her. Soon it will be my name coming from her lips.* Rade read it over and over trying to figure out its meaning.

Rade thought if he left early enough, he would be able to get in touch with Chris to find out where these threats were coming from. Rade requested Chris to meet him at the office the minute he received the text. For two days, they worked only to end up with nothing. So after two days, Rade finally told Chris to go home and get some sleep. They were both utterly exhausted. Michael was smarter than Rade had initially suspected. The text messages were untraceable. With no sleep and no answers, the strain was taking its toll on Rade. Wherever Michael was, Rade needed to find him, before something bad happened to Dylan. Each threat Michael made was becoming more aggressive than the last.

Rade was planning on going to the penthouse to grab a few hours of sleep himself, but was pulled away from his plans when Keeve stopped by Dylan's office with some important information that he needed to tell him. Rade tried to convince him that it could wait, but when Keeve insisted that it couldn't. Rade had no other option but to satisfy Keeve's request, but first he needed to take care of his own needs.

No matter how drained and tired Rade was, he only wanted to see Dylan, but with Keeve's request, his time with her was shortened. She was the only person that could brighten his day

Shutting the door to Dylan's office, Rade walked to where Dylan was sitting behind her desk. With one quick pull, he had her out of her chair and in his arms. Dylan would never get tired of his scent. Even though he was still in the clothes from two day before, he still smelled amazing with his signature woodsy and spice cologne.

Placing his hand on her cheek, Rade gently rubbed his thumb across her soft skin. Nudging her forward, he placed his lips on hers and took what would always be his. Given the threat of the text, letting her out of his sight was no longer an option. Now more than anything he needed to stay close to her.

Dylan knew by the passion in his kiss that he was hiding something. She wasn't sure if it had to do with the private club or something else. Whatever it was, she was determined to find out.

"Rade, is something else going on with you other than going to *The Castle?*" Dylan questioned.

"It's nothing for you to worry about Sweetness," Rade whispered as he continued his assault. "I need to get to Keeve's office and find out what's so important that it can't wait."

Dylan wasn't convinced it was nothing. With the meeting Rade was going to have with Keeve, Dylan knew that his day was going to get worse. She wasn't sure if she should shed some light on what Keeve had to tell him or wait until the meeting was over. Even though she had promised Keeve not to say anything to Rade about his private business arrangement, she needed to at least tell him something to prepare him for what was about to happen.

"Rade," Dylan said just before Rade got to the door. "Whatever Keeve tells you, don't be too hard on him."

"Do you know what this meeting is about Dylan?" Rade asked as he lifted his brow.

"It's not my place to say," Dylan admitted.

Rade was confused by Dylan's admission, but let it go for now. If anything his curiosity was piqued.

* * * * *

When Dylan arrived at the penthouse, Rade was nowhere to be found. She thought for sure he would have showed up at the penthouse before she did. Pulling her cell from her purse she decided to call him and find out where he was at. When she got no answer, her next move was to text him.

Dylan: Where are you?

Rade: At the office, will be home late.

Dylan: How late? I can wait up for you.

Rade: Not sure. Don't wait up.

Rade knew that his explanation was cold and to the point. After his meeting with Keeve, his day went from bad to worse. Knowing that his father was going to have a part of Spectrum didn't sit well with him. Instead of getting the much needed sleep he needed, Rade spent the last four hours trying to figure out how he was going to make the deal he had with Keeve and Mason work out. Mostly he wanted it for Dylan. She had worked so hard on the account, that he couldn't let her end up with nothing. His best bet was to get in touch with his father and see if he could compromise with him.

Grabbing his suit coat, Rade headed out of his office to the Four Seasons where his father was staying. Even though his father wasn't yet fully recovered, the authorities agreed to house him at the Four Seasons per Rade's request. An officer remained with him 24/7. Rade could no longer stand having his father so close to him. He needed distance.

Rade was surprised to see Chloe answer the door instead of the officer. Rade knew that she was staying with his father. Rade wasn't sure what her game was, especially since she had an apartment of her own.

"Rade, how nice to see you sweetheart," Chloe said with a fake smile.

"Where's my father and the officer that's suppose to be watching him?" Rade barked.

"What…no how are you? How's the baby?" Chloe questioned.

"I'm not in the mood for your games Chloe," Rade cursed as he stepped past her.

Stepping further into the suite, Rade found his father sitting on the couch with a crystal glass in his hand and the assigned officer on the chair next to him fumbling with his cell phone. "Do you really think it's wise to be drinking while you're on medication?" Rade inquired.

"Since when do you care about my health," Garrett hissed downing the rest of his drink.

"I don't give a shit about your health. I only care about one person and that's Dylan," Rade huffed.

"What is this about son? I know it's not a courtesy call," Garrett asked.

"You're right. I'm here to talk some sense into you about your partnership with BlackStone," Rade began. "I would like to buy out your controlling interest."

"Now why would I want to let go of control?" Garrett asked amused.

"Because, it would be the right thing to do," Rade pointed out. "I think that the guy that came looking for you at BlackStone came after you for a reason. The only tie you have with them is the partnership. I think it would be smart to let that go."

The officer quit typing, interested in the conversation between the two men. This may be information he needed to listen to.

"You can't be certain that the shooting had anything to do with my partnership with BlackStone. I think you are grasping at straws. You will do and say anything to have control over BlackStone or at least the deal with Spectrum," Garrett argued.

Rade knew is father was way off base. Rade had no intension of keeping controlling interest in BlackStone. If his father agreed to his demands, Rade would gladly split control with Keeve and Mason giving them equal control. The only thing he cared about was the potential revenue he would have once the voice recognition app was up and running.

"Be a smart man. The money I would give you to end your partnership would allow you to start your own business. If having a partnership is so important to you, then partner with me. There are several companies I have been looking into that I would be willing to let you have controlling interest in." If Rade could offer his father a deal he couldn't refuse, there might be a chance he would let BlackStone go.

"So if I allow you to buy out my partnership with BlackStone, you would be willing to partner with me instead?" Garrett inquired.

"That about sums it up."Rade confirmed.

"How do I know that you won't shove me under a bus?" Garrett asked

"I'll provide you with all the information you need before you make a decision. It would be stupid for you to not take advantage of this. This is a onetime offer. If you choose not to do this, I won't offer it again," Rade declared.

By the time Rade left his father's suite, he was second guessing his offer. He knew he needed something to entice his father into letting go of controlling interest in BlackStone. There was still another card Rade hadn't played yet. If his father agreed to his proposal, Rade figured that within six months, his father would be penniless. All he needed, was to wait for his father to take the bait.

Chapter Fifteen

"Something is wrong," Chloe said feeling a sharp pain in her stomach. *"This can't be happening again. I thought for sure being four months pregnant, the baby would be okay. Oh God, what is happening to me?"*

It was the middle of the night when Chloe began feeling the sharp pain in her belly. It took all her strength to get from her bed to the kitchen where her phone was. She needed to contact Dr. O'Brien. If she was about to lose the baby, she wanted to make sure plan B was in order.

"Cali, its Chloe. Something's wrong. How soon can you get here?" Chloe pleaded.

"On my way. I'll be there in fifteen minutes," Cali said calmly.

An hour later Chloe was in Dr. O'Brien's office resting. Cali needed to make sure that Chloe was okay before letting her go back to her apartment. Chloe prayed that she wouldn't lose the baby again, but when Cali O'Brien came into her room, she knew exactly what happened. The baby was gone and so was her initial plan to get Rade.

Chloe had waited for months for Rade to give up his infatuation with Dylan. She thought for sure the night at *The Castle* would bring Rade to her. With Dylan out of the way, she knew Rade would soon be hers. But then Dylan forgave him and she was right back in his bed again.

Even though she lost the baby, she still needed to continue with her plan. Rade needed to think she was still carrying his child. Soon they would be together. Soon Dylan would be gone forever. Not even Rade would be able to stop what she had planned for his little schoolgirl. With Alex gone, there was only one other person who could help her get Rade for good.

* * * * *

The planned London trip was only a week away. Dylan still hadn't mentioned what she would like to do for her birthday and Rade was getting worried. He wanted to take her somewhere special, he just didn't know where. He only had until tomorrow to find a place. A place she would never forget.

Over the last week Rade had been working endlessly trying to find the whereabouts of Michael Stewart and thinking of nothing else. With no leads in sight, it was beginning to take a toll on him. Every time he thought he was close, it ended up being a dead end. His only hope was that soon Michael would get sloppy and make a mistake.

At least one thing was going his way. His father agreed to hand over his fifty-one percent interest in BlackStone Industries over to Rade. This was the first step in cleaning up Keeve's little side business venture. It would only be a matter of time before Keeve Black and Mason Stone would have equal control over their company once again. If it wouldn't have been for the love he had for Dylan, Rade would have kept the fifty-one percent interest himself. She deserved his equal share.

Another matter was Chloe. They still had to figure out how to get into Chloe's deposit box without getting caught. All they needed was admittance in order to get a look at what was inside the steel box.

Rade was finalizing the paperwork with his attorney when a call came in on his cell. "Dylan, I was just thinking about you," Rade confirmed.

"I hope I'm not interrupting you," Dylan asked.

"You could never interrupt me sweetness," Rade said. "Can you hold on for just a minute?"

Rade finished up his meeting with Miles, letting him know he would be in touch to schedule a meeting with Garrett Matheson once the agreement was ready.

"So, what's on your mind Sweetness," Rade asked as Miles left his office.

"I was just wondering what your plans were this evening. I thought it would be nice to go out to dinner," Dylan suggested.

"I think that's a wonderful idea. How about I pick you up at your office in an hour," Rade said looking at his watch for the time. He still had a few things to wrap up before he left for the day.

"That would be fine. I'll see you in an hour," Dylan replied.

Nothing brightened Rade's day more than hearing Dylan's voice. Even though they hardly spoke to each other the past week, Rade was ready to spend an evening with her. This friction between them needed to change. He needed to put his problems to the side and focus on the woman he loved. He knew he was more than neglecting her and he was beginning to feel the animosity Dylan was having towards him.

Rade pulled up to the BlackStone building in just under an hour. Tonight he needed to focus only on Dylan. His mood these last couple of days had been nothing but tolerable. He wanted to change that.

When Rade walked inside the building, Dylan was already waiting for him in the lobby. Looking at her gorgeous body, all Rade could think about was how much he wanted to take her right then and there. Dylan was wearing her stiletto Louboutins and a red pencil skirt which enhanced the beauty of her already gorgeous legs. How Rade would have loved to have those soft silky limbs wrapped around him as he thrust deep inside her.

As Rade walked up to her, he could see that she was in deep thought. Rubbing his thumb down her cheek, he leaned over slightly and gave her a soft kiss. Turning towards Rade, Dylan took in his form. Being left alone again this morning, Dylan didn't get a chance to see him. Looking at him now, she wished she was back at home in their bed.

Rade and Dylan left the BlackStone building leaving behind, the problems of the day. Rade wanted to take Dylan somewhere special. Even though her birthday wasn't until tomorrow, he wanted to start it tonight.

Dylan wasn't sure where Rade would be taking her for dinner, but when he pulled up to a modern style building on Duane Street, she knew he had chosen one of the most expensive restaurants in New York. Before Dylan could exit the car, a valet opened her door and assisted her out. Standing just outside the restaurant, a hostess greeted them requesting the information for the reservation. Dylan knew that it took months to get a reservation at this restaurant, but when Rade told the hostess who he was, they were led in with no question. Dylan just rolled her eyes knowing that Rade pretty much owned New York and it didn't matter where they went, everyone bowed to him.

Once they were seated at their table a waiter presented a bottle of red wine which Rade accepted after he tasted the sample that was poured in a wine glass. The taste of the wine was out of this world. It was like nothing Dylan had ever tasted. Dylan was surprised to find that no menus were presented to order from, but when their first course showed up minutes later, Dylan suspected that Rade had placed their orders ahead of time.

Just as they were finishing their dessert, Rade's phone began to ring. "Richard, I hope this is important. I'm having dinner with Dylan," Rade said, none too happy about the interruption.

"It's about Garrett sir. Someone broke into his suite. There's no sign of a struggle other than the officer being found tie and unconscious in the closet. There was a note. The person who has him is requesting fifty million dollars in exchange for his life," Richard stated firmly. "The police are sweeping the room for any clues. Peter and I will stand by and let you know if they find anything."

"When is this shit going to stop. Let me know the minute you hear anything." Rade's body stiffened knowing this thing with his father was far from over.

"What is it Rade? What happened?" Dylan questioned.

"My father. He's been taken."

"Who? Where?" Dylan asked concerned.

"Not sure, but whoever has him, wants money and a lot of it," Rade hissed. "We need to get out of here."

It wasn't long that the waiter brought Rade the check and they were in Rade's Martin driving back to the penthouse. Rade needed to get Dylan home so he could think of what to do. He still hadn't heard back from Richard on whether or not the police had found anything. If Rade had to guess, they didn't.

It had been a long night for both of them. Dylan decide to turn in early. She tried to convince Rade to come to bed with her, considering his lack of sleep, but he refused. He said he wouldn't be able to sleep anyway. Dylan knew that she wasn't going to be able to sleep either. Not with everything going on. Pushing from the bed, she grabbed her robe and headed back to the kitchen. She thought maybe a glass of wine would help her sleep.

When she got to the kitchen, she noticed Rade staring out the floor to ceiling window. She would have missed him standing there except his form was visible by the light shinning off the full moon. Placing her wine glass on the counter, she walked over to where he was standing. Fishing her hand around his waist and under his arms, she encircled his body with hers. Rade didn't move. The only thing that Dylan could feel was the tension in his body. It felt like every muscle in his body was on stress overload.

Rade slowly turned his body so that he was facing her. Taking his hand, he gently rubbed the soft skin along her cheek. "Why is everything so messed up Sweetness?" Rade asked with difficulty. "The only thing good in my life is you."

Dylan didn't know how to answer him. So she showed him instead. Rising to her tip-toes, she placed her lips on his. Showing him just how much she loved him, Dylan captured his pain. Sliding her hands up his chest and over his shoulders, Dylan pulled him even closer to her. This must have been what Rade needed, because before she knew it, he had her up of the floor and in his arms nudging her legs around his waist.

Unable to hold back, being without his skin next to hers for far too long, Dylan tugged his shirt over his head feeling the warmth of his skin through her thin robe. Giving him everything she had, Dylan parted his lips with her tongue and began sharing the love she had for him. With parted lips, feeling the eagerness to explore her as well, he wondered if she could feel the pain he was carrying.

In one swift swoop, Rade had Dylan's robe off her, exposing her soft breasts that he so loved. Lowering his head, he seized her taut nipple and began sucking and licking until it swelled into a hard peak. Satisfied, he moved to the other side and lavished her nipple in the same way. He knew she wanted him as her back began to arch in his arms giving him the access he needed.

Tugging his jeans from his body while holding her to him, he freed his ironclad cock from its barrier. Erect and waiting, he took hold of Dylan's lacy underwear and with one tug, ripped them from her body. Fully naked, he pressed her body against the cool glass and began devouring her like she was his only meal. With added force, he deepened his kiss further, sending then both into the land of pleasure. Their hands were all over each other. Feeling and touching with such fire, neither one of them could break free, nor would they ever want to. Rade gently moved Dylan's body upward and with precision, separating her slick folds with his thundering mass consuming her warm channel. The minute he entered, he could feel the tremble in Dylan's body as his name parted from her lips. They say absence makes the heart grow fonder, right now this minute, no words felt more true. They had been under so much stress, that the time for each other was put on hold. Rade knew, that no matter how bad things got, he would never go a day without having Dylan beneath him ever again.

Still fully lodged inside, Rade began working on his own release. The release he had been deprived of. The release his body now craved. Increasing his thrusts, he was delighted by another explosion of ecstasy from Dylan as she tightened around his throbbing cock. With the window as his brace, he pushed her harder against the glass and moved his hands up her slick body. Meeting her taut nipples, Rade took one in each hand adding a hint of pressure to the hard buds. Helpless, he lowered his mouth and took her nipple in his mouth drinking in her essence. Rade increased his movements, bringing him closer to his own release. With an earth shattering scream, Dylan once again greeted his release with one of her own. Lowering Dylan to her feet, Rade felt her knees weaken, so he lifted her into his arms and carried her to their safe haven. A place where he could once again devour her. A place where nothing else mattered but her.

* * * * *

The morning came in with a crash as Dylan woke to the sound of her cell. Reaching over to the nightstand, she searched for the annoying sound with no luck. Having no other choice but to get out of bed, Dylan pulled the sheet from the bed in search of her phone. Even though her phone was on the kitchen counter, the volume was so loud that she heard it in the bedroom. Just as she was ready to pick it up, the ringing stopped, but not long enough before another wave of noise echoed through the room. Dylan knew she shouldn't have let Lilly pick the ringtone when she called. This early in the morning waking up to *The Chicken Dance* was not the least bit cute.

"Remind me never to let you pick my ringtone for you," Dylan said half asleep.

"Happy birthday to you, happy birthday to you. Happy birthday my bestie in the whole wide world. Happy birthday to you," Lilly sang happily out of tune.

"If you promise never to sing to me again, you can pick my ringtones. Do you know what time it is?" Dylan asked.

"Yeah is 10:00 am," Lilly said matter-a-factly.

"Girlfriend, you do realize you are six hours ahead of New York time," Dylan reminded her friend.

"Oh God Dylan, I totally forgot about the difference in time. If I told you I'm coming to the states to see you, will you forgive me," Lilly asked calmly as if she was asking Dylan to pass the milk.

"Wait, what? Did you just say you're coming to New York?" Dylan asked, now fully awake.

"Yepper. I should be there by tomorrow afternoon," Lilly confirmed.

This couldn't be a better birthday for Dylan. Her best friend, whom she hadn't seen in weeks, was coming to New York. Even though they talked almost every day, Dylan still missed Lilly. By the time she finished her conversation with Lilly it was close to 5:30 am. No longer feeling tired, Dylan decided to use some of the added energy and burn a few calories. Walking back to the bedroom, Dylan saw that Rade was no longer in bed. She was afraid that the sound of her phone may have woken him up. When she saw Rade step from the bathroom door, her suspicion was confirmed. His wet body was wrapped in a plush white towel. Soaking up his god-like body, Dylan could feel the wetness forming between her legs.

"I didn't mean to wake you," Dylan apologized for the early morning call.

"Why would you pick *The Chicken Dance* as a ringtone. Unless you really like that annoying song," Rade said, unamused.

"Or someone who really likes to annoy me, like Lilly," Dylan confessed. "She forgot about the difference in time."

"Well that explains everything," Rade replied. "So how is Ms. Davis these days?"

"Good. Really good. She's coming to New York. She should be here tomorrow afternoon, which brings me to my next question. Can she stay here with us?" Dylan asked stepping closer to Rade.

"You don't need to ask Sweetness. This place is yours as much as mine. How long is she staying?"

"Just a few days. There are a few paintings her dad wanted her to pick up for the gallery. She's leaving the day before we leave for London," Dylan said sadly.

Wrapping his arms around Dylan's waist, Rade kissed the top of her head."So have you decided what you want for you birthday?" Rade asked in a soft tone trying to think of anything but his father's ransom.

"Maybe when we get back from London, we could go to Paris," Dylan suggested then thought twice about her request. "On second thought, with everything going on with your father, it can wait.

"I think that could be arranged. In the meantime, I have something planned for this evening for your birthday. Nothing is going to interfere with my plans, not even my father being taken. I'll pick you up at your office around six o'clock," Rade confirmed.

Rade kissed Dylan one more time on her head before he broke away from her. Feeling rejected from Rade's sudden withdrawal, Dylan put on her workout clothing and headed to the gym. She wasn't going to let anything ruin her day. She understood Rade's concern for his father, but his mood swings were becoming an annoyance.

* * * * *

When Dylan arrived at work, she was greeted with a beautiful bouquet of red roses. She knew that they must have come from Rade. When she lifted the small card from the vase, she was surprised to see that they came from and unknown person. As she read the card, Dylan wondered who could have sent them.

My Dearest Dylan,

I hope your day is filled with happiness on this special day. My only regret is that I wasn't able to share it with you. Soon all my days will be filled with your happiness.

My undying love,

OXOXOX

171

Whoever sent them spared no expense. They had to be from Rade. There must have been at least three dozen in all. Placing the card back in the envelope, Dylan lowered her purse from her shoulder and began her work day. The minute Dylan sat down, there was a ping on her cell phone. Reaching for her purse, she took out her phone and entered her four digit code.

> *Rade:*   *I will be in meetings all day, but there will be a delivery for you.*
>
> *Dylan:* *If you mean the roses, they are beautiful.*
>
> *Rade:*   *Sorry Sweetness, I didn't send you flowers.*
>
> *Dylan:* *I thought for sure they came from you. What did you send me?*
>
> *Rade:*   *It is a surprise. Make sure you are promptly ready by six o'clock.*
>
> *Dylan:* *I will.*

Finishing his message to Dylan, Rade thought about who might have sent Dylan roses. It could have been a number of people after all it was her birthday. He pushed the thought away. What he had planned for her tonight, was going to seal their life together. He never thought that his life would come to this. He only knew, he could no longer deny his love for Dylan. And in three days, Chloe would also know there would be no other woman in his life but Dylan.

It was getting close to six o'clock and Rade needed to get to the BlackStone building if he was going to be on time to pick up Dylan. He had never been more excited for an evening than the one he had planned for her. This was going to be a birthday she would never forget. Already changed, Rade grabbed his tux jacket from the back of the chair and headed to the garage. Rade had left instructions for Richard to make sure his limo was ready to go.

Entering the parking garage, Richard was already waiting for Rade. He was dressed in his black chauffer suit, another request from Rade. Walking to the passenger side of the car, Richard opened the door for Rade.

Before Rade slid in, he asked, "Is everything ready for this evening?"

"Yes sir. Everything is ready per your instructions," Richard confirmed as he handed Rade an envelope and a small box.

"Good. Everything needs to perfect," Rade advised.

Richard nodded in acceptance assuring Rade that it would be. He knew how important this night was for him.

When the packaged arrived, Dylan knew it was the surprise Rade had sent her. Removing the gold ribbon, Dylan saw the Gucci emblem embossed on the lid. Whatever was inside, Dylan knew it would be over-the-top expensive. Lifting the lid, a gasp of air escaped from Dylan's body. Removing the gown from the tissue, Dylan held the most beautiful gown she had ever seen. It was scarlet red with small Swarovski crystal diamonds on the bodice and up the shoulder strap. The gown itself was form fitting flaring out just below the knees. Also inside the box was a pair of matching red stiletto heels and a matching clutch.

Dylan couldn't believe her eyes, but it was nothing compared to how it looked on her once she put it on. She felt like a princess in it. Touching up her make-up, Dylan was ready to go with five minutes to spare. Dylan placed her office clothes and her other belongings inside her desk drawer, locking then up for safe keeping, and taking only what she knew she needed, she placed them inside the small clutch.

Stepping off the elevator, Dylan was greeted by the handsomest man she had ever seen. Dylan wasn't sure what Rade had planned for her, but she couldn't wait to find out.

Rade looked up from his watch and about lost it. He couldn't believe a woman could be more gorgeous than the one standing before him. His heart skipped a beat just at the sight of her. She was an angel. His angel. Unable to take his eyes off her, he approached her with certainty; no other woman would ever fill his heart more than Dylan. "God, you're breathtaking," Rade whispered, lowering his head and kissing her on the cheek.

"Thank you," Dylan said softly.

"Are you ready?" Rade asked, taking her hand in his.

"Yes. Where are we going?" Dylan questioned.

"That my Sweetness is a surprise," Rade confirmed with a grin.

When they stepped out onto the sidewalk, Dylan couldn't believe what was waiting for them. A sleek black limo. Leaning against the front fender, Richard was waiting for them. This must have been an important evening for him as well. Dylan had never seen him in a suit other than the first time he picked her up months ago.

Rounding the car, Richard opened the back door for them, but not without sharing his thoughts. "You look beautiful tonight Ms. Adams."

Dylan looked up at him with a smile. "Thank you Richard."

Once they were settled inside the limo, Richard pulled away from the curb. Moments later, the partition that separated the driver from the passengers went up, leaving Dylan and Rade privately to themselves.

Rade reached in front of him to a small bar. Pulling out a bottle of Dom Pérignon and grabbing two champagne flutes, Rade began pouring the crystal liquid. Handing a flute to Dylan, he proposed a toast. "To your birthday and a wonderful evening ahead."

Dylan nodded her head in acceptance as she took a drink of the bubbly wine. Taking in her surroundings, Dylan was in awe. She had never road inside a limousine before. The inside looked to be very expensive with its leather interior, lighted bar and small flat screen television in the corner. Rade went through a lot of trouble for her birthday, she thought as she looked out the window and watched the New York City lights pass by.

The ride came to an end when Richard pulled in front of the Metropolitan Opera House. Exiting the car, Richard opened the back door and assisted Dylan out of the car. When she set foot on the curb, Dylan couldn't believe her eyes. The building was beautiful with its arched windows and the magnificent chandeliers lighting the lobby. They were breathtaking. Dylan had never been to the Metropolitan Opera House. She heard so many wonderful things about it. This was another place on her bucket list that she wanted to visit.

As they walked through the entrance, Rade presented two tickets to the host for the performance. The young gentleman ushered them to a box seat nearest the stage. Dylan only wondered how much the seats had cost. As they took their place, Dylan noticed two additional seats in the booth. She wondered if maybe someone else would be joining them. Pushing away her thoughts, she took in the beautiful theatre. Every seat was covered in red velvet. The walls were painted in gold and the curtain that hung so elegantly on the stage was also draped in gold. The entire place was very regal. When the orchestra began playing music and the lights began to dim, her question was answered. It would be only them occupying the small booth. She knew Rade must have purchased the entire seating to make sure they would be alone to enjoy the performance.

Dylan watched with amazement at the performers began singing in what she assumed was Italian. Even though she couldn't understand what was being sung, it wasn't hard for her to follow the story line. It was a sad story of love and betrayal. When the last scene ended, everyone in the house rose to their feet with a rumble of applause. Dylan also rose to her feet, wiping away the tears that fell. Rade stood beside her taking her hand in his and softly kissing the back.

This was an evening Dylan would never forget. It was more than she ever dreamed of. It was the best birthday present ever.

As the exited the building, Dylan saw the beautiful fountain that was displayed in front of the building. She wasn't sure how she missed it when they arrived.

Walking around the enormous water display, Richard was already waiting for them. Rade took Dylan's arm in his and escorted her to the limo. The night had just begun as far as Rade was concerned.

Richard opened the car door, helping Dylan inside. Rade slid in right beside her. Once they were inside, Dylan looked to him with tears of joy.

"This has been the best birthday ever Rade. Thank you so much for bringing me here," Dylan said softly overwhelmed with happiness.

"It was my pleasure Sweetness. There is one more place we need to go," Rade confessed pulling Dylan close to him.

Looking into her beautiful green eyes, Rade lowered his lips to hers. With tenderness he consumed her softness as he parted her lips with his tongue. Entwining his tongue with hers, he could feel her desire channel through him as he deepened their kiss. Needing to feel her, he placed his hand under the hem of her gown and began working the silky material up her smooth legs. "I need to take you Sweetness. I can't wait any longer." Dylan could no longer hold back her desire for him either. Lifting her bottom, she wiggled out of her panties and lifted her gown higher on her hips giving Rade the access he needed. Before she knew it, he lowered his body, positioning himself between her legs. Her body began to tremble, knowing that soon his mouth would be consuming her heat. Rade wanted to worship her. He knew they had plenty of time before they got to where they were going. Beginning at her ankle, he placed soft kisses on her silky skin, pushing Dylan close the edge. He had to taste every part of her. Working his way up, he trailed kisses up her calf, then her sexy knee, switching his seduction from her left and then her right leg. When he reached her inner thigh, he knew he had her. The heat from her sexy cunt radiated through him as he landed each kiss closer and closer to his target.

"I will never get enough of your beautiful pink cunt," Rade confessed moving closer to her wetness.

Dylan took in a deep breath as Rade's mouth clamped over her clit. If only he knew, she too would never get enough of his mouth devouring her sex. His tongue was like magic as he lapped and sucked her sweet juices. Just when she was on the verge of her release, Rade pulled his mouth from her clit and dipped it fervently inside her tight channel. Now more than ever Dylan needed to come. "Please Rade," she whispered as her control for him dissipated.

"Tell me want you want Sweetness. Do you want me to suck you pretty little cunt until you scream my name?"

"Yes, God yes!"

"Do want me to plunge my hard cock inside you tight pussy and feel the warmth of your milky cream coating me?"

"Yes, please Rade."

"Then your wish is my command."

Before Dylan could utter another word, Rade had her straddled across his lap and his cock deep inside her. She was more than ready to take is length. Her wetness coated his shaft as it dripped freely from her tight channel. Pulling her closer, his lips met hers. There was no hesitation as she parted her lips for him, tasting her own juices, she lapped her tongue with his. Grabbing her by the hips, Rade began pumping deep inside her. Dylan was so close to her release the deeper Rade push inside her. His grip on her hips tightened as her walls cinched down on his cock. Trying to control his own release, he thought of nothing but her pleasure. Slowing his movements, Rade slipped his hand from her hip down the front of her body. Pushing the silky material out of the way, he found what he was searching for. Coating his finger with her nectar, all he wanted was the feel of her clit between his fingers. Pinching the swollen nub, he applied more pressure until he could feel the strength of her walls tighten even more around him. He knew she was close. "Let go Sweetness," he said, holding on to his own bliss. Hearing his name escape from her lips, he covered her mouth with his to shield the scream of pleasure. Even though the partition was up, the limo wasn't sound proof. The last thing he wanted was for Richard to know what was taking place behind him.

Richard pulled up to The Plaza Hotel not a minute to soon. Dylan had barely pulled her gown down while Rade was safely tucking his shaft back inside his trousers. When Richard opened the passenger door to assist them out of the car, they both grinned at Richard. Taking his awaiting hand, Dylan stepped from the car. The hotel was beautiful with its majestic castle-like appearance, but it was the inside of the hotel that took Dylan's breath away with its marble floors, cream walls and plush furniture.

While Dylan was taking in the sights, a gentleman walked up to them. "Mr. Matheson," he said as he tipped his head.

"Yes," Rade greeted the gentleman.

"Your room is ready for you per your instructions. Please follow me," the gentleman requested.

As the man led them to the elevator, he handed Rade a keycard. Once on the elevator, Dylan could only imagine how much the room was costing Rade. Rade placed his hand in Dylan's as they stepped off the elevator. When the gentleman opened the door to the room, Dylan's mouth hung open. She had never seen anything so beautiful and regal in her entire life. Dylan took in the space as Rade gave additional instruction to the gentleman, slipping him a couple hundred dollar bill. Dylan assumed by their conversation he was the butler that came with the expense of the room.

Once the hotel butler left the suite, Rade led Dylan to the second floor where a table set for two awaited them on the terrace. This evening couldn't be any more surprising to Dylan. This by far was the best birthday ever for her.

Dylan took in the city lights as Rade busied himself with the bottle of champagne resting inside a stainless steel bucket of ice beside the small table. Everything was perfect. Hearing the pop of the cork, Dylan directed her attention back towards Rade as he poured the champagne into the crystal flutes.

Handing a glass to Dylan, Rade made a toast. "To my Sweetness, may you remember this evening forever."

As Dylan took a sip of her champagne, something inside the crystal glass bumped her lip. Looking oddly at Rade, she held the glass to the candles lit on the small table to see if she could see the foreign object. When she realized what it was, her eyes began to swell with tears. Taking the flute from her hand, Rade drank the sparkling wine catching the object between his teeth. Lowering to one knee, he confessed his love. "My Dearest Sweetness, you are the sunshine that wakes me every morning even on the gloomiest day. You have captured my heart when I thought I had none. You have shown me what it means to love again. I was certain that it was lost forever, but you showed me how to find it. You are my life, the air that I breathe, the feeling of fulfillment whenever you are near me. With all my heart, I ask, please say that you will share the rest of my life with me. Will you marry me?"

Dylan was in shock, not only by his words, but also by what he meant to her. He was her sunshine as well, the air that she breathed, her life. Nothing in the world would stop her from loving this man. Lowering herself to his level, Dylan softly whispered, "Yes."

Chapter Sixteen

Dylan woke with a smile on her face as she gazed over to Rade and then to the beautiful ring on her finger. She couldn't believe the size of the diamond. It had be at least three karats. With the additional smaller diamonds along the band and the platinum setting, she knew it cost more than she could make in a year.

When Dylan rolled over after admiring her ring, she was greeted by the biggest smile she had ever seen. Positioning his body over hers, Rade asked softly, "Are you happy Sweetness?"

"If I were anymore happy, I think I would burst at the seams," Dylan confessed.

Wedging his body between her legs, it was time to test her theory. Placing his mouth over hers, he got his first dose. Soaking in her softness, Rade parted her lips with his tongue and took in her warmth. Lapping his tongue with hers, he could feel her body press into his as her taut nipples brushed against his chest. The soft whimper of pleasure echoed as Rade continued to sweep his tongue inside her warmth. Continuing his promenade, Rade lowered his hand down the curve of her plump breast for a quick caress before moving to the contour of her firm stomach, and stopping just below her belly button. Dylan's hands grasped the soft Egyptian sheets, feeling the slow decent of Rade's mouth on her body. Reaching the apex of her mound, Rade playfully began lapping his tongue over her sensitized nub. When Dylan's back arched off the mattress, he knew he had her where he wanted. Nothing thrilled him more than Dylan's need for his touch. "I'm going to taste every inch of you Sweetness, and when I have had my fill, I'm going to fuck you until only my name will burst from your sexy lips."

Dylan's body was on fire. Every nasty word from Rade's mouth brought her closer to the edge. Her hands were no longer grasping the silky sheets, instead they were intertwined in Rade's hair, holding him close to her, wanting to feel more of his mouth on her cunt. "Oh God, Rade. I can't hold on," Dylan moaned, wanting this moment to last longer.

"You are only allowed to come when I say Sweetness," Rade ordered, lifting his head from between her folds.

Taking Dylan's hands entwined in his thick hair, he took her by the wrists and moved his body up her silky softness. Nuzzled between her legs, Rade pushed Dylan's arms above her head and held on to her wrist with one hand while he caressed her pert nipple with the other. Dylan's back bowed off the bed to the pressure she felt on her taut peak as Rade gently nipped her pink bud. Unable to hold on any longer, Dylan came with such force that Rade's name echoed off the bedroom walls. Dylan was certain the walls shook as they absorbed her cry of ecstasy as thunder crashed within her core.

Even though Dylan let go without permission, Rade smiled down on her knowing that he was going to enjoy her punishment. Flipping her over with ease, he commanded, " On your knees."

Dylan did as she was told and lifted her upper body from the bed and placed her palms on the soft mattress. Without warning, Rade's hand came down on her soft cheek. Dylan could feel the sting all the way to her sex. She knew before long she would be dripping with desire. Plunging two fingers inside her wet channel, once again Dylan came without permission. Her wetness was all it took, Rade was buried inside her with one deep thrust. Grabbing her by the hips, Rade continued his ascent inside her tight channel. He could feel her dripping with arousal. A few more thrusts and she would be his. Close to his own escape he whispered, "Come." It only took that one word and Dylan exploded with fury with Rade right behind her. This was what he needed. With no word on the ransom, all the tension left his body.

Dylan was sad; their time at The Plaza was over. She wanted this moment to never end, but she knew that Lilly would be arriving at JFK soon. Gathering the beautiful gown Rade had purchased for her, Dylan placed it inside the garment bag and zipped it close. Rade's birthday gift was planned to the smallest detail, which included another change of clothing for both of them. While Rade was dressed in black jeans, a white button-down shirt and a black leather jacket, Dylan was dressed in a flare skirt, a knit top with a matching sweater.

Walking out on to the terrace, Dylan took one last look at the beautiful sights of New York. She would never forget what took place at this very spot. It will be a memory she would never let go of. Just as she was ready to turn. A strong arm wrapped itself around her waist. Smiling to herself, she turned her body and gazed up into the most gorgeous hazel eyes she had ever seen.

"Are you ready to go Sweetness," Rade asked.

"I am," Dylan replied, pushing to the balls of her feet and placing her lips on his.

Hearing a knock on the door, Rade and Dylan descended down the staircase. A young bellboy stood outside the door waiting to take their bag down to the lobby. As they exited the room, Dylan said goodbye to the hotel butler that came with their room, standing just outside the suite door. Even though she didn't see much of him, he made sure they had everything they needed for their short stay.

The elevator doors promptly opened allowing them to enter. Rade took Dylan's hand into his and squeezed it gently. When

Dylan looked up at him, she could see the love he had for her. She knew it because it was the exact same look she had given him.

Richard was no longer driving the limo, but instead the Bentley was parked waiting to take them to the penthouse. It would have to be a quick trip for them since Lilly's plane was due to land in a couple of hours and Dylan wanted to make sure she was on time to greet her friend. Rade had offered to go with her, but Dylan thought it would be best if she went alone. So he insisted that Richard be with her. Dylan wasn't sure how Lilly would react to her engagement to Rade given that he wasn't one of her favorite people.

* * * * *

Dylan waited patiently at the baggage claim for her friend with Richard at her side. She was concerned that she would miss her with the amount of passengers milling around waiting for their luggage. Walking up and down the baggage claim area, Dylan finally spotted her friend. It was a wonder that she had seen her at all. Everything about Lilly had changed. Her hair was cut and styled in a shoulder length bob whereas before it draped down her back. It also looked as though Lilly may have been working out. Dylan knew for a fact how much Lilly hated the gym. The only time she ever accepted Dylan's invitation to go with her was to check out the hot guys.

The closer Dylan got to Lilly, the more tears fell. Dylan didn't realize how much she really missed her friend until she was standing right in front of her. Lilly must have felt the same way, because her eyes were also filled with tears of joy.

"Oh God Lilly. I've missed you so much. You look amazing," Dylan said as she pulled her friend in for a hug.

"I've missed you too," Lilly babbled between sobs.

Finally able to contain their emotions, Dylan helped Lilly with her luggage. One thing that didn't change with her friend was the amount of clothing she packed for a few days.

Just like he said, Richard was waiting in front of the door leading outside of the terminal. It didn't take long for Richard to load Lilly's bags in the back of the Bentley. As Richard made his way through the airport, Lilly and Dylan caught up on what was happening with them. It was when Dylan lifted her hand as she explained her night with Rade at the Met, that Lilly noticed her left ring finger.

"Oh my God, Dylan, is that what I think it is," Lilly said in surprise as she pulled Dylan's hand close to her.

"It is. Rade asked me to marry him, and I accepted," Dylan confessed watching the reaction on Lilly's face.

When Lilly pulled Dylan in for a hug, Dylan's apprehension disappeared. The last thing she wanted was for Lilly to disapprove of her decision to accept Rade's marriage proposal.

"I'm so happy for you Dylan. Somehow I just knew you two would be together," Lilly admitted. Even though Rade and she got off to a bad start, Lilly knew how Rade felt about Dylan. She also knew he would stop at nothing to keep her safe.

"So," Dylan began as she turned to face Lilly. "How are things with you and Peter?"

Lilly looked away from her friend focusing on her hands that rested crossed in her lap. Lily knew that it was a matter of time before the she would be faced with telling Dylan the real story between Peter and herself. "Things are....Let's just say, nonexistent," Lilly said regretfully. She hated the way things ended between them, but she knew with his secrets and her moving to Paris indefinitely, there would be no chance for them to be together. It didn't matter that she still cared for him deeply.

"What do you mean nonexistent? I thought you both were going to work things out," Dylan confronted her Lilly.

"There's just too many secrets and with the distance between us, it's better that we broke it off," Lilly said with a hint of sadness.

Dylan wasn't sure what secrets Peter could possibly have. She knew that some of the things he did with his job required him to keep information confidential, but that didn't explain him having secrets. Pushing her thoughts aside, Dylan decided it was best to let it go. She wanted to spend time with her friend on a happy note, focusing only on their time together and not Peter.

Richard pulled into the designated spot in the parking garage at the Crystal Hill Tower. Dylan noticed that Rade's Martin wasn't parked in its spot next to her Audi. He must have gone to work. At least that was what she was telling herself. She hoped that he wasn't trying to avoid Lilly and decided to make himself scarce.

Dylan pulled her phone from her purse and decided to give him a call to let him know that they were at the penthouse. Just as she was getting ready to dial, she heard the familiar sound of his car nearing them. Looking behind her, she stopped and waited for Rade to park his car. Her eyes glowed as he stepped out of the car. He could have posed for a car magazine the way his body looked as he stood. He was absolutely gorgeous. Dylan could see her friend was even taken by his form. "Lilly, your mouth is hanging open, "Dylan warned, before Rade saw the affect he had on her. Lilly's eyes rolled at Dylan's observation.

Taking her in his arms, Dylan didn't hesitate to wrap her arms around his shoulders as he pulled her in for a kiss. With a soft whisper, Rade asked, "Miss me?"

Dylan answered his question by placing her lips on his. The kiss lasted a little longer than normal because they were reminded of their PDA when Lilly cleared her throat. Smiling over to her,

Rade said with a smile, "It's good to see you again Lilly. I hope you had a good flight?"

"It was fine, thanks," Lilly returned the smile walking up to Rade wrapping her arm through his. "So what is this I hear about you proposing to by BFF?"

Rade couldn't understand Lilly's change of heart. Before she left for Paris, they weren't on the best of terms. Rade pushed his feelings aside and welcomed the change of attitude and pulled her in for a quick hug as he whispered, "Thank you for letting me take Dylan home."

Even though his comment was vague, Lilly knew exactly which night he was referring to. "You're welcome."

Rade had called ahead of time to make sure Maria had prepared them something wonderful for dinner, so when Dylan opened the door to the penthouse the air was filled with the aroma of something spicy and wonderful. Rade took Lilly's luggage to the guest bedroom, while Dylan and Lilly went to investigate the mouth water smell coming from the kitchen. Opening the oven door, Dylan took in the scent even further. Inside the oven was a Mexican casserole dish and a pan of cornbread waiting to be devoured. Dylan knew the meal was just warming since Maria put the oven setting on the lowest temperature. Pulling the two pans from the oven, Dylan set them on a ceramic warming stone sitting on the counter. It was then that Rade appeared, catching the two girls taking in the scent of steam as Dylan lifted the aluminum from the glass dish. "You two look like you've died and gone to heaven," Rade observed watching the drool practically running from their mouths.

By the time the meal was done, nearly all of the tasty dish was gone, most of which was consumed by Dylan and Lilly. Looking over at Rade's plate, Dylan could see that he had hardly touched his plate. The more she thought about it, he hadn't talked very much during the meal either. Dylan knew something was wrong, but she didn't want to get into it in front of Lilly. Dylan put it on the back burner until she could talk to Rade about it privately.

Rade excused himself and went upstairs to his study. Dylan thought this was odd of him considering they had a guest. This confirmed her suspicion that something was bothering him. Even Lilly could tell that something was up with him as well.

Taking their place at that couch, Lilly decided it was time for catch up. "So are you going to tell me what's going on with Rade?"

"You know Lilly, I'm not sure," Dylan admitted. "Unless it has to do with Chloe the devil woman."

"Yeah, about that. How are you doing with it?" Lilly asked placing her hand over Dylan's.

"As best as I can. I'm just taking it one day at a time. I'm just worried what is going to happen once she finds out that I'll be going to London with Rade. I'm pretty sure she had plans to get her claws into him," Dylan admitted with disgust.

"However it goes Dylan, remember that Rade loves you and not that bitch," Lilly confirmed. "Not even Chloe can change that."

It was close to midnight when Dylan decided to call it a night. Lilly was only in town for a couple of days and she wanted to do something special with her while she was here. Dylan had a full day planned for them and it was going to start early in the morning with a spa treatment and then a shopping spree.

Giving Lilly a hug, she made her way to her bedroom. When she opened the door, the bed was still made. Dylan knew that Rade was still in his study. Changing into her nightgown, she decided to find out what was keeping him awake so late. As she approached the door, she could hear yelling on the other side. If she could hear it, Dylan could only imagine what Lilly was hearing. Quietly, Dylan opened the door to see if she could hear what was going on.

"I'm not giving up. I know he's still in the city. Money or no money, I'm going to find him," Rade cursed in anger. "If you hear anything Peter, let me know. I don't care what time it is."

After what Dylan just heard, she wasn't going to let this go. There was something Rade was hiding from her and she wanted to know. Dylan didn't understand what Lilly meant about Peter having secrets, but it was plain to see that he knew something about what was going on. Knocking lightly on the door, Dylan stepped inside the room without an invitation. Walking up to Rade's desk, she could see the tension in his body. She needed to find out who Rade was referring to in his conversation with Peter.

"Rade, are you going to tell me what's going on. I could hear you yelling all the way downstairs." Dylan may have over exaggerated, but there was no way she could let Rade know that she was listening in on his conversation.

"I'm sorry Dylan, I didn't mean to wake you," Rade said, rounding his desk and pulling Dylan in for a hug.

"I wasn't asleep. When I'd seen you weren't in bed, I came up here," Dylan confessed. "So what's going on?"

"Nothing you need to worry about," Rade said. The last thing he wanted was for Dylan to find out the real reason behind the call with Peter.

"Rade, if I'm going to be your wife, you need to start being honest with me. I know something is going on that you aren't telling me," Dylan said forcefully.

"Dylan, you need to let this go," Rade said, kissing her forehead. "Let's go to bed."

Dylan still didn't have the answers she needed when she woke the next morning. Rade had been so withdrawn from her that their night was spent miles apart as Rade laid on one side of the bed and Dylan on the other. So it was no surprise to find him MIA from the penthouse.

Strolling into the kitchen, she found Lilly already awake and ready to go. Pouring herself a cup of coffee, Dylan pulled up a seat at the breakfast bar next to Lilly. Lilly couldn't stand the silence any longer. Looking over to Dylan she said, "Spill."

Once Dylan began talking, her emotions got the best of her because the waterworks began falling. She had no idea what Rade was keeping from her. "Why won't he tell me Lilly. We're engaged now. That has to mean something," Dylan sobbed.

"I know girlfriend. Men and their secrets," Lilly said perturbed.

"Well, I'm not going to let this ruin our day. I'm going to get ready for our day of complete bliss," Dylan said as she turned in the direction of her room.

The spa was packed when Dylan and Lilly arrived. It wasn't as high end as *La Mirage*, but it was still classy. After their mani-pedis, facials, and Brazilian waxes, Dylan and Lilly head out for their shopping spree. In-between shopping, they managed to grab lunch at Harlow's. Even though it took some time to get seated, it was well worth the wait. As Dylan looked around, she could see several men dressed in business attire as well as women. It wasn't until she looked over to her right that she just about lost it. Chloe was sitting three tables away with another attractive woman. Trying not to stare, Dylan looked closer at the other woman. It was then that she realized that she recognized the woman from the park. With the chatter that was taking place, Dylan couldn't hear what they were talking about.

Chloe looked up catching Dylan looking right at her. Dylan tried to act inconspicuous, but she was caught. Pretending to look at the menu, Dylan ignored the fact that Chloe was walking towards her table.

"Fancy seeing you here schoolgirl," Chloe hissed.

"I don't know why you continue to call me that, but I'm guessing it's because you feel threatened," Dylan hissed.

"That's where you're wrong. I'm not threatened by the truth. In a few days it will only prove that you are nothing but a distraction. London is beautiful this time of year. Rade is going to love it," Chloe declared.

Dylan didn't comment. She knew that Chloe would be in for a rude awaking. Dylan was almost ready to announce her engagement with Rade, but decided that it was more fuel for the fire. Dylan couldn't wait to see the look on Chloe's face when she showed up at her parent's house with Rade on her arm and her diamond ring in plain view. Now more than ever, she couldn't wait to go to London.

"Who the hell was that Dylan? Was that Chloe? What was she taking about Dylan?" Lilly asked confused.

"It doesn't matter because that bitch is about to get a taste of her own medicine," Dylan said with disgust.

"Well she looked like she was pregnant. What did she mean about Rade loving London? Aren't you leaving with Rade to London in a few days?" Lilly asked trying to figure out what was going on.

Dylan thought it would be best to tell Lilly what was going on. She hated keeping things from her, but knew it was only a matter of time before Lilly figured out the real truth about Rade's relationship with Chloe.

"Lilly, there's something that I need to tell you and you have to promise not to judge until I tell you everything," Dylan advised.

After Dylan explained everything to Lilly, she was more confused than she was a minute ago. She couldn't believe what she was hearing. "So let me understand this. Chloe is having Rade's baby, but only because she somehow got him to have sex with her. But since he was drugged and can't remember, there's no way to prove she took advantage of him, and the only person who knows for sure, is dead," Lilly explained exasperated.

"Yep, that about sums it up," Dylan replied.

"I don't know about you girlfriend, but that is so messed up," Lilly admitted.

Dylan tried not to think about Chloe and what she said. Instead she focused on her friend and how things were going in Paris. Dylan admired Lilly for leaving New York and going to France. It was a place Dylan dreamt of going ever since she was a little girl. Hopefully when the dust settled, she would seriously think about going. It would be nice to go there with Rade. *"How grand it would be to get married in Paris."* Dylan thought to herself.

* * * * *

Dylan was sad to see her friend leave. Spending only two days with Lilly wasn't near long enough. It was nice having someone that she could talk to. Lilly was the only friend Dylan had. Even as they grew up together, they shared everything.

Richard drove them to the airport. Dylan would have loved for Rade to ride along, but as always, he had a pressing matter that he needed to attend to. Dylan felt empty and alone on the ride back to the penthouse. She hated goodbyes. It was always so difficult for her, especially when she had to say goodbye to Lilly, who was more like her sister than her best friend.

Getting to the penthouse, Dylan was greeted with silence. She thought for sure that Rade would have been home. With only tomorrow left before they left for London, Dylan decided to take the time to get ready for the long trip. Rade hadn't let her know the specifics about the visit. Dylan wasn't even sure how long they would be staying, but if she knew Rade, it was going to be a very short visit.

After doing research, Dylan found that the weather in London was a little on the chilly side with temperature running around sixty degrees. It was also more than likely that the weather would be rainy at times. She wanted to make sure she packed accordingly. The last thing she wanted was to be underdressed for the weather conditions.

It was getting late and Rade was still not home. Dylan decided to send him a quick text.

Dylan: Where are you?

Rade: At the office.

Dylan: When are you going to be home?

Rade: Late, don't wait up.

Dylan: Okay. Love you.

Dylan waited for a response, but was disappointed when her cell showed no new texts. She thought it was odd that Rade didn't respond to her. Pushing her thoughts aside, Dylan decided to call it a night. She had a big day tomorrow at work. She needed to tie up some loose ends before leaving on her trip overseas. What she really needed was an assistant. Someone who wasn't Asian or gay.

It was after two in the morning when Rade finally got to the penthouse. He was beat and no closer to finding out where Michael was. Richard had received a tip from an old friend who spotted Michael going into a bar off of Twelfth Avenue. The problem was, by the time he and Richard arrived at the sports bar, Michael was long gone. When Richard had asked the bartender if she recognized the man in photo he showed of Michael, she said she did and that he must have stepped outside for a smoke because he hadn't paid his tab yet. An hour later, Rade was paying Michael's tab with frustration. Michael managed to slip through his fingers. One consolation was that he was a regular and usually came in every night around ten. At least this was something. Rade knew he couldn't spend every night in the bar until Michael showed up so he instructed Peter and Josh to watch the place for him.

Walking in the bedroom, Rade could see Dylan's perfect form lying in the bed. He could also see that she had his pillow nuzzled close to her body. God, he loved this woman. Removing his clothes, he slipped into bed beside her warm body. Pulling her close to him, he heard her soft whimper. Unable to hold back, he nestled his woody between her soft heat. He knew it was late, but he couldn't wait any longer. Feeling her heat, he pushed her panties to the side and pressed his hard shaft between her thighs. Dylan stirred at the invasion. Rolling on her back, she slipped her hands down her stomach and quickly glided her panties from her body. It didn't matter that it was late. All she wanted was to feel Rade inside her. Rade cupped her face and lowered his lips to hers. Kissing her tenderly, he whispered. "God, I will never get enough of you." With that, he resumed his kiss and took in the warmth of her mouth.

Positioning his body over hers, Rade spread her legs wider as he gently thrust inside. Her folds were wet and ready to consume him. Lowering his head, he captured her nipple and began kissing and sucking it into a taut peak. With one hand on her other breast; he slid his free hand down her body until he was met with her wetness. Tweaking her clit, he moved his finger deeper and deeper inside her. He needed more. He needed to taste her sweet honey. Sliding down her body, leaving tender kisses in his wake, Rade took what was his. Feeling her back arch, Dylan gave Rade what he was searching for. As soon as his mouth captured her clit, her body began to burn like a raging fire. There wasn't one inch that didn't feel like it was going to combust. Powerless, she let the surge take over, leaving her body weak and sensitized, yet thirsting for more.

Rade pulled Dylan's limp body to his, positioning her tender folds over his throbbing cock. He needed to be inside her. Raising her hips, Rade carefully lowered her body down on him. The minute her warmth shielded him, he was lost. Never had he experience the way her body took him. The way her walls gripped his cock as he moved inch by glorious inch inside her. Thrusting harder, Rade was close to his own explosion. Dylan accepted him as he plunged deeper within her channel. Deeper than he had ever been before. When her walls tightened, it was all she wrote. He was hers as he spilled his seed deep within her.

Chapter Seventeen

When Rade's Gulfstream landed at Heathrow, Dylan couldn't be happier. Even though she had slept most of the way, she was glad to finally touchdown after the seven hour flight. Rade invited Richard along not only as a driver, but also to keep an eye on Chloe. Rade knew once Chloe found out that Dylan came with him to London, she would be planning her next move.

It wasn't a surprise that a black Land Rover was waiting on the tarmac when they landed. Richard exited the private jet first making sure the luggage was transferred from the plane to the SUV. Emerging from then plane, Dylan took in the clean air that London offered. The air was humid, but refreshing. Richard put the luggage in the back of the SUV while Rade assisted Dylan into the vehicle.

As Richard drove, Dylan took in the sights of London. Even though it was September, the trees were beginning to change. The countryside was breathtaking. The drive took only thirty minutes, once Richard maneuvered out of the airport. Dylan continued to look out the window taking in the architecture of the old English style buildings. Passing the Natural History Museum, Dylan was in awe at the large building with its beautiful design. It was the most amazing exhibition of Victorian architecture she had ever seen. So many of the buildings they passed were just as amazing. Even when they drove through Hyde Park Corner, Dylan couldn't believe the structures and statues she saw. It was beautiful. Everything about the city was beautiful. Dylan hoped that they would be able to visit some of the sights while in London.

Richard pulled up to the Claridge Hotel leaving Dylan even more impressed. The hotel was magnificent with its timeless elegance. As Rade exited the Land Rover, he was greeted by a friendly man with an English accent. Assisting Richard with the luggage, a bellboy rolled a brass luggage cart through the double doors of the hotel. If the outside of the building wasn't impressive enough the inside left Dylan beyond speechles with its marble flooring and impressive archways. Even the chandeliers sparkled with grandeur.

Once checked in, Rade and Dylan were led to a set of elevators where the bellboy pushed the top floor on the panel. When the doors opened to reveal their room, Dylan was again speechless. The penthouse was more beautiful than the hotel. Walking to the double doors that led to the outside, Dylan would never get use to the sight in front of her with the panoramic view of Brook Mews, Davies Street, and the Houses of Parliament. Taken in by the view, Dylan didn't hear Rade walk up behind her.

"How about we freshen-up and go out to eat. I know of just the place along the River Thames," Rade said, placing a soft kiss on Dylan's neck as he pulled her to him from behind.

"That sound wonderful," Dylan admitted turning to face him.

"Tonight it will be just us," Rade began. "Tomorrow we will meet with Chloe's parents and soon they will know the truth about us."

Rade thought it would be romantic to take a carriage ride through the city, so it was only fitting to make the arrangements. With a little effort and a lot of money, he was able to get a local carriage company to accommodate his request.

Nothing could have prepared him for the look on Dylan's face as the coachman pulled up in front of the hotel in a horse drawn carriage. Rade wanted to make sure this was a night that Dylan would never forget.

When they arrived at the restaurant, the coachman was dismissed. Even though the ride was a little chilly for Dylan, nothing could have stopped her from experiencing another first.

Rade escorted Dylan into the restaurant knowing that he had made points with her. A hostess with an English accent greeted them and led them to a table outside the restaurant. The evening was a little cool, but having dinner along the River Thames was going to be another first Dylan wasn't going to pass up.

After Rade had placed their order, which Dylan had no idea what he ordered since he ordered it in French, Rade raised his wine glass. "Here's to a wonderful evening."

The evening was perfect and the meal was exceptional. Dylan never had wild duck before. It was so delicious, she couldn't describe the way it melted on her tongue. After they finished the main course, the waiter brought a Caramel soufflé and Armagnac ice cream. Dylan thought she had died and gone to heaven the way it took over her taste buds.

Finishing their meal, Rade suggested they take a walk along the river to burn some of the meal they consumed. There was so much to see on London that Dylan knew there was no way she would be able to see everything on their short visit. As they walked on the brick pathway, Rade pulled Dylan to his side. Stopping just short of the Tower Bride, Rade turned to face her. Dylan was confused by his sudden pause, but when she looked up at him, she knew it was to capture a kiss. When his lips met hers, it took everything she had not to beg him for more. She knew they were in a public place, but with the feel of his lips on hers, it didn't matter. All she wanted was him. "Take me home," Dylan softly said.

Rade must have called for Richard, because no sooner he broke from her, Richard pulled up to the curb ready to take them back to the hotel. It wasn't long before they arrived back to the room with their hands all over each other. Entering the penthouse, Rade pushed Dylan against the wall causing a picture to tip that was hanging on the wall. His need for her took over as he began tearing away at her clothing. Pulling her top over her head, his mouth was on her taut nipple sucking and kissing unable to get enough of her. Ripping her lacy bra, he needed more of her. With his other hand he found the clasp of her skirt and ridded her of it within seconds. Her panties were next, only he couldn't wait until they were off. He wrapped the delicate material around his fingers and with a forceful tug, the scrap of lace was removed. Dylan knew the minute the material dug into her skin, a mark would be left behind, like so many times before. There were no words that could express the hunger they had for one another. Rade's hands fell to Dylan's ass, clutching the soft flesh until her body was lifted from the marble floor. With unhampered desire, Dylan wrapped her legs around Rade's waist needing to be closer to him. It didn't take long for Rade to slide his trousers down his legs and thrust his engorged cock inside her warm channel. Dylan just about came undone at the sudden invasion. Trying to adjust to his large girth, Dylan adjusted her hips so that she was better able to take his ample shaft. "God, do you know how good you feel right now," Rade moaned with desire.

Unable to hold back his control, knowing that he might hurt her, Rade plunged to the hilt, swearing that he could feel her womb as he pressed deeper inside her tight channel. Hearing Dylan's scream, he knew he was home. Dylan's juices spread like wild fire as her walls tightened around him. Letting her walls consume him, he thrust one last time before his own need took over, spilling his seed inside her.

Rade gently lowered Dylan to the floor still holding on to her. Meeting her lips with his, he claimed what was his. His hunger for her strengthened with each pull of her body. Lifting her once again from the floor, he carried her in his arms to the bedroom. Laying her gently on the bed, He went to his suitcase and removed a tie from one of the compartments. It was the only item in the suitcase that he instructed the hotel butler to leave. He wanted to make sure he could obtain it in a hurry. He didn't want to waste time hunting it down.

"Put your arms above your head Sweetness," Rade instructed as he moved closer to her.

Taking her wrists in his hand, Rade began to loop the silky material around her wrists. When he was satisfied that the cloth was tight, her secured the ends to the headboard. Lowering his body between her legs, he spread them wide to accommodate his body. Looking down on her, he was ready to worship every inch of her perfection. Beginning at her feet, Rade placed wet tender kisses on her soft skin. Admiring her red toenails, he started moving up her body leaving no part of her soft skin untouched. By the time he got to her knees, Dylan was beyond frustrated. All she wanted was to have him inside her. "Please Rade, I need you," Dylan moaned.

"I want to hear you beg Sweetness," Rade said demandingly.

"I need you inside me Rade. Please, I need you to fuck me," Dylan pleaded.

Continuing his assault, Rade wasn't done taking what was his. He knew it was killing Dylan not to have his cock inside her, but this was what she needed. It had been to long since she felt his control. He needed to let her know that her body was his, her desire was his, her orgasms were his.

Hoping to gain his attention, Dylan began rocking her hips. She wasn't sure what it would take for Rade to give her what she needed. "You need to be still Sweetness, otherwise this will stop," Rade ordered.

Giving into his demand, Dylan stopped her movements and took what Rade was willing to give her. She knew that if it became too much for her, she could use her safeword. Just when she thought she couldn't hold on any longer, Rade slipped between her wet folds, careful not to enter her. He needed to show her who was in control. Once again Dylan's hips began to buck trying to lure Rade's cock inside her. "Be still," Rade commanded.

"I need you Rade, Please," Dylan cried in frustration.

Feeling her desperation, Rade slowly entered her tight channel. It took everything he had not to explode. Her wetness coated his hard shaft like a blanket. Pumping inside her, her hips began to meet his thrusts. He knew she was close. He contemplated on letting her go, but decided it would be worth more for her to hold on as long as possible. "You can only come on my demand Sweetness," Rade instructed. He knew every minute he kept her from coming was more time she had to feel the pleasure he was giving her.

"Rade please, I need..."

Before Dylan could finish her plea Rade whispered, "Come."

Letting her body take over, Dylan came. Warmth took hold of her body taking her beyond the scope of ecstasy. It wasn't long after that Rade too met his own release.

* * * * *

Rade wished that he could rewind the events from last night. What waited for him today was something he wasn't looking forward to. He knew it was a game he had to play. Sure he would take on the responsibility of being a father, but that didn't mean his commitment extended to Chloe or her family. The only reason he agreed to meet her family was because she agreed to the additional blood test.

Rolling on to his side, all his anxiety lifted once Dylan came into view. She looked like and angel lying beside him. Her body was barely covered by the sheet. Her taut nipples rose with every silent breath she took. He could have watched her for hours, absorbing every beautiful part of her. When she began to stir, he was knocked from his trance. Leaning over her, he gently placed his mouth on her taut nipple sucking and kissing the hard bud. He knew this would get her going. He would never get enough of her. In a soft voice she asked, "What time is it?"

"It's still early. Go back to sleep and I'll order breakfast," Rade said bending over to give her a tender kiss on the lips.

"Okay. Whatever you say," Dylan murmured as her eyes fluttered shut.

Dylan wasn't sure how much longer she slept, but when she woke, the air was filled with the scent of bacon, eggs and mocha. Pushing from the bed, Dylan grabbed Rade's white button-down shirt that was draped across the chair. Dylan walked to the bathroom to relief herself and checked her appearance in the mirror. For someone who was thoroughly fucked and exhausted, she looked better than she had in a long time. Maybe it was the happiness than flowed through her. Brushing her teeth, she took sight of the diamond ring sparkling under the light. She couldn't believe after everything that her and Rade had gone through that they would end up like this. Soon they would be bound together, belonging only to each other.

Dylan walked into the living area of the London penthouse feeling more energized than ever. Looking over to her man, she couldn't help but take in his perfection. He was shirtless which only added to his perfection. Dylan took in every hard line of his muscles. It was only after she took a deep breath that she realized she was gawking at him like a love crazed teenager. Walking closer to where he was standing, Dylan wrapped her arms around his waist from behind.

"Good morning Sweetness," Rade said feeling her warmth next to his body.

"Can't we just stay like this forever," Dylan asked nuzzling closer to his body.

"I would love nothing more, but we have an appointment with the she devil in a couple of hours. As much as it pains me to go, I'm almost looking forward to seeing the look on Chloe's face when she sees you, and we announce our engagement," Rade said, turning to face Dylan.

Dylan wanting nothing more than to see the look on Chloe's face, but it also left her wondering what Chloe would do. Dylan knew what Chloe was capable of, she just hoped they weren't making a mistake.

The drive to Chloe's parent's home in Oxford was silent. Dylan looked out the window admiring the countryside, while Rade finished some last minute emails needing his immediate attention. Dylan wondered what the day would bring. She was certain that whatever it brought, it wouldn't be good. Pulling up to the massive brick mansion, Dylan couldn't believe the size of the beautiful home. Just as they pulled around the circular drive, they were greeted by an older gentleman in a dark gray suit wearing white gloves. Opening the door, the older gentleman held out his hand and assisted Dylan out of the SUV.

Nodding his head as Rade exiting the car, he said with a formal greeting, "Lady Dupree and Sir John are waiting for your arrival in the study. Please follow me."

The butler led them through the house to a set of double wooden doors. Dylan had no idea that Chloe came from money. Her parent's house was something you would only imagine seeing in pictures. With its high ceilings, marble flooring and dark wood, the home was very inviting. High above the front door was an etched stain glass window which displayed a shield of some sort. It looked to have a harp and lions incased in a blue and red coat of armor. It was beautiful nonetheless.

Making their way to the back of the house, the butler stopped and gestured for them to enter a large room. As they entered the butler announced, "Madam Adams and Sir Matheson." It was all very formal.

Dylan took in the room as an older couple rose from the sofa. Looking at the couple, Dylan didn't expect them to look the way they did. They looked refined and well educated. Mr. Dupree was much older than his wife with gray hair and a slim built. His eyes were dark, just like Chloe's. Mrs. Dupree, on the other hand, was much younger. She looked to be in her early forties. She looked stunning for her age, with blond hair and green eyes. There wasn't anything about her that reminded her of Chloe. Dylan assumed that she was Chloe's step-mother. As the two approached Rade and Dylan, they made their introductions.

"Mr. Matheson, Chloe has told us so much about you. It's nice to finally meet you," John Dupree said as he held out his hand. "This is my wife Elizabeth."

"Nice to meet you," Rade said shaking his hand. "This is my fiancée, Dylan Adams."

"It's nice to meet you Mr. Dupree, Mrs. Dupree." Dylan smiled as she greeted them.

"Please call me John. No need for the formality," he confessed. " We were just about ready to have some tea. Please join us."

Dylan and Rade followed them to the sitting area taking their place on a sofa across from where they were previously sitting.

"Pardon me. If I can be so bold, but this is a little bit unexpected. We were under the impression that you and Chloe would be making wedding plans," John Dupree said, puzzled by Dylan's presence.

"Your daughter's relationship with me only goes as far as providing for the child she's carrying. I'm sorry if you thought otherwise," Rade admitted.

Before the conversation continued, Chloe stepped inside the room. The look on her face was priceless as she looked over to the sofa and saw Dylan seated next to Rade. Rade could already see the steam coming from her ears as her gaze turned into rage.

"Rade what is this?" Chloe let out, staring directly at Dylan with hatred.

"I'm sorry Chloe. I couldn't leave my fiancée behind. She is as much a part of this as I am," Rade gloated with a grin.

Rade watched as Chloe's anger went from rage to fury. If the look in her eyes could kill, they would both be dead. Rade knew the announcement of his engagement would infuriate her, but no way was he prepared for what she did next.

Picking up a crystal decanter of liquor from the beverage cart, Chloe threw it aiming it in Dylan's direction. Dylan ducked her head causing the glass to shatter against the fireplace, spilling its contents everywhere. Dylan was thankful that Chloe's aim was off, otherwise she may not have survived the force of the heavy crystal hitting her in the head.

"Chloe, you need to get a hold of yourself. This is no way to act in front of our guests," John warned.

Chloe drew her attention away from Dylan and focused on her father's words. "You're right father. It must be the hormones taking over," Chloe maintained with a sneer. "I guess congratulations are in order."

Dylan could see right through Chloe. She knew Chloe was no more happy about Rade's announcement then she would have been getting a root canal. Looking at Chloe, Dylan could see that something was off with her, She didn't look right. She looked tired and almost sickly. Being pregnant was supposed to make a woman gleam. There was nothing glowing at all with Chloe. Matter of fact, Chloe looked like she had lost weight.

After a wonderful dinner, Rade and Dylan decided to head back to the hotel. John and Elizabeth were nothing but charming. Dylan couldn't understand how different Chloe was from her father and step-mother. During the conversation, Dylan learned that John had married Elizabeth after the death of Chloe's real mom. It turned out that Elizabeth was actually Chloe's nanny before she married John. Dylan had no idea what Chloe's mother was like, but if she was anything like Chloe, it was probably a good thing that there was one less person like her around.

Heading back to London, the change with Chloe was bothering Dylan. She needed to get it out before it consumed her thoughts.

"Rade, did you noticed anything different about Chloe?" Dylan asked.

"Other than her change in attitude, not really," Rade confirmed.

"Something has been bothering me. For a woman who is four months pregnant, she didn't look right. Most women would be glowing. She looked sick. She lost weight as well," Dylan hinted.

"Come to think of it, she didn't look like herself," Rade admitted.

Rade would need to look into what could be going on with Chloe when they got back to the states. For now, he just wanted to spend the few days they had in London with Dylan.

* * * * *

Dylan had never been so exhausted in her life. When she told Rade that she wanted to take in the sights of London, he didn't miss a beat. Dylan had no idea that there was so much to see. They visited the Tower of London, Kensington Palace, Westminster Abbey, and even a tour through the Windsor Castle.

But what really excited Dylan was catching the changing of the guards at the Palace. This was an experience she would never forget.

It was late when they got back to the hotel. Even though it was exhausting, Rade managed to fit everything in one day, taking Dylan to every place she wanted to visit. Entering the penthouse, Rade went to the master bedroom en suite bathroom and ran a bath for Dylan. Tomorrow they would be leaving for the states and Rade wanted to make sure that Dylan would be ready. With the amount of sightseeing they did, he knew that her body would be sore. A warm bath would help loosen her sore muscles.

While Dylan took a bath, Rade decide to make the arrangements for their flight back to the states. Just as he was getting ready to call Richard, his phone buzzed.

"Peter, this is unexpected," Rade said surprised.

"I was going to wait until you returned back to the states, but I thought you may want to know, we were able to get inside Chloe's safe deposit box at World National," Peter began. "You aren't going to believe what we found."

"I'm ready to put this shit behind me. I hope you found what is necessary to do that," Rade replied.

"We did, and more. Everything you need to put Ms. Dupree away for a long time was in that box. It baffles me that she kept all that incriminating evidence," Peter confessed.

"Well, you never know what thoughts go through the mind of a woman mentally unstable," Rade admitted. "I'll get with you tomorrow after we land. It will give me more time to sort through what you found."

Rade couldn't be happier. It looked like his wish was going to come true. Chloe would be spending the rest of her days in jail and their child would know the truth about its mother.

Chapter Eighteen

As much as Dylan enjoyed London, she was glad to be back in New York. The flight home was just as tiring as the flight to England which left Dylan sleeping most of the way. Dylan was glad to see Peter as he pulled up to the Gulfstream, driving the Bentley. It was only when she saw the Mercedes pull up behind the SUV that Dylan became confused. Rade could see her confusion, so he thought it best to explain.

"Josh is going to take you back to the penthouse. There are a few things I need to take care of at the office. I shouldn't be too long," Rade advised.

"Okay, but can't it wait until tomorrow?" Dylan question, wanting Rade to herself tonight.

"It can't," Rade admitted cupping Dylan's cheek in his hand before pulling her in for a kiss.

Rade, Richard and Peter parted as the SUV pulled away from the black Mercedes. Dylan wasn't sure what was so important that couldn't wait until the morning, but that didn't mean she wasn't going to find out as soon as Rade got home. Now that they were engaged, she wasn't going to let him keep things from her. She knew that Rade was thinking about his father's kidnapping. Rade thought being in London would ease his mind, but it only made him more tense, not hearing back from the kidnapper.

Josh didn't stick around once he helped Dylan with the luggage and escorted her inside the penthouse. Dylan began to relax once she poured herself a much needed glass of wine. With Rade gone, she decided to take a hot bath. Taking her wine with her, she headed to the bathroom. Before she could fully strip off her clothes a text came in on her phone.

> *Rade: I'll be home in an hour. I want you naked and waiting for me.*

Dylan smiled as she typed her reply.

> *Yes sir.*

Throwing her cell on the bed, she headed to the bathroom for a quick bath. Engulfed in the soothing lavender bubbles, Dylan must have drifted, because when she opened her eyes, Rade was standing above her with his arms crossed over his chest. *Shit, shit, shit.* Dylan quickly pushed to her feet, just as Rade swooped her from the tub.

"You have a hard time following orders Sweetness. For that you will be punished," Rade said sternly.

Without letting Dylan dry off, Rade had her stretched and tied to the bed. First were her ankles and then her wrists. Her body was face down on the bed which only meant that soon she would be receiving her punishment. Dylan couldn't see what was happening, but she could hear Rade behind her. When a lash of his belt on her butt cheek, she knew she was in for it. The sting of the belt sent her body soaring as another strike hit her other cheek. Dylan knew that she was wet. Pleasure took over the pain. She needed him. "I'm sorry Rade. I must have dozed off," Dylan apologized, hoping he would have mercy on her before she came without permission.

"What should your punishment be Sweetness? Ten lashes. No, I think double that is more appropriate for your defiant behavior," Rade said with a smirk.

"Can't you just fuck me instead?" Dylan pleaded.

"Punishment first," Rade replied as he laid another strike to her backside. "Count Sweetness."

"One, Dylan moaned feeling the sting. "Two." Dylan gripped the pillow beneath her head the best she could with her restraints, trying to muffle the sounds of pain.

By the time the last lash hit her ass, Dylan was burning with desire. There was no denying the pool of wetness between her legs. By the time she counted to twenty, she was dripping.

"I think my Sweetness enjoyed her punishment," Rade affirmed, slipping his fingers between her slick folds.

Loosening the ties around her ankles, Rade took hold and flipped Dylan over in one move. Spreading her legs, he took her bindings and re-secured her ankles to each side of the bed leaving her wide open for him. He was going to enjoy this time with her. Her control was going to be tested. She was going to learn what it meant to do as he commanded. Lowering his body between her legs, he began placing tender kisses across her heated flesh. The more he kissed her, the more she struggled. "You need to hold still Sweetness or I will stop," Rade ordered. Dylan gritted her teeth, but did as she was told. Placing his mouth along her jaw line, Dylan took in the scent his breath left behind. The smell of musk and scotch filled her senses, making her need him that much more. "Rade, please," Dylan cried with desire.

"Please what Sweetness?" Rade whispered in her ear while pushing his body into to hers.

"I need you."

"I want to hear you say what you want."

"I need you inside me, please Rade. I need you to fuck me."

Rade wasn't ready to give her want she needed. He only just begun his play with her. Lifting his body from hers, he left the room, leaving her bound to the bed. Dylan raised her head, wondering where he went. If he was going to leave her unsatisfied and bound to the bed, she would surely pay him back for this. Dylan was struggling with her binds when she saw Rade appear in the doorway. Holding a tumbler of what Dylan assumed was scotch, he took a sip. She could have killed him for the length of time it took him to finish his drink. "Are you going to fuck me or just stand there," Dylan yelled, needing to be taken.

"Are you getting impatient Sweetness?" Rade snickered.

He knew she was on the edge. He loved seeing her powerless. He loved having control over her. Taking his time, Rade walked over to the bed and placed his glass on the night table, not before taking an ice cube into his mouth. Straddling his body over hers, Rade lowered his head and captured one of Dylan's taut nipples, With the cube in his mouth, he pushed it forward between his teeth letting the coldness spread across the rosy bud. With a small gasp, Dylan's back rose from the bed as the shock of the cold sensation running across her pert nipple took hold. Changing his position, Rade picked up his glass and took another cube in his hand. This time he lowered his hand to her folds and took the tip of the cube making sure to rub it against her swollen nub. Once again Dylan's body rose at the sudden jolt of coldness. "Oh God, I can't take any more. Please Rade, just fuck me," Dylan moan with desperation.

"You can and you will Sweetness. Only I can tell you when you can come," Rade whispered as he captured Dylan's mouth with his.

Her need for him grew as he deepened the kiss, clashing his tongue with hers. Her soft moans just about set him off. Pulling from her, Rade lowered his pants and stripped his body bare. He needed to feel her as much, if not more, than she did. With her legs spread for him, he lowered his mouth to her swollen clit and began licking and sucking the hard nub. The taste of her sweet honey was on his lips as he continued his assault on her womanhood. Placing his fingers along her folds, he slipped inside her. God she was perfect the way her pussy tightened around him. Matching her movements, he slipped another finger inside. Dylan's body came undone as he felt the spurt of her arousal coat his fingers. "My Sweetness needs to show more control," Rade said as he lapped up her sweet juices.

Just when Dylan thought there was nothing left, her body surged with another orgasm. Unable to hold back himself, Rade plunged deep inside her. His intension to take it slow with her passed the minute her body exploded with yet another orgasm. Pushing deeper inside her tight channel, Rade felt the onset of his own release. Needing to be deeper, to take all that was his, he undid her binds and flipped Dylan onto her stomach. Pulling up on her hips, he drove his cock to the hilt, with no mercy, until he was consumed by his own heart retching release, only to be greeted by one of her own.

Rade's body collapsed onto Dylan's. He was fully sated. He had fully fucked her. Pushing to his elbows, he rolled over and gently pulled her limp body close to his. "I love you Sweetness," Rade whispered, before he fell into a deep sleep.

* * * * *

Dylan's day back to work turned out to be a day from hell. Even though Rade had talked his father out of his intension to take over shares of the Spectrum merger, BlackStone was getting heat from the CEO of Spectrum. Wayne Morris wasn't happy with the way things were going. Even though he didn't have a say in what happened with the project and Keeve still felt he had an obligation to him to keep him happy. So when Wayne Morris decided to hop a plane to New York to check the new location of Spectrum himself, Keeve was more than willing to accommodate his request.

Dylan was working diligently on a financial report when Keeve poked his head in her office.

"I'm on my way to the Hilton to meet with Mr. Morris. I should be back in about an hour," Keeve informed Dylan.

"Okay, is there anything you need me to do?" Dylan asked.

"I think everything has been taken care of. When I get back, Rade should be here and then we can leave for the new Spectrum site. I'd like to get this over with as soon as possible," Keeve admitted. The less time he had to spend with Wayne Morris the better.

Focusing on her work, Dylan heard her phone ringing. Pulling it from her purse, she didn't recognize the number. Going against her better judgment, she went ahead and answered it.

"Hello," Dylan said hesitantly.

"Dylan, it's Garrett."

"Oh my God, Garrett, where are you? Everyone has been so worried about you after the break-in at the hotel. How are you even calling me?" Dylan asked frantically.

"I'll explain later. I've been trying to get in touch with Keeve. Do you know where he might be?" Garrett ask with concern.

"He just left to meet with Wayne Morris. What is this about Garrett? Where are you?"

"I think I may have figured out who took me." Garrett confessed.

"You need to contact the police? There was a ransom note. Why would you need to talk to Keeve about this? What's going on Garrett?" Dylan questioned.

"It was Wayne Morris who took me. The minute he appeared at my hotel room, I recognized him. A few years ago, I did some things that I'm not proud of. I basically stole from him. I think he wanted revenge," Garrett admitted.

"Oh God Garrett, if what you're saying is true, then Keeve could be in danger. I need to call Rade."

"Maybe you'll have better luck than I did. We need to get to Keeve. Do you know where he was meeting Wayne Morris?" Garrett inquired.

"At the Hilton," Dylan advised him.

"I'll call the police and head there. Try to get in touch with Rade and let him know what's happening," Garrett requested.

Dylan hung up the phone with Garrett and immediately dialed Rade. When the call went to voice mail, she began to panic. She then tried to get in touch with Keeve, but the call also went to voice mail. Dylan was a mess. Her concern for Keeve was beginning to set in. It was then she decided to call Richard. She was thankful when he picked up.

"Richard, I just hung up with Garrett and I can't get a hold of Rade or Keeve," Dylan said frantically.

"What is this about Ms. Adams," Richard asked getting irritated.

"Garrett escaped somehow. He said the man who took him was Wayne Morris. Keeve is on his way to the Hilton to meet with him. If Garrett is right, then Keeve could be in danger," Dylan explained already in panic mode.

"I'll let Rade know. In the mean time, I'll send Peter to come and get you and take you back to the penthouse where you'll be safe," Richard commanded.

"Okay. Be careful Richard," Dylan said, worried about what could happen.

Just like Richard said, Peter was waiting to take Dylan back to the penthouse where he knew she would be safe. Once inside the car, Dylan tried again to get in touch with Rade with no success.

It was unlike him not to answer his phone when she called. Placing her phone by her side incase Rade did call back, Dylan began thinking about all the bad things that could happen. Peter could see the worry in her eyes.

"It will be fine Dylan. If I know Richard, he will have it all under control, before Mr. Morris does anything," Peter assured her.

"I hope you're right Peter," Dylan said, not comforted by his confidence.

Entering the penthouse, Dylan tried once again to get in touch with Rade. She was just about ready to give up, when he finally answered.

"Rade, I was so worried about you. Your father called me. He said Wayne Morris is the man who took him. He also was the one who shot Keeve and Mason at BlackStone," Dylan said hysterically.

"I know, Richard told me. I've been in conferences all day and had my phone muted. Where are you?" Rade asked.

"I'm at the penthouse with Peter," Dylan advised. "What about you? Where are you?"

I'm with Richard. We're on the way to the Hilton. I don't want you going anywhere," Rade ordered.

"I can't sit around and wait for something to happen to you," Dylan interjected.

"The last thing I need Dylan is to worry about you. Please stay where you are," Rade commanded.

"Okay, but stay in touch with me so I know you're okay," Dylan huffed.

"I will," Rade said before ending the call.

On the way to the hotel, Rade ran every scenario possible as to what could go wrong once they got there. Thankfully Richard contacted his friend at the NYPD to meet him there. Rade wasn't sure what was in store for them so he had Richard take the extra precautions.

Once inside the hotel, Rade spotted Keeve right away. He was glad to see that Keeve was alone. This meant that Wayne Morris hadn't met up with him yet. Walking up to Keeve, Rade placed his hand on his shoulder.

"What are you doing her Rade?" Keeve asked surprised.

"Garrett shared some information about Wayne Morris. We thought it best to have reinforcements," Rade confessed.

"Reinforcements for what?" Keeve answered confused.

"Wayne Morris was the man who shot you and Mason and killed the IRS investigator," Rade began. "He was also the one who took my father for ransom. We didn't want to take any chances on him having another opportunity to finish the job he started.

"I knew there was something familiar about the shooter. Shit.., motherfucker," Keeve belted.

"Lower your voice Keeve. The last thing we need is to cause a scene," Rade advised looking around the lobby.

Rade and Keeve stood patiently in the lobby while they waited for Wayne Morris to appear. Keeve surveyed the area looking for any sign of him. Giving up, Rade and Keeve began heading towards the restaurant, thinking they may have missed him. They spotted him sitting at a table. Morris must have known something was up, because he stood and headed in the opposite direction walking away with accelerating speed.

The only escape was through the kitchen doors. Morris swung the door open and proceeded inside the kitchen. Richard had already contacted his friend and they were manning all the exits incase Mr. Morris tried to escape. Morris went through the exit door in the kitchen. Rade and Keeve weren't far behind when they came upon him. Wayne Morris was already cuffed and being read his Miranda rights. With the information they had against him and Garrett's testimony, there wasn't any chance that Wayne Morris would be going back to LA anytime soon. The only thing left to do was find the gun he used to shoot Keeve, Mason and the IRS investigator. Once they found it, Morris could count on spending the rest of his days behind bars. The authorities had already been contacted in LA to get a warrant to check his home.

Rade couldn't be happier that things went the way they did at the hotel. He contacted Dylan as soon as they left the Hilton to let her know that the police had Wayne Morris in custody and that he was on his way to the penthouse. It had been a long day and Rade was ready to do nothing but consume Dylan.

Arriving at the penthouse, Rade saw Dylan busying herself in the kitchen. She must have gone on a cooking warpath because pots and pans covered every inch of the counter space. On the dining room table were several prepared dishes which they couldn't possibly consume in one setting. Stepping behind her, Dylan was pulling a soufflé from the oven. Bending over, Rade gently kissed her on the neck which caused her to gasp with surprise. Dylan frowned as she watched the center of the decadent dish collapse.

"I wanted this meal to be special," Dylan said with regret as she placed the ruined dish on the stove.

"It's okay Sweetness. I'll just eat you," Rade whispered pulling her closer to his body.

Dylan could have melted from his touch. Turning her body, she lightly kissed him on the lips. "I hope you're hungry after all that excitement. I might have gone a little overboard with dinner," Dylan mumbled between kisses.

"Only for you Sweetness, Only for you," Rade replied.

As much as Dylan hated to, she pulled away from Rade's embrace before they got wrapped up in each other. She needed to know what happened.

"Are you going to tell me what happened at the hotel?" Dylan asked.

"Later, first I want to consume you," Rade argued holding Dylan tighter to his body.

"Rade, I want to know what happened, now," Dylan objected standing her ground.

Pulling away, Rade stepped to the side and pulled a wine glass from the cabinet. Pouring himself a glass, he took his place next to Dylan.

"There really isn't much to tell. Wayne Morris didn't have anywhere to go once we found him. The police took him to the station. The authorities were notified in LA and with a court order. They are going to search his home for any evidence tying him to the shooting. He already admitted to the kidnapping, so all they needed to do is get him for the shootings," Rade said taking a drink of his wine.

"So what do you think they will find?" Dylan questioned.

"Hopefully the gun he used to shoot Keeve and Mason. Maybe more," Rade advised.

"Well whatever they find, I hope it's enough to put him away for a long time," Dylan said.

Dylan's words made Rade think about Chloe's safe deposit box and what Peter had found inside. With the full day he had, he still hadn't talked to Peter about what to do about its contents. Once more day wasn't going to make a difference. Right now all he cared about was getting Dylan beneath him. Setting his glass on the counter, Rade pulled Dylan into him and lowered his lips to hers. Biting her bottom lip, a soft moan escaped her mouth. Adding more pressure, Rade parted her lips with his tongue and slide inside. The heat between them took over as Dylan's hands began snaking through Rade's thick hair. Sending the pots and pans to the floor with a crash, Rade lifted Dylan's body onto the counter. Just the scent of her made him hard. Taking the hem of her shirt, Rade pulled it over her head, taking her lacy bra with it. With her pert breasts presented before him, it only took one second before his mouth was over the pink bud. While his mouth worked one nipple, his fingers were caressing the other. Dylan's head fell back when Rade took the hard peak between his fingers and pinched the tender skin. This was enough for Dylan to want more. Even though they had a wonderful meal waiting for them, she only wanted him.

Placing her hands on his chest, Dylan began unbuttoning his crisp shirt. By the time she got to the third button, her self-control took over and the remaining buttons began flying in the air until they bounced on the floor. "I need you inside me Rade," Dylan said with fervent desire. Sliding Dylan's body off the counter, Rade swiftly lowered her leggings with one tug and bent her over the cold granite. A groan escaped Dylan's lips as her warm flesh hit the cold stone. Pulling his belt from his pants, Rade had his pants down exposing his raging cock. "Place your hands behind your back Sweetness," Rade ordered, barely able to contain his control.

Once her hands were in place, Rade wrapped the belt around her wrists and watched as they rested on her lower back. Sliding his fingers between her folds, he could feel that she was more than ready to be consumed. In a heated thrust, Rade was inside her. He could feel her walls begin to stretch, accepting his cock with each thrust he drove inside her sweet pussy. Another moan echoed, filling the air with a hunger only they could share. Rade took hold of her hips pushing further and further inside her. The slickness of her pretty cunt coated his balls the deeper he pushed causing the slapping sound of his sac to radiate against her folds. "God, you feel so good Sweetness," Rade moaned with pleasure. "I'm going to fuck you until you scream my name."

Dylan was lost in the feeling. With her channel stretched to the point of ripping her in two, she couldn't hold on any longer. Screaming his name, just as he commanded, her gates opened and ecstasy ripped through her body. It was like no other feeling she ever experienced.

Barley able to stand on her feet, Rade pulled from her and twisted her body so she was splayed across the cold counter. Finishing where he left off, Rade plunged inside her dripping pussy and took what was his. Dylan wanted nothing more than to feel him. "Rade, Please, untie me. I needed to hold you," Dylan cried.

Pulling her body to his chest, Rade undid her restraints and waited for her arms to wrap freely around his shoulders. With her hands free, Dylan gripped Rade's hair and pulled herself closer to his body causing him to go deeper inside her. Before she could say, "I love you," Rade spilled his seed inside her. Holding her tightly in his arms, he softly whispered. "I will forever love you Sweetness."

Chapter Nineteen

It was the weekend and Rade needed to get in touch with Peter about the contents in Chloe's deposit box. Dylan was still asleep as he slipped from the bed and into the shower. After their lovemaking episode, he thought it best to let her sleep in. It never failed him, even when he wasn't thinking about Dylan his dick was. Sporting a full erection, Rade took care of his needs as he stroked his cock while under the warm stream of water. He would have preferred to empty his seed inside Dylan's tight pussy, but given their explosive night, he opted to give her a break. There would be plenty of bumping and grinding later.

Only partially satisfied, Rade finished his shower and put on a pair of lounge pants. As he left the bedroom, Dylan was still asleep. God, he could have stared at her sleeping for hours, but there was something important that he needed to take care of first. With coffee in hand, Rade jogged up the steps to his office to call Peter.

When Rade got to his office, he quietly shut the door and called Peter. It was no surprise that Peter answered on the first ring.

"Hewitt," Peter greeted.

"Peter, its Rade. I wanted to finish our talk about what was found in Chloe's safe deposit box," Rade said determined.

"We got her Mr. Matheson. There's no doubt with the incriminating pictures of her and Mr. Moreno, and with the flash drive showing everything that was done to Ms. Adams and you, she can plan on making prison her new home. Give me the word and we can get put them in the right hands so Ms. Dupree never sees the light of day," Peter advised. "Oh, one more thing I forgot to show you. There were adoption papers inside. I'm not sure if it means anything to you."

"It does Peter. I think Chloe was going to go through with having a child. No matter whom it came from. Was there anything else?" Rade asked.

"Yeah, there were various men items in the box. A tie, money clip and a set of cufflinks with RM engraved on them. I don't know Mr. Matheson, if these things belonged to you, then Ms. Dupree may be more unstable than we thought," Peter cautioned.

"Give the items to Richard. He'll make sure they get to the right person. We needed to find Chloe and keep an eye on her. With her reaction in London to my engagement announcement, who knows what will set her off? She should be back from London by now. It shouldn't be too hard to track her and inform the authorities," Rade said, wanting this thing with Chloe to be finished once and for all.

"When we have her, I let you know," Peter said, letting Rade know he would find her.

Dylan woke up to an empty bed, but was greeted by Rade's scent as she pulled his pillow to her chest. The scent of coffee also filled her senses. Rising from the bed, Dylan grabbed her silk robe and headed to the kitchen. Disappointed that Rade wasn't there, she filled a mug to the rim with coffee and added her favorite creamer. When she was satisfied that she had it the way she wanted it, she headed up the stairs to Rade's study. She knew it was the only place he could be. Knocking lightly on the door, she waited for her cue to enter. When it didn't come, she turned the knob and pushed the door slowly open.

Rade was on his cell, when Dylan walked through the door. Taking a seat on the couch, she waited for his call to end.

"Peter will get everything over to you and let you know his plans. I told him to let me know when he finds her so the appropriate action can be taken," Rade commented.

Dylan assumed it was Richard that Rade had been taking with. "What's going on Rade?"

"The key you gave me was to Chloe's safe deposit box. Peter found evidence that Chloe had a part in what happened at *The Castle* the night you were assaulted and also what happened to me," Rade said as he rounded his desk to be closer to Dylan. "I asked Peter to get the information to Richard to make sure it gets into the right hands. She's going to be spending the rest of her life in prison for what she did."

Dylan was in shock. She wasn't sure what Peter had found in the box, but she needed to know. She wasn't ready to relive that horrible night, but she couldn't face the nightmare if what happened to her ever got out either. "Rade, what did she have in her box regarding the night at *The Castle*," Dylan asked feeling uneasy.

"It's not good. Everything that happened was saved on a flash drive," Rade said as he sat next to Dylan.

"I need to see it Rade. I need to see for myself what's on that flash drive, I need to know. If any part of that night is on there Rade, it would kill my dad if he ever found out what happened. I can't let that happen," Dylan pleaded.

"Richard is on his way over so we can look at it. Together," Rade said comforting Dylan as he pulled her close to him. When Rade met with Peter after the trip to London, he couldn't bring himself to watch it.

The last thing that Rade wanted was to put Dylan through that terrible nightmare. If he had to he would find another way to pin it on Chloe without the evidence, but first he needed to see what was on the drive for himself.

Knowing what they did, took Rade everything he had to calm Dylan. This was the last thing he wanted for her. Taking her by the hand, he led her back to the bedroom and stripped her of her robe. Making sure the temperature in the shower was just right, he pulled her body close and lifted her to him so that her legs were wrapped around his waist. He needed to let her know that no matter what happened, he would always be there for her. Entering the hot stream of water, Rade gently placed butterfly kisses along her neck while holding her close to him. Leaning her body against the cool tile, he slid his hand down her slick body until he found her clit. With circular movements, he placed his thumb on the swollen nub while using his index finger to glide between her folds. It amazed him how she was always ready for him. Her folds were slick with wetness. Adding another finger he glided it inside her tight slit, entering her warmth. "Just feel Sweetness. Think of nothing else but this," Rade whispered.

Capturing her mouth with his, Rade slipped his tongue between her parted lips feeling the emotion consuming her. Sucking and licking, intertwining, gravitating together, their kiss deepened with voracity, taking them to a place they both needed to be. Just the two of them, no one else, no other sound other than their hearts beating, colliding together as one. Desire and need took over as Dylan exploded with fury. Placing her on her feet, Rade twisted her body, placing her hands above her head as her breasts pressed against the smooth marble. Spreading her legs with his own, he gripped his shaft and slowly filled her with his velvet hardness. Dylan's walls tightened around him, launching his body into the cosmos and beyond. Pushing deeper, with hard heeded thrusts, Rade plowed further and further into her core. Dylan's walls clamped down on his throbbing cock causing Rade to lose his control and relentlessly spew inside her.

"That was just what we needed Sweetness," Rade said sated. Pulling from her, Rade grabbed the soapy bath sponge, watching the creamy liquid drip from her spent body. Lightly, Rade rubbed the sensitive skin between Dylan's legs, and gently began washing away the product of their desire.

Their timing couldn't have been better because just as they put on their last stitch of clothing, a knock came at the door. Rade went ahead and answered the door, while Dylan finished drying her hair. Opening the door, Richard appeared carrying a manila envelope which Rade knew contained the items from Chloe's deposit box.

"Come in Richard. Dylan is drying her hair and should be done soon. In the meantime, tell me how much of what happened to Dylan is on the flash drive," Rade asked concerned.

"It's all there. What was done to her was unspeakable. I'm not sure if it's wise for her to relive that night again," Richard cautioned. "Death for Mr. Moreno was too charitable for him. He should have had his balls ripped off first."

" I agree. Somehow we have to find another way to tie Chloe to that night," Rade shot, taking the envelope from Richard as they headed to Rade's study.

Rade prayed that he would be able to review what was on the flash drive before Dylan came looking for him. If it was as bad as Richard claimed, he couldn't watch it together with Dylan. Settling in the leather chair behind his desk, Rade turned on his computer, and push the flash drive into the USB port. Seconds later, the files began to appear. One thing he had to say, Chloe was organized in that she labeled each file according to the incident. Clicking on the file that read *The Castle,* Rade watched as the video of that night appeared. Watching what happened was making him sick. Rade slammed the cover to his lap top and went to his liquor cabinet and poured himself a double shot of Glenfiddich. He needed to hold it together. His heart broke as he watched the woman he loved assaulted in such a vile manner. Dylan had explained to him what had happened to her, but seeing it for himself, just about caused him to lose it. His body was totally numb

Downing the remainder of his drink, a knock came on his study door. Before he could say anything, Dylan appeared. Based on the expression she had on her face, Rade knew she saw the guilt spread across his, it was no use hiding it.

"What's going on Rade," Dylan asked almost afraid of what he would say.

"The night at *The Castle*....the whole thing was taped. From the moment you walked into that room, to when you passed out. I'm so sorry Dylan, I had no idea how bad it really was. I think it's best that you don't watch it. We'll find another way to get Chloe for what happened to you," Rade choked, disgusted that he could have let something like this happen.

"I need to see it Rade, if I'm ever going to get past this, I need to see it," Dylan begged.

"I can't let you Dylan. It could break you forever," Rade urged.

"This is not your decision to make Rade. I need to do this," Dylan argued.

Against his better judgment, Rade pushed from his desk and took Dylan in his arms. "Are you sure you want to do this Sweetness?" Rade asked, afraid of what this could do to her.

As soon as Dylan was settled, He opened the file and the video began playing. Rade watched as Dylan sat silent. Her face went from radiant to pale within minutes. When he saw the tears fall from her face, he knew she had seen enough. Before he could shut the file, Dylan was out of the chair and down the steps. Without hesitation, Rade followed her. When he got to the bedroom, he saw that she was in the bathroom crouched on her knees in front of the toilet. He knew he should have demanded that she not see the footage of that night. She may have been mad at him, but at least she would eventually forgive him instead of going through what Rade knew for certain would happen.

Walking next to her, Rade gently pulled her hair from her face as she continued to spill her guts. When he knew she couldn't expel anymore, he took her in his arms and set her on the vanity to help clean her up. Thoroughly satisfied she was clean, he carried her to their bed where he gently placed her on it. Holding her as tightly as he could, he whispered, "I'm so sorry Sweetness. The last thing I wanted was for you to see that,"

"I will do whatever I have to..., to make sure she never sees the light of day," Dylan blurted with vengeance in her voice.

"I will do everything I can to protect you Sweetness. I will find another way to get her," Rade confirmed.

Rade stayed with Dylan until she fell asleep. Heading back to his study to look at the rest of the information on the flash drive, He searched for something, anything that would show Chloe's part in Dylan's assault.

After spending hours reviewing the evidence, Rade was about to give up on finding anything on Chloe when it came to him. When they had been looking for Dylan's assailant, they were looking for a man. It never occurred to them to look for Chloe. Picking up his cell, he dialed Dane's number.

"Dane, hey old friend. I have a favor to ask of you. Remember looking at the security footage for Dylan's abuser?" Rade asked.

"I remember. What is this about Rade?" Dane asked confused.

"There was someone else involved. Chloe Dupree," Rade advised.

"Chloe Dupree? Are you shitting me?" Dane answered surprised. He had known Chloe for a long time. He couldn't believe that she would have done anything so horrible.

"Yeah. Can I meet with you to go through all the footage from that night. I have a feeling that we will find something interesting on it," Rade advised. "If we could follow the footage from the time she entered to when she left, I think it will prove she was a part of the plan to get Dylan in the dungeon."

"Whatever you need my friend," Dane said.

Once the arrangement was made with Dane to go over the security footage, Rade went to check on Dylan. When he got to the room, he wasn't surprised to see that she was still resting. Watching the video was like reliving the event all over again. He hated seeing her like this. Dylan had put this incident behind her, but reviewing the video brought the horrible memories of that night back. Rade wasn't sure if Dylan would be able to get through this again. Even though she was a strong woman, and she would never let anything or anyone break her again, he knew this was something that would haunt her.

Rade left Dylan to rest while he went to his study to catch up on some work. He needed something to occupy his mind. Rade advised Richard to get the information to his friend at the NYPD minus the file of the night at *The Castle*. Once he had the evidence he needed against Chloe on that matter, he would let Richard know, but for now he couldn't risk the information going public.

As Rade was going through his emails a buzz came from his cell. It was Peter. Hopefully he had some news for him regarding Chloe.

"Hey Peter. I hope you have something positive to report considering the day I've had," Rade suggested.

"I'm afraid I don't. Ms. Dupree is MIA. We know she had a flight booked back to the states, but we have no information other than that. We checked her flight schedule and she should have been on the plane that landed about an hour ago at JFK. Her luggage arrived, but she didn't," Peter said. "Personally, I think she got wind that we got the information against her and she disappeared."

"Get with Richard. See if he can find out if she boarded the plane from London. They should have airport surveillance cameras. This should give us an idea where to look for her," Rade ordered. "If she's hiding out, sooner or later we will find her, especially in her condition."

"On it. I let you know what we come up with," Peter said before ending the call.

Darkness fell when Rade finally emerged from his study. He was drained from what the day brought. The bit of news that Peter shared, was no more comforting than a kick in the gut. It seemed no matter what Rade did, something always happened, and not in a good way. Walking to the kitchen, Rade pulled a bottle of wine from the wine cooler and popped the cork. Taking the bottle and a glass, he settled on the floor behind the couch. Propping against the back of the couch, Rade gazed out the floor-to-ceiling windows. *"How could a city with so much to offer be filled with so many fucked up people?"* Rade thought to himself as he poured the wine into his glass.

Lost in thought, Rade didn't hear Dylan come up beside him. Lowering her body next to his, she asked, "Tell me everything will be okay Rade."

Staring out the window, Rade didn't know how reassuring he could be knowing that he questioned that himself. "I can promise you that I will do everything I can to make sure it will be," Rade responded honestly, pulling Dylan onto his lap.

Looking into Dylan's eyes, Rade could see the uncertainty behind them. "Dylan, everything will work out," Rade said sternly, hoping it would ease her mind.

Cupping her face, Rade placed his lips on hers. Kissing her, he let her know that no matter what, he loved her with his very soul. Before he knew it, Dylan pulled him closer asserting the need she had for him. Breaking for a moment, Dylan lifted Rade's shirt up over his head exposing the rippled muscles beneath. Smoothing her hands down his chest, she took in every hard line of his body. With soft movements, she began at his neck and worked down placing sweet tender kisses on his smooth skin. Taking his taut nipple in her mouth, she lightly sucked the hard pebble while gently biting the hard peak. Unable to contain his own desire for her, Rade removed her shirt, throwing it onto the floor. He didn't care that the wine bottle and wine glass were now spilled over the white marble. Reaching behind her back, he unclasped her bra and threw it to the floor where her discarded shirt lay. With the Manhattan lights shining through the windows, Rade could see the perfect curves of her body. Pushing from the floor, Rade took her in his arms and carefully laid her on the floor. Kissing her, the heat from her desire radiated though his body. *How could any woman be more perfect than her?* Stroking her cheek, he looked into her eyes. "I love you so much Sweetness," Rade confessed.

Taking her lips, his passion ignited as he swept his tongue between her lips while gently nipping at her bottom lip. When her lips parted, he moved inside her warmth and consumed her fully. Mingling his tongue with hers, they moved rhythmically like a well orchestrated symphony. Concentrating on her, he removed her pants and tossed them next to the collection of clothing already discarded. She deserved to be worshiped and he was the only man who would ever do just that. She was his. Trailing tender kisses down her soft body, Rade accepted the soft whimpers as his cue to continue to delight her every way possible. With soft kisses, Rade tenderly took Dylan's nipple in his mouth and gently pulled on the taut peak with his teeth. Dylan's back arched off the floor, pushing her breast closer towards him, allowing him to cherish her in complete bliss.

Every inch of Dylan's body was electrified. Only Rade's touch could make her body react to the pull he had on her. Like a magnet drawing out every sensation she didn't even know her body could feel. The minute Rade's mouth found her clit, her heart raced as he freed the torment that had been building inside. Dylan's tears began to fall as her emotions finally gave way.

Rade was right there, absorbing the pain she kept buried for so long. With undeniable love, he kissed her trembling lips filling his own heart with her pain. "I will forever love you Sweetness," Rade whispered softly.

"Then show me Rade," Dylan murmured.

With utter tenderness, Rade spread Dylan's legs and gently entered her. His movements were slow. This was about showing his love and commitment to her. He needed this as much if not more than her. Rocking with unhurried movements, Rade needed to feel every inch of her. Increasing his movements, Dylan's body began to move against his. Rade could feel moisture build as her walls tightened without mercy around his throbbing cock. He knew his release was close, so when Dylan screamed his name with her explosion, Rade followed with violent force. "Fuck," Rade wailed as his seed spilled inside her.

* * * * *

Rade wasn't sure how much more bad news he could take. Not only had Chloe escaped sometime after the flight back to New York, the airport surveillance footage only picked up her boarding the plane. This only meant one thing, somehow Chloe got off the plane without being noticed. The only way she could have done that was through the door leading to the gate apron. Someone had to have been at the entry door to let her in. Since there were no cameras in that area, there was no way to know who it could have been. Rade only knew one thing, Chloe was somewhere and he needed to find her.

After hearing this information, Rade thought it best to not tell Dylan. The last thing she needed was to know that Chloe was nowhere to be found. Rade knew it would push her over the edge. Ending his call with Peter, Rade headed to the kitchen to make Dylan something special for breakfast. This was the time of day he enjoyed the most. Not only did he enjoy cooking, he also enjoyed spoiling Dylan. It was something he looked forward to and took advantage of every chance he got.

Pulling several ingredients from the refrigerator, Rade began preparing her meal. Turning on the Bose stereo system that his iPod was connected to, he began chopping to the beat of Maroon 5. Lost in the song, Rade forgot about his dilemma as the song took him to a different place. He was so in tune to the music that he didn't hear Dylan's screams in the background. When the song ended, it was then that he heard her pleas for help. Shutting off the burner, he rushed to the bedroom. Opening the door, Dylan wasn't in the bed, instead he found her on the floor with her knees pulled to her chest. She looked like a child huddled in the corner. Her eyes were red and her facial expression was hollow as she stared into space.

Rade was pretty sure seeing the video caused her to react the way she did. She was having a nightmare. Careful not to startle her, he walked up to her slowly and settled on the floor next to her. He didn't say anything as he watched Dylan rock back and forth. Trying to get her to focus on him, Rade gently placed his hand on her flushed cheek. "Dylan, look at me."

Aware of her surroundings, Dylan came out of her trance, focusing only on Rade. Dylan unlatched her arms that were tightly wrapped around her knees and clasped them tightly around Rade's neck. "It's okay Sweetness. I'm here. No one's ever going to hurt you again."

Looking up at his concerned face, Dylan faintly said, "It was so real Rade. Alex was here. I couldn't get away from him. He was too strong."

"It was only a bad dream Sweetness. He can never hurt you again," Rade assured her. "Let's get you off the floor." Rade gently took her arms that were still tightly wrapped around his neck and helped her from the floor. "Take a shower Sweetness and I will finish making breakfast."

Dylan looked up to Rade with terror in her eyes. It was a look he only saw one other time. The night at *The Castle*. Taking her by the hand, Rade led her into the bathroom and turned on the water to the shower. When it was hot enough, he carefully lifted her nightgown over her head and helped her inside. "Are you going to be okay?" Rade asked with concern.

"I think so, " Dylan answered softly.

"If you need me, just yell my name," Rade insisted, hesitant to leave her alone.

Heading back to the kitchen, Rade kept thinking about how Dylan looked sitting on the floor moments ago. He should have demanded that she not watch the footage. Dylan could be very stubborn and he knew he shouldn't have given into the argument.

Concentrating on something else, Rade proceeded where he left off in preparing Dylan's breakfast. After they were done eating, he vowed to take her away from the penthouse to a place where she could get her mind off of the events of that horrible night.

As they ate the wonderful meal he had prepared, Dylan's mind was elsewhere. Her thoughts went back to her life and how it came to this point. Even though she loved Rade with her mind, body and soul, she wondered if things would have been different if they hadn't met. Trying to push her thoughts aside, she looked over to Rade and asked, "Can we get out of here? I need a change of scenery."

"I was thinking the same thing Sweetness," Rade smiled as he took her hand and kissed it lightly.

Without cleaning up the dishes, Rade grabbed the keys to the Audi and they left the penthouse. Even though it was a two hour drive, he thought it would be nice to spend time at his home in the Hamptons. He knew Dylan always liked it there.

As they drove through the streets of Manhattan, Rade confessed, "I thought it would be nice to go to the house in the Hamptons. If that's okay with you?"

"I would love to go there. I love your home there," Dylan said enthusiastically.

"Good. You know, it's your home too," Rade informed her. Everything he had was hers.

"I've been doing some thinking Rade. With the amount of money you have, don't you think you should think about a pre-nup?" Dylan asked.

"Sweetness, I'm not going to have a pre-nup. If anything happens to us, everything I have wouldn't be worth having if I can't share it with you," Rade declared. "Where is all this coming from anyway?"

"I just thought it would be something that needed to be done," Dylan explained. "Aren't billionaires supposed to protect their assets?"

"Only if there is a threat that they would be taken to the cleaners Sweetness. It doesn't matter to me," Rade confessed as he pulled her hand to his lips and kissed it tenderly.

Reaching the gate two hours later, Rade punched in the code. He instructed his security staff to change the code to Dylan's birthday when he found out that Chloe was missing. The last thing he needed was for Chloe to show up uninvited again. The last time they were here, it wasn't under the best of circumstances. It was when Dylan learned that Chloe was pregnant with his child.

Rade drove up the tree lined drive and pulled in front of the huge house. Dylan always questioned the purpose for the enormous house, but now it didn't matter because once she and Rade were married, she planned to fill each room with an abundance of children. She and Rade never really talked about having children. Before they got out of the car, Dylan placed her hand on his hand.

"Rade, I know that we never really discussed this, but I was just curious, it's not like it's super important, but it kind of is, I mean if we…."

"Dylan, just say it," Rade said, concerned about her inability to get to the point.

"Okay, so here's the deal. I want lots of kids and we never really talked about it so it only makes sense to ask, do you even want kids?" Dylan asked hesitantly.

"No kids Dylan. End of story," Rade barked.

"But…"

"End of story Dylan. Let's just have a good time while we're here," Rade said avoiding the subject.

Dylan didn't know why Rade was so set on not having any children, especially since he was going to be a father in five months. Maybe it was just with her that he didn't want to have kids.

Instead of waiting for Rade to accompany her inside the house, Dylan went round the back. Walking down the flagstone steps, she made her way to the beach. Given what she just learned, she wasn't sure that she could marry a man who didn't want to have children. It was a part of being together, starting a family, getting old, having grandchildren. It was all a part of life, how it was meant to be.

Staring out at the blue ocean, Dylan didn't hear Rade come up behind her. Pulling her to his body, he placed his chin on her shoulder. "Sweetness, I don't want you to be angry with my decision not have any children, but I hope that you can accept the reason I don't. With what happened to Isaac, I can't risk it happening to our children," Rade spilled.

"But you're going to have a child with Chloe, why would this be any different?" Dylan quizzed.

"Because, I had no control over her pregnancy. My only obligation to that child is to make sure it is well provided for. Nothing more," Rade affirmed.

"But it's your child Rade. How could you not love him or her?" Dylan couldn't believe the words that were coming from him. Even though the circumstance behind him becoming a father was less than consensual, it is nonetheless, still his child.

"I won't allow myself to get close enough to feel that hurt again Dylan. Let's go back to the house," Rade said as he held out his hand so he could lead her back.

"I think I'd like to say here for a little while longer," Dylan dared, going against his wishes. She needed a few moments alone so she could sort out her feelings. *Would she be able to share a life with the man she loved knowing that they would never share the joy of having children together? Was she willing to give up her dream of motherhood?*

Chapter Twenty

When Dylan finally came back to the house, she no more had the answers she needed than when she walked a mile down the coastline. She didn't want to think about anything anymore. Her mind was completely drained. Opening the patio door, Dylan saw Rade leaning against the fireplace, where a fire was already going. Even though it was still September, there was a chill in the air. Fall was right around the corner. Approaching him, she could see that he had a drink in his hand.

"I'll take one of those," Dylan said, standing just a few feet from where he was standing.

"I was wondering when you were going to come inside," Rade said, walking over to the liquor cart. Removing the top from the crystal decanter, he poured a shot of scotch into a tumbler for her.

Handing Dylan the drink, Dylan said, "Thank you." Needing to let him know how she felt, she began, "About what you said, I understand how you feel, but can we not close the book on this discussion and just save it for another time." Dylan knew that if she could discuss it with him again once they were married and his child was born, she would have a better chance to argue with him about having children of their own.

"I don't want to fight with you about this Dylan, so yes, I will allow this to be brought up at a different time. Besides, I brought you here to get your mind off of things and not add to them," Rade confessed.

Even though Dylan's mind was off of the video, something else was consuming her thoughts. Worrying about whether or not children were ever going to bless their relationship was no better than thinking about that horrible night. Sitting on the couch in front of the fireplace, Dylan drank her scotch. Feeling the burn of the amber liquid, Dylan welcomed the taste as it began dulling the pain she felt in her heart. Tossing back the last of her drink, she held up her glass for a refill.

Rade walked over to her with the decanter and filled the tumbler about a quarter of the way full. Taking a seat beside her, he gazed at the fireplace and watched as the flames danced in the confined area. Looking over to Dylan, he took the glass from her and ordered, "Remove your clothing."

It didn't matter how she felt, Rade always had this pull on her that caused her to do whatever he said. Standing to her feet, she began peeling the clothing off her body. Starting with her shirt, she slowly lifted it up over her head. Leaving her bra in place, she began unzipping the zipper on her skirt and lowered it slowly down her legs. With her dressed in only her bra and panties, Dylan stared at Rade.

"All of it Sweetness," Rade commanded, taking in her beautiful curves.

Dylan reached behind her and unclasped her bra, lowering the straps down her arms; she did it hesitantly, wanting to tease Rade by removing it slow and seductively. Patience, that's what he was always telling her. Once her bra was off, Dylan slowly placed her thumbs through the lacy straps of her panties and gingerly began gliding them down her silky legs. She could tell Rade was getting frustrated with her little strip tease. Before she had her panties down her legs, he pulled her to him and abruptly placed her over his thighs so that her stomach was resting across his upper legs. With her panties around her thighs, he wrapped the thin material around his hand and ripped the material off her body. Dylan knew that was going to leave a mark.

"I know what you're doing Sweetness." Rade smirked, laying his hand across her bottom before Dylan could protest.

"Ouch," Dylan yelped.

"That's for making me wait," Rade said as he planted another swat to her ass. "And this is for teasing me with your gorgeous body."

Dylan knew that Rade couldn't see her face as she smiled to herself. She knew exactly what she was doing. Feeling his hands on her body, she knew she was soaked.

"Looks like you're enjoying your punishment," Rade advised as he ran his finger between her slick folds. "On your knees Sweetness."

Dylan pushed off of Rade and knelt between his legs. Watching him, she knew what he wanted. Licking her bottom lip, she waited for him to lower his pants down his muscular legs. Fully erect, his cock popped free from his boxers sending her arousal in motion. Placing her hands on his knees, she brought her body forward. Slowly, she glided her hands up his upper legs until she was met with the base of his shaft. Taking hold of his cock in one hand, she cupped his balls with the other. The feel of his hard shaft felt like velvet in her small hand. Stroking him lightly, she began placing wet kisses up his leg as she alternated from the right leg to the left one. When she reached the base of his shaft, she lifted his balls and began kissing lightly at the soft skin. Moving upward, she continued her assault, lapping her tongue around his girth. Like a lollypop, Dylan licked and sucked him to no end. Reaching the top, she placed her mouth over the head and lowered her mouth just enough to feel the tip hit the back of her throat. She loved the way he tasted. Increasing her movements, Dylan pushed her mouth lower and retreated slowly, sucking him until her cheeks collapsed.

"God Sweetness, I love your mouth," Rade moaned.

Dylan continued her ministration. She knew he was close. She could feel the throbbing of his cock the more she went down on him. With a loud pop, Rade pulled her from his length and placed his hands under her arms, lifting her onto his lap. Positioning her over his engorged hard-on, he lowered her body on to his. She was so tight for him. Just the feel of his cock inside her sweet pussy made his control go out the window. Placing his hands on her hips, he moved her up and down as he watched his cock pump in and out of her. This was the biggest turn on for him. Watching her pink folds open for him as he glided deeper inside her.

Moving his hands up her body, Rade cupped the tender skin of her nipples drawing them closer to him. With his mouth, he kissed the taut peak, lapping the bud with his tongue while nipping lightly. Rade could feel the strength of her walls tighten harder around him. Holding his control, he whispered, "Come for me Sweetness." Dylan's gate opened coating his cock with her sweet juices. Seconds later, Rade expelled his own juices inside her, filling her tight channel with his seed.

*****

It was late by the time they went to sleep, so it was no surprise that Dylan woke to the alarm clock exhausted. "Rise and shine sleepyhead," Rade coaxed as he rose from the bed.

"Just a few more minutes," Dylan gruffly moaned.

"Nope. No can do. If you want to make it to work on time, we will need to leave in an hour. I'll get coffee ready. Up and Adam," Rade demanded in a cheery voice.

"Urrrr," Dylan groaned as she pushed herself from the bed.

Showered and as ready as she was going to be, Dylan headed down the stairs to the kitchen. Rade was already seated at the table reading his morning paper with a cup of coffee in hand. One thing Dylan knew for sure, she would never get tired of seeing him half naked every morning reading the stock report. His body held so much power. Power that Dylan was more than familiar with.

Grabbing her own cup of java, Dylan walked over to where he was sitting and pulled up a chair next to him. Without looking, Rade said, "You smell good enough to eat."

Dylan swatted his paper causing his face to come into view. Greeted by his smile, she had to find out what put him in such a good mood. "So are you going to tell me why you're so happy this morning?"

"You Sweetness. Only you," Rade confessed as he pushed from the table and rose to his feet. "I'm going to take a quick shower, then we can leave," he added as her placed a light kiss on the top of her head.

Dylan sat at the table a while longer while she waited for Rade to finish his shower. It was a beautiful day outside as she gazed out the window. She would have loved to play hooky today from work, but she had an important meeting with Keeve and Mason that she couldn't miss. With everything that went on with Wayne Morris, they needed to think about finding another person to run the Spectrum office in LA. It was decided that, with the amount of exposure LA provided, that it would be beneficial to keep the Spectrum facility open. The new facility in New York was already underway. Hopefully within a year, it would be fully operational. The multi-million dollar building would be bringing in over a hundred jobs, which would boost New York's economy. Even though Dylan was looking forward to it being finished, she wasn't looking forward to the ciaos that came with hiring people to staff the new facility.

The drive back to Manhattan was uneventful. Most of Dylan's ride was spent sleeping. The silence left Rade with time to think about what Dylan had asked for. Having children was the furthest thing from his mind when he asked Dylan to marry him. He couldn't think about the possibility of having children with Dylan. Not only because of what happened to his brother, but also the lifestyle that a child would be born into. Even though he told Dylan that the D/s lifestyle wasn't important to him and that he could live without it, he was only fooling himself. This was what he knew and what he was accustom to. When Dylan agreed to let him train her, it was like he could have his cake and eat it too. Adding a child to the mix, would complicate things.

Just outside of New York, Dylan began to wake-up. The two hour nap made her feel more rested than she did this morning. Pulling up to the BlackStone building Rade turned to her and said, "I have a few things to take care of at the office, but I should be back in time for the meeting."

"Okay," Dylan answered with a faint smile.

Just as she pulled the handle on the door, Rade lightly grabbed her arm causing her to turn his way. Leaning over, he gently placed a soft kiss on her lips. Right when Dylan was ready for more, Rade pulled way. Placing his hand on her cheek he affectionately said, "Love you."

Those words melted Dylan's heart as she countered. "Love you too."

The meeting was in full swing by the time Rade arrived. He could hear the bickering and yelling down the hall. Opening the door, Dylan was the only one yelling while pointing her finger at Keeve. Rade smiled as he watched her argue with the two men. It was no surprise to Rade, given Dylan's fiery personality.

"I'm not going agree to that Keeve. Are you on drugs? Clearly you aren't thinking straight," Dylan belted.

"What's going on? I always miss all the fun," Rade interjected, watching three sets of eyes glare at him.

"This is far from fun, Rade," Dylan began. "Keeve has it in his head that I should be the one to run the Spectrum facility in LA. I think he has gone completely nuts."

Rade had to agree with Dylan, but he was still curious as to why Keeve felt so strongly about it. "Keeve, why would you want Dylan to run the facility in LA?"

Dylan looked over to Rade, perturbed that he would even consider asking such a question. "Rade are you serious?" Dylan said, giving Rade an evil eye.

"Let's hear him out Dylan. I'm just trying to understand what his thought process is," Rade confessed, knowing perfectly well he would never agree to Dylan moving to LA. Not only because he wasn't willing to leave New York, but also because he already had someone in mind to head the office.

Rade knew that Dylan was on pins and needles wondering what Rade was thinking as he listened to the bullshit Keeve was feeding him. "I'm not going to stand here and listen to this. I have more important things to do," Dylan said, aggravated with all three of them, even though Mason wasn't chiming in on the conversation, he looked every bit as guilty.

All three men watched Dylan walk out of the board room. Rade pulled up a chair and began pitching to the guys. "Okay, here's the deal. There's no way I can allow Dylan to relocate to LA. I know you guys want her there, but I have a better solution. I have a guy in mind that is more than qualified for the job. He's coming to New York at the end of the week. His name is Logan Fisher. I think you guys will be please with his credentials once you meet him."

Rade ended the meeting with Keeve and Mason and made his way to Dylan's office where he knew she would be stewing. He kept her in the dark long enough. It was time he let her in on his plan. Knocking lightly on the door, he pushed it open. With her eyes drawn on him, he entered her office and pulled up a seat in front of her desk. Crossing his leg over, resting his ankle on the opposite knee, Rade looked at Dylan. "Don't be upset Sweetness. There's no way I would agree to have you go to LA to head the Spectrum office. I already have someone else in mind. I'm sorry I didn't let you know before, but the look on your face was priceless," Rade admitted with a smile.

Dylan didn't know what could have been so amusing. She wasn't sure if she should be angry with him or relived that she wasn't going to California. Walking around her desk she plopped her ass on his lap and wrapped her arms around his neck. "That was pretty underhanded of you Rade. You're lucky I'm too tired to fight with you."

"Good. How about I pick you up later and we spend a quiet evening at home?" Rade suggested.

"That sound wonderful," Dylan agreed as she lowered her lips to his, kissing him passionately before leaving his lap and getting back to work.

Rade pulled her close to him one last time, taking her lips with his. Biting her lower lip, he coaxed her lips to part, willing him to gain entry into her warmth. Mingling his tongue with hers, he deepened his assault on her mouth. Dylan was lost in his touch. There was always something about his kiss that sent her body on arousal overload. In a breathy whisper she said, "If I am going to be ready for you later, we better stop, otherwise I won't be able to get anything done."

"Rade pulled back from her with a smile. "Just this once Sweetness," he declared setting her on her feet, but not before giving her a light spank on the ass.

Rade left Dylan's office sporting a hard-on the size of Mount Everest. Adjusting his pants, Rade moved his fully erect cock to a more comfortable position. He was hoping that Jessica and

Lucy would be away from their station. The last thing he wanted was to make small talk with them in his current condition. His prayer was answered as he quickly dipped into the elevator with a grin on his face. Leaving Dylan's office left him not only in an uncomfortable state, but also gave him inspiration on how the evening would go once he had her home. It had been awhile since they played and he was more than ready to appease his desire for her.

* * * * *

Dylan didn't know what she was thinking, but she would have been better off taking advantage of Rade's bout of affection. After he left the office, there was no use in getting anything done. The only thing on her mind was the thought of having Rade deep inside her. When she looked at the clock and it was approaching five, she couldn't be happier. Grapping her purse and her coat, she turned off her lights and headed to Keeve's office to let him know she was leaving for the night.

Right on time, Richard was waiting for Dylan in front of the BlackStone building. As soon as he saw her, he exited the Bentley and rounded the hood to assist her in. As he opened the door, Dylan was greeted with the most gorgeous sight. Rade was sitting in the back seat thumbing through emails on his phone. Sliding in beside him, Dylan took the phone from his hand and tossed it aside. She wanted his undivided attention. Taking hold of his chin, she turned his face so that he was facing her. Without hesitation she placed her soft lips over his and whispered, "I missed you." Even though they had seen each other less than four hours ago, her body had been on fire all day just thinking about how much she wanted him.

Pulling her onto his lap, Rade deepened the kiss as he ran his fingers through her thick red locks. He couldn't wait until the day when she was officially his. Unable to resist her, he tugged at the hem of her blouse freeing it from her skirt. Shifting her body

245

slightly, he began maneuvering his hand up the inside of her shirt to her abdomen until he reached her glorious mound. Releasing her breast from the lacy cup of her bra, he began caressing the taut peak. Aware that Richard was in the driver's seat, Rade shielded his movements so that Richard was none the wiser as to what was taking place in the back seat.

Sending Dylan in flight, Rade pinched the hard bud. Dylan's soft whimper said it all. Lowering his head, Rade whispered softly, "You need to be quiet Sweetness; otherwise Richard will know what's going on."

Trying to tame her desire, Dylan placed her hand over her mouth. It wasn't until Rade slipped his free hand beneath her skirt that she lost it. She knew that if he continued to rub her clit, she would be coming like a roar of thunder. "Rade, I can't hold back," Dylan moaned as quietly as she could.

Placing his mouth over hers, Rade muffled the scream that was going to escape Dylan's mouth. Unable to hold back any longer, Dylan broke free and yelled, "Oh God!"

"Is everything okay back there," Richard said concerned.

Looking at each other, Dylan began to giggle as Rade said, "Everything is perfect."

Rade worked to get Dylan's clothing adjusted while she tried to compose herself. This was the first time she had made-out in the back seat of a car knowing that someone else could hear what was going on. She never thought she would ever be that adventurous, but being with Rade, anything was possible.

Arriving at the penthouse with no other incidences, Rade and Dylan exited the SUV. It wasn't until they reached the elevator that they continued where they left off. Rade had Dylan's body up against the wall the minute the elevator door shut. Wrangling her hands through his hair, Dylan used what little strength she had left to pull Rade to her. They were all over each other as the car rose. Rade's lips were on hers, thrusting his tongue between her swollen lips. When Dylan parted for him, he mingled his tongue with hers like there was no tomorrow. Grabbing her ass, he lifted her from the floor and guided his hand beneath her skirt. With one pull of her panties between his fingers, he had the delicate material completely off. Holding her body to the wall, Rade began unbuckling his belt with his free hand. When his cock was free from the barrier of his pants, he positioned it between Dylan's slick folds and entered her channel with no mercy. She was so wet and ready for him that going slow wasn't an option for him. He needed to be hard and rough with her. It was something that he had craved for a long time.

"I won't be able to go slow Sweetness," Rade groaned.

"Take me however you need," Dylan panted.

The need for each other didn't end once the doors to the elevator opened. Setting Dylan back on her feet, they were at each other, removing every layer of clothing they had on. Unable to break away from each other, their desire continued down the hall. Leaving a trail of clothing on the marble floor, Rade and Dylan finally made it to the bedroom. Something unleashed inside of them. The passion and love they had for each other grew stronger with every kiss, every touch they laid upon each other. Cupping Dylan by the ass, Rade gently laid her on the fluffy comforter. Taking his tie that he held on to during the shedding of their clothing, Rade began wrapping it around Dylan's wrist. Once he felt it was secure, he ordered, "Roll over on your stomach Sweetness." Dylan did as she was told and carefully rolled onto her stomach. With Rade kneeling behind her, he pulled up on her hips and guided her to her knees while pushing between her shoulder blades to keep her head lowered onto the pillow.

Dylan's perfect ass, on perfect display with her pink folds glistening with her juices caused his cock to throb. Taking his finger, he coated the tip with her wetness and gently glided toward her small pucker. Her soft moan signaled her hesitation. It wasn't like she hadn't had him there before, but it had been awhile and she knew it would take a little persuasion for her to relax enough to take him again. Lowering his body over hers, he skimmed his lips over her earlobe and whispered, "Relax Sweetness."

With reassurance, Dylan began to slowly relax. Dipping his finger inside her tight passage to the first digit, Rade could feel her tightness grip his finger. With a little more pressure he slid further inside her. Slowly Dylan began to relax and accept more of his finger. With his finger fully inside her tight channel, he began adding another. Rade could feel Dylan push against him, her body needing more of what he was giving her. Angling her hips a little higher, he positioned his cock between her folds and slowly began pushing inside her . Giving him the resistance that he needed, he inched his way deeper and deeper inside. "God Dylan, you're so fucking tight and even tighter with my fingers up you beautiful ass," Rade said, moaning his words as he pressed deeper and deeper inside. As he pushed inside her, his finger drove deeper into her tight pucker giving him an even tighter hold on his cock. Dylan's scream of pleasure bounced off the walls signaling the euphoric delivery of her release with Rade close behind.

As they settled together in each other's arms Dylan admitted, "That was amazing. I will never be able to get enough of this."

"It was pretty amazing," Rade agreed pulling her closer to him.

"Rade?" Dylan began as she pushed from the bed so she could look him in the eye. "I want to go back to *The Castle*. We haven't talked about it much, but I really want to go back."

"Dylan, do you really think you're ready to go back there?" Rade questioned.

"I'm as ready as I'm going to be. The longer I wait, the less likely I'll go. I need to do this for me, for us," Dylan argued.

"Okay Sweetness. When do you want to go?" Rade asked unsure if he was ready to take her back to the place that held so much pain for her.

"Can we go tomorrow night?" Dylan requested. "We don't have to do anything necessarily. I just want to know that I can go back there. If I feel comfortable enough, then we can play."

"Tomorrow night it is then. On one condition," Rade began. "The minute you feel uncomfortable, we leave."

Chapter Twenty-One

"We need to meet. I'm done with this shit. I need her out of the picture once and for all," Chloe hissed. Chloe was done playing games. Rade may have been engaged to Dylan, but he would be forever hers.

"Where do you want to meet?"

"There's a spot just outside of New York City. It's deserted so no one will see us. The last thing I need is to be found," Chloe admitted.

"Yeah, you and me both. I won't take another risk like I did at the airport."

"Sorry about that. I didn't have anyone else I could call," Chloe advised.

* * * * *

Even though Dylan woke to a gloomy windy day, she was excited. Tonight was the night that Rade would be taking her back to *The Castle*. Even though she was a little nervous about how she would react, her stomach was doing summersaults knowing what could happen.

Rade was sleeping soundly beside Dylan. This was a nice surprise for Dylan. Usually when she woke in the morning, he was already awake or gone. Rolling over, Dylan nuzzled up to Rade's warm body wanting to feel his skin on hers. The best part of her morning was waking up with Rade next to her. Feeling him stir, Dylan began kissing his hard body, beginning with his exposed chest. God, how she loved the lines of his muscles. Kissing the smooth hard skin, Dylan worked her way down the hard plain of his incredible chest. Placing her mouth over his nipple, Dylan began sucking and licking the hard disc. As she continued her assault, his hands went to the nap of her neck until he ran them through her thick hair. Lowering her hand down his ripped stomach, Dylan wasn't surprised to find that he was hard. Kissing her way down his abs, she stopped at the base of his cock and began tenderly caressing the smooth skin with her tongue, making sure every inch was given attention. With no hesitation, Dylan slowly worked her mouth to the tip of his cock where his arousal was beginning to take hold. Taking his shaft into her mouth, Dylan began enjoying her morning indulgence. Sucking and licking, she could feel the throbbing of Rade's cock between her lips. The more she sucked the harder he became. Slowly inching down his shaft, she used her free hand to gently cup his balls, giving them a tender caress. A small groan escaped Rade's mouth as Dylan felt the movement of his hip against her mouth. She knew he was close when the grip he had on her hair began to tighten.

Dylan could feel her own arousal fill her body. Taking Rade deeper inside her mouth, she could feel the onset of his release as the movement of his hips increased. "Fuck, what are you doing to me Sweetness," Rade moaned with pleasure. Lifting his shoulders off of the bed, Rade wrapped his arms around Dylan's waist and pulled her away from his cock. He needed to be inside her. Flipping her over onto the bed, he pressed his body on top of hers and entered her tight pussy. Nothing could take the place of her tight cunt. Not even the feel of her mouth on his cock. Pumping inside her with eagerness, Rade let his semen spill inside her.

Still hard and needing more, Rade pulled out of her dripping channel and flipped Dylan onto her stomach. He wanted to see her pretty little cunt as he thrust deep inside her. Entering her, he snaked his hand under her stomach and glided it between her legs. Finding her clit, Rade began circling it with his finger. A small whimper sounded as Dylan pushed her hips back and forth mimicking the movement of Rade's cock driving inside her. Dylan's did know how much longer she could hold out. Holding onto the pillow with everything she had, she tried to control her need to let go, but it was no use. The harder Rade pumped inside her the harder it was to hold back. "Rade," she breathed. Rade knew she was close. With a few more hard thrusts he whispered, "Let go Sweetness," As soon as those words left Rade's mouth, Dylan's body let go the pleasure she held in. Doubling in strength, Rade's release greeted her with the same force.

Collapsing on the bed, Dylan took in a deep breath as she waited for her body to come down from her explosive orgasm. Rade managed to collapse beside her. The last thing he wanted was to smother her. Rolling towards each other, they began to laugh.

"Wow," Dylan said softly. "What a way to wake up in the morning."

Leaning into her and kissing her tenderly on the lips, Rade said, "No argument there."

Pushing up from the bed, Rade held out his hand. Dylan placed her hand in his. It amazed her how strong his hand was and how gentle it could be. Pulling Dylan from the bed Rade said, "Shower."

Dylan nodded and followed Rade into the bathroom. As they stood in front of their designated sinks which meant Rade was on the right and Dylan on the left, they both began brushing their teeth. Dylan would love for it to be like this with Rade every morning. She hated when he was gone in the morning. This was something she loved sharing with him. Turning on the water to the shower, Rade entered the shower first with Dylan close behind. Dylan washed her hair while Rade scrubbed her body clean. When he was done, they switched places and Dylan did the same for him. This was something that Dylan could get use to.

* * * * *

Rade dropped Dylan off at work making sure that she got inside the building safely. Since he drove her to work. He called Peter to make sure he would be at BlackStone in time to stay with Dylan and make sure she remained safe. With Michael still out there and Chloe missing, now more than ever he needed to make sure Dylan was protected.

Heading to his office, there was a call coming in. Syncing his Bluetooth, Rade answered the call.

"Matheson," he said as he greeted the caller.

"Hi Rade, it's Dane. I just wanted to let you know that all the preparations for tonight have been made," he confirmed.

"Good. What about the added security?" Rade asked as he pulled into the RIM Global parking garage.

"Done. I requested that Peter and his men secure the building. I know that you trust them, so I got with Richard to make sure they were available."

"I do trust them. They are very good at what they do," Rade confirmed.

"Well, I'll let you go. See you tonight then," Dane said before ending the call.

With Peter and his men watching *The Castle,* Rade had every confidence that this evening was going to go as planned. Rade knew that Dylan would appreciate the extra security. After meeting with Dane and looking over the security camera, it was confirmed that Chloe was the one who lead Dylan to the dungeon. With this bit of evidence, the video of Dylan's assault didn't need to be handed over to the police.

Parking the Martin in his designated spot, Rade grabbed his briefcase and headed to the elevators. When he entered his office, Gwen was already seated at her desk working away.

"Good Morning Gwen," Rade said warmly.

"Good morning Mr. Matheson," Gwen replied. "I have your schedule ready for you. Not too much for today. Just a couple of meetings and a conference call."

"Excellent. I was planning on leaving early today," Rade confirmed as he took the schedule form Gwen.

Gwen was the best secretary that he could have asked for. She had put up with a lot through the years. Rade sometimes wondered why she continued to work for him. Leaving her to her work, Rade headed to his office. Just as he was getting settled behind his desk a text came in on his phone.

Dylan: Thank you for a wonderful morning.

Rade: You're most welcome Sweetness.

Dylan: I wanted to know if there is anything special that I need to wear tonight.

Rade: You should be asking what you shouldn't wear tonight.

Dylan: OK, I'll bite. What shouldn't I wear tonight?

Rade: Underwear. I'll just rip them off anyway.

Dylan: Of course you will. Love you.

Rade: Love you too Sweetness

Rade smiled as he placed his phone on his desk. Just thinking about Dylan with no underwear made him hard. He needed to think of something else. The stack of files Gwen left on his desk to review for his meetings should do it.

After the last text from Rade, Dylan couldn't stop thinking about this evening and what it would bring. She knew that Rade wouldn't let anything bad happen to her. After what happened last time, he assured her that he wasn't going to take any chances. Knowing that there would be extra security, made Dylan feel a lot better. Rade also swore that he was never going to leave her side. That alone confirmed his commitment to keep her safe.

Dylan's thought were interrupted by a knock on her door. "Come in," Dylan said.

Mason's head peeked in behind the door. "Are you busy? I just needed to visit with you for a minute."

"No, of course not," Dylan replied watching Mason take a seat.

"I just wanted to tell you that Keeve and I spoke and we would like you to head the hiring for the new Spectrum facility."

"Wait, what? Why me? I don't know the first thing about hiring people," Dylan asked confused.

"We've spoken to Rade, and he thinks it would be a great idea. All of us will be available for you during the process. You won't be alone in this," Mason confirmed.

"You guy's sure do have a lot of confidence in me. First the transfer, now this. You know I'll do anything to help out, but taking on this is a big responsibility Mason," Dylan stated nervously, concerned about what he was asking of her.

"You'll be fine, and like I said, we'll all be here to help you," Mason admitted.

"Okay, I hope you guys know what you're getting into," Dylan accepted hesitantly, unsure of what she was getting herself into.

After Mason left her office, Dylan was worried about taking on the responsibility of hiring the staff for the Spectrum facility. She needed to talk to Rade about this new task given to her. She knew that he would be in meetings all day and didn't want to disturb him. She would need to discuss it with him when he picked her up from work, which reminded her that she needed to get some work done otherwise she wasn't going to be getting out of there in time for their date at *The Castle*.

It was close to five and Dylan's mind was swimming with numbers and graphs. She knew that Rade would be picking her up at 5:30 to take her to dinner and then to the private club. With all the work she'd done, she thought it was time to quit. This would give her time to freshen up and clear her mind. The only thing she wanted to think about was Rade and what he was going to do to her.

* * * * *

Rade took Dylan to a local restaurant before their evening of pleasure. The food was exceptional, but with what was in store, Dylan had a hard time eating. Her nerves were going a mile a minute. Paying the check, Rade took her by the hand and led her out of the restaurant to where his car was parked. Assisting her in, he made sure she was buckled in. Dylan felt like a little kid the way he was always fussing over her.

"Rade, you need to stop treating me like I'm going to break," Dylan exclaimed.

"I can't help it Sweetness. You mean everything to me," Rade confessed.

Rade knew this was going to be a big night for Dylan. It was going to test her limits. He hoped that she wasn't taking on more than she could. With the memory of what happened to her so fresh in her mind, the last thing he wanted was for her to close herself off from him.

"I know, and you mean everything to me. Everything will be fine. With all the security and you with me, nothing bad is going to happen," Dylan said convincingly.

Rade looked to Dylan leaning over and kissing her on the lips. Her softness enveloped him as he slid his tongue between her parted lips. Placing his hand on her cheek, Rade pulled her closer as he deepened the kiss. Dylan moaned softly feeling the heat rooting inside her. Tearing his lips from hers, Rade placed his forehead against hers.

"We better get going Sweetness," Rade said regretfully.

Turning on the engine and putting the car in gear, Rade pulled away from the curb and began heading to *The Castle*. As Rade drove, he looked over to Dylan several times making sure she didn't seem uneasy. It was hard telling how she felt.

"Are you doing alright Sweetness?" Rade asked with concern.

Looking over to him, Dylan replied, "I'm fine."

Rade wasn't convinced that she was. It may have been the nervousness of what the night would bring or the fear of going back to the place that held bad memories. Either way, as much as he wanted to please Dylan, he wasn't sure if this was the right thing to do.

"We can turn around and go another time," Rade suggested hoping she would change her mind.

"No Rade. I want to do this. It's important," Dylan objected.

Pulling up in front of *The Castle*, Dylan saw the fountain she remembered. It still left her breathless. Dylan also noticed that the parking lot where the limos and expensive cars were usually parked, was mostly bare.

Turning off the engine, Rade looked over to Dylan and asked, "Are you ready?"

"I'm ready," Dylan replied, hoping Rade didn't hear her uncertainty.

Opening the door, Rade exited the car and rounded the hood to Dylan's side. Assisting her out, Rade took her hand. Leading her to the iron door, Rade took in a deep breath. He was more nervous than he should have been. He had been here on more than one occasion. There was no reason for him to be nervous, other than worrying about what this place was going to do to Dylan.

The iron door opened with a small creak before Rade had a chance to open it himself. On the other side was Dane. Dylan recognized him from the last time they were there. Dylan remembered him being a gentleman when it came to her care. Dylan still felt a little embarrassed by what happened. Even though she knew it wasn't her fault, she knew that Dane was the one who assisted her out of the dungeon. He also saw her naked before Tessa wrapped her in the black cape.

"Rade, good to have you back," Dane said, shaking Rade's hand.

"Good to be back," Rade replied.

"Dylan, you look as lovely as ever," Dane complimented as he placed a small kiss on her cheek.

Dylan smiled back at him, comforted by his kindness. Maybe this wasn't going to be as bad as she thought. With everyone looking out for her, she knew she had nothing to worry about.

"Your room is ready Rade," Dane said looking back at him.

Closing the heavy door, Dane led them upstairs to one of the private rooms. Standing in front of a door, Dane turned the knob and pushed the door open. Rade ushered Dylan in first before entering himself. Giving Dane a quick nod, Rade closed the door to the room.

Dylan took in her surroundings. This room was nothing like the one she had been in before. Where the dungeon room was cold and musty, this one was warm and inviting. With the candles lit thought out the room, Dylan felt her body begin to relax. Looking around the room, Dylan spotted a cross just like the one she had seen in the dungeon. There were also ropes dangling from a bar that was secured by bolts on the ceiling. There was also a king sized bed draped in red satin and black pillows. It looked to be very comfortable. The one thing Dylan didn't see was the sawhorse like contraption, which she later found out was a spanking bench. There also was no table displaying various sex toys. Rade must have planned their evening down to the last detail, knowing that these things could trigger flashbacks for her.

Coming up behind Dylan, Rade slid his hand under Dylan's skirt. Feeing her bare skin he smile and said, "You will be greatly rewarded for following orders Sweetness. I want you to strip."

Dylan could feel the flutter of excitement taking residence in her stomach. With shaky hands, she began removing her clothing. When she was fully naked, she toed the heel of her shoe ready to remove them as well. She was stopped abruptly when she heard Rade say, "Leave those on."

Standing in front of him fully naked, aside from her high heel shoes, Dylan lowered her eyes. Taking her hand, Rade led her over to where the St. Andrews cross was.

"Turn and face the cross Sweetness with your legs spread apart," he ordered.

Dylan did as she was told and turned to face the cross. With her legs spread, she could feel the leather cuff wrap around first her right and then left ankle. When her ankles were secured, Rade lifted her right hand, kissing her palm and placing the cuff above her head around her wrist. He took extra care in securing the other wrist as well. With her body restrained spread eagle, Rade asked softly, "Are you good?"

CHAPTER TWENTY-ONE

"Yes," Dylan replied.

"Yes, what Sweetness?" Rade commanded as he landed a soft spank to her backside.

"Yes Sir." Dylan corrected herself.

"Good girl. Remember if at any time you feel uncomfortable, you will need to use your safeword. Do you remember it?" Rade whispered in her ear.

"Yes."

Dylan couldn't see what was going on behind her, but she could here Rade. Feeling him behind her, she took in a deep breath. When a black scarf was presented in front of her eyes, Dylan said nervously, "No blindfold sir, please."

Rade stepped back from Dylan throwing the scarf on the floor. "No blindfold Sweetness," Rade said, reassuring her. The last thing he wanted was to make her feel uncomfortable. She had been bound and blindfolded the last time she was here. This was something he should have anticipated would make her uncomfortable.

Walking over to the small table, he grabbed a flogger. With intricate movements, he began gliding the soft leather down her back and over her bottom, before he landed a gentle swat to her cheeks. Dylan whimpered softly at the sudden strike. It didn't hurt, it just caught her off guard.

Moving closer, Rade placed light kisses on her shoulder, down her back to the two small dimples above her butt. Dylan's body shuttered at the light touch. Placing his hand between her legs, Rade could feel the moisture that had already coated her sex. With his finger, he rubbed it along her seam and plunged it inside her wet pussy. A small gasp filled the air as Dylan's desire began taking control of her body. Slipping another finger inside her, Rade began pumping them in and out of her tight channel making sure to hit her special spot. Dylan's moans of desire grew the more Rade played with her. Unable to hold back any longer Dylan's voice rang. "Rade, please."

Removing his fingers from her tight channel, Rade backed away from her. Her body was electrified. This is how he wanted her. Bound and hungry for him. Transfixed on her beauty, Rade unzipped his pants and pulled his cock from his boxers. Stroking his cock while he took her in, he needed more than what he was getting. He had deprived himself long enough. Stepping closer to her, He glided his hands down her back, stopping to tweak her nipples on the way down. Dylan's sensitized body jolted as Rade pulled her nipples into hard peaks. Moving down her body, Rade felt the pulsating sensation in his shaft. It was Dylan that did this to him. She was the only woman who could make him feel this way. Unable to hold back, Rade plunged his fingers between her folds gathering enough of her juices to coat his fingers. Positioning his cock at her entrance, he slowly began entering her tight channel while his wet fingers searched for her tight pucker. With his cock buried inside her, he pushed his index finger inside her pucker. Her body tensed sending a heighted grip on his cock. He needed her to relax. With his free hand, he reached around and placed his hand over her mound while taking his fingers and rubbing them against her swollen clit. He wanted to have every part of her. Soon she would be screaming his name.

Once Dylan was relaxed, he pushed his finger further inside her. "God Sweetness, you feel so good," Rade confessed, pushing deeper inside her wet pussy.

"Rade, I need to..." Dylan moan as her control tool over and her body exploded with fury.

"Shame, shame Sweetness. That's going to cost you," Rade warned, still deep inside her. Slamming inside her, he needed to be freed. He pulled his shaft from her wet pussy and watched as his seed coated her creamy skin. The milky liquid ran down her back into the valley of her ass.

Leaving her, Rade went to the bathroom to grab a washcloth so he could clean her off. Returning, Rade gently wiped down Dylan's sated body. Once he was satisfied she was clean, he undid the leather cuffs. Her body fell into his. With little effort, he picked her up from the floor and placed her on the bed. Removing her shoes, he began massaging her ankles and then her arms.

"That was incredible Rade," Dylan said softly still half dizzy from her orgasm.

"Yes it was," he replied.

Planting a gentle kiss on her lips, Rade was far from having his fill of her. Working down her body, he placed his mouth over her nipple, sucking and lapping his tongue around the hard peak. Dylan's body was so sensitized, she wasn't sure how much more she could take. His touch felt so good on her body. Reaching over her, he grabbed the flogger that he placed on the floor beside the bed. With gently sweeps, he began caressing her body with the soft leather. The touch was just enough to make her go insane. Dylan's body needed more. When the flogger touched the apex of her sex, she came unhinged. "Rade please," she moan, needing more.

Before Dylan knew what was going on, her wrists and ankles were bound to the bed. Rade continued his assault on her body with the flogger, making sure to barely touch her skin. A small grin curved on Rade's face with satisfaction knowing that he was the one in control. He could see that Dylan was getting frustrated with him. She knew he was teasing her, sending her body over the edge with hunger. Thinking she may have had enough, Rade placed the flogger on the bed. With her legs spread, he had full access to her luscious pussy. Lowering his body down the bed, he positioned himself between her legs and began feasting on her. Lapping his tongue between her folds, he continued his course in driving her crazy. Dylan's hips began to move telling him that she needed more. With only the tip of his tongue touching her, tasting her, he knew it would be a matter of time before she screamed his name. Not out of pleasure, but out of frustration.

The problem with his play, was that he was also feeling the onset of his own arousal which he knew he needed to satisfy soon before he exploded. Taking in more of her juices, Rade confirmed between licks, "I could stay just like this forever."

"No," Dylan pleaded, raising her head from the bed. "I need you to fuck me Rade, please."

"Only if you promise not to come until I give you permission," Rade ordered.

"Yes, yes, I promise," Dylan panted.

Moving up her body, Rade took hold of his throbbing cock and plunged it inside Dylan's wet channel. He could feel her body tense. "Remember Sweetness, you can't come until I say," Rade groaned, feeling the dawning of his own release.

"Yes... Oh God, please Rade let me come," Dylan panted between breaths.

With increased thrusts, Rade's release spilled with a violent crash. "Fuck," Rade groaned. "Let go Sweetness."

Dylan's release sent stars shooting though her mind as the explosion of fireworks emanated from her body. Never had she experience such an intense orgasm.

Fully sated, Rade released Dylan from her binds and rolled over beside her. Taking her body and pulling it close to his, he whispered, "I love you Sweetness,"

"I love you too Rade. Thank you," Dylan said as exhaustion took over.

Rade wasn't sure how long he had been asleep, but he knew he needed to get Dylan home. Letting her sleep for a little while longer, Rade pushed from the bed and headed to the shower.

When Rade finished, he walked back over to the bed to wake Dylan. Kissing her lightly on the lips, she began to stir. "Sweetness, we need to get going. You take a shower and I'll be back by the time you're done. I need to visit with Dane," Rade whispered."

"Okay, don't be long," Dylan said softly still half asleep.

Shortly after Rade left, Dylan got out of bed to shower. She knew he would be back soon, so she took a quick shower. Just as she finished getting dressed, there was a knock at the door. Leaving the bathroom she said, "Just a minute Rade, I'm coming." Rade must have locked the door before he left, Dylan thought to herself.

Opening the door for him, she lost it. "Michael," she said unable to breathe. His arms went around her pushing her back inside the room. Dylan tried to fight him off, but her mind was still processing that he was alive. Suddenly her body began to give way as he placed a white cloth over her mouth. Soon all she saw was darkness.

Chapter Twenty-Two

"Why does this keep happening to me? God, please tell me what to do? How can the man I once loved do this?"

"It's dark in here and cold. My head hurts really bad. I think it might be from what he used on me. I don't know for sure. I wish I could see where I am. If only I could get to the small window. Maybe then I would know. Oh, God, please help me."

"There's light coming through the small window now. I can see the room I'm in. The floors are hard, cement, I think. There is so much grim, I can't tell for sure. If only I could loosen these ropes, maybe then I can see where I am. They are so tight."

"It's dark again. I know now that this is my second day here. I haven't seen anyone. I really need to go. Wait, is that a toilet? If I could just get over there. Oh, God… why? Maybe if I yell, someone will hear me. Help, someone, please help me."

"The sun is back. I'm so hungry. Wait what's that? I need to get over there to see. Food, its food. Just a little further. I made it. All I need to do is push up on my knees, if I slide my hands around by butt and over my legs then I can eat with my hands. Just a little more. Got it"

"The water is warm and….What is that? Looks like mush. God, it's disgusting. I need to eat. I can do this. Get it down Dylan. You can do it. Scoop it in your mouth and just swallow. I feel like a dog. God, please let Rade find me, please"

"It's dark again. Oh, God, someone's at the door. I need to hide. There's nowhere to hide. It's too late. He's here. What does he want? He's coming closer. Oh, God, please help me."

* * * * *

Rade was frantic with worry. When he got to the room and Dylan wasn't there, he almost lost it. When he saw the cloth on the floor, he knew she had been taken. He recognized that scent. It was chloroform. *Someone got to her, but how?* Rade thought to himself.

"Peter, tell me you found her," Rade asked in desperation.

"Sorry sir. Whoever took her, got in through the delivery entrance," Peter began. "Nothing was reported since it was a scheduled delivery."

"That's not good enough Peter. We have to find her. Do you understand? If Michael has her, who knows what he'll do to her," Rade responded frantically.

"We'll start with the delivery company, maybe he still has the truck. Hopefully they have a GPS system and we can track where he went." Peter replied with confidence.

"Whatever it takes Peter, whatever it takes."

When Rade hung up with Peter, his mind was whirling. He had to find Dylan. Pacing the floor in Dane's office, he didn't know where to start looking for her. He was thankful that Peter was doing something to find her. The only thing Rade could think about was how alone she must feel. If it was Michael who took her, she must be confused as well. Rade knew he should have told her Michael was still alive. He shouldn't have been so selfish. He knew that if he told her, she would leave him. He couldn't lose her. He just couldn't risk it.

Rade needed something to calm his nerves, walking over to Dane's liquor cabinet, he grabbed the bottle closest to him and poured it into a glass. He didn't care what it was. All he cared about was making the pain he had in his heart to go away. Tipping the glass back, he drank the amber liquid until it was gone. Even the burn of the alcohol didn't faze him. Pouring himself another, he walked over to the window and cried out, "Sweetness where are you?"

As Rade tried to calm himself so he could think rationally, Dane entered the room. Rade turned to watch him pour himself a drink. Rade knew that in some way Dane blamed himself for Dylan being taken. Rade didn't blame anyone but Michael and his obsession with her.

Walking over to where Rade was standing, Dane placed his hand on his shoulder and said, "I'm so sorry Rade. I thought I had everything covered. I didn't even think about the deliveries."

"I know Dane. It's not your fault. I'm not blaming you for this," Rade assured him. "We just need to find her."

"Whatever you need my friend, just let me know and I'll do it," Dane said with anguish.

It was late by the time Rade left *The Castle*. He knew that he needed to go home and get some rest. He just didn't know if he could stand being in the penthouse without Dylan. He was afraid that everything would remind him of her and her absence. So his next plan was to either spend the night at the office or at a hotel. After throwing his idea back and forth, he finally settled on a hotel.

After driving to no particular place, Rade spotted a hotel. Pulling into the parking lot. He exited his car and headed to the lobby. It wasn't his preferred five-star hotel, but by the way he felt, he could care less. The host at the front desk greeted him with a toothless smile.

CHAPTER TWENTY-TWO

"I need a room for one night," Rade requested.

"No checks, no credit cards, cash only. It will be eighty bucks for the room and an extra twenty for use of the internet," the man grumbled.

Rade didn't argue about the cost of the room. He just needed a place that he could think. Throwing a hundred on the counter, Rade was given a key to his room. Before he left the lobby, he asked, "Is there a liquor store nearby?"

"Yeah, there's one a couple of blocks up the street. Better hurry if you want anything. They close in fifteen minutes," the man informed him.

Walking the short distance to the liquor store, Rade returned to his room with a bottle of their finest scotch, which only cost Rade twenty bucks for a fifth of something he never heard of, but was assured it was the best they carried.

This was the life, drinking cheap scotch from a plastic cup, which he would probably get charged for. At least he had one thing going for him, the room was clean.

By the time Rade went to bed, he had consumed the entire bottle of scotch, ending up with a headache and not the numbness he was searching for. Too tired to even think, his body finally gave in.

* * * * *

It had been exactly three days, six hours and twenty minutes since Dylan was taken. Rade tried everything he could to find her, but he came up with nothing. The delivery van that was taken showed up near an empty warehouse. One thing Rade knew for sure, based on the description if the man who knocked the delivery driver out and stole the van, it was Michael. He also knew that the longer Dylan was gone, the slimmer his chances were in finding her. This was tearing him apart.

Staring out the living room window, his cell began to ring. Looking down at the screen, he saw that it was Richard. Swiping the screen he said desperately, "I'm going crazy Richard. Please tell me you have something for me."

"We may have a lead. Remember the bartender from that dive bar?" Richard asked.

"Yeah. What does she have to do with anything?" Rade asked confused.

"Well, Mr. Stewart showed up there a couple of nights ago. Josh tried to get to him, but he slipped out the back. Anyway, the bartender shared some information with him. She said Michael was with a woman, and based on the way she was dressed, didn't belong there. This is what raised her curiosity. She overheard what they were talking about," Richard explained.

"So what did she hear?" Rade questioned.

"She heard them talking about the old sewer plant and how it would be a great place to hide someone." Richard began. "When Josh asked her to describe the woman, she gave a perfect description of Chloe. They must be working together. I think that as much as Michael wanted Dylan, Chloe wanted her out of the way more."

"You might be on to something Richard. If they are working together, it only makes sense that she would want to help Michael. We need to get over there. Pick me up at the penthouse," Rade requested before he hung up.

Rade looked like hell. Taking a much needed shower, he quickly rinsed the grime off his body, three days worth. Looking in the mirror, he didn't even recognize himself. He looked like a mountain man with his unshaven face and hollow eyes. Tossing his appearance aside, he walked out of the bathroom to his closet and got dressed. Wearing a pair of worn jeans and a t-shirt, he headed down to the parking garage to meet Richard. Even though he wasn't a religious man, he prayed that this piece of information would lead them to Dylan.

Rade exited the elevator just as Richard pulled up. Getting into the Yukon, Rade looked over at Richard and said, "Let's go."

"Can I just say, you look like shit," Richard admitted.

"Yeah, well you would look like shit too if the woman you loved was taken from you," Rade belted out.

Richard didn't dare remark. He knew Rade didn't need any more criticism. Concentrating on his driving, Richard proceeded out of the covered garage. Pulling onto the street, they began heading out of town. The old sewer plant was on the outskirts of town. Richard already contacted Peter to make sure he was in route to meet them there with his men. Richard wasn't sure what would be waiting for them, so he wanted to make sure they were well prepared.

Driving up a dirt road into the sewer plant, Richard and Rade scanned the area. From what they could see, there were no other vehicles around. Not seeing a vehicle didn't mean that Dylan wasn't being held there. Driving around the back, there was still no sign that anyone was around. Pulling his cell from his pocket, Richard dialed Peter to find out where he was.

"Peter, where are you?" Richard asked.

"We should be there in five. Don't do anything until we get there," Peter demanded.

"Will do," Richard replied.

Just as Richard hung up with Peter, Rade opened his car door. Looking over to him, Richard asked, "Where are you going?"

"I'm going to find Dylan," Rade said point blank.

"Peter is going to be here in five minutes. He said to stay put. I think we should listen to him and wait before we make a move," Richard suggested, knowing he was wasting his time.

"We may not have five minutes," Rade hissed as he continued to exit the SUV.

"Then I'm going with you," Richard acknowledged as he opened his door.

Heading to the back of the Yukon, Richard opened the hatch and pulled out a rifle and a hand gun. He didn't have much time to prepare, given Rade's demand to find Dylan.

"Here take this," Richard demanded as he handed Rade the hand gun. "You're not going in there unarmed."

Rade took the gun from Richard checking the magazine for ammo. He wanted to make sure the gun was fully loaded. Pulling back the slide, he loaded a bullet into the chamber.

Fully armed, Rade and Richard began walking toward the building. Just as they reached the entry door, Peter and his men pulled up. Exiting the truck, Peter walked up to the two men.

"I thought I told you to wait. There's no way of knowing what is waiting inside," Peter hissed quietly.

"I couldn't let Rade go alone," Richard admitted.

"Mr. Matheson with all due respect..." Peter began.

"Save it Peter. You're not here to give me orders," Rade affirmed.

Looking at Rade's body language, Peter knew that arguing with him was going to get him nowhere. He could only imagine what Rade was going through. Peter didn't want to make the situation any worse than it already was.

"You follow us in. No discussions," Peter directed, looking right at Rade. The last thing he wanted was to for Rade to play hero and end up getting hurt.

Rade didn't argue with Peter. He trusted Peter would keep them safe. Walking up to the steel door, Peter pulled it open. Checking out the area for any movement, Peter signaled to the rest of the men that the area was clear. As they made their way down the long hall, Peter and his men checked the rooms for any sign of Dylan. All the rooms were clear.

Heading down the steep staircase, Rade was beginning to panic. He had this gut feeling that Dylan wasn't there. She may have been there at some point, but something was telling him that she was no longer there.

Making their way down the metal stairs, Peter was listening for any kind of sound or movement. Reaching the bottom, there were only a few closed doors. The smell of the area definitely smelled like a sewer. Pushing open the first door, Peter saw nothing. It wasn't until they reached the second door, that Peter saw where Dylan must have been kept. Inside the room was a soiled mattress nestled in the corner of the room with a make-shift toilet consisting of a bucket and the top of a toilet seat in the other. Peter could see two bowls on the floor. One contained dirty water while the other only contained remnants of what Peter assumed was food. The whole place was disgusting. Pulling a flashlight from his waistband, Peter inspected the room further. Shinning the light in the room, he noticed that something was scratched on the wall. Stepping closer, he tried to decipher the message.

HELP ME TAKEN BY MICHAEL DOMINO SU

Peter was trying to understand what the message meant. Walking up behind him, Rade also read the message. The only thing that made sense was that fact that Michael had taken her. The other part of the message didn't mean anything to the men.

After they walked through the plant for more clues, Rade was giving up hope when they came up with nothing other than the clue Dylan left on the wall. Rade was able to get a good picture of the message from the camera on his phone. Once he was back in the SUV, he googled DOMINO SU. All he could do was hope that he would get a hit. Coming up with nothing except a well know pizza place, Rade cursed to himself. His lack of sleep and patience were taking hold. He needed to find Dylan.

Richard felt his tension. Looking over to him he said, "We will find her Rade. Let me do some checking. Maybe someone will know what her message means."

Running his hands through his hair, Rade nodded and then turned away from Richard. Rade was completely numb as he looked out his door window. His felt the pressure on his heart as he thought about how alone and scared Dylan must be. When he found Michael, he was going to make sure he paid for what he put Dylan through.

Reaching the penthouse, Richard dropped Rade off while he went to Peter's and hashed out the message that was found on the wall. Nothing would make him happier than to figure out what it meant.

Rade entered the quietness of the penthouse. This was the last place that he wanted to be. Without Dylan, the quietness was too much of reminder of what he didn't have. Looking at the message he took with his phone, Rade stared at it trying to figure out what it could possibly mean. With nowhere else to go with it, he decided to contact Evan. Maybe he would be able to shed some light on the message. Evan's experience as a freelance investigator couldn't hurt.

Dialing his number Rade waited for Evan to answer. "Hello," Evan greeted Rade, surprised by his call.

"Evan, I need your help," Rade began. "There are some things that I haven't told you. They pertain to Dylan. She's been taken."

"What do you mean she's been taken," Evan asked confused.

"Can we meet? I'll tell you everything," Rade asked.

Hanging up with Evan, Rade decided it was best to meet him at *Riley's*. Grabbing his jacket, Rade headed out of the penthouse. Rade knew he should have been honest, not only with Dylan, but also with his brother. Even though they got off on the wrong foot, they were still family. The only family Rade had.

Driving through the city, Rade ran through his mind how he was going to explain everything to Evan. Coming up short, he decided to just tell him. Plain and simple. Once Rade reached Evan's place, he drove around the block and turned into the alley where he parked behind the bar. Exiting his car, Rade entered the establishment through the back door. Evan's office was in the back of the bar, so it didn't take long for Rade to reach him.

The door was already open, so Rade entered Evan's office knocking lightly on the door. Evan looked up showing concern on his face.

Rising to his feet, he rounded his desk and said, "You look like hell brother." Walking over to his bar, he poured him a drink. "Here, looks like you could use this."

"Thanks," Rade said walking closer to Evan to accept the glass of whiskey.

Taking a seat, Rade downed the entire contents before he began explaining. "Remember when we were looking through the security footage?" Rade paused for a response. As Evan nodded, Rade continued. "I wasn't exactly honest with you. I was looking for something in particular. A man. Dylan was engaged. His name is Michael Stewart. He disappeared shortly before they were supposed to be married. He stole ten million dollars from one of my companies and in order for him not to get caught, he plotted his own death, only he couldn't stay away. He's the one who wrote Dylan that note. He was here. Your security footage showed him entering. He has her, Evan."

Evan sat back in his chair, swiping his hand through his hair. He couldn't believe what he was hearing. "So does Dylan know this?" Evan asked concerned.

"No, I had every intension on telling her. Once we were engaged, I was going to tell her everything," Rade confessed.

"Wait. What? You two are engaged?" Evan asked surprised.

"Yeah," Rade replied.

"So I guess congratulations are in order. What do you need from me?" Evan asked.

Pulling his phone from his jacket, Rade pulled up the picture he took of the message Dylan left on the wall. Handing the phone to Evan, he asked, "Do you know what this could mean?"

As Evan stared at the message, Rade waited for an answer. "I'm not sure," Evan began. "Let me look into it and get back with you. Something about it…. seems familiar."

Once Evan finished jotting down the message, Rade let his office. He wasn't sure where to go next. One thing he knew for sure, he couldn't go back to the penthouse. There was too much of Dylan there. Heading out of the city, there was only one other place he could go. Somehow he was always able to find the answers he needed.

What was normally an eight hour drive, took Rade six hours. Just like the last time he was here, his speed exceeded the allowable limit. Rade thought about the last time he visited his brother's grave, it had been because of Dylan as well. It was the first time he thought he lost her, but by some miracle, he got her back.

Walking up to the grave, Rade knelt in front of his brother. "Isaac, tell me what to do brother. Help me find the answers I need to find her. I love her so much. If I ever lost her, I don't know what I would do. How I would ever be able to live my life."

Lowering his head, Rade felt defeated. With anger he yelled at the top of his lungs, "Dylan, please help me find you."

Rade didn't know what time it was, but the heat of the sun was warm against his face. Looking up, he realized that he had fallen asleep beside his brother's grave. Pushing to his feet, he kissed his index finger and placed it on Isaac's headstone.

Rade didn't speed on his way back home. Instead he took his time. He was mostly lost in thought trying to find the answers he needed. He thought for sure visiting his brother's grave would give him the answers that he needed.

Eight hours later he was in the parking garage at Crystal Hill Tower. Pulling into his parking spot, Rade looked over to Dylan's Audi. He remembered the day he bought it for her and the hard time she gave him. To this day, he still hasn't cashed any of the checks she gave him for payment. Chuckling at himself, he slid his hand along the smooth surface of the car before heading to the elevator. He had to find her.

Chapter Twenty-Three

Dylan woke with another headache. The only thing she could think of was Rade. She hoped to God that he found where Michael had taken her and the message she had written. Even though she wasn't able to finish scratching it into the concrete wall, she hoped it would be enough of a clue for him to find her.

The new place that Michael had taken her was no better than the last. The only difference was the smell. At least the room she was being held in was a step up from where she had been held before. She had an actual toilet and the mattress was off the floor and on a small cot. Taking in her surroundings, she found an old plastic cup on the floor. Tearing off the edge, Dylan walked over to the painted window, hoping that she would be able to scrape some of the dark paint off the window so she could at least see where she was. Based on the conversation she overheard, Dylan was pretty sure they were at the Domino Sugar Factory.

Hesitating in her efforts, Dylan heard someone coming. Making her way back to the small cot, she took a seat and acted like she was just waiting. When she heard the door open, her stomach began to churn. Watching the handle turn, she waited for the person to enter.

Michael stood before her. Dylan still couldn't believe he was actually alive after all this time. As he approached her, she tried to move further onto the cot. She didn't know why. There was no room to escape him. Looking up at him, she could tell that he had lost weight. He also looked horrible. Like he had been living without a shower and clean clothing for a long time.

Walking up to her, Michael sat next to her on the cot. Placing his hand on her cheek, Dylan tried to pull away. When he felt her apprehension, he pulled back.

"I'm not going to hurt you Dylan," Michael said in a soft voice.

"Then let me go," Dylan pleaded.

"I can't do that. I can never let you go. You belong to me and not him." Michael barked.

"What do you want Michael? Why would you do this? Fake your death and take me," Dylan question, furious that he did this to her.

"For you. I did it for you," Michael began as he stood and began pacing the floor. "I wanted a better life for us. It was simple to take the money. Matheson had more money than he deserved. I worked my ass off for his company and not once did I get any recognition. I figured he owed me. It was the least he could do for me."

"What are you taking about Michael?" Dylan asked confused.

"Don't pretend you didn't know. Isn't that why you're with him?" Michael cursed.

"I have no idea what you're talking about," Dylan replied.

"You mean to tell me that he didn't tell you about the money I stole from him. He didn't tell you that he's been trying to get it back for months," Michael hissed directing his animosity for Rade towards her. "That's why he pursued you. He thought you could give him the answers he needed."

Dylan was trying to digest what Michael was saying. "Are you telling me that the only reason Rade is with me is because he thought he could find out where you were. It doesn't make sense. I don't believe you," Dylan blurted.

"I'm telling you the truth Dylan. I've done some pretty shitty things, but I've never lied to you. I didn't mean to make things so bad. I needed the money so I could get out of debt. I never should have gone to Chen Wu for the money. That guy would have never broken into your apartment if I hadn't," Michael confessed.

"Wait, you knew about that?" Dylan asked dazed. She wondered how much else he knew.

"I've been following you Dylan. Ever since the day I disappeared. I've been watching everything you've been doing. I forgive you for everything. I know you were lonely and needed someone. I'm here now. You don't need him anymore."

"Are you crazy Michael. I could never be with you after what you've done."

Just as Michael was about to say something, someone else entered the room. Dylan couldn't believe it. Could this be anymore fucked up? Chloe came through the door and she no longer had a baby bump. Dylan looked from Chloe's belly to her face speechless.

Chloe pulled Dylan from her thoughts as she said, "Don't look so surprised Dylan. I lost the baby. It's all your fault. You shoud have stayed away from Rade. He belongs to me and soon I will have him."

"How could you possibly think that he would ever want you? We know everything Chloe. We know what you did to me, what you did to Rade. You're sick," Dylan barked.

Chloe was done hearing Dylan's harsh words. Stepping up to her, she slapped Dylan across the face with all her might. When Dylan finally realized what happened, she could taste a tinge of blood coming from her lip.

"You have no idea. I should have killed you when I had the chance, but Michael insisted he would be able to control you," Chloe informed Dylan, rubbing the palm of her hand.

Dylan looked from Michael to Chloe. She had so many questions. *How the hell did they even know each other?* She thought to herself. This whole situation was messed up.

Before Dylan knew it, Michael was grabbing her by the arm and escorting her out of the small room. As they walked, Dylan looked around trying to figure out a way to escape. The old factory was run down. Dylan knew that it had been abandoned for some time. She also heard somewhere that a developer purchased the property. Guess he never got around to developing it.

Walking down a long corridor, Michael pushed Dylan though a door. When they entered the room, Dylan could see that it was a locker room. She wasn't sure why Michael had brought her here. Looking over to him in confusion, Michael walked up to her so that he was standing directing in front of her.

"I'm going to untie you Dylan. I thought you might want to shower. The water isn't very warm, but at least you'll be clean. I bought you some clean clothing as well," Michael said as he began loosening the ropes that were holding her hands together. "Don't try anything. I don't want to shoot you, but if I have to, I will."

Dylan rubbed the feeling back in her wrists as she watched Michael pull a gun from behind his back. Feeling uncomfortable with him there she said, "Can you at least turn around so I can get undressed?"

"Dylan, it's not like I haven't seen you naked," Michael began. "Go ahead and strip."

It didn't take Dylan long to remove her clothing considering he had a gun pointed at her. Being fully naked, Dylan could feel Michael's eyes burn into her. She couldn't stand looking at him. Walking up to the shower, she slowly turned on the water. Rust colored water sprayed from the nozzle. Dylan waited for a minute for the water to eventually run clear. Placing her hand under the stream, the water was cold, but not cold enough to warrant forgoing a shower. It had been four days since she was taken and a shower would make her feel better.

Michael must have thought ahead of time, because there was a bar of soap and a small bottle of shampoo and conditioner sitting on the shelf that was mounted on the shower wall. Dylan hurried as quickly as she could. The least amount of time she spent in the shower, the least amount of time she would be exposing her body to Michael.

When she was done, she turned off the water and slid back to shower curtain. Scaring her half to death, Michael stood on the other side, holding a towel out to her. Grabbing the towel from him, she kept her eyes pointed toward the floor. She in no way wanted to make eye contact with him.

It wasn't long before she was dressed, tied up again and heading back to the small room. Once the door was locked behind her, Dylan went to the cot and curled up in a fetal position. Her tears began to fall as she prayed that Rade would find her.

Dylan's days ran into nights. The only way she could tell that another day had past was by the hint of light that had shown through the window where Dylan managed to scrape the paint away. Counting the days, Dylan knew that she was taken six days ago. Her heart was beginning to sink. She thought for sure that Rade would have found her by now. Michael came to check on her periodically to visit and bring her food. Dylan was in no mood to talk or eat, but Michael wouldn't leave until she at least ate something. So she did.

Needing answers, Dylan asked as she took her last bite of food. "What happened to you Michael?"

CHAPTER TWENTY-THREE

Michael looked up at her. "I'm not sure I understand what you're asking Dylan."

"I just want to know what happened to you that made you this way." Dylan clarified.

"I don't know. I dug a hole so deep that I felt the only way to make it out was to do whatever I needed to survive. Plain and simple," Michael choked.

"Is that why you stole the money and faked your death?" Dylan asked.

"Partly, but mostly I did it for us. I thought if I could just get ahead, we could make a good life. I didn't know that once I started, I wouldn't be able to stop. First it was a couple of hundred dollars here and there. Then it turned into thousands. Soon I was so deep in debt, that the only thing I could do was find cash fast. Owing a loan shark was my only option until I figured out a way to get money from Matheson. It was easy really. Having access to the financial records at Smith, Whitaker and Associates, they trusted me with codes and passwords. It was just a matter of transferring funds from one account to another. The problem was I couldn't stop. By the time I did, it was too late, I had to disappear. I thought if they knew I was dead, they would stop digging and I would just need to lay low for a while. Then Matheson started digging. He found out about you and that was when I had to stop him, but every time I tried to get close to you, he was there. Then the guy I borrowed money from started sending his goons your way." Michael sighed lowering his head.

"Why didn't you just go to the police and turn yourself in," Dylan asked.

"Because I couldn't be without you and I certainly couldn't let Matheson have you. No matter what you think Dylan, you are mine," Michael affirmed sitting next to her on the cot.

"And Chloe, how did you get involved with her? Dylan asked in disgust.

"She actually found me. I'm not sure how, but I wanted you and she want Rade. It was a perfect partnership," Michael admitted with a smile.

Cupping her cheek with his hand, he lowered his head and kissed her. Dylan tried to pull away, but he held her close. Sinking his tongue between her parted lips, he began consuming her. No matter how hard Dylan tried to pull away, he was just too strong. Finally Michael broke away. "God I've missed you so much Dylan."

"Michael you need to let me go. If you really care about me, please let me go," Dylan pleaded.

"No, I'm never letting you go Dylan," Michael said sharply. There was no way he was ever going to let her go. Walking to the door he turned back to her. "Get use to it Dylan, you're mine."

Dylan slumped over on the cot. She needed to figure a way to get out of there. It had to be when she was alone with him. Maybe if she could make him think that she was finally giving in, she could get the gun away from him.

* * * * *

It was going on the eighth day and Rade was no closer to finding Dylan than he was a week ago. Evan still hadn't come up with anything on the message that Dylan left for Rade on the wall at the sewer plant. If he knew Michael, soon he would be moving her, if he hadn't already. Rade was running out of time. He couldn't sit and wait without doing something.

Gwen came into his office several times to make sure he was doing okay. It made sense, since Rade basically locked himself inside his office. He could no longer stand being in the penthouse, so most of his nights were spent in his office.

Pulling up his search engine, he tried again to search the information he had. First he tried DOMINO SU, New York. His results were the same as before. "Damn, what could it mean? Help me out Sweetness. What were you trying to tell me?" Rade said out loud to an empty room. Running his hand through his hair, Rade stepped away from his desk. Pacing back and forth in front of his desk, he tried to think about what it meant. Coming up with nothing, he grabbed his suit jacket and headed out of the office. On the way out he called Richard.

"Richard, have you got anything for me yet?" Rade asked.

"Not yet sir, Still trying to decipher the message from Ms. Adams," Richard explained.

"How about, Peter, has he come up with anything?" Rade questioned

"Just spoke to him. Still has nothing," Richard confirmed.

"Fuck, we are running out of time Richard. If we don't find the meaning of that message soon, I'm afraid Michael is going to take her somewhere else. He tends to stay in one spot for only a short period," Rade advised.

"We'll find her Rade," Richard assured him.

Rade wasn't convinced that Richard or Peter would be able to find out where Dylan was before Michael decided to move. Getting into his car, he decided to touch base with Evan. Even though he knew Evan would have called if he came up with anything, he couldn't wait around until he did.

Turning the corner by Central Park, Rade decided to make a pit stop. Pulling the car into a parking spot, Rade headed down the path to where he found Dylan for what seemed like a life time ago. Taking a seat on the park bench, he began thinking about Dylan and what his life would be like without her in it. The thought of losing her ripped him apart. He needed to stay strong. If not for himself for Dylan. Sitting there, he decided to put his time to good use. Pulling out his phone, he once again tried to search DOMINO SU. Looking out over the park, he spotted the rooftop of the Belvedere Castle. It was then an idea came to him. He typed 'New York old buildings-DOMINO SU'.

Rade was surprised by what came up. Three links down from the top, he saw it, '**Domino Sugar Refinery – Abandoned Building gets new remodel.**' That had to be it. That had to be where Michael was holding Dylan. It was at least worth a chance to check out.

Pulling up Richard's contact, he waited for Richard to answer. As he explained what he found to Richard, he agreed that it was worth a shot. Richard knew of the building. It had been abandoned for some time. He knew that it was suppose to be renovated into apartments or something by a developer. Something happened with the zoning that postponed the renovations.

After Rade hung up with Richard, he headed back to his car and dialed Peter to let him know of their plan. There was no time to waste, so Rade told him he would meet him at the old building. Peter cautioned Rade not to make a move until he got there. Rade agreed, but only to get Peter off the phone. Something inside told Rade that Dylan was there. There was no way he was going to wait for Peter or Richard to get there.

Pulling out of the park, Rade put Domino Sugar Refinery into his GPS. Rade knew that his quickest route would be to take Lexington to Queensbro. If the traffic wasn't too heavy, he could make it in about twenty minutes.

Popping the gear shift into first, Rade drove out of the park, down East Drive towards Center. So far so good. Traffic was minimal. It wasn't until he got on the Queensbro Bridge that his efforts slowed. He did the best he could, honking and weaving in and out of traffic. Based on the expressions of the drivers he passed, they must have thought he was a lunatic.

Twenty-five minutes later, Rade pulled up to the run-down warehouse. There was a black Tahoe parked around the back of the building. Rade grabbed his phone and texted the license plate number to Richard. Waiting a few minutes for a response, Rade scanned the building for an entrance. Unable to wait any longer, Rade opened his car door. As he walked up to the building a text came in from Richard. The SUV was stolen. It didn't surprise Rade that Michael would be driving a stolen vehicle to transport Dylan in.

Rade didn't know what he was thinking. Trying to enter the building with no protection was asking for trouble. Running back to the car, he popped open the glove box and took the handgun Richard had given him at the sewer plant. Rade was glad that he decided to hold on to it instead of giving it back to Richard. Pulling back the slide, Rade engaged a bullet into the chamber. Locking the car, Rade proceeded to the old building. Checking the only entrance he could see, he found that the steel door was securely locked with a chain and padlock. Rade had to find another way into the building. Walking down the side, he could see that one of the windows had been propped open. Removing the piece of wood, he lifted the window and climbed through it.

The building was filled with remnants of what use to be a booming industry. There was still a hint of molasses in the air mixed with the scent of mold and rot. Most of the inside of the building had been gutted. Rade had heard of an exhibition being held her last year displaying a sculpture of a sphinx made out of refined sugar.

Casting away the history behind the factory, Rade focused on finding Dylan. Even though most of the warehouse was torn down, there were still a lot of places where Michael could be holding her. Rade moved onward in his search for Dylan. Leaving the main floor, he headed up the stairs. Coming across the old administrative area of the warehouse, he came across the locker rooms. Entering what must have been the women's locker room, Rade spotted Dylan's clothing on the floor. Picking them up, he took in her scent. His only conclusion was that Michael allowed her to shower. Based on the used bar of soap, shampoo and conditioner in the shower, his assumption was correct.

He was comforted knowing that she was still alive. Michael wouldn't have allowed her to shower if he planned on killing her. Leaving the locker room, Rade headed down the hallway where other administrative offices were. Just as he was about to turn the corner leading to more offices, he heard voices, He recognized them right away. "Chloe and Michael. What the fuck?" Rade said under his breath.

"We can't stay here. Sooner or later they're going to find us," Michael said.

"I know. The passports are ready, I just need to pick them up. I'll go get them and meet you back here. Are you sure she won't be a problem while we're gone?" Chloe asked.

"Dylan isn't going anywhere. It won't take me that long to get food," Michael confirmed.

"Okay, see you later then," Chloe said.

Rade watched as the two of them headed past the room he was hiding in. Once they were out of sight, Rade proceeded in the direction they came from. His only hope was that he would be able to find Dylan before they came back.

Opening the doors that he could, he looked inside the rooms for any sign of her. The doors he couldn't open, he yelled for her. Door after door he came up empty. There was one last door at the end of the hallway that had a lock on it. Rade thought it was kind of strange seeing a lock on it since none of the other doors had one.

Pulling on the lock, he was unable to pull it loose. Once again he yelled for Dylan, "Dylan are you in there?" Turning around, he went to check another hallway. Just when he was about to give up hope, He heard her voice. It was faint, but it was Dylan.

Backing up, he went back to the locked door. "Dylan, is that you Sweetness?" Rade asked hoping with desperation that she was on the other side of the door.

"Rade," Dylan answered with a muffled voice.

"I'm, going to get you out of there Sweetness," Rade answered.

Pointing the gun at the lock, he pulled the trigger. The bullet hit the lock square and the lock dropped to the floor. When Rade opened the door, his emotions took over. Looking at her, he couldn't hold back his need to hold her. Pulling her to his body, he held her tightly, kissing every inch of her face. Holding her back slightly, he looked her over. "Are you okay? Did he hurt you?" Rade asked with concern.

"No, I'm fine. He didn't hurt me. I knew you would find me," Dylan said with tears in her eyes. "I just knew you would find me."

Rade pulled her close to him one again unwilling to let her go. Gradually he knew he had to let go and get her out of there. Undoing her bindings, he said softly, "We need to get out of here before they come back."

Heading down the hallway and to the lower level, Rade knew he missed his chance to escape. As soon as he and Dylan hit the bottom of the stairs, Michael was waiting for them.

"It's no use Rade, you have nowhere to go," Michael shouted.

"Michael don't do this. If you let us go, I won't say anything. You can take the money and be on your way," Rade said, trying to compromise.

"You think I'm going to believe you," Michael spat.

"I'll go with you Michael, Please don't hurt Rade," Dylan begged.

"I'm not letting you go with him Dylan. I would die first," Rade confessed still holding on to her.

"You know that can be arranged," Michael smirked. "They way I see it, you can go ahead and shoot, but I might be able to get a shot off. I won't think twice about shooting Dylan. Nobody will ever have her. So if I die, so does she. Your choice, drop the gun or shoot."

Rade had no other choice. He couldn't risk losing Dylan to this psycho. Dropping his gun, Rade slid it over to Michael.

"For a smart business man, you're pretty stupid. Now I guess, I get to kill you," Michael said as he raised the gun. Just as he was ready to pull the trigger a shot rang inside the empty warehouse echoing off the metal walls.

Michael looked right at Dylan as blood began spilling from his mouth. As he fell to the floor, Rade saw Peter standing behind him with his gun drawn. Nothing made Rade happier than to see Peter.

Dylan went to Michael and held his head as he took in his last breaths.

"It didn't need to be this way Michael," Dylan said as tears fell down her face.

"It's okay Dylan, I've always loved you. Now the hurt will go away," Michael groaned. His last words consumed him as his body went limp in Dylan's arms.

Looking at her hands, Dylan stared down at her blood covered hands. Michael was really gone. This time he was really gone.

Rade knelt beside Dylan taking her in his arms. He knew no matter how angry she was at Michael for what he did, the last thing she wanted was for him to die. Getting to their feet, Rade helped her out of the warehouse, while Peter called his men for damage control.

As they got outside, Richard was leaning against the Yukon with his arms crossed over his chest. As Rade passed him, Richard turned and watched as Rade escorted Dylan to his car. As angry as Richard was for what Rade did, he also felt for him. He knew that if it was him in Rade's spot, he would have done the same thing. Before Rade got too far, Richard yelled, "Rade," and waited for him to turn around.

"I know what you're thinking Richard. Save it. I'm taking Dylan home," Rade informed Richard.

"I was just going to say, drive safely," Richard said walking around the hood.

Chapter Twenty-Four

Pulling up to the parking garage at the penthouse, Rade looked over to Dylan to see her looking out the side window. Taking her by the hand, he pulled it to his lips. When Dylan turned his way, he asked with concern, "You doing okay Sweetness?"

Leaning into him, Dylan said, "I couldn't be better. I just want to forget about everything."

"I think that's a perfect idea," Rade agreed with a smile.

Leaning closer to Dylan, he captured her lips with his and took her in. With the thought of almost losing her, he was never going to let her out of his sight. "Come on let's get you out of those horrid clothes and into a nice bath," Rade demanded.

"Yes sir," Dylan replied.

Once they were inside the penthouse, Rade went to the bathroom and began drawing Dylan a bath with an abundance of bubbles. He was going to worship her. Dylan stayed in the bedroom and took off her clothing. When Rade appeared back in the bedroom, he picked up her discarded clothing and took them with him as he exited the room.

"How about a nice glass of wine while you soak?" Rade yelled behind him.

"That would be perfect. Can I have Rade Matheson with that too?" Dylan asked as she walked into the bathroom.

"Your wish is my command," Rade advised.

Going to the kitchen trash, Rade threw the ugly gray sweats into the trash. He never wanted to see them on Dylan again. He bet she didn't want to see them ever again either. Grabbing a white wine from the fridge, Rade popped the cork and pulled two wine glasses from the cupboard. Filling the glasses, he went back to the bathroom to begin showing her his love.

As he walked into the bathroom, Dylan was talking on her cell phone. He tried not to interrupt her. Rade knew that she was talking with her father. He had been frantic about what happened to Dylan. When Rade couldn't find Dylan after the second day, he contacted Ray to let him know what was going on.

When Dylan finished her call, tears clouded her eyes. Rade quickly undress and slipped in behind her. Once he was settled, he reached over and handed her a glass of wine.

"Are you okay Sweetness?" Rade asked.

"Yeah," she began. "I just hate it when my dad worries so much. It can't be good for him. I do have some good news though." Dylan turned to face Rade before she told him the good news. "Dad and Sally are getting married."

"Well that is good news," Rade said as he lifted his glass for a toast. "When is the big day?"

"They are flying to Las Vegas next week. They didn't want to have a big wedding since they both have been married before. I would like to be there for them though," Dylan explained.

"I think that would be great. We should be there to share their special day," Rade agreed.

Taking Dylan's glass from her, He leaned her body toward him with her back to his chest. Adding body wash to the bath sponge, he began cleansing Dylan's body. For close to eight days, he was denied the privilege to do this. To thoroughly worship every inch of her gorgeous body. Moving the sponge upward, Rade began tenderly caressing her beautiful breasts. With his free hand, he took her breast in his hand, and began pinching the hard pebble between his fingers. When Dylan's head fell back against his shoulder, he knew she was enjoying his play. Dropping the sponge in the water, Rade lifted Dylan's body and cradled her in his arms. Looking into her beautiful green eyes, Rade entangled his lips with hers and seized her with such passion, knowing that he could have lost her.

Dylan severed their embrace, but only to adjust her body so that she was straddling him. Lifting her hips slightly, she lowered onto him and watched as his thick cock slid inside her. She needed him. Being held captive in the small room allowed her to do a lot of thinking. She needed to find out the truth from Rade, but more importantly, she needed him. Pumping her hips up and down, Dylan took more and more of him as she glided down his cock. Circling her hips, Dylan consumed him as she felt the impact of his thrusts against her sweet spot. Closing her eyes, unable to breathe, Dylan's body released with fury, taking with it all the pain and torment, leaving her body feeling free and alive. Everything that had happened over the past months was now over. They could finally live their life together, the way it was supposed to be.

It wasn't until she pulled her body from Rade that she realized it wasn't over, Chloe was still out there. When Peter shot Michael, Chloe was nowhere. Once again she managed to escape.

Getting out of the tub, Dylan grabbed a towel and wrapped it around her wet body. Leaving Rade in the tub, Dylan walked to the bedroom and began changing into something comfortable. When Rade appeared from the bathroom carrying a confused look, it was then that Dylan decided she couldn't wait any longer to get some answers.

"Rade, I need to know something, and you need to be completely honest with me," Dylan started. "Michael said that you knew he was alive. He said that he took money from you and you only were interested in me to get to him. I need to know if what he said is true."

Rade walked over to Dylan dress in only a towel. Dylan was serious about getting the answers that she needed, but with Rade exposed in this manner, she wasn't sure she would be able to resist him. All she wanted was to feel his lips on hers.

"You better sit, before I explain everything to you," Rade said, taking Dylan by the hand and leading her to the bed. As soon as she was seated, he began. "Some of what he said to you was the truth, only my intensions changed. I was going to use you to get information on the location of Michael and the money he stole from me. Things changed the moment I saw you. Right then, I knew that I needed you. There was something about you that drew me in. You were so innocent." Rade acknowledged as he took both of Dylan's hands in his. "Slowly we began gathering information on him. He somehow got involved with Chen Wu."

"Does this Chen Wu have anything to do with David Wu?" Dylan asked.

"Yes, David Wu was Chen Wu's son. Chen Wu said that he hadn't spoken to his son in years. Anyway, Michael stole the money from me to pay him back, only he never did. Chen Wu sent one of his men to search your apartment for the money. Unfortunately, you walked in on him. I didn't know Sweetness. When you got hurt, I had to find out who did this to you. We finally found him and got him to confess to what he did to you. Richard made an anonymous call to the police."

"You knew about this guy and you didn't tell me? Did you know Michael was alive too?" Dylan asked, angered that he hid this from her.

"I wanted to tell you Sweetness, but I needed to protect you as well," Rade admitted.

"What about the charms? Did you know about them?"

"No. We tried to find out who was sending them to you. We thought it was Chen Wu, but he said he had nothing to do with it. It wasn't until I was kidnapped, that I found out it was Alex along with Chloe," Rade explained.

Dylan was silent trying to understand everything that Rade was saying. She couldn't believe that after all this time, he knew that Michael was alive and he didn't tell her.

"Dylan please say something?" Rade said concerned.

"I don't know what to say. I can't believe you would keep this from me," Dylan said, tears beginning to form in her eyes. Wiping them away, Dylan sat tall, she couldn't be with a man who kept things from her. Looking at him, she wasn't about to give him the same consideration. She needed to tell him about Chloe. "Chloe was at the sewer plant and the warehouse. She's not pregnant. She lost the baby," Dylan said in a strong voice.

"I knew she was at the warehouse. I overheard Michael talking with her. I didn't get a look at her. How did you know about the baby?" Rade asked.

"Because, unlike you, she told me and it was evident that she was no longer pregnant," Dylan said as she stood from the bed, ready to leave the room.

Grabbing her arm, Rade pleaded, "Wait, please?"

"I need to think Rade. I can't do that here," Dylan confessed.

"Let Richard take you. With Chloe still out there, I can't chance something happening to you." Rade demanded.

Instead of arguing with him, Dylan nodded her head. Leaving the room, she walked out the front door down to the parking garage where she knew Richard would be waiting. She had a lot of thinking to do. Everything between her and Rade had been built on a lie. She knew she loved him, but she didn't know if that was enough.

Watching Dylan leave the penthouse was the hardest thing that Rade had ever done. He knew that telling her the truth would hurt her. Now that she knew everything, he just needed to wait. Give her time to process everything, it was what he needed to.

* * * * *

Rade was beside himself. He was going crazy. It had been four hours since Dylan left. He contemplated calling her several times, but decided against it. He would give her another hour and then he would call her. Heading to his study to do some work to get his mind off of her, he heard the front door open. Looking over to the door, Dylan walked into the penthouse. A relief swept over him. Walking down the two stairs he had climbed, he walked over to her.

Stopping him before he got closer, Dylan held out her hand. "Please Rade, let me say what I need to say," Dylan asked sternly.

Rade looked down on her with worry. He was afraid of what she was about to tell him. He knew by the look on her face that it wasn't good.

"I love you Rade, more than I've ever loved anyone," Dylan confessed trying to get the rest of what she had to say out. "You hurt me by not trusting me enough to tell me the truth about Michael, about everything. I can't be with someone who hides things from me. I can't be with you. Not like this," Dylan said hesitantly knowing it was the right thing to do even though her heart told her differently. Pulling the diamond ring from her finger, Dylan handed it over to Rade.

Rade stood there unable to move. Looking down at the ring resting between her thumb and finger, he couldn't bring himself to take it. It was only when Dylan took his hand and placed the ring inside that he it hit him. Nothing could have prepared him for what was happening.

"Dylan, please don't do this. I was trying to protect you. I love you so much," Rade said in agony.

"I love you too Rade," Dylan said placing her lips on his. Giving him a kiss she left with once last word. "Goodbye."

Rade watched as Dylan turned and walked out the door. He had to make this right. He would make this right. Holding the ring in his hand, he walked to the bedroom and put it in a safe place. One day, very soon he would have it on her finger again.

It was late and Dylan had nowhere to go. She didn't know what to do. She needed to talk to someone. Pulling her phone from her purse, she dialed Lilly. Waiting for her friend to answer, she told the taxi driver to take her to the BlackStone building.

"Hello girlfriend," Lilly greeted Dylan.

"Hey," Dylan said feeling lost.

"Something's wrong. What is it Dylan?" Lilly asked concerned.

"I need a place to stay and I thought if you're apartment is available, you would let me stay there," Dylan asked hopeful.

"You're in luck. My sub moved out about a week ago. You're more than welcome to stay there. What going on Dylan?" Lilly tried to remain calm. She knew Dylan too well. Something was up.

After Dylan explained to Lilly what had happened over the past week, they were both in tears. Dylan, because she already missed Rade, and Lilly because she could only think about what it would be like without her friend.

By the time they ended the call, Lilly was determined to come back to New York to be with Dylan. Of course Dylan convinced her that there was no need. Dylan just needed a little time and she would be okay.

Telling the driver to take her up town to Lilly's apartment building, she sat back relieved that she had a place to stay for a while. When the driver pulled in front of Lilly's building, Dylan paid the driver and headed inside. Lilly called the security guard to let him know that Dylan would be staying at her place for a while. When Dylan walked up to the security desk, she was handed a key to Lilly's apartment. The security guard called her by name, remembering her staying with Lilly many months ago.

When Dylan opened the door, she was greeted with silence, which only added to her feeling of emptiness. Turning on the light, nothing had changed. Everything was the same as it was a few months ago. Sinking to the floor, Dylan's emotions finally gave way leaving Dylan consumed with heartache.

Dylan tried to pull herself together. Once the tears stopped, she managed to push herself from the floor and head to the bedroom. Curling up into a ball, Dylan began running through everything. The kidnapping. The night at *The Castle*. Rade coming clean with the truth. The fact that she did see Michael in her apartment only to be convinced by Rade that she was mistaken. The unforgettable night at the opera and then The Plaza.

She thought about everything leading up to this point. Most of which were good. Dylan didn't have any more energy to think. Her mind was exhausted. She tried to go to sleep, but then she thought about everything all over again. She couldn't stand it anymore, Getting up, she decided to raid Lilly's kitchen. What she wouldn't give for a glass of wine or a shot of whisky. Opening the cupboards, there was nothing. The last thing Dylan wanted to do was to go out. It was still early enough that she could walk up the street and grab a bottle of wine. Grabbing her purse, she left the apartment.

* * * * *

Rade had been staring out the window for hours. He couldn't sleep. All he could do was think about Dylan. Even with the amount of alcohol that he had consumed, his mind was filled with despair. He knew exactly what he did. He just didn't know how he was going to be able to make it right again.

With Richard following her, at least Rade knew she was safe. Richard called Rade about an hour ago letting him know that Dylan was staying at Lilly's apartment. Finding out where she was, was one less thing that Rade had to worry about. Rade instructed Richard, Peter and Josh to watch over Dylan by taking turns keeping an eye on Lilly's apartment building. No matter what happened between them, Rade would forever make sure she was protected.

Rade didn't know what time it was, but he was finally able to sleep. Stretching the kink he had in his neck from sleeping on the couch, Rade regretted not making it to his bed. Based on the way he felt, he must have drunk the entire bottle of his fifty year old scotch. His only regret was that he didn't have more of it on hand. It was the only way that he could numb the pain he was feeling inside.

Coming to his senses, Rade knew that he couldn't drink his problems away. He was going to fix this thing with Dylan. Pushing from the couch, Rade headed to his bathroom to bring some life back into his body.

Feeling almost himself again, he put on his gray suit, light blue tie and black Zelli Aviano shoes. Looking at himself in the mirror, he had to admit he looked pretty good. He almost left the beard, but decided against it. He wanted Dylan to see the man she fell in love with. Heading out, he grabbed the keys to the Martin and got inside the elevator.

It didn't take long for Rade to reach Lilly's apartment. He wasn't sure if the security guard would allow him up to Lilly's apartment, but he had to at least give it a shot. When he entered the building and saw that no one was manning the desk, Rade began to panic. If he could get to Dylan without being stopped, then anyone could.

Rushing to the elevator, Rade pressed the up button, willing the door to open. When it finally did, Rade hit Lilly's floor and hoped like hell that Dylan was okay. With Chloe still free, his heart began pounding faster. If Chloe ever got near Dylan again, he would kill her.

Reaching Lilly's apartment, Rade lightly knocked on the door. Greeted by Dylan, Rade's heart just about broke. Dylan was no longer the happy vibrant woman that he fell in love with. She looked tired with the look of hopelessness spread across her beautiful face. She looked like she had been crying. Rade hated seeing her like this. What he hated more was that he was the cause of her pain.

With his hand, he gently rubbed her cheek. Leaning in, he lowered his lips to hers only to be denied. Dylan turned her head, rejecting his touch.

Looking back at him Dylan asked softly, "What do you want Rade?"

Rade ran his fingers through his hair trying to choose the right words. "Can I come in? I really need to talk to you."

Going against her better judgment, Dylan stepped to the side and allowed Rade to enter the apartment. Once inside, Rade walked over to the window and gazed out to the city, not really seeing anything in front of him. Turning, he set his eyes on Dylan standing with her arms crossed around her waist. The only thing Rade could see was how vulnerable she looked.

Waking closer to her, he again tried to show her how much he loved and needed her. "Don't Rade," Dylan whispered as she walked away from him.

"Dylan, I know that I've hurt you. I know nothing I say or do is going to change that. I'm so sorry Dylan. I thought I was doing what was right. I thought that by keeping what I knew about Michael from you...." Rade paused. "I was afraid that if you knew about Michael, I would lose you. In the beginning, I did seek you out to find out about him, but that changed. I started to fall in love with you. I had to keep you safe. I didn't know what he was capable of. When he started sending messages, I knew I should have told you. I should have let you know he was alive. I kept thinking, how could he leave you? If he really loved you, why would he be with any other woman?"

As soon as Rade said those words, Dylan looked up at him. "What are you talking about Rade?"

Instead of explaining it to her, he showed her. Pulling out his phone, He showed her the picture of Michael and the curvy blond he was with in St. Croix. He thought that he could keep this from her, but with her knowing the truth, he needed to tell her everything.

"He was with someone else?" Dylan said questioning what she was seeing.

"I didn't want you to show you this Dylan, but you needed to know that Michael wasn't the man you thought he was," Rade admitted.

Slumping on to the couch, Dylan just stared at the picture of Michael locking lips with the attractive blond. Knowing that Dylan had seen enough, Rade pulled his phone from her grasp and sat beside her withdrawn body. Putting his hand on her chin, he turned her face towards him. Looking in her tear filled eyes, he lowered his lips to hers. This time he was greeted with her pain. He took it all. He vowed to never hurt her again. "I will never keep anything from you again Dylan. I promise. No more secrets."

Rade deepened the kiss as Dylan opened up to him. It was like they were kissing for the first time. Feeling the passion that bonded them together. Pulling from her slightly, Rade said softly, "I love you Dylan. You are my world."

If Dylan wasn't an emotional wreck before, she was now. She loved Rade more than anything. Wrapping her arms around his shoulders, she pulled him closer, placing her mouth over his. Being without him wasn't going to happen again. No matter how much they fought, she was never going to be without him. He meant everything to her.

Picking her up from the couch, Rade carried her to the bedroom. Laying her gently on the bed, Rade showered her with the love he had for her. He began removing her clothing while keeping his lips on hers. He couldn't break away. He needed to feel her. Pulling his own clothing off, he regretted having to withdraw from her, even for a moment.

Placing his body over hers, Rade began to worship her. With soft kisses, he layered her body. There wasn't an inch of her softness that wasn't cherished. Spreading her legs wider, Rade positioned his body between them. Resting his elbows beside her head, he held her gaze and declared, "I love Sweetness. I'm going to prove to you everyday just how much I do."

"Mmmm, then you better start now," Dylan moan with pleasure.

Lowering his hand, he found her clit and began rubbing his finger against it in a circular motion. Sliding his hand lower, he pressed one then another finger inside her tight channel. "God, you feel so good Sweetness," Rade breathed. Removing his finger, he took hold of his cock and gently plunged it inside her wet pussy. Pushing forward with gentle movements, he began driving deeper and deeper inside her. Rade wanted to take it slow. He wanted to harness every feel of her body as he felt the hold she had on him. Feeling the squeeze of her walls, Rade lifted Dylan's hips, taking her legs and placing them over his shoulders. Deeping his assault, her pussy began tightening, clinching on to his hard shaft the more he moved inside her. Pulling out so that only the tip of his cock was imbedded inside her, he repositioned his body, taking her farther into paradise. Hitting her sweet spot just right, he heard the sound of pleasure take over as his name spilled from her lips. Feeling the onset of his own release, Rade spilled his seed into her tight channel, never feeling more fulfilled than he did at that moment.

Once at the remnants of their lovemaking had been cleaned away, Rade pulled Dylan into his chest and took in her warmth. Staying that way for just a moment, Rade remembered the reason he came. Getting out of bed, He picked up his pants from the floor and removed the platinum ring from the pocket. Slipping in beside Dylan, he took her left hand and placed the diamond ring on her ring finger. Kissing her tenderly on the lips, he whispered softly, "I don't want you to ever remove this again."

With a nod of acknowledgement, Dylan kissed Rade with love, before they both feel into a blissful sleep.

Chapter Twenty-Four

It was the start of a new day and the sun was shining brightly through the window. Dylan was lying beside the man she loved more than anything. Even though Rade had kept things from her, she trusted their relationship together, she trusted that there would no longer be secrets between them.

Nudging Rade awake, she needed to get back to the penthouse. When she left the other day she neglected to grab a change of clothing. She was over wearing the same clothing .

Rade's eyes slowly began to open. When his eyes focused on her, he knew he was in heaven. Leaning over, Rade captured her mouth. "Good morning beautiful. How about some coffee?"

"I'll make it. You stay and just look gorgeous," Dylan demanded.

Walking to the kitchen, Dylan began making the coffee. Finishing, she poured two cups. Lilly didn't have her favorite creamer, so Dylan settled on cream and sugar. Dylan walked back to the bedroom with coffee in hand. When she got to the door, she heard the shower going in the bathroom across the hall. Turning, she stepped to the closed door and opened it to find Rade's naked body on display in the shower. God, he was gorgeous. Placing the two cups on the counter. Dylan slipped off her panties and shirt and joined Rade in the shower. The shower in the bathroom wasn't big enough for two people, but that didn't stop them from making enough room.

An hour later they were in Rade's car and on the way back to the penthouse. Traffic was minimal, so it didn't take long to reach his building. When they got inside the penthouse, Dylan changed quickly and freshen-up her make-up. By the time she exited the bathroom, Rade had been dressed and ready to go.

Heading down to the parking garage, Rade took hold of Dylan's hand while they waited for the elevator to make its final stop. Richard was waiting for them in the Bentley which he pulled up to the front of the elevator.

As the both slipped into the SUV, Richard watched from the front seat. Safely inside, Richard proceeded out of the garage and on to the streets of Manhattan. Looking back at them in the review mirror, he was glad that they were able to make their amends. Even though he didn't agree in the beginning with Rade's plans, he was glad the way things ended.

Richard dropped Dylan's off first at the BlackStone building. He waited while they said their goodbyes. Rade had made plans with Dylan to have a quick drink at *Riley's,* before heading home. It had been a while since Dylan had seen Evan. Last night when they were in each other arms, Rade explained to her how he went to Evan for help when he couldn't figure out the message she left him. It's funny how things turned out between them. Rade never thought he would have another brother that he could share his life with.

When Dylan entered the office, Jessica and Lucy were hard at work. With everything that had happened, they were left with more than their share of work. Now with the new Spectrum building getting ready to open, Dylan needed their help more than ever. Applications after applications were coming in with people interested in filling the positions that Dylan had posted on-line. She knew that once she had the initial staff hired, more positions would need to be filled. At least this was a start for her.

Taking the applications that Jessica had pulled on-line, Dylan headed to her office to weed through them. Sitting at her desk Dylan began going through them. A lot of what she was seeing was good. More than half of the applications that were filled out held promise. There were some that didn't have any experience, but then there were those that had more than enough.

By the end of the day, Dylan had chosen about a dozen potential applicants. It was too late in the day to call and set up appointments to meet with them, so she decided to come in tomorrow early and start the interview process.

When Dylan got to the lobby, she was greeted by the most gorgeous smile she had ever seen. Rade was standing, all six-foot-four of him, in the lobby reading some kind of health magazine. When he saw her, he dropped the magazine on the small table and began walking towards her. Taking her in his arms, he laid his mouth on her lips and kissed her. What was meant to be a quick peck, turned into a passionate kiss that left Dylan wet between the legs. She was just about ready to forgo their plans to go to *Riley's* when Rade pulled away and asked, "Are you ready to go visit your future brother-in-law?"

On the way to *Riley's*, Dylan went though her day with Rade. She talked about the abundance of applications she had received and the ones she had chosen to come in for an interview. She also suggested that he help her with the final decision on hiring the staff that would be working at the new site.

"It sounds like everything is going well with the application process." Rade said.

"I think it is. At least I hope so. There are so many potential candidates. I just hope I can choose between all of them." Dylan said.

"I have all the faith in the world in you Dylan." Rade admitted as he raised her hand to his lips and kissed her.

Richard pulled in front of *Riley's,* dropping Rade and Dylan off in the front. Before they exited, Rade instructed Richard to come back in a couple of hours to pick them up. Leaving the car, Rade and Dylan headed inside. It was still early enough in the evening that the place hadn't filled up yet. Taking Dylan by the hand, they began walking to the back of the bar. Evan's office door was already open when they got there. Evan was looking at the security monitors on his desk so with a light tap, Rade knocked on his door.

Evan looked up from the monitor and greeted them."Hey you two?"

Rounding his desk he stepped in front of Dylan and pulled her in for a quick hug, while holding his hand out to Rade.

"We thought we would stop by and have a drink and say 'Hi,'" Rade explained, shaking his brother's hand.

"Well I'm glad you did. I had to see for myself that my future sister-in-law was okay," Evan declared.

"I'm fine. Can you join us for a drink?" Dylan asked.

"I'd love to," Evan responded with a smile.

Leaving Evan's office, Dylan walked ahead of them as Rade and Evan continued their conversation. Dylan could hear what was being said. Rade was going through the event of Dylan's rescue and the death of Michael. Hearing what happened, brought tears to Dylan's eyes. As much as she hated Michael for what he did, she didn't want him to end up dead. She wished that he would have turned himself in.

It was about eight o'clock by the time they left *Riley's.* Dylan wasn't in the mood to go out to dinner, so Rade suggested they order in. When the food arrived, Dylan was just getting out of the bath. Cuddling up behind her, Rade let her know that their dinner had arrived. Dylan's body was warm and smelled of lavender and vanilla. Rade could have eaten her instead of the Italian food that he had ordered from *Russo's*.

"Our dinner is here Sweetness," Rade said, kissing her neck between each word.

Turning around, Dylan captured his lips with hers, giving him something else to kiss. Dylan loved the feel of his lips on her. The way he lightly nibbled on her bottom lip. The way he could make her come completely undone with every sweep of his tongue against hers.

Regretfully, Rade pulled from her. Placing his hand on her cheek he said, "Finish up. I'll get our dinner ready."

Rade was dishing the food onto two plates when his cell began to ring. Looking down at the number, he contemplated not answering it, but then decided that it could be important.

"Hello," he said greeting the caller.

"Rade, it's you father," Garrett began. "When were you going to tell me that you and Dylan were engaged?"

I didn't tell you because I don't want you to have any part of it. Dylan is the most important thing in my life. I'm not going to allow you to take that from me."

"Aren't you being a little harsh. I would never hurt Dylan," Garrett confessed.

"Just like you would never hurt Isaac? Good-bye father," Rade hissed.

"Wait," Garrett pleaded.

"What do you want?" Rade asked.

"I heard what happened to Dylan. I want to help you find Chloe. She trusts me. She also knows our history. Let me help you find her," Garrett offered.

"Why would you help me? Finding Chloe isn't going to change anything between us," Rade confirmed.

"Because, no matter how much you hate me, you are still my son. You deserve to be happy. Let me help you," Garrett pleaded.

"I'll think about it," Rade said ending the call. He knew that his father had an agenda in helping him and it wasn't out of the kindness of his heart.

Just as Rade hung up with his father, Dylan was standing a few feet away. Looking down on her, Rade was pretty sure she heard the conversation based on the look she had on her face.

"Rade, why won't you let him help you? The sooner she is caught, the sooner we can live a normal life," Dylan said, trying to reason with him.

"I don't want anything from him Sweetness. Just like with everything else, there's a reason he is so willing to help," Rade confirmed.

"You don't know that. Maybe he's changed Rade. Don't you think he deserves another chance to make things right? " Dylan asked.

"No, He doesn't deserve anything from me." Rade turned away from her, grabbing two glasses from the cupboard.

Rade and Dylan ate in silence. Neither one of them knowing what to say. The only thing Dylan wanted to talk about was Rade's conversation with Garrett, but given that they had just recently made up, she wasn't willing to have another fight with him.

Trying to make conversation, she said, " So tomorrow I'm going to begin calling in people for interviews. I would like it very much if you could be there when I interview them." Dylan confessed taking a bite of her pasta.

"Whatever you want Sweetness. Just let me know when and I'll have Gwen rearrange my schedule," Rade said looking down at his plate.

Dylan was glad dinner was over. She was thankful however, that even though she only got a few words out of Rade, at least they didn't end up fighting. Dylan thought maybe she would reach out to Garrett and have him work on finding Chloe anyway. The only thing that stopped her from doing just that was that she hated the idea of going behind Rade's back. They had promised to be honest with each other, which also meant no secrets. The last thing she needed was for Rade to find out what see did.

Dylan cleaned up the dishes while Rade went to his study. He had a full day tomorrow and wanted to be sure to get a head start in case Dylan had set up interviews that he needed to be there for. When he looked at the email that Gwen had sent him of his schedule, he responded right away asking if any of his appointments could be rescheduled for a later time, in case he needed to leave. Rade knew that unless Gwen was sitting by her computer, he wouldn't receive a response from her until the morning.

Finishing up what he was doing, Rade shut down his laptop and headed downstairs. When he got to the bedroom, he could see that Dylan was already fast asleep. While he was in his study, he considered what she said. Maybe it was time to put aside his feelings towards his father. Thirteen years is a long time to hold a grudge against someone. The feelings he had for his father wasn't going to bring his brother back. At twenty-nine, it was time to set aside his anger and forgive.

Slipping off his clothing, Rade slipped into the bed beside Dylan. Pulling her near, he took her in. Breathing in her scent was the only thing that could calm him. She was the antidote to his affliction. The sunshine on his cloudiest days.

In a hushed voice he said, "I love you."

Dylan woke the next morning with Rade no longer beside her. Rising from the bed, she put on her robe and headed to the kitchen where she thought for sure he would be. The only greeting she got was the fresh smell of coffee brewing and a note leaning up against her coffee cup.

Sweetness,

Sorry to have left so early this morning, but I wanted to get things done in case you needed me today.

I also thought about what you said. I've decided to give my father a chance. Thirteen years is a long time to have ill will towards him.

I contacted him early this morning and agreed to meet with him to see what he had in mind about finding Chloe.

If I don't see you before this afternoon, I want to take you to lunch. I'll be at your office at one o'clock.

Have a good day Sweetness.

All my love

R

Dylan took the note and held it to her chest. She was glad to hear that Rade was willing to give Garrett another chance. Hopefully they would be able to work out their differences. Lifting her cup from the counter, she poured herself a cup of coffee and headed back to the bedroom to get ready for work.

Getting to work thirty minutes early, Dylan began scanning through the applications she had chosen for the next phase of the hiring process. Separating them into piles according to job title, Dylan began contacting the future employees.

Hanging up the phone, Dylan scheduled an interview with the last of the applicants. Most of her interviews were scheduled for next week. She wanted to make sure plenty of notice was given to them as well as to Rade. More than anything, she wanted Rade present when she spoke with them. Cleaning off her desk, the time was approaching one o'clock and she didn't want to be late for her lunch date with Rade. She knew how he felt about punctuality. Grabbing her purse, she stopped by Keeve's office, then Mason's to let them know she was going to lunch. Both of them were so deep in work, she wasn't sure that they even paid attention to her.

Waiting for a short time in the lobby, Richard pulled up to the curb. Rade exited the Bentley once the car came to a complete stop. Dylan walked towards the entrance, meeting Rade at the door. Something was different about him. Dylan couldn't put her finger on it, but he looked more relaxed than he had in days. Rade had been through a lot the past week and Dylan was happy that this part of their life together was finally over.

Kissing her on the cheek, Rade walked behind Dylan to the SUV. Once they were settled, Dylan couldn't hold back any longer. She needed to find out how Rade's meeting with his father went.

"So how did things go with your father?" Dylan asked, looking into Rade's eyes.

"It was good. He's going to try and reach out to Chloe. He's going to convince her that he has some information for her, but he can't disclose it over the phone. He thinks her curiosity will get the best of her and she would be willing to meet him to find out," Rade explained.

"Do you think she will do it?" Dylan asked.

"I don't know. If she finds out it has to do with me, she might," Rade said in a hopeful manner.

"I hope you're right Rade. She's the last threat against us," Dylan responded.

"One way or another, she's going to get caught," Rade said convincingly.

Dylan hoped that Rade was right. Chloe was smart. She would know when there was a trap waiting for her. Just like everything that happened, Chloe was always one step ahead of them.

Rade didn't have a whole lot of time for lunch. He could have canceled his date with Dylan, but he had to see her. Leaving as early as he did, he didn't get a chance to spend the much needed time with her this morning.

They choose to have lunch at the bistro that Dylan loved so much. Dylan remembered the first time they came here and how she convinced Rade to order one of their signature sandwiches. Dylan would never forget the look on Rade's face when he took a bite.

A short time later they were seated and eating their delicious sandwiches. When they had finished, Rade had something else in mind instead of going back to the office. Taking Dylan by the hand, he led her to the woman's restroom. He was glad to find that there was only one bathroom. Pushing her inside, he locked the door and lifted her small frame onto the countertop. Dylan was weak against his touch. Taking him in, she pressed her lips against his. Their kiss became more demanding as Rade slid his hands under her skirt. Taking hold of her panties, he pushed them to the side to gain better access to her slick folds. Placing his fingers between her seam, he began rubbing her until his finger dipped inside her.

Feeling the warmth of her tight channel, he curved his finger in search of her g-spot. As her body arched, he knew he had found it. Needing more, he removed his fingers and lowered to his knees, replacing them with his mouth. Lapping his tongue on her clit, he consumed the taste of her. Rade could feel that she was close when her hands tighten around his head. The grip she had on his hair was painful, but not enough for him to stop what he was doing. Dipping his fingers back inside her, he felt the tight grip of her walls as he moved in and out of her. Moving his mouth upward, he took hold of her clit, licking and sucking until her control took over sending her over the edge. Releasing her hands that were so firmly gripping his head, Dylan pulled him up to her until her lips met his. With ushered tenderness she whispered, "I love you."

Helping Dylan to her feet, Rade kissed her one last time before he unlocked the door. Looking first right, then left, Rade and Dylan escaped unnoticed. By the look on the patron's faces, Dylan knew that they were aware of what they had been doing and it wasn't a quick trip to the restroom.

After the explosive orgasm Rade had given Dylan, it was hard for her to focus on work. Her thoughts kept deviating towards Rade's mouth on her. *God, his mouth could work magic,* she thought, making herself wet all over again.

By the time the clock hit five, Dylan was all kinds of wet. Several times she had to go to the restroom to splash water on her face. She didn't know what was going on with her. She felt clammy, almost nauseated. She blamed it on the sandwich she ate and the stress she'd been faced with over the last couple of days.

Heading out, she saw that Richard was already waiting for her. When she got to the Bentley, she could see that Rade wasn't in the car. Looking over to Richard she asked, "Where's Rade?"

With a smile, Richard replied, "He's working late. He instructed me to make sure you got home safely."

"Did he say how long he would be?"

"I'm sorry, he didn't Ms. Adams," Richard replied pulling away from the curb.

Dylan sat back against the seat wondering when Rade would be home. Needing to know how long she would be alone, she decided to call him.

"Hello Sweetness. Are you on your way home?" Rade quizzed.

"Yeah, Richard just picked me up. When do you think you'll be home?" Dylan asked.

"Hopefully not too late. Don't wait up for me. When I get home you'll know because I'm going to worship every inch of that beautiful body," Rade said with a mischievous voice.

"I can't wait," Dylan said with a smile.

When Dylan got to the penthouse, she looked in the cupboard for anything that would settle her stomach. Pulling out a box of soda crackers and a can of ginger ale, she started feeling better.

By the time she went to bed, she felt like herself again. Knowing that Rade would be waking her when he arrived, she wanted to make sure she was dressed in her sexiest lingerie. Crawling into bed, Dylan grabbed her book from the nightstand. She tried to stay awake as long as she could. Looking at the clock, she could see that it was almost midnight. No longer able to keep her eyes open, Dylan fell into a deep sleep.

Rade wanted to get out of the office and on his way home before midnight, but with everything going on, he ended up staying a lot longer than he wanted. With his new found relationship with his father, he needed to try and save the company he used as leverage to gain full interest in Spectrum. Once he was satisfied that everything was taken care of, it was close to two in the morning. Grabbing his jacket, Rade finally headed out. He needed to be near Dylan. Rade knew she would be fast asleep when he arrived at the penthouse. As much as he wanted her, he couldn't bring himself in waking her up, so when he got to the penthouse, instead of consuming her, he took a cold shower.

Chapter Tewnty-Five

Rade was so exhausted that when he hit the bed, it was all she wrote. As tired as he was, it was no wonder that he slept though the alarm on his phone. It wasn't until Dylan snuggled up against him that he became fully awake. He didn't care what time it was. He needed to satisfy his need for her, especially since he missed out last night. Rolling Dylan over onto her back, he removed the sheet from her warm body and began taking what was his. Seeing her, she was like an angel beneath him. Lowering himself down her body, he slowly lifted her nightgown up her body while tenderly placing soft kisses along her body. When her breasts were exposed, he couldn't help but stop and worship the taut buds. Placing his mouth over one nipple while caressing the other, he was well on his way to satisfying his need for her.

Dylan began to stir, raising her back off the soft bed. Taking hold of his hair, she forked her fingers through his thick hair needing to satisfy her need to touch him while being touched. Missing him, she whispered softly, "Rade, I need you inside me." Pulling her hands from his hair, he lifted them above her head. Pulling her nightgown over head, Rade encircled her wrist in the silky material. Slipping the ends of the material through the iron spindle, he knotted the two ends together securing her hands to the headboard. Continuing his decent on her, he lowered his mouth down her body, touching her very lightly with his lips. When Dylan began to squirm, he warned her, "You need to stay still Sweetness."

Doing as he asked, Dylan held her body still while Rade continued to worship her. As much as she wanted him to stop, she wanted him to continue more. Every breath he blew on her sent her body to places she never knew existed. The pleasure that was consuming her was almost too much for her to take. It was only when he bit down gently on her clit that she lost it. She came with such force, she could have sworn that the angels above were talking to her. Taking her out of her trance, she heard Rade's voice. "My little beauty came without permission." Rade wasn't going to punish her this time. With all the emotions going every which way, he knew there wasn't any way she would have been able to hold back her release.

Kneeling between her legs, it was time for Rade to get his fill of pleasure. Guiding his thick cock between her legs, he plunged inside her inch by inch. He wanted the pleasure he was about to take from her to last. He made sure his movements in and out of her were slow and precise. Pulling out just to the tip, he slowly moved back inside her. He knew her release was close. Her back began to bow off of the bed, sending her closer and closer to another unforgettable release. This time she would need to wait. He wanted them to come together, his seed mixing with her juices. "I want you to wait until I tell you to come," Rade ordered plunging deeper inside her.

Taking her where he needed her to be, in a soft voice he whispered "Come for me Sweetness." With her screams of ecstasy filling the room, Rade lost his control and came with her.

Their little morning pick me up caused both of them to be late for work. Dylan only had a couple of days to get caught up at work. Soon she and Rade would be leaving for Vegas to join her dad and Sally in their vows of marriage. Dylan was excited for her dad. He deserved so much. Mostly he deserved to be happy.

Thinking about her dad, made Dylan think about when her happy day would arrive. With everything that was going on, she wasn't thinking about making wedding plans. The only friend

317

she had was Lilly. Dylan didn't care too much about having a big wedding. She wanted something small with only family. This was something that she needed to talk to Rade about. They would need to decide on a date so that Dylan could begin planning. She didn't really even know where to start. She didn't know whether she get a wedding planner or try to plan it herself.

Pushing away her thoughts of wedding cakes and wedding dresses, Dylan dug into her work. With all of her interviews set up for next week, she could finally concentrate on other tasks like re-evaluating the financial records for BlackStone. When the IRS investigator came to the office to do a review of the financials, it worried Keeve and Mason. They wanted to make sure that everything would be in order for the next audit. They wanted to make sure it went more smoothly then this audit did. It was for this reason they suggested Dylan go through the records and make sure everything was in order.

Half way through the review Dylan had to take a break. Her brain was swimming with numbers. Pushing from her desk, she decided to take a quick walk to the corner deli to grab some lunch. As she was heading out of the building, she noticed that Peter was sitting on the couch on the lobby. Walking up to him, Dylan said, "I'm going to grab something to eat."

Rising to his feet, Peter said. "I'll join you."

Rade insisted that Dylan be protected 24/7. With Chloe still out there and her psycho tendencies, Rade wasn't about to take any chances that she would be coming after Dylan.

As they walked down the sidewalk, Dylan had to wonder what actually happened between Lilly and him. She wanted to ask Peter, but felt like she may be intruding on his privacy. Then she thought about Lilly. Lilly was her best friend. Dylan would do anything to make her friend happy.

When they got to the deli and placed their order, Dylan went for it and asked Peter, "Can I ask you something?"

"Sure. Go for it," Peter said taking a bite of his sandwich.

"What happened between you and Lilly? You two seemed so happy together," Dylan asked.

Wiping his mouth with his napkin, Peter looked at Dylan. "I honestly don't know. One minute we were together and the next she was on her way to Paris."

"Lilly seems to think that you were keeping things from her," Dylan said bluntly. If she was going to find out what happened between them, she wasn't going to hold back. Based on Peter's look, he wasn't expecting her to be so direct.

"I did keep things from Lilly. Sometimes my job requires me to keep things confidential," Peter said choosing his words wisely. He knew what he was keeping from Lilly didn't pertain to work, but Dylan didn't need to know that.

"That's what I told her, but she seemed to think it was more. If you still care about her, you should talk to her," Dylan suggested.

"I'm dangerous Dylan..," Peter paused. "I mean with the kind of work I do."

"Do you still care about her?" Dylan asked.

"More than you'll ever know," Peter said affectionately. "Can we not talk about this?"

Dylan and Peter walked back to the office building in silence. Something she said must have affected Peter because his mind was elsewhere. What Dylan didn't understand was why Peter wouldn't fight for Lilly. If he really cared for her the way he admitted, why wouldn't he make every effort to be with her? People have long distance relationships all the time and they seem to find a way to make them work out. It wasn't like Lilly would be living in Paris forever. Dylan knew Lilly would be coming back to the states to help her with her wedding plans and there was no reason why Peter couldn't go to Paris to be with her.

Dylan was working diligently when Mason stepped into her office. Looking up from her computer, Dylan greeted him. "Hey Mason, I'm going through the BlackStone financials. Everything looks good so far."

"Well that's good to hear. Do you have a minute to take a break? I want to talk to you about something," Mason asked, taking a seat in front of her desk.

"I always have time for you. What's on your mind?" Dylan asked with a smile.

"Well, I've thought a lot about this. How would you feel about heading the Spectrum facility here in New York? I know that you have put a lot of time in getting it up and running and with the interviews coming up, I think you would be a perfect fit for the position." Mason admitted confidently.

"I don't know anything about running a business Mason. I'm just a financial advisor," Dylan replied honestly.

"You aren't giving yourself enough credit Dylan. Look at everything you've done already. It doesn't take a genius to see that you were meant to head the office here. I haven't spoken to Keeve or Rade about it yet, but I'm almost positive they would agree that the CEO position should be yours," Mason argued.

"I don't even know what to say Mason," Dylan choked, trying to hold back her doubt.

"Just think about it. In the meantime, I'll let Keeve and Rade know of my proposition," Mason said as he stood and left Dylan's office.

This news was just too much for her. Being the head of a company was the last thing she ever expected she would be offered. Even though Dylan had put a lot of time and effort into Spectrum and she knew it inside out, she was still not sure if she was ready to take on such a big responsibility. It was one thing to know everything there was to know about the financial stuff, but to actually run a company, that was a whole different ball game.

Five o'clock was approaching and Dylan was ready to call it a day. Gathering her things, Dylan headed down to the lobby. Taking her phone from her purse, she decided to send Rade a quick text.

> Dylan: *I'm heading home. Will you be there by the time I get there?*
>
> Rade: *Running a little late. Should be there soon after you.*
>
> Dylan: *I will cook dinner. What would you like?*
>
> Rade: *You.*
>
> Dylan: *Very funny. I'll surprise you. Love you.*
>
> Rade: *Love you too!!*

Dylan wanted to share the news with Rade and get his thoughts on what Mason was offering her. Since Rade didn't mention it in his texts to her, she thought it was better to get his opinion before Mason had a chance to bring it up first. She decided that if Rade didn't bring it up after they finished dinner, it would be a good opportunity to talk to him about it.

Entering the penthouse, Dylan placed her things on the barstool and poured herself a glass of wine. Scanning the contents in the fridge, she decided on chicken Alfredo and a Caesar salad. Dylan wanted to make something special for Rade. As much as he liked making her breakfast in the morning, Dylan enjoyed cooking him dinner at night. It was a way that they could decompress and share the events of the day together.

While Dylan was watching the water boil for the noodles, she kept thinking about Rade and what she planned to do to him. She wasn't sure what was going on with her. Lately, she had been feeling really needy when he was around. All she could think about was Rade touching her body and being inside her. Maybe it was everything that had been going on with them. Whatever it was, the only thing she could think about was jumping his bones.

Preparing their meal, Dylan didn't realize that there was someone else in the penthouse. It was only when she turned to place the plates and tableware on the counter that she saw her.

"Hello, schoolgirl. Bet I'm the last person you expected to see? You should have listen to me," Chloe seethed in a low voice as she took one of the knives from the knife block running her thumb over the sharp edge.

"How did you get in here?" Dylan asked hiding her fear.

Chloe reached in her pocket and pulled out a keycard. "You left this behind at *The Castle*. You know, you should really be more careful. Someone could just walk in," Chloe said arrogantly.

"I didn't leave it. You or Michael took it from me," Dylan confirmed.

"No matter," Chloe smirked.

"What do you want Chloe?" Dylan asked afraid to find out.

"You out of the picture so Rade and I can finally be together once and for all," Chloe hissed as she rounded the breakfast bar.

Dylan swayed back and forth trying to judge which way Chloe was going to come after her with the knife. Turning away from where Chloe was, Dylan thought she could escape her. Running toward the front door, Dylan was stopped abruptly by Chloe's claws in her hair. Taking hold of Chloe's wrist, Dylan tried to alleviate some of the pain caused by the pull of her hair. It was no use, the harder Dylan tried, the harder Chloe pulled. Chloe had her where she wanted. With her hand gripping Dylan's hair, Chloe was able to pull Dylan's body closer to hers. The knife was so close to Dylan's throat, she thought for sure she was going die.

"You ruined everything. You made me lose the baby. Rade and I would have been the perfect family hadn't it been for you." Chloe's words echoed thought the room as she pressed the knife against Dylan's skin.

Dylan knew she had to do something. The blood from the cut to her throat began to trickle down her neck. Dylan wasn't sure how badly Chloe had sliced her, but she wasn't ready to die like this. Stepping back with her left foot, Dylan was able to throw Chloe off balance. Turning her body, Dylan tried to get the knife away from her. When Chloe wouldn't release it, Dylan punched Chloe in the face hoping that the jolt would cause her to release the weapon. The only thing it did was make Chloe angrier. "You fucking bitch," Chloe yelled as she started swinging the knife radically at Dylan.

"It doesn't have to be like this Chloe. You can have Rade. I'll stay away. I'll tell him I don't love him anymore." Dylan knew she could never leave Rade, but she had to try anything to convince Chloe differently.

"You think I would believe you. I know exactly what you're doing schoolgirl. It's not going to work. The only way I'll have Rade, is if you're dead." Chloe cursed as she lunged forward.

Dylan looked down to her side seeing blood slowly seeping through the material of her blouse. Looking up at Chloe, Dylan was angry that Chloe got a piece of her. Dylan didn't know where her strength came from, she charged at Chloe causing them both to tumble to the ground. Struggling back and forth, Dylan tried to get the knife away from Chloe. Blood was everywhere, coating the white marble floor with Dylan's blood. Dylan began to lose her strength. With the amount of blood that was on the floor, she was surprised that she managed to fight Chloe off this long.

Unable to fight anymore, Dylan was ready to give up. By the smile on Chloe's face, she knew she was inches away from finishing her off. It was then that Dylan heard Rade's voice.

"Dylan," Rade yelled hysterically.

Chloe looked up at Rade with apologetic eyes. Returning her focus back to Dylan, she lifted the knife above her head, ready to plunge it inside Dylan. Dylan's eyes shut knowing that soon her life would be over. As Dylan waited for the pain of the knife to dig into her skin, she only felt the warmth of Rade's arms wrap around her.

Dylan didn't know what happened. When she was able to open her eyes, she saw Chloe lying on the floor and the knife was no longer in her hand. Looking back at Rade, Dylan asked softly, "Is she dead?"

"No," Rade said with regret, pushing her hair from her cheek with his hand. "When I saw what she was going to do, I grabbed her arm and punched her. She's going to be out for awhile."

Rade pulled Dylan closer to him. When he felt something warm, he looked at her. He thought for sure the blood on the floor was from Chloe based on how much covered her clothing. Dylan's eyes slowly closed. Lifting his hand to her cheek, his hand was covered in blood. Turning her body, he could see that she was the one bleeding. Chloe stabbed her. "Oh God, Dylan hold on baby."

Rade pulled his phone from his pocket and dialed 9-1-1. After talking to dispatch letting them know what happened, he placed his phone on the marble floor and held Dylan close to him. He thought by holding her, she would be ok. He was there now. To protect her.

The paramedics finally showed up along with the police. Rade refused to let go of her. It was only after they told him he could ride to the hospital with her in the ambulance, he let them do what they needed to take care of Dylan.

The police wanted to question him about what happened, but Rade wasn't going to leave Dylan's side. Rade told the police that until he knew for sure that she was going to be okay, he wasn't going to leave her side. It was then that the police officer gave in and agreed to meet him at the hospital for questioning.

As Rade followed the paramedics out of the penthouse, he looked over to Chloe who was now handcuffed by the police. Before he got into the elevator he heard Chloe's voice crackle. "Rade," she said sharply.

Looking at Chloe's defeated body, he cursed, "I have nothing to say to you Chloe."

"But, I thought you loved me," Chloe cried with a confused look on her face.

"You can rot in hell for all I care," Rade claimed with vengeance. "I hope when they lock you up, they throw away the key."

Chloe lowered he head. She knew Rade was angry with her, but he would forgive her eventually. She knew he loved her or at least her demented mind thought he did. Soon they would be together.

Chapter Twenty-Six

Rade had been pacing back and forth for what seem like hours. He still hadn't heard anything. With his clothing covered in Dylan's blood, he looked down at his appearance. He needed to make sure she didn't see him like this, but for now he didn't care. All he wanted to know was how she was doing.

Richard showed up two hours later. He wanted to let Rade know the status of Chloe and to find out about Dylan. Putting his hand on his shoulder, Richard asked sympathetically, "How is she doing?"

"I don't know. They haven't let me know anything," Rade admitted painfully, trying hard to hold it together,"

"She's a strong woman Rade. She'll get through this," Richard reassured him.

Leading him over to the waiting area, Richard convinced Rade to take a seat. Pacing the floor wasn't doing him any good. Richard spotted a coffee cart and asked Rade if he wanted some coffee. Rade nodded his head in acceptance. With two cups of coffee in hand, Richard took a seat beside Rade. Handing him one of the cups, he filled him in on Chloe. "When the police took Chloe away, she went crazy. She started confessing to everything she did to you, to Dylan. She even confessed to how she got pregnant. How she drugged you and then had her way with you. She even confessed to persuading Michael to kill the guy they found by the Brooklyn Bridge."

"Oh God, she did get a piece of me" Rade cried out with disgust.

"Rade, you were drugged. It was the only way she could get you to submit to her. This was by no means your doing."

"I should have never followed through with my plan to seduce her. All it did was give her the opportunity to take what she wanted. Me," Rade confessed.

"Wasn't that you plan. To get her to fall for you and confess everything she had done to Dylan," Richard asked.

"Yeah, but not like that. I guess I should have thought that one through," Rade said with agony.

"Anyway, they had to call in a doctor to sedate her. He's evaluating her now. Don't be surprised if she spends the rest of her days in a mental institution," Richard advised.

"Better there than anywhere near Dylan or myself," Rade admitted.

Just as Rade was ready to get himself another cup of coffee, the doctor appeared. It was the same doctor that saw to Dylan's care when she had been beaten so badly. "Mr. Matheson, I didn't expect to see you here again," the doctor said surprised.

"Cut the crap and tell me how Dylan is." Richard placed his hand on Rade's shoulder trying to calm him. Richard knew how much Rade loved Dylan, but there was no reason for the harsh words that he flung at the doctor. "Sorry, I didn't mean to be rude. I've just been sick not knowing how she is."

"That's understandable. I need to ask you a question. Did you know that Ms. Adams was pregnant?" the doctor asked concerned.

"What? No," Rade answered confused.

"It's hard to tell how far along she really is, but when we did the blood test on her, it showed positive. It's common protocol to do a pregnancy test when pain medication is going to be administered. We don't want to endanger the fetus in the event the patient is pregnant," the doctor explained.

Rade was shocked by the news. He had no idea that Dylan was pregnant. She was always so careful in taking her pill every day. She always kept the small disc with her in her purse. It was then that Rade realized that Dylan couldn't have taken them while Michael had her. Her purse was left behind. He remembered seeing with her things in the private room at *The Castle*. It should have dawned on him then that she didn't have access to her pills. Pushing away his thoughts he asked. "How are they doing? Dylan and the baby?"

"Both of them will be fine. Dylan has lost a lot of blood, but we were able to stop the bleeding. Her body should be able to regenerate the lost blood in a couple of weeks. Being it that it's so early in her pregnancy, the baby wasn't affected by the knife wound. We were able to repair the small cut to her large intestine," the doctor confirmed.

"When can I see her," Rade asked.

"She's still in recovery. I'll have a nurse come get you when they move her to a room," the doctor advised.

Rade looked to Richard trying to find the answers that he needed. Dylan was pregnant. Rade didn't know how to feel about it. It was something that Dylan wanted. Even though the discussed it, Rade wasn't sure he was ready to love another being. All he could think about was, what if something happened to the baby?

It was as though Richard knew exactly what Rade was thinking, patting him on the shoulder, he said understandingly, "Not everything turns out bad, Rade. Dylan gave you her love, something you thought you would never find again. Now you have been given the gift to share the love you have for her with another being. A being both of you created out of that love. Don't treat this as an omen, treat it as a second chance to live free from your demons." With those choice words, Richard left Rade to his thoughts.

Moments after Richard left, the nurse came and got Rade to take him to Dylan's room. After Richard left, Rade had time to think about what he said. He knew Richard was right. Rade knew that he needed to put his fears aside and release the demons that had been haunting him for so long. He made the first step in forgiving his father, now he just needed to move forward and let the happiness that was going to fill his life happened.

Before he entered Dylan's room, he asked the nurse if they had something he could change into. The last thing he wanted was to have Dylan see him covered in blood. When the nurse came back with a set of scrubs, Rade ducked into the men's restroom to change. He couldn't see any reason to save his discarded clothing so he deposited them inside the trash bin. Taking a quick look at himself, he said softly to his reflection, "You're going to be a father, and you're going to be the best father your child is going to ever have." Pushing from the counter, he headed to the room where is future wife was.

Stepping across the threshold, Rade looked over to the most gorgeous woman he had ever set eyes on. Even in her paper thin hospital gown, she was beautiful. Taking her by the hand, he lowered his lips to her head. Dylan was pale and looked so fragile as Rade gently swept his hand across her cheek. Dylan's eyes fluttered open at his touch.

Focusing her eyes, she saw the man she loved more than life itself. "Hey," she whispered softly.

Rade put down the bed rail and sat beside her on the bed, careful not to disturb the wires she had running from her body. Looking into her peaked eyes, Rade answered, "Hey Sweetness. How are you feeling?"

"Tired," Dylan sighed softly.

"The doctor said you lost a lot of blood, but that you both would be okay," Rade told her as he rubbed her hand.

"Both?" Dylan asked confused.

"Yeah, we're going to have a baby Sweetness," Rade said smiling down on her.

"Baby?" Dylan replied back.

With Dylan's one word sentences, Rade was beginning to think she wasn't rested enough to understand what was going on. Maybe by tomorrow she would feel better and understand what was happening to her.

"Just rest Sweetness. We can talk about this tomorrow when you're stronger," Rade demanded softly.

Even when he was tender, he was demanding. This was how he would always be with her. Leaving her side, Rade called Richard to have him pick up some appropriate clothing for him. No sooner he was gone, Dylan was back resting soundly.

When Richard came back with a change of clothing, Rade asked one of nurse's sitting at the nurse's station if there was somewhere where he could take a shower and clean-up. Giving into his request, one of the nurses was more than happy to show him a bathroom with a shower that he could use. She would have probably helped him wash his back.

Rade came back to Dylan's room to find that she was still resting comfortably. While Richard was out getting him a change of clothing, Rade also requested that he pick up his laptop from the penthouse. Rade wasn't willing to leave Dylan's side, but there was still work that he needed to do. Going through his emails, he saw that he received one from Mason. Opening it up, Rade began to read the message.

After reading what Mason was proposing, Rade thought it was the best idea he had yet. Making Dylan the head of the New York facility was going to be the best thing for her. Rade was more than confident that she could handle the job. Emailing Mason back, Rade told him that he couldn't agree more. He also suggested that they come up with a different name for the new facility. He also thought that Dylan should have the honor of naming it.

* * * * *

After being in the hospital for a week, Dylan was ready to go home. Just like before, Rade made all of the arrangements for her transportation. And just like before he insisted on carrying her to the penthouse once Richard had dropped them off. As much as Dylan was feeling better, she was still sad that she missed her dad's and Sally's wedding. They had offered to postpone their trip and wait to get married when Dylan could be there. Dylan knew how important it was for them, so she insisted that they continue with their plans and to take a lot of pictures.

When a video came over on her phone of the wedding ceremony, Dylan began to cry. She had never seen her dad as happy as he was. The way he looked at Sally, Dylan knew that he loved her very much.

After watching the video for the fourth time, Dylan decided to take a nap. Even though she felt better, she was still tired. She blamed her tiredness on the fact that she was going to be a mom. She still couldn't believe it. There were no signs that she was even pregnant. She was thankful that she hadn't reached the stage where morning sickness set in. Thinking about her pregnancy, she wondered how Rade really felt about it. He was constantly asking how she was feeling and if she needed anything, but he never talked to her about the baby.

Closing her eyes, Dylan wondered what it would be like to have a baby in their life. Her dreams began to fill with white picket fences, big blue balloons and stuffed tigers and bears. Dylan continued to dream about playmates and birthdays. Then her dream swayed into a different direction. Chloe entered her dreams. She was standing outside the white picket fence with a knife in her hand. Walking through the gate, Dylan just stared at her unable to move. Then it happened, the knife plunged inside her. All Dylan could here were the cries of a child. The cries of a child she hadn't yet given birth to.

Screaming from the dream that seemed so real, Dylan placed her hand on her stomach knowing it was just a bad dream. Rade had told her that Chloe went crazy at the police station and that she would more than likely spend her days in an institution. Dylan knew she was crazy. As much as she hated Chloe, she hoped that she would find peace with herself there.

Rade came flying down the stairs, hearing Dylan's screams. When he got to the couch, she was sitting up. Rade sat beside her and took her into his arms. "I heard you screaming Dylan," Rade said worried.

"I had a bad dream. I dreamt that Chloe was at our home and she killed our child. Just like she stabbed me. I could hear the baby crying," Dylan explained. Wiping away the tears that had fallen.

"It was only a dream Sweetness, Chloe is never going to hurt you or our child again," Rade assured her.

"Rade," Dylan began, turning her body towards him. "I know we haven't talked about the baby, but I need to know that you want this as much as I do."

"I know I said that I didn't want any children Sweetness, but something change. You lying in that hospital bed with our child made me think about how lucky I was to have both of you. I want this baby more than ever," Rade confessed. "I'm thinking about selling the house in Hampton Bay. I want to buy you a home that we can have together. To build happy memories. Something closer to the city, but out in the country."

"Really, you would sell the house you love so much for me?" Dylan asked with sadness.

"For us Sweetness. You, me and the baby," Rade confirmed.

"Let's get married Rade. I don't care where." Dylan demanded, out of nowhere.

"Are you sure? What about Lilly and your dad and Sally? Don't you want them to be there?" Rade asked understandingly. He didn't want Dylan to miss out on the wedding she really wanted.

"Of course, I do. I didn't mean right now. I just don't want to wait any longer than I have to." Dylan replied.

"How long do you need to get everything ready?" Rade asked. More than anything he wanted to make Dylan his. He didn't care where it was done.

"A couple of weeks. Maybe less. I just need to make a few calls and make sure Lilly can be here." Dylan confirmed.

"Okay, I can live with that. I love you Sweetness," Rade said, kissing Dylan lightly on the lips.

* * * * *

"It's hard to believe that two weeks have already passed by," Lilly said as she looked down on Dylan.

"We did it girlfriend. I wouldn't have been able to do this without your help," Dylan confessed, taking Lilly by the hand that held the veil she was about to place on Dylan's head.

"Okay, No tears. You're going to ruin my masterpiece. Are you ready to put that gorgeous dress on," Lilly asked wiping away her own tears.

"Yeah. I can't believe you brought it from Paris for me. How did you even know that I would like it?" Dylan asked.

"Because I know you. Now let's get it on you and see how it looks," Lilly ordered.

Dylan carefully stepped into the dress, while Lilly carefully worked the silky material up her body. Pulling the delicate material around Dylan's neck and zipping up the back, Lilly smiled at how perfect the dress fit her. It was like it was made for her. The dress was elegant with a beaded halter neckline and a trumpet style skirt, and a long flowing train edged with the same beads. It was breathtaking alone, but with it on Dylan, it was mesmerizing. She looked like and angel in it.

"Dylan, I have never seen a more beautiful bride," Lilly confessed with a tear in her eye.

"Thank you for knowing me so well Lilly. It's beautiful," Dylan said hugging her friend.

There was a light knock on the door. Lilly walked over to the door and opened it. Sally was on the other side. As she stepped into the room, Sally took in a deep breath placing her hand over her heart. "Oh my God, sweetheart, you're absolutely beautiful," Sally said with affection. "Everyone is waiting for you. Are you ready?"

Dylan nodded her head and stepped out of the room. Rade and Dylan decided to hold the wedding at the Hampton home. They thought it was fitting to spend one last time at the home Rade loved so much before the new owners took possession. Walking down the staircase, Dylan spotted her dad dressed in a black tux and blue bowtie. Dylan wanted Rade to wear the tie that had brought so many wonderful memories. It was only fitting that her dad and Evan wore the same shade of blue. Looking at her dad as he waited for her to reach him, Dylan could see the love in his eyes.

Pulling her in for a hug, Ray said, "You look absolutely beautiful pumpkin. You look so much like your mother did on our wedding day. Are you ready?"

"I am," Dylan said as she looked to her dad with teary eyes.

As Dylan and her dad stepped onto the patio she could hear the sound of violins playing Jason Mraz "*I'm Yours*." As Dylan took in her surroundings, she had to admit that with the help of Lilly and Sally, they did a wonderful job in putting everything together for the wedding. Every seat in the ceremony area was occupied. Most of the guests she knew, but there were also some that she didn't recognize. The weather had been perfect for the wedding. Walking between the perfectly positioned rows, Dylan smiled at the guests as they rose to their feet. Smiling as she passed them, she held her gaze to the one man that would change her life forever. Soon she would be Mrs. Dylan Matheson.

Ray gave Dylan a kiss on the cheek as he handed her off to the man she was going to spend the rest of her life with. As the ceremony began and the minister said the traditional ceremonial pledge, it came time for Dylan and Rade to confess their love to each other. When the minister let the guests know that they had written their own vows, he looked to Dylan to proceed.

Looking at Rade, with her hands held by his, she began to confess her love. "A chance meeting, that was what my father said the day he met my mom. With so much love, they gave life to a young girl who grew to be a strong, yet stubborn woman," Dylan smiled as she continued. "That woman fell in love with the most amazing man. A man who has shown her what true love really means. I love you Rade with all my heart. I see you in the sun that wakes me every morning. I feel you in the breeze that touches my skin. You are my everything. You are my heart, my body and soul. For that I am thankful because, that one chance meeting brought me to you."

The minister looked over to Rade, giving him his cue to begin his own vows to Dylan. "My Precious Dylan. I knew from the moment I saw you, you were an angel sent to rescue me. You've shown me what it means to be love. Through the love that you have given me, I found myself again. You once said something to me that I will never forget. It allowed me to find the one thing I thought I would never have again. For this, I vow to show you everyday what you have given me. So my promise to you is this; Never will I leave you. Always will I hold you tight. Forever will I love you. You my Sweetness are my heart, my body and soul."

After the vows were exchanged there wasn't a dry eye among the guest. As Rade place the ring on Dylan's finger and Dylan placed the ring on Rade's, their love for each other was finally sealed.

"Mr. Matheson, You can most definitely kiss your wife," the minister said as the guest cheered.

Epilogue

"Sweetie, you have to go ask you Daddy," Dylan said looking into her son's eyes, reminding her so much of Rade.

"But mommy, Dada say no."

"Isaac, you need to listen to what Dada says," Dylan replied, completely drawn to his sad look. "Tell you what, you can have half now and half after supper."

Dylan watched as Isaac's eyes lit up like a Christmas tree. Breaking the cookie in half, Dylan watched as his tiny fingers took hold of the sugary treat.

"What do you say Sweetie," Dylan asked him.

"Tank you mommy," Isaac said taking off with his cookie in hand.

She would never be able to refuse him. Rade was constantly after Dylan for spoiling their son. It had been only yesterday that she caught Rade doing the same thing. When those hazel eyes looked up at her, she couldn't help but give into his demands. Like father, like son.

Dylan thought about all the hearts he was going to break when he got older. Lost in her thoughts, she watched as her phone began vibrating on the counter. Picking it up, Dylan looked at the caller and smiled.

CHAPTER TWENTY-SIX

Rade: Are you ready for tonight?

Dylan: I wouldn't miss it for the world.

Rade: When is Lilly coming over to watch Isaac?

Dylan: At eight.

Rade: Perfect. Miss you already.

Dylan: Me too!!!

Dylan thought it was adorable the way Rade texted her, even though he was only a few feet away in his study. Setting her phone down, she continued working on the financial report for the new app that Malcolm had been working on. Malcolm had been one of the people Dylan had hired as the new tech guru. Since she took over the new Spectrum Facility, which was now Tetralogy Innovations, nothing but positive things had happened. Rade, Keeve and Mason had faith in her to run the company so Dylan felt it was only fitting to name it after the four of them.

Since giving birth to Isaac, Dylan spent most of her days working at home so when Rade suggested they have a weekly date night, Dylan was all for it. Since their marriage two years ago, they set one day a week for play. Everything about their life was perfect. The house that they picked out together was close enough to work, yet far enough away from the city to enjoy the county life. As soon as Rade saw the house he knew it would be perfect to raise a family. It wasn't as large as the home he had in Hampton Bay, but it was beautiful nonetheless. There was plenty of room to have a family, with five bedrooms and four baths, it gave them room to grow. Evan even came over and helped Rade build a tree house before Isaac was even born. Dylan knew that it was more for Rade's benefit than for little Isaac's.

Having ten acres of land, Rade also thought how nice it would be to build a horse stable and fill it with a couple of horses that he and Isaac could ride once he was old enough. There was so much of Rade that Dylan saw in the little man and she knew that Rade loved him with all his heart.

Maria came into the kitchen just as Dylan was powering down her computer. Maria was a great help with Isaac. She wasn't only their housekeeper, she was also little Isaac's nanny during the day.

"Señora Dylan, little Isaac has been feed and bathed. I'm going to take off. See you mañana," Marie said grabbing her things.

"Good-bye Maria, See you tomorrow," Dylan replied.

Walking into the study, Dylan was greeted with a picture perfect sight. Rade was holding his son in his arms while working on his laptop. Dylan guessed he was getting him ready to take over his business one day. Stepping closer to them, Dylan said. "It's time for bed sweetie."

"Mommy, Dada teach me puter," Isaac said excitedly as he pounded his little finger on the keys.

"That's wonderful sweetie, but time to go to lala," Dylan said softly.

"Otay. Wuv you Dada," Isaac said as he gave Rade a hug.

"Love you too big guy," Rade replied with pride kissing his son on the head.

Dylan took Isaac from Rade. "Dinner is ready, I'll put him down, then we can eat," Dylan said as she left the study.

After Dylan was satisfied that Isaac was settled comfortably in his crib with his favorite stuffed animal, she headed down to the kitchen. Rade was already there dishing them each a plate of Maria's famous Mexican casserole.

As they were finishing up, the sound of the door bell chimed. Rade pushed from his seat to answer the front door. Lilly had arrived to watch little Isaac. Rade had been looking forward to this day all week.

Rade and Dylan left their home twenty minutes later on their way to the place Dylan loved, now that all the bad stuff was gone. Helping Dylan into the car, Rade kissed her tenderly as he reached over to make sure she was safely buckled in. Rade still had his Martin. It was the one thing that didn't change.

Half an hour later they were at *The Castle*, ready to begin their night together. Rade assisted Dylan out of the car and up the concrete steps to the iron door that Dylan was so familiar with. Once inside, they were greeted by Dane, who was now more of a friend than the Master of the house that held so much pleasure.

Leading Dylan up the stairs to their favorite room, Rade had an evening planned that Dylan would never forget. Closing and locking the door behind them, Rade commanded, "Strip and get on your knees Sweetness."

"Yes sir."

"Let's see if we can make some more babies."

Dylan smiled at his words. If he only knew that he was going to be the proud father of twins.

Acknowledgement

To my husband, who has been so supportive of my writing. If it weren't for him my dream of writing would have never been fulfilled. I love you sweetheart. And to my family whom I also love dearly. Through their love and support, I can continue my passion for writing. To the many readers who took a chance on me and purchased my books. I hope that I can continue to fill your hearts with the passion I have grown to love.

About the Author

A. L. Long lives in Greeley, Colorado sharing a home with her wonderful husband and granddaughter. When she isn't reading or writing, she enjoys spending time with friends. She also enjoys her morning jogs and family weekend outings. Out of everything, she enjoys driving in her little two-seater convertible with the top down which she received from her gorgeous husband of twenty-one years.

Watch for A. L. Long Newest Series:

Jagged Edge Series

More books by A. L. Long

Next to Never
(Shattered Innocence Trilogy)

Next to Always
(Shattered Innocence Trilogy Book Two)

Get all the latest news on new releases:

Twitter:

A L Long@allong1963

Facebook:

www.facebook.com/ALLongbooks

Official Website:

www.allongbooks.com

Lightning Source UK Ltd.
Milton Keynes UK
UKOW02f1925190116

266721UK00001B/12/P